KT-370-882

ISLES
OF THE
FORSAKEN

CAROLYN IVES GILMAN

ChiZine Publications

FIRST EDITION

Isles of the Forsaken © 2011 by Carolyn Ives Gilman
Cover artwork © 2011 by Erik Mohr
Cover design © 2011 by Corey Beep
Interior Image © 2011 Robin Ahle
All Rights Reserved.

This book is a work of fiction. Names, characters, places, and incidents are either a product of the author's imagination or are used fictitiously. Any resemblance to actual events, locales, or persons, living or dead, is entirely coincidental.

LIBRARY AND ARCHIVES CANADA CATALOGUING IN PUBLICATION

Gilman, Carolyn, 1954-
    Isles of the forsaken / Carolyn Ives Gilman.

ISBN 978-1-926851-36-5

   I. Title.

PS3557.I426I85 2011   813'.6   C2011-902566-3

CHIZINE PUBLICATIONS
Toronto, Canada
www.chizinepub.com
info@chizinepub.com

Edited and copyedited by Sandra Kasturi
Proofread by Samantha Beiko
Printed in Canada

Simon Butler

ISLES
OF THE
FORSAKEN

1
SOME KIND OF HERO

At last, the war was over.

All day long the festive volleys of firecrackers had ricocheted off the tawny brick walls of Fluminos, until it sounded like a new attack was under way. Despite the March chill, the celebrations spilled out into the streets, and as sunset drew near, crowds carrying blankets and hampers of food headed down toward the harbour. Two of the great Inning warships that had conquered the Rothur navy were to be anchored in the river, and a fireworks re-enactment of the climactic battle would take place at sundown. When big, wet snowflakes began to fall, it did not cool the atmosphere at all; it simply seemed like the sky was throwing confetti to congratulate Inning on its great victory.

It had just begun to snow when Nathaway Talley emerged from the ancient, arched door of the law school and paused on the steps, books slung under his arm, to survey the drunken troop of students making their way across the quad toward the college gate to carouse. He was a spindly, gawky figure, all arms and legs. A long knit scarf wound around his neck and dragged like a tether behind him; his untrimmed blond hair was topped with a moth-eaten cap, and he fumbled to push his spectacles up past the bump on his monumental beak of a nose. As he set off through the slippery streets toward the Talley family home, his stiff, stalking gait would have telegraphed disaffection to anyone watching. No one was. Everyone was in far too good a mood to spare him a glance.

In contrast to the rest of the city, Nathaway was gripped by a feeling of failure. Others could take vicarious pleasure in the nation's victories; for him, they only rubbed in how badly he had failed to measure up.

The family residence of the Talleys was a rambling brick townhouse at the very heartbeat centre of Fluminos, facing Holton Street, just around the corner from the opulent chambers where the High Court met. Its main floor was almost as public as the court itself, buzzing at all hours with the comings and goings of dealmakers, schemers, visionaries, and, lately, military attachés. Political quorums were apt to assemble in the library, and scientific experiments jostled with state dinners in the dining hall. The chaos was barely kept in control by the strong managerial hand of Nathaway's mother and her competent and tolerant staff.

When he got to the courthouse square, Nathaway found Holton Street nearly blocked by a crush of carriages delivering elegant visitors to the brightly lit doorway of his father's home. Dodging assorted footmen and a large ornamental dog on a leash, he thumped down the stone steps to the service entrance under the front stairs. The policeman stationed there nodded at him familiarly, so Nathaway reflexively pretended to recognize him.

Inside, the kitchen was a staging area as tightly organized, and nearly as noisy, as a military campaign. Liveried servitors manoeuvred down the steps with empty bottles and trays, and up again with loads of food and drink for the guests. Nathaway strolled past the counters, helping himself to canapés until Betts, the cook, slapped his hand and snatched the cap from his head. "You look like some fishmonger that wandered in, in that filthy thing," she said. Which was, of course, the point of wearing it—to look like anything but what he really was.

"Has Corbin come yet?" Nathaway asked.

"No, they're all up there waiting to toast him," Betts said. "If we don't run out of wine before he comes."

"Who *is* here?"

Betts ticked off Talleys on her fingers. "Tarbison, Fithian, Hallowell, and Mandregan. And your sister, of course."

"A regular reunion," Nathaway said morosely.

"Try not to let it spoil your day," Betts said tartly. You had to be tart in this household, just to be heard.

"Where's Rachel?"

"Upstairs somewhere. Go off now, make yourself look like a Talley."

Nathaway gave a cynical snort and headed for the back stairs. Before he could escape, Mumford the housemaster saw where he was headed and broke off a conversation with three maids to impart a message. "Tell your brother Mr. Hallowell that he needs to clear his fossil bones off the banquet table, or we'll have to do it for him," Mumford said.

"All right," said Nathaway.

He took the servants' stairs two at a time, up past the muffled sound of conversation on the first floor, and to the second. He peered out into the hallway, and finding it empty, slipped out. It was clear Hallowell had returned from his tour with the fleet, because the hall was lined with shadowy crates of scientific instruments, specimen books, and an enormous kite. A creature that looked like a cross between a small dog and a lizard saw Nathaway approaching its cage and spread its ruff with a menacing hiss.

He peered over the balcony railing into the main floor below, and saw his father receiving guests in the lamp-lit foyer. Tennessen Talley radiated enjoyment of the moment. The judge knew everyone; he had a joke or observation for every occasion; his trademark laugh rang out at regular intervals, giving everyone in earshot the impression that they were surely at the most entertaining event on earth. He was not being Chief Justice tonight, for he was dressed in civilian clothes; but he couldn't stop being the perfect politician, since that was no act. Tennessen dominated the room so instinctively that it was hard to remember he was not the guest of honour, only the hero's proud father.

When Nathaway peered into the first door down the hallway, he found a cabal of Mandregan's political friends intently debating something over wine. They broke off when he entered, and turned to see who it was; but since it was only Nathaway, they resumed their conversation.

"An army would be a threat to our liberties, and would have to be disbanded," Mandregan was saying. "But a navy is a different matter. Each ship is its own fiefdom. A navy is more a confederation of little warlords than a single machine. It gives a necessary outlet to dangerous men who crave glory, but in the end it is easy to disunite and defeat *in camera*."

"It seems to me your brother the admiral is the living argument against you," one of his co-conspirators said in a low tone. "The way things stand, he could walk into any office he chose, the nation is so entranced with him. Emperors are acclaimed, remember—it is the people who choose them, not the law."

"Corbin will never be emperor," Mandregan said with a secretive look that made the others draw closer, sure that he knew something they didn't. He had a lean, vulpine face that always looked like he was hiding something. His deep-set eyes were like the ones in paintings that always watched you. "Do you think the court hasn't been in a knot about that very question? What do you *do* with a man who has earned the adulation of the nation? It is a very risky situation."

"What does your father feel?" one man whispered. "As Chief Justice, will he support the nation, or his son? Does he see a dynasty as his legacy?"

Nathaway knew that Mandregan could never answer the question, since answering it would deflate the drama of the moment. Stirring up suspicion and mistrust was Mander's hobby. Sure enough, Mandregan turned to him. "Did you want something, Nat?"

"Have you seen Rachel?" Nathaway said.

"I think she's down listening to Hal's tall tales," Mander said.

Having been put in his usual place of irritating little brother, Nathaway turned to leave. The conversation would not go on anyway, he knew. This convocation had achieved its purpose of bringing everyone to a shivering precipice of uncertainty about the future of the Inning lexocracy. To continue would be redundant.

Out in the hall again, he paused at the side table where a chess game was set out in progress. It was black's turn, since the salt cellar was sitting on that side of the board. Nathaway studied it for a minute, then made the next logical move, and set the salt on the other side for the next passer-by.

A peal of infectious laughter from down the hall told him where Hallowell was holding forth to his scientific friends. As Nathaway approached the door, he heard his brother's commanding baritone saying, ". . .these tiny organisms, far too small for the naked eye to resolve, will sometimes bloom in such abundance that the whole surface of the sea turns red. The natives regard it with the utmost superstition, imagining that the sea has turned to blood. . . ."

As Nathaway appeared in the doorway, Hal saw him and rose to his feet. "Nathaway, upon my word!" He picked his way through the chairs to throw his arms around his younger brother. Hal was the one that most took after their father, both physically and in temperament. He would have been a natural in politics, but that had never interested him. Natural history was the realm Hal had set out to conquer.

"Upon my word," he repeated, holding Nathaway at arm's length. "You've grown like a *Leguminosae*. You're three feet taller than when I saw you last."

Nathaway shrugged self-consciously and said, "Mumford wants you to shift your bones."

"I beg your pardon?"

"Your fossil bones. The staff will have to give them to the dogs if you don't move them."

"Ah." With his arm still around Nathaway's shoulders, Hal turned to the others in the room. They were an assortment of university professors, a publisher, a well-heeled collector, and an officer of the learned society that had funded Hallowell's research. So in fact, Hal was not as oblivious of politics as he made out. The one woman in the room was Nathaway's sister Rachel.

"My friends, we had better take the chance to view the *mastronomicon* before some ignorant chap throws it in the dustbin. If you will follow me . . ."

They all rose on cue and crowded after Hallowell out the door. Nathaway let them pass and waited till Rachel came close. "I've got to talk to you," he said quietly.

Together they crossed the hall and made for the back stairs again. They had to go single file up the twisting flight to the third floor, where the family bedrooms lay. It was a much more spartan place up here. A well-worn carpet runner covered the board floor in the hall, and the walls were simple plaster. The line of doors made it look like a dormitory—which, when they were all growing up, it had been.

Nathaway headed for his own room on the side that overlooked the harbour. The window was nearly dark, so he lit the oil lamp, then turned to Rachel, who had settled down cross-legged on his bed. "Well?" she said.

The famous Talley family resemblance that gave the seven brothers their distinctive looks had had an unfortunate effect in Rachel's case. The pronounced nose that looked noble on the men simply looked horsey on her face; the blonde hair had no life nor curl to lend her beauty, so she wore it in a limp braid. The brothers all grew up tall and recognizable; Rachel was just lanky and homely. But she was Nathaway's confidante and ally.

He closed the door and turned to tell her. "I did it," he said. "I quit law school."

"Oh no," she breathed. Her face gave him a preview of the horror that would ripple through the Talley household at the news.

"I was going to flunk contracts and legislative theory anyway," he said. "So better to save everyone the embarrassment." They had all grown up knowing that everything they did reflected on the others. Their father had always said it didn't matter what they chose to do in life, so long as they were better than anyone else at it. It had seemed like a fair enough rule till Nathaway had had trouble figuring out what, if anything, he was any good at.

"How are you going to tell the judge?" Rachel said, meaning their father.

"Wait, you haven't heard it all." He drew a deep breath. "I'm leaving Fluminos."

"What? Where?"

"They're recruiting law students to go to the Forsaken Islands," he said.

"The Forsakens!" she protested. "There's nothing there but pine trees and savages."

"That's the whole point. The Court's going to be expanding our presence in the Forsakens, developing some of the poor and primitive areas. They need observers to make sure it's all going according to the law. We're to be like Justices of the Peace, adjudicating disputes and so forth. They have no courts or judiciary there, no advocates or trial by jury. It's barbaric, and unscrupulous people could take advantage."

"But can you do that without a degree?"

He shrugged. "They took me." Of course, like everything else, he could not know whether it was because of himself or his name. "I'm to leave in two weeks."

"Oh, Nat," she said. "This is . . . it's crazy."

He looked out the window, where the snow was falling in earnest now, big fat flakes gathering on the sill. "I'm sick of this city," he said, his voice low and intense. "I'm sick of being the last Talley in line, the only one who's not some kind of hero. It's all so false, like theatre. I don't want to play a part; I want to do some actual good in the world."

"You will," Rachel said. "You'll be a hero, Nat. Just give yourself time."

He sat on the bed facing her, crossing his long legs underneath him, his bony knees sticking up. "You should have heard the recruiter talk about the Forsakens," he said. "We've supposedly ruled them for years, but we've done nothing to help them, just left them in a state of poverty and ignorance. They have no schools, no doctors. We've let the most horrible superstitions persist. Did you know they still practice a kind of human sacrifice?"

"No!"

"Yes. There's a race of islanders that are like their chattel, kept in bondage because of a belief that their blood can cure disease. So whenever the islanders grow ill they bleed these slaves, sometimes to death. The administration has tried to put a stop to it, but the practice is too ancient. And as long as they have no alternatives, what are they supposed to do but keep their traditional cures? I've thought that I could pick up some medical books before I leave, and show them there are better ways."

His dry description did not do justice to the thrill of horror he had felt at the recruiter's much more lurid account. He did not mention the overtones of sexual slavery. It was his outrage at the needless suffering, his pity for the victims, his disgust at the ignorance, that had told him this was what he had to do. Never had he felt so strongly that he was called upon to act. All his life had been an aimless, pampered game up to now. Something had sent this message to him, to fetch him to the place where he was needed.

"This is real, Rachel," he said. "There are people who need us, right now. We're sitting around drinking wine and shooting off firecrackers while people are suffering, people we're responsible for. How can we call ourselves civilized if we let this kind of thing go on?"

She saw his passion, and her expression changed. She was taking him seriously now; but if anything, her concern had only deepened. "What kind of conditions will you have to live in?"

"I don't care," he said. "I can survive." In fact, he longed for the challenge of hardship. He wanted to test himself, and learn his limits. "It has to be a sacrifice. I can't do this in comfort and have it mean anything."

"Oh, Nat." She took his hand and squeezed it.

"You think I'm not ready for this."

"No, I think you're noble and brave. But—"

"Nobody can be noble and brave just by talking. You've got to *do* something."

To his surprise, her reply was bitter. "You Talley men are all so damned stubborn."

"Excuse me," he said defensively, "it's not just the men."

"Yes, but you can be stubborn in spectacular, self-destructive ways Mother and I can't."

They were interrupted by a loud explosion from the harbour, the first volley of fireworks. The echo bounced off the tall buildings, redoubling the sound. They both knelt on the bed and peered out the window to see if they could catch sight of the rockets.

Watching the next shell arc into the sky and detonate, consuming itself in an ecstasy of fire, it felt to Nathaway like a moment of pending transformation. He didn't aspire to fireworks to mark his deeds. He wanted something more intangible: to explore himself, and find out who he was apart from his family. He didn't want to conquer other nations like his brother; he wanted to conquer his own self.

The thought of wilderness filled him with a peace and space he had never known in crowded, artificial Fluminos. There would be elemental powers of sea and sky to test him, the true judge and jury of mankind. He would surrender himself to them—to scour him clean of civilization's taint and refine his being into essences. Only then would he be pure enough to give away his life to serve others. The thought of a life devoted to sacrifice filled him with an exaltation whose white-hot light burned all ambition to cinders.

The snow was just beginning to fall when Harg Ismol, soon to be former captain of the Native Navy, peered out the window of Holly's Hole, a waterfront tavern favoured by islanders. Behind him, the smoky room was packed with loudly celebrating men, newly paid off and released from the service. In one corner, several of them were holding a competition to see who could drink a pitcher of beer in one breath; but their shouts were almost drowned out by the roaring of another group watching two men pantomime what looked like an act of sexual congress with a cannon.

Harg was the only one in the room still in uniform, since his appointment to pick up his pay and papers was still an hour away. He had come to the window ostensibly to check the weather, but really to check his watch. It was a mark of his strange position that he couldn't make a simple gesture like taking out his watch without subterfuge. Among the men down here, the fact that he could afford a watch would make it seem like he was putting on airs; the fact that he needed one would not excuse him, only set him apart. Time belonged to the Inning world; men who simply took orders didn't need to worry about it.

Pocketing the incriminating instrument, he glanced up the wooden stairs at his left. He knew the chamber above was a sea of grey and blue uniforms like his own, since that was where the officers were celebrating. But it wasn't just rank that separated the men below and the men above; it was race as well, the omnipresent factor among islanders. Above, they were all Torna; here, the crowd, like himself, was Adaina. He had already been upstairs for a while, and knew they had no problem with him—the rank and reputation he had earned outweighed old prejudices. But he had drifted downstairs to find more relaxing company, only to discover that his fellow Adainas rather bored him. Only two things had kept him downstairs: the sweet knowledge that it looked, for the first time in his life, like he was snubbing the Tornas; and the delirious pride of his fellow Adainas that he would do so.

There was time for a last carouse before he had to leave for his parting interview. But where should he go—back to his table with the boatswains, pilots, and gunners, or upstairs to mend fences with the officers? The men with whom he had joined the navy, or the men with whom he left it? He felt like he was walking along a wharf with one foot on the dock and the other on the deck of a shifting, unmoored boat. One of these days he was going to tip into the drink.

And so he took the third alternative: he slipped out the door into the snow without a goodbye to either group. Let them try and interpret that.

It was cold outside, so he buttoned his broadcloth uniform coat and put on his hat. The street was full of revellers, vendors, aimless men, and shameless women—most of them immigrants from the various dependencies of the far-flung Inning empire. Presumably some Innings lived in Fluminos—probably somewhere in the tall brick buildings on the hill above the harbour—but so far Harg had seen little evidence of them. Everything here seemed to be run by conquered peoples.

The route to the Navy Office took him past the hospital, and his steps slowed as he came abreast of the gate, knowing he had time to go in, wanting above all to avoid it. But the thought of walking by, in all the enjoyment of his success, would leave him feeling soiled, so he turned in.

The people on duty in the hospital recognized him by now, and didn't need to ask where he was going. Outside the door to the second-floor ward where Jory was, Harg met an orderly he had paid to give his friend some extra comforts. "How is he?" Harg asked.

The man shrugged. "Bad day, Captain. He was raving earlier, and we had to restrain him. Sorry."

Harg grasped the man's shoulder to show there was no ill feeling; he knew how violent Jory got in his fits. He slipped a coin into the man's pocket. "Thanks, Captain," the orderly said, nodding in deference.

The ward was a long room lined with a double row of wooden beds. Looking down it, Harg had the bitter thought that the revellers setting off the fireworks tonight would turn silent in shock and shame if they knew what it had really taken to win the war. His boots sounded loud on the plank floor as he walked down the line of beds. Jory was sitting up, his shaved head drooping, his wrists and ankles tied to the bed frame with strong strips of cloth. When Harg came to a halt at the foot of the bed Jory looked up, and for a moment his face was a mask of paranoia and hostility. Quickly, Harg removed his hat to make himself more recognizable.

"Oh, Harg," Jory said, his words slightly slurred. "You didn't look like yourself, dressed that way."

Jory didn't look like himself, either. There was a caved-in place on his skull where the shell fragment had penetrated the brain. No one had thought he would live, but here he was. The wound was almost healed on the outside now, but the havoc on the inside would never go away.

Harg sat on the side of the bed and said, "How are you doing?"

"I don't like these," Jory said, pulling the restraints tight.

"Well, you shouldn't attack people then," Harg said matter-of-factly.

"I know." Jory shook his head in angry frustration. "It's like I've turned into you, isn't it?"

Jory was never violent when Harg was around; the hospital staff had commented on the difference in his behaviour. But Harg had seen enough evidence to know that what he saw was the remnant of the old Jory, not the new one.

They had grown up together, best friends, though Jory's mother had disapproved of Harg's influence on her son. But it was Jory who had come up with the crazy scheme to run away and join the navy seven long years ago, and Harg who had followed unthinkingly. They had had to steal away at night and hide in the hold of the recruiter's boat to escape the sure pursuit of Jory's family. No doubt the whole village had blamed Harg, since Jory was such a good boy.

And he had been—good-natured, pliable, like clay in the hands of the navy trainers, while Harg had struck sparks, like flint, against everyone he touched. Jory had accepted rules and strove to please; Harg had rebelled and suffered the harsh consequences. It had looked like they were headed in opposite directions— Jory to honourable service, Harg to the brig or even the gibbet—until the day when it had occurred to Harg that he could outwit this system, and beat the Torna officers at their own game. After that, it had all changed.

Outside on the street, someone set off a string of firecrackers. Jory tensed, eyes wide and panicky, thinking they were under attack.

"Don't worry, you're safe," Harg said. Then, to distract him, "Think you'll be ready to leave soon?"

"Leave? For where?"

"Home. Remember, I'm taking you back to Yora."

"You keep saying that."

"Well, I mean it. I'm on my way to get my discharge right now. Then, whenever you're well enough, I'll book passage for us both, back to the islands."

Jory had little reaction. "I thought you would stay in the navy. You're so good at it."

This was an understatement; Harg was brilliant. Three years ago, he had taken command of the frigate *Wolverine* when its captain and lieutenant had both died of the fever, and he had not brought it back till he had obliterated a Rothur cruiser. After that, unrestrained by age-old precepts about how to conduct war at sea, he and a core of other islanders had used pirate tactics, seamanship, subterfuge, and insanely vicious attacks to more than equalize the size difference between the Native Navy's sloops and the Rothur warships. It was an open secret that the Native Navy, not the lumbering and hidebound Inning Navy, had turned the course of the war.

And now he was giving it all up, the only thing he had ever been successful at. He gave a slight, cynical laugh. "I'm tired of all this *civilization*." He gave the word a flick of contempt. "It's all false, like theatre—an Adaina playing a Torna playing an Inning. It's best to get back to the South Chain, where things are genuine."

"What will you do there?"

This was an excellent question; Jory sometimes surprised Harg with simple insights. "I don't know," he laughed. Mine peat? Fish? What did aimless war heroes do?

He checked his watch again; he was late now. Well, what could they do, discharge him? But out of long habit he rose and said, "I've got to get going. I'll be back tomorrow."

"Take care, Harg," Jory said, his face wan.

Harg always felt guilty leaving, and slunk out faster than he had come in. But when he came to the gate he felt a burden lifted; he had met his obligation for the day.

The Navy Office building was bustling when he arrived, though it was nearly evening and all the clerks were working by lamplight. To the young Torna adjutant who looked up from his desk when Harg entered Commodore Buckrush's antechamber, he said, "Don't you ever get to leave?"

"As long as the Admiral's in the building, so is everyone else," the adjutant said dourly. It should have seemed odd for Admiral Talley, the hero of the hour, to be still at work with all the celebrations pending in his honour, but the man had the reputation of a fearsome taskmaster. He had burned through any number of subordinates by failing to understand that real humans required more than three hours of sleep at night. Harg had never seen him; officers of the Native Navy had little to do with the Inning hierarchy not assigned to them.

Commodore Buckrush was in charge of the Native Navy. He was a grizzled veteran on the verge of retirement who had been given the undesirable appointment to oversee what was supposed to be a second-class squadron for guarding the coasts and escorting merchant vessels. And yet, under him the Native Navy had metamorphosed into a lethal striking force that had done the ungentlemanly work of actually beating the enemy. It was to this Inning that Harg owed his promotion; and yet, he had never been able to bring himself to like the man. There was something too old-school and patronizing about him. Harg had never been able to square the rule-breaking creativity of his orders with his bluff, conventional demeanour.

When the adjutant showed Harg into the inner office, the Commodore was trying to button the bright scarlet and blue coat of his dress uniform over his ample paunch, doubtless in preparation for some party. "Ah, Ismol," he said. "At last."

Harg saluted with a shade less than the usual precision. "Sir."

Buckrush went to his desk, where Harg's papers were lying, but he seemed reluctant to hand them over. "Well, you've come a long way, haven't you, Ismol? Frankly, I think it's a miracle you survived the first two years."

He didn't know the half of it. It was several miracles piled on top of each other. But it seemed ungracious to bring it up now.

The Commodore went on, "I daresay there aren't too many captains in the navy who have been flogged for insubordination. Three times."

Thanks for mentioning it, Harg wanted to say, but instead stayed silent.

"I've got your papers here," Buckrush said, fingering them. "But I'd prefer not to have to give them to you. Sure you won't re-enlist? You could have a fine career in the navy. We need men like you."

"No thanks, Commodore," Harg said. "I've made other plans."

Buckrush picked up the papers, but still didn't hand them over. "In that case, there's someone else who wants to talk to you. Come with me."

He walked past Harg and out the office door. Mystified, Harg followed him down the hall and up a staircase to the second floor of the building, where Harg had never set foot. They passed under a brass chandelier and across a carpet to a set of painted wooden doors at the front of the building. This was the realm of the Inning Navy, the separate elite branch where natives like himself served only as seamen.

Buckrush knocked, then opened the door and entered, leaving Harg to follow after. Inside was another antechamber with a grim-looking Inning in civilian clothes, sitting at a secretary's desk. It took Harg a moment to realize the man really was the secretary. Buckrush handed him Harg's papers, and he scanned them. Harg watched longingly, wondering if he would ever get a chance to touch his own discharge. But the secretary rose and took the papers into the inner office.

"Well, this is it, then," Buckrush said, turning to Harg. "We probably won't meet again; I'm retiring after this. Good luck to you, Ismol." He actually held out a hand for Harg to shake as if they were old friends. Then he went out by the door they had come in, leaving Harg alone in the antechamber.

The secretary returned from the inner office without the papers. In a monotone he said, "Admiral Talley will see you now."

Harg didn't move at first. He couldn't help the reflexive thought that he must have done something truly heinous this time. But try as he might, he could not think of a single reason why the legendary head of the Inning Navy should want to see him. The secretary had to say, "You may go in, Captain," before Harg could shake off his paralysis.

The office he entered was simply furnished—a functional, orderly place devoid of ostentation. Despite the snow falling outside, no fire burned in the fireplace. Harg came to a halt just inside the door and saluted as precisely as he ever had. A fleeting gratitude that he had bothered to shave passed through his head, and disappeared.

If he had ever pictured Admiral Corbin Talley, Harg had imagined something imposing, along Commodore Buckrush's lines; but the reality was completely different. The man who stood behind the desk scanning Harg's papers was slightly built, with close-cropped, greying blond hair and wire-rimmed spectacles. Had he not been dressed in a splendid, gold-trimmed uniform, he would have looked like a botanist or watchmaker. But any impression of myopic intellectuality disappeared the instant he looked up to study Harg. He had startling blue eyes as probing as lancets. Harg felt that every cell of his body was being inspected separately. He kept his face impassive.

"Captain Ismol," said Admiral Talley, "I am glad to finally meet you."

He made it sound like he had actually heard Harg's name before this very instant. "Likewise, sir," said Harg.

"Did Commodore Buckrush go over these with you?" Talley asked, referring to the papers.

"No, sir."

Talley picked up a small wooden box from the desk and came around to Harg's side. He handed the papers to Harg, clearly assuming that Harg could do more than puzzle out a few simple words. Embarrassed, Harg studied the top paper as if he could make sense of it. It didn't look like the other discharge papers he had seen; it was embossed with fancy gold lettering. The next thing Talley did, explained it. He opened the box and held it out to Harg. In it lay the epaulette and cockade of a squadron commander. Harg stared at them, unable to move.

"Go ahead, take it," Talley said. "You earned it."

Harg took the box, but still couldn't touch the insignia in it. It was not that he had been promoted to Commodore; that would have been explainable. It was the colour of the epaulette. Instead of the silver of the Native Navy, this one was the gold of the Inning Navy.

"This . . . this is a mistake," he said.

"No it's not," Talley said calmly. "We're abolishing the Native Navy as a separate institution. The segregation is divisive and inefficient. From now on the Native Navy will simply be a branch of the regular navy, on the same standing as the other branches."

Such a sweeping reform would send seismic shocks through the whole organization. It was no wonder Buckrush was retiring; probably a good many other Inning officers would as well, out of protest. Harg looked up at the man who had ordered the overthrow of such ancient and accepted institutions, and spoke as if it were merely a bit of housekeeping. Harg found it impossible to imagine having such power.

"A great victory gives one some opportunities that might not otherwise arise," Talley said with a slight smile. "I felt the Native Navy deserved some recompense for its part in that victory."

Harg looked down again at the epaulette, and this time dared to touch it.

"Of course," said Talley, "if you decide to take your discharge now, this rank will be merely ceremonial, with the thanks of your grateful nation. However, if you decide to stay . . . Would you like hear more?"

All of Harg's plans were whirling around his head, scattered by this revelation. "Yes, sir," he said.

"Have a seat, Commodore," the Admiral said urbanely. "Would you like some coffee?" Without waiting for an answer, he knocked on the door of his secretary's office, apparently a well-known signal. The door opened and the long-faced secretary appeared with a samovar which he placed on a low table flanked by wing chairs. Talley sat in one and poured two cups. "I daresay I am going to need this," he said, leaning back in his chair. "I have several obligations tonight."

The coffee was a smooth, pungent ambrosia unlike any Harg had tasted before. He was disarmed by the whole setting, and the unexpected civility of the man before him. Most Innings affected a rough simplicity when dealing with islanders, but the Admiral made no such concessions. Harg wondered why people were so terrified of Corbin Talley.

He had figured out that the rank he had been offered was the same as that which Buckrush was vacating, but he still didn't know if he were being offered Buckrush's job, and couldn't think how to ask. So he said, "How will it be organized?"

"That's necessarily a little fluid now," Talley said. "It will be designed as best suits the accomplishment of its new mission. You see, the Court has honoured the navy with a new assignment."

"Already?" Harg said, surprised. They had barely gotten home from the last war.

Admiral Talley seemed to get some hidden amusement from Harg's reaction. Drily, he said, "I'm glad to see I am not the only one . . .shall we say, impressed by the Court's alacrity. But yes, they have handed us our next orders, and the Native Navy, or whatever it is to be called, will have to play a crucial role. You see, we have been instructed to turn our attention to the Forsaken Islands."

Even over his wince at the condescending Inning name for his homeland, Harg felt a dull throb of alarm at this news. "What does Inning want with the isles?" he said.

"It seems the Forsakens are rich in resources that our merchants are eager to develop."

"What resources?" Harg had never noticed any but peat and sand.

"Timber. Lead. Iron. Hemp. Cheap labour."

Timber for building ships, Harg thought. Lead for bullets, iron for cannons. Hemp for ropes. It sounded like Inning's imperial ambitions had not been stilled by the victory over Rothur.

"And of course, the fisheries are phenomenal," Talley added.

"Of course."

"As you know, Inning has claimed the Forsakens for years, but we have never tried to administer them. We have left control entirely in the hands of the native civilian governors, but even they have never been able to extend the law to the outer archipelagos. While our attention was diverted in Rothur, the unadministered territories have become a nest of pirates and brigands who are preying on the coastal shipping almost as far south as Fluminos. The present administration in Tornabay seems unable to cope with the situation, and has come under criticism for corruption and autocracy. Altogether, some sort of police action is warranted. The regular navy is the wrong tool for the job; the Native Navy has a far better chance of success."

The explanation, so reasonable-sounding, left Harg with terrible misgivings. "We'd be fighting against our own people," he said.

"No, you'd be fighting *for* your own people. To free them of tyranny, corruption, and lawlessness. To create a new nation that cuts across all the old divisions of race and religion. To unite your people behind the ideas of rational self-government and justice for all."

For a moment Harg imagined himself returning home with a liberating army to topple Governor Tiarch and her despised Torna cabal from power, to restore the ancient greatness of his land. It was an intoxicating thought for a young man who had been no more than a sullen troublemaker when he left. But he couldn't quite believe it. "What do you want me for?" he said.

Talley answered, "I want you to do Buckrush's job, only do it right. With some understanding of the people under you, and some initiative. You've proven you can handle islanders, command them when others can't. The Native Navy has tremendous potential; by the time we have to go to war again, it could be the most valuable weapon in our arsenal."

So the Innings saw it as a sort of training exercise. Merely a prelude to the real geopolitical mission, whatever that would be. Harg thought of all the things that were wrong with the Native Navy, and of having the power to set them right. But there was one huge obstacle.

"I'm Adaina," he said. "The officer corps is almost all Torna. They wouldn't accept me."

"They would if I told them to," Talley said, coolly setting down his coffee cup.

How could he explain this to an Inning? "No, you see, there are racial divides in the isles, old prejudices that run deep. . . ."

"Do tell. I never would have known," Talley said with ice-smooth sarcasm.

Harg realized he had just patronized the head of the Inning Navy. "Sorry, sir," he said. "Not many Innings pay much attention to us."

"Please assume that I have been paying attention," Talley said in a voice that could have cut glass.

Looking into those cold blue eyes, Harg felt a revelation strike him with physical force. It was not Buckrush who had engineered the transformation of the Native Navy, as everyone had assumed. It was this man—this ruthless, razor-like mind. Buckrush had been merely a puppet, a cloak for the machinations of his commander. Talley had needed a weapon more versatile and nasty than the gentleman's club of a navy he had inherited, so he had created one.

"It's me that hasn't been paying attention," Harg said, as much to himself as to Talley. But how could he have known? He had been a tool as well, manipulated without knowing it. He remembered how cool Buckrush had always seemed about his promotion to captain. Now he guessed why: Buckrush had had no choice about it. Talley had been micromanaging the Native Navy all the time.

Clearly, all Harg's assumptions had to change. With this man, absolutely everything was intentional. He had to assume no gaps in knowledge, no mistakes.

"You *want* an Adaina in charge," he said, eyes narrowed. "Why?"

Talley smiled at the change in tone, but he was still assessing Harg, testing. "I fancy you can see my reasoning."

"If it were me," Harg said slowly, "I'd want an Adaina because the great majority of the population is Adaina, especially in the Outer Chains—the parts beyond Inning control. If a Torna navy showed up in those islands to impose the law, they would explode into rebellion. But having Adaina officers might just give the navy some credibility. It couldn't be just one officer. You would have to promote a whole cadre of Adainas."

"That would be your first priority," Talley said. "But tell me, how much of a threat could the Adaina truly be?"

"Look at your pirates. Are they a threat? They wouldn't fight you like a navy would, head-on. They would strike invisibly, pick off targets of opportunity, and then melt back into the population. If they had local support, you could be fighting them for decades. I don't think you want that."

"No indeed. So what do you recommend?"

"First of all, avoid sending in the Northern Squadron, Tiarch's navy. You can't imagine how they're hated in the outlands. The Southern Squadron has no history there; it wouldn't be seen as a provocation. Then, long-term, you have to think like the Adaina. There are ancient traditions of leadership in the outlands, things people would respond to and respect, if you got it right."

"Yes. What traditions?"

There was a tap on the door, and it opened a crack so that the secretary's nose was visible. "Excuse me sir," he said, "the Chief Justice has sent a carriage to fetch you to the reception."

"Let them wait!" Talley shot the words like bullets at the secretary's head, and the door quickly closed. As if nothing had happened, the Admiral said, "Please go on."

But Harg had realized that he was giving an Inning a blueprint for conquering his homeland. Once again he had been manipulated, lured to the edge of betrayal. He said, "I think perhaps the Chief Justice might be more important than me right now, sir."

There was a short silence. Harg was thinking that if he took this man's bait he would still be an Inning tool. Still obeying them, doing their dirty work. He would become what the Innings had made him forever.

"Well, thank you for your insights," Admiral Talley said lightly. "It is seldom enough that an islander will speak to an Inning as an equal."

Harg stared, disarmed again. But that wasn't what had been happening. He had been talking to Talley as if they were both Inning.

"You don't need to give me your answer today," Talley said pleasantly. "Think of the offer, sleep on it. I'll be here tomorrow."

"No," Harg said, standing. "I can give you my answer now, sir. I appreciate your offer, but I'll take the discharge."

For the first time since Harg had walked in the door, Talley looked like something had not gone precisely as he had expected. A slight, ominous line appeared between his brows. "You understand, if you refuse, the offer must go to someone else."

"I understand that. I don't want it. Sir."

Talley saw that he was in earnest, and his pleasant mood vanished. "Very well," he said. He took the gilded commission off the top of the pile of papers, crumpled it into a ball, and threw it with furious force into the fireplace. He handed Harg the discharge and pay slip, then went back to his desk and began writing as if he were alone in the room. Harg stood for a second, then assumed he had been dismissed, and went to the door.

"Ismol," Talley said as Harg's hand touched the knob. "You forgot your epaulette."

He had left the wooden box sitting on the coffee table. "I thought—"

"It's yours, you earned it," Talley said.

Harg went back and took the box.

"Perhaps we'll see each other in the Forsakens," Talley said neutrally, signing a document and placing it deliberately on a pile.

"You're going there?" Harg said, astonished. "I thought—"

Talley looked at him across the desk, his face unreadable. "Oh, yes, I'm going there. I go where my nation sends me. And right now it seems my nation wishes me to be very, very far away from Fluminos."

This statement made no sense. From what Harg had seen, the Inning nation adored this man, and Fluminos desperately wanted him close. As if to prove it, the first explosion of the fireworks rang out across the harbour.

Then Harg realized that when Talley said "my nation," he didn't mean what everyone else did. He didn't mean all those people eager to write him poems and lift up their children to see him. He meant some group invisible to everyone else, who had the power to work even him like a puppet. Harg could hardly imagine who they might be.

"Thank you, sir," Harg said, glancing at the box.

"You're entirely welcome," Talley said, and turned back to his writing.

Out on the street, Harg had to step around the carriage waiting to whisk the Admiral away to wherever his nation waited. Looking back at the window of the office he had just left, Harg saw the light still burning. He felt cautious respect, perhaps even admiration, but no warmth. In fact, deep down where it mattered, Corbin Talley terrified him.

THE SANDS
OF YORA

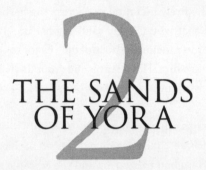

Spaeth Dobrin woke, as she always did, to the sheer, sensual joy of being alive. The relaxation of her naked limbs, the texture of the bed linens—every sensation pleased her, since that was how she had been created, for enjoyment and delight. It was a cool morning, but the bed was warm, and still smelled a little of Goth. She rolled over to his side and buried her face in the pillow, trying to capture his scent, as if it could conjure up the man. Just the thought of his touch made little thrills scamper across the surface of her skin.

But his scent did not summon him, and the bed now seemed empty and abandoned, as it had for over two weeks. Feeling the restless hunger his absence left in her, she got up. Almost at once the cool air distracted her by nipping at her nakedness. She raced to the back door of the cottage and out into the morning, bare feet slapping on the stone doorstep. The sun fell lightly on her skin, making it shine the pearly grey of an oyster shell; the warm wind ruffled the tarnished silver of her hair. The Yorans called her Grey Girl. Outwardly, she looked like a mature woman just out of her teens, but she had been created only seven years before.

Spaeth was a creature of impulse, and now the impulse struck her to climb the hill above Yorabay and lie in the sun on the boulders there. She was halfway to the main path when she remembered that she needed to wear some clothes. The village women had been harping at her about it, especially since the Tornas had arrived and begun building their dock, busy as burrowing rodents. "They don't respect you like we do," Tway had said. "They have baser impulses."

Spaeth had been curious to know what a base impulse was, but Tway had seemed so convinced no good could come of it, that she had promised to be careful. Now she backtracked to the weather-beaten, moss-grown timber cottage and rummaged in a drawer till she found a sleeveless undershirt and a cloth to wrap around her hips. Thus clad in a bare minimum of decency, she returned barefoot to the path, turning uphill toward the early sun.

The dome of Yorabay Hill rose like a man's bald head above the fringe of woodland along the shore. As Spaeth climbed, the dewy grass clutched playfully at her legs, and alongside her, carefree little gusts of wind played porpoise. When she reached the top and climbed onto one of the great grizzled boulders that ringed the crest of the hill, she could see the entire world spread out like a rumpled cloth fringed in white where it met the sea. Off to the north, a single sail dotted the azure expanse of the Pont Sea. This was the extent of Spaeth's universe, all she had known since her creation.

A distant boom sounded, as a charge of explosives went off at the work site near The Jetties, and Spaeth turned that way, frowning. The Tornas had been at it for a week, digging and building. She could feel the island's hurt in an aching spot under her breastbone, a new and unwelcome sensation. What had Yora ever done to the Tornas, that they wanted to gouge out holes and pound stakes into its sands? She wished her arms were big enough to circle the whole island, to shelter it forever from change.

It occurred to her that the stones might know what to do. She stretched out on the licheny surface of the boulder under her, making her mind a floating net for passing stone-thoughts. She thought the Whispering Stones were her friends. She had been feeding them and watering their roots for three years now, and they were thriving. Some had even grown, and they scarcely ever left off passing their secrets to and fro on a windy night. But the warm appreciation she usually felt from them was gone now; instead, there was only a strange, cold silence.

Another distant explosion rattled the sky. "Stop it!" Spaeth shouted in helpless rage. If Goth were here, he would know what to do. Why had the Grey Man chosen this moment to be gone?

He had disappeared into the other circles before. It was his only escape from the ties that otherwise kept him a prisoner on Yora. But he had never been gone so long. Every day of his absence, Spaeth's gnawing sense of loss had grown—and her worry about what would happen to her if he did not come back.

Rolling over, she put her arms around the boulder, pressing her cheek against its rough surface. "You miss him too, don't you?" she whispered.

Behind her there was the pad of a stealthy paw. "Silly girl," a voice drawled. "The stones don't care."

"Ridwit!" Spaeth sat up, but was almost knocked over again when the panther leaped onto the stone and rubbed up against her. She put an arm around Ridwit's sharp black shoulders.

"The stones don't care about much of anything," Ridwit said. "Not even this island—what do you call it?"

"Yora."

"Yora." Ridwit punctuated the word with a purr halfway through. "They are older than the sea, older than the bones of Hannako. This is just one stop on their long march down from the north. If the island sank today, they would just go on their way."

"Where are they going?" Spaeth asked.

"Don't ask me. I am only a god." Ridwit laid a heavy head on Spaeth's shoulder and purred deafeningly in her ear till she began to scratch the velvet fur between the panther's horns.

Spaeth liked Ridwit, but knew better than to trust such a lawless being. In past centuries they would have been adversaries. But the enmity of the Mundua for the Grey People had grown so ancient it was almost a kind of friendship now—and friendship, Goth always said, was a good way to understand your enemies.

"Ridwit," Spaeth said, "Do you know where Goth is?"

"He is gone."

"I know he is gone. Where?"

"To a place where the sea is wet and the night is dark."

Generations ago, they had called the horned panther The Riddler. Now Spaeth began to scratch in that particular place by the ear that the cat could never resist. Ridwit's back leg began to jerk and her eyes to film over in delight. "Is he dead?" Spaeth whispered.

"Scratch again."

"Answer me first."

"Did you keep a stone for him?"

"No."

"Then answer the question yourself."

It was true. If Goth had gone forever, he would have left a stone for her to keep his soul.

"Why should you care about him?" Ridwit asked a little peevishly. "You have me." She rubbed her sinuous body against Spaeth's, then jumped down and rolled playfully onto her back in the grass.

"Because," Spaeth said softly, "he is my lover and my creator. He is my bandhota."

Ridwit twisted around into a crouch, glowering at her. "Oh, you Grey People and your dhota. It makes me sick." She rose, bits of grass clinging to her fur, and stalked between the stones, into the centre of the ring.

Spaeth had always known what the Grey Man did. She had often come with him, carrying the tools of dhota, the bowl and the knife. She had sat silent in the shadows, watching as he used them. He had told her about dhota, how it came about and what it meant.

Oh yes, she had known. She had seen his face chalky and drained after losing too much blood, and held him as he tossed in his bed in the grip of someone else's pain. She had fed him when his hands were too palsied to lift a spoon. She had seen the feverish longing in his eyes when his bandhotai were too long gone, and the foolish, unjudging love that made him a victim of their ills again and again. He had taken on all the hurts of Yora, little and great, for forty years. It was not healthy or right, but he was as addicted to giving dhota as the Adaina were to receiving it.

The panther was sitting in the stone circle with the tip of her tail twitching. Spaeth climbed down from the rock to sit beside her.

"You Grey People have gotten degenerate," the god said. "Once, you had the power to protect the isles. But you will never use your power again. You don't care about the world any more. All you think about is giving dhota."

"Don't talk as if I am one of them," Spaeth said.

"Goth is Lashnura. He made you from his own flesh. So you are Lashnura. But you've never given dhota, so you don't know. Once you do it, you'll turn like all the others, soft and sentimental. There won't be any outside world for you; all you'll care about is your bandhotai. You'll just be a slave." She looked at Spaeth mournfully. "I like you now. I wish you didn't have to change."

"I *won't* change!" Spaeth said fiercely. "I'll never give dhota." The idea made her horribly uneasy. Goth, wonderful man that he was, was helplessly bound to the tiny community of Yora. Spaeth felt panic at the thought of becoming like him, enslaved by a thousand invisible bonds. She didn't want to be just an ignorant village dhotamar. She wanted freedom.

"You all say that," Ridwit growled. "You all think you'll stay free. But it only takes one claim, and you change your minds."

"If anyone asks, I'll refuse to do it," Spaeth said. "I'll deny their claims."

"You won't be able to," Ridwit said. "Your ancestors saw to that."

Spaeth put her hands over her ears. "I'm not listening to you. I'm not one of them."

The cat suddenly stiffened as if a shot had gone through her. In a single contortion of muscle and fur she was crouching between two of the stones with her tail lashing to and fro, her amber gaze directed down the hill. "One of *them* is coming," she snarled.

Startled, Spaeth followed her gaze. A tall, lean figure dressed in a frock coat and broad-brimmed hat was making his way toward the hilltop with a stiff, purposeful stride. Spaeth gazed, transfixed. She had never seen anything like this novelty before. It could only be one thing. "They say the Tornas brought an Inning with them."

"Is that what you call them?" Ridwit's eyes narrowed. "He's wearing a very ugly body."

"I think all Innings look like that."

"Didn't he get enough sun? He grew spindly."

Spaeth stroked down the cat's bristling back fur. "Be still, or you will start a hurricane." All the world knew it was the lashing of Ridwit's tail that stirred up the wind.

"I *want* a hurricane," Ridwit said maliciously. "It's been a long time."

"Go north, then, and don't trouble us. We have enough worries."

Ridwit's keen eyes turned from the approaching figure to Spaeth. "They are our enemies, you know," she growled low in her throat. "They want to keep me from my kingdom, to tie me in bonds. I hate them. If you bring this one to me, I'll help you."

Spaeth frowned. "What do you want with him?"

"To feed on his terror."

"I can't do that. You know that."

The Inning was at the base of the steep dirt path that led to the Whispering Stones. Ridwit turned to hiss at him with primeval malevolence, then with a single movement stepped out of reality into myth. Where she had been, a dried bush of wild pea rattled in the wind.

The young man climbing the grassy slope was tall, rawboned, and blond, with an awkward gait and spectacles that gave him a slightly baffled look. He had not yet spied Spaeth, so she crouched to slip away. But curiosity stopped her. She had never seen someone from beyond the isles. And so when he reached the crest of the hill she was perched on one of the granite boulders with her arms around her legs.

He stopped to catch his breath, leaning on the oak walking-stick he carried. By now Spaeth had remembered what the islanders called him: Nathaway Talley, the Justice of the Peace who had come to teach Yorans about Inning law.

"Hello," he said breathlessly.

"Hello," Spaeth answered.

After a tortured pause he said, "I came up here to see the ancient curiosity." He waved his stick at the stones. "What are they, a fortification?"

"I don't think so," Spaeth said.

He waited a moment for her to say more, but when she didn't, he went on, "Are they a holy site, a shrine?"

"No," said Spaeth.

"Is it all right if I look at them?"

"You have to ask them," Spaeth said.

He gave her an odd look, and didn't follow her advice. Instead, he began to walk around the circle, taking out a small notebook to record the positions of the boulders. He paced out the diameter and circumference of the ring, writing down numbers. Spaeth crouched like a cormorant, watching him. Ridwit was right: he looked uncomfortable in his body, as if it fitted him too loosely. It was a ramshackle assemblage of limbs and defensiveness.

At last he climbed atop the largest boulder to survey the view. "Granite isn't native to the South Chain," he said. "Do you know where the stones came from?"

"From the north," Spaeth said, repeating what Ridwit had told her.

Shading his eyes with one hand, the Inning looked down the steep slopes and ravines between the beaches and the hill. "How did they get up here?"

"Up the path from Lone Tree Point. The stones came of their own accord."

He turned to her with such a sceptical expression that she felt obliged to explain. "The Altans caught the stones in nets and sang them to the surface of the sea. When they reached the land, the stone-fishers danced ahead along the path, and sang so sweetly that the stones came after to hear."

"I see," Nathaway observed noncommittally, then turned back to the stone he stood on. "They must weigh several tons apiece, but the natives then had no wheeled vehicles, no pulleys, and no ropes strong enough for the task. It must have been an extraordinary feat."

Since she had already told him how it was done, Spaeth wondered if she were not expressing herself very well, or if perhaps he were a trifle stupid.

He was studying her, though when she looked at him he glanced quickly away. She knew he was curious. "You're not Adaina, are you?" he said at last.

"No."

He jumped down from the boulder and came over. Fascination and morbid curiosity mingled in his gaze.

"You're one of the Grey People. Lash—how do you pronounce it?"

"Just the way it's said. Lashnura." She still sat on the boulder, but their eyes were almost on a level.

"Are you the only one on the island?" he asked.

"There was Goth Batra, but he has gone somewhere."

"So it is your duty to perform the sacrifices?"

She didn't have the faintest idea what he meant. When she didn't answer, he grasped her left wrist and turned her arm so he could see the veins. Her grey skin was unblemished. With a pang, she remembered the sight of Goth's arms, so scarred there was scarcely a place left to cut.

"They haven't preyed on you," he said, with evident relief.

Offended, she pulled her arm away. His ignorance cheapened and desecrated the whole idea of dhota. Though only moments ago she had denied it, she now felt a need to defend the custom. "A dhotamar gives willingly, as a gift to those he loves," she said. "It is a beautiful act, a sacrifice of loving kindness, and Goth is honoured for it."

The Inning seemed arrested by what she said. He pinned her with startling, earnest blue eyes through his shaggy bangs. "Truly? It is voluntary? You are not forced?"

She wanted to say, *No, a Grey Person is never forced*; but that was only the ideal, not the flawed reality. She had to look away, disconcerted by the strange intensity of his gaze.

Gently, he said, "Well, you don't need to fear that you will be forced now. The law forbids it."

The presumption of this statement was seemingly lost on him. Did he really believe that he could come from some faraway land and make a rule forbidding something woven into every strand of Yoran life? It was like saying that eating was now forbidden. "I suppose you think that everyone will obey you," she said, mocking his certainty.

"Well, yes," he said, clearly startled by her tone. "It's not me, it's the law."

"Your law has nothing to do with us."

"Oh, but it does!" The subject seemed to really interest him, because his face suddenly became animated, as if he had forgotten all about himself and his own discomfort, in his zeal to inform her. "The law is the great gift we are bringing to your people; it will benefit you beyond anything else, if you use it wisely."

Spaeth had always assumed that "law" meant just a batch of rules, but in his face she could read that there was more to it. She had an intuition that, to an Inning, law was like a set of magisterial spells that could be used by learned practitioners to control the behaviour of others. If an islander had claimed such powers, she would have thought him foolish; but this Inning was a very peculiar sort of man, and might have abilities she knew nothing of.

"Are you a lawster?" she asked.

"Lawyer," he corrected her. "No, I'm just a student of the law."

Even Goth, a great namora who had powers of creation and curing, never claimed to be more than a student. It now seemed significant to Spaeth that even Ridwit had feared and hated this Inning lawgician.

"Will you take apprentices to learn your law?" Spaeth said.

"Yes!" he said, delighted at her interest.

"Teach me something simple," she said.

"All right." He seemed to cast about in his mind. At last he hitched himself up onto the boulder beside her, his long legs dangling.

"In a simple society," he said, "everyone cooperates for the mutual good. But as society grows complex, it's necessary to set up rules and procedures to govern disputes, to prevent concentration of power, and to insure equity and promote the general welfare."

He glanced at her to make sure she was following. She recognized his words as the preamble every tutor of esoteric knowledge used to explain the origins of his powers, and nodded.

Reassured, he continued, "Now, you and your neighbours have been living without law, except your customary practices. This served you well as long as your needs were simple; but now things are going to change, and you need the protection of Inning law. It will be like a shield, a roof over your heads, something you can use to defend yourselves even if someone tries to exploit you or take away your rights. The thing you need to know is that in the Inning lexarchy, everyone is equal under the law: rich or poor, Adaina or Torna, woman or man, young or old. It is the most beautiful and just system ever invented."

Down at The Jetties there was another explosion. The concussion rolled up the hill.

"So," Spaeth said slowly, "if we wanted to protect Yora from the Tornas digging their mines and cutting the trees, could we use the law to drive them off?"

Nathaway seemed uncomfortable with this question, from which she knew it was the right one. "Well, yes," he said, "but you'd have to convince a court the Tornas had done something wrong. At the moment, there is also an obstacle because there are no property titles here. In fact, the real estate records are nonexistent: everyone agrees there are private claims, but there are no deeds, no surveys, no probate records—it's a complete mess. We have to set up everything from scratch, and in the meantime there is a window of vulnerability."

His language was incomprehensible, as the language of the arcane often was. "What's a property title?" Spaeth asked.

"It's a document, a piece of paper that guarantees your ownership of something, say your home."

"But we *live* in our homes."

"Yes, of course, but what if someone dies? What if they want to sell, or get in debt, or there is a dispute?"

"Oh. Then people feud. For generations, sometimes."

"Well, you see, we can put an end to that."

Spaeth mulled this over. "You will give us pieces of paper, and then we will all agree?"

"Oh, no. But instead of shooting each other, you can hire lawyers."

"And they will shoot each other instead?"

"No, they'll argue before a court." Ruefully, he added, "For generations, sometimes."

Spaeth was having a hard time understanding. Seeing her expression, Nathaway said, "Look, the law is all about making sure the world is fair. It's about seeing that no one feels cheated or unhappy with the way they are treated."

Even dhota could not cure unhappiness. "Law must be a great and powerful thing, then," Spaeth said.

"Yes! Yes, it is."

As he sat beside her, she had been trying to intuit his mora—a thing Goth could have done in an instant, but which she was less practiced at. Mora had no single translation; applied to a person, it meant something like fundamental character, but Spaeth thought of it as a governing *mood*. Her own was joyful and thoughtless; Goth's was a vast sadness that seemed to encompass all creation. As for Nathaway, there was something yearning about him—a feeling of incompleteness, as if he were homesick for a home he had never known. It felt half spiritual, half sexual, and Spaeth suddenly wondered how such a rigid, angular Inning made love.

"Would you like to have sex with me?" she asked.

He stiffened as if she had slapped him, and a flush crept up his neck to his face. Spaeth had never seen anyone react so strangely. It made her feel defensive. Did he think there was something wrong with her?

What he said was, "I . . . you see . . . that is . . . it's . . ."

Perhaps he couldn't do it. Now she was wildly curious, but feared he might have a convulsion if she asked.

"I know your customs are different from ours," he finally stammered out. "But in my country, we don't just . . . do it with anyone."

Spaeth couldn't resist saying, "Is that one of your laws?"

"Well, yes, in a way. Marriage laws."

Spaeth stared in disbelief; she had thought it was a joke. "You have *laws* about who to make love to?"

"In a way. You get a marriage license. I'm not explaining this very well."

Probably he wouldn't be very good anyway, she decided. Jerky. Awkward. Or maybe methodical, like a machine. She thought of the pile driver the Tornas had set up at The Jetties. Yes, like that. As if he were thinking the same, the Inning twitched nervously.

A new thought struck her. "You're not expecting us to go to you for a piece of paper every time we want to—"

He interrupted hastily. "Once you understand our ways, you'll see it's really better. It protects women, encourages fidelity. Harmony. Commitment."

The thought of Innings peeking into bedrooms to see who was with whom was too absurd to contemplate. Spaeth slipped off her rock. This conversation's usefulness had ended.

"Stop!" he called out as she started down the hill. She turned to see what he wanted, but he seemed at a loss for words. "What's your name?" he asked at last.

"Spaeth."

"Where do you live?"

"In Yorabay, with Goth."

"Are you his daughter?"

"No, I'm his lover," Spaeth said. Then, mocking him, "But we don't have a license."

The grass whispered ribald comments around her as she started down the path to the village, and a seagull was laughing somewhere.

Yorabay looked tranquil and idyllic in the morning sun, but Spaeth felt uneasy as she entered it; there were a faint scent of tension in the air. The cottages were nestled back in the trees on either side of the main path. Because it was such a fine day, the shutters and doors were thrown wide, and people were working in their gardens. A dog rushed out from one house to greet Spaeth, and she waved at its owner. When she came abreast of Agath's house she walked faster, hoping to get by without being seen, but Agath was out splitting firewood, and hailed her.

"Any sign of him?" Agath asked.

Spaeth didn't have to ask who she meant. She shook her head.

"Did he ever say where he was going, or why?"

"No. But he has to get away from all of you sometimes. You ask too much of him."

Agath was one who had abused Goth's gifts. She had claimed dhota again and again, till he was deliriously blind to her faults, unable to refuse her anything. It had galled Spaeth to have to live with his love for such a demanding, bitter woman.

Now, Agath's face looked strained and pallid, as if years had been added to her burden in just the time Goth had been gone. Her hands, gripping the axe she had been using, looked bony and mottled. "Yes, Goth takes on too much," she said. "He should let you share his work."

It was a reproach, very nearly an accusation, and it shocked Spaeth. She wondered how many people had been thinking this, and not saying it. "It's not why he made me," she said defensively.

"Yes, I know what he made you for," Agath said. "But we've all got to grow up. Life isn't all pleasure."

There was something hungry in her eye that terrified Spaeth, and she took a step back. She had seen that look before, but never directed at her—only at Goth. It made her feel not like a person, not like Spaeth, but like a source of blood.

"I'll let you know if he comes back," she said, and turned away. She could feel Agath's eyes on her back as she hurried on down the road.

After that, she felt watched as she passed the homes on either side—and it was not the secure and protected feeling she had always had. Now, she felt the whole village's needs and longings following her, pushing her onto a path she didn't want to take. By the time she reached the home of Strobe the shipwright, opposite the dock at the very heart of Yorabay, she was quivering with nervous tension.

Strobe's was a rambling, driftwood-grey board house that seemed to be sinking into the grass around it. It was surrounded by the carcasses of half a dozen derelict boats that the shipwright was scavenging for parts. The mossy door was standing open to the sunlight. Spaeth entered the main room, a large, homey kitchen presided over by Tway, Strobe's daughter. At the moment, Tway was in the midst of canning some vegetables.

They didn't greet each other; that would have seemed too formal, as if not-welcome were the normal state of things and Tway were making an exception for Spaeth. In fact, normal was people wandering in, sitting for a talk, then going on. Spaeth sat down at the table and helped herself to some nog that stood in a pitcher on the table for everyone.

Tway was a vigorous, solid young woman who wore her fine brown hair cut short just at her jawline. She had not yet married, but few criticized her for it, since she was like everyone's sister. It took her only a glance to see that Spaeth was upset. "What is it?" she asked.

Spaeth poured out the story of her encounter with Agath. At the end, she said, "Dhota's supposed to be a gift, not an obligation. It's supposed to be given freely. I don't want to be her dhotamar, milked like a cow for blood. I want to be me."

"You know Agath," Tway said. She sat down and poured a mug of nog for herself. "Her life is all about blaming other people for her ills. She's been like that ever since Jory left."

"But it's not just Agath!" Spaeth said. "Do you think I don't see them eyeing me? Do you think I don't hear the conversations breaking off when I come near? They're all thinking it, all wanting it. All but me."

Tway cradled her mug between her hands. "It's not everyone. There are people on your side, Spaeth. There are some of us who think this has gone far enough. Too far, in fact. I used to think Yora was a blessed island, because we had so many healthy, rugged old people, so full of opinions. But now I see them all getting querulous and peaked, and Goth's only been gone a couple of weeks."

Her voice dropped low, and she leaned forward. "He's been prolonging their lives beyond what's natural. You know, for seven years no one has died on Yora for any reason other than their own choice. It's a problem, but we've never talked about it, because Goth was always there, always willing." She gave a little, humourless laugh. "Who would have thought it was such a curse to have a saint in our midst."

"I can't be a saint," Spaeth said. "I don't want to."

"And you shouldn't," Tway said, reaching across the table to squeeze her hand. "It's not good for them, or for the island. The problem is, some people are going to die if he doesn't come back soon."

Hearing it put this way, Spaeth only felt her desperation deepen. She could see no way out. Either she would become bound to them by the unbreakable knots of dhota, or she would be blamed for their deaths. One way, a slave; the other way, a pariah. She looked out bleakly to the sea, hemming her in. "Where can I go?"

Tway smiled and patted her shoulder. "You can always come here. No matter what happens."

Looking down, Spaeth said, "That Inning thinks he's going to tell us to stop giving dhota."

At this, even Tway frowned. "You should stay away from him, Spaeth. He's already sticking his nose into too many things. He needs to leave you alone."

Never had Spaeth felt this way. Always her life had been a carefree dance of sensual delights. Now, responsibility was tangled around her like a fishnet, pulling her down. She closed her eyes and breathed a little prayer. "Goth, please come back."

It was beautiful sailing weather for the last leg of the journey to Yora, across the Pont Sea from Thimish. There was a steady west wind to fill the close-hauled sail, and the prow of the boat slapped rhythmically against the waves. The sun massaged Harg's stiff muscles, and the breeze ruffled his hair playfully. He wondered if this was what it felt like to be content.

He had barely slept for two weeks, and had been on edge the whole time, keeping an eye on Jory almost round the clock to prevent him detonating and harming someone. They had had to take passage all the way north to Tornabay and then backtrack, catching rides on the little coastal vessels that always cruised between the islands. They had stayed last night in Harbourdown and could have waited four days for a trader to Yora, but Harg had opted instead to spend some of his money and rent a dinghy.

It was odd, but one of the many things Jory had lost in the injury was his boat-sense. As soon as they were in the dinghy together Harg had realized that Jory was like an inert sack of flour—able to follow instructions, but unable to feel the needs of the boat instinctively. Raised on the sea since before he could walk, Harg had never even been conscious of how he adjusted to a boat's tilts and tensions—leaning into the wind, adjusting the sheets, feeling the tension of the tiller—as if they formed a living system together.

The closer he had gotten to home, the more he had begun to wonder if he were making a terrible mistake by bringing Jory back. With his hair grown in, the young man looked perfectly normal, which only made him more like a hidden mine. But what alternative was there? After two weeks alone with him, Harg longed to be rid of the responsibility, even though that meant someone else's life was about to change for the worse.

"There it is," Harg said, pointing. Jory turned to look. There was a low, blue bump on the horizon, seeming to float on a white line of morning mist. Yora. Gentle, unassuming little island, just a teardrop-shaped smudge of sand in the wide Havenwater. There were no treasures here, no new realms. Nothing much even grew in its windswept soil but swordgrass, burdock, and legends. It had survived the centuries by being inconspicuous when the powers got angry. Harg reflected that he had never quite picked up that knack. Survival, yes—inconspicuousness, no.

He felt an odd mix of emotions at the sight of home. He had cherished the memory of Yora; it had been an anchor during the nightmare times when he had thought he must escape the navy or go insane. But he hadn't escaped, and now, looking back, it seemed as if he *had gone* insane for a while—the time that had coincided with his most spectacular deeds of glory, when stories had stuck to him like burrs. It came back in flashes now that made him flinch. Even his superior officers had been a little frightened of him, all the while they had egged him on.

Jory was not the only walking weapon he was smuggling back to Yora, where such people should not exist.

In an hour they were close enough to see the Whispering Stones, an uneven circlet crowning the hill. Soon they rounded Lone Tree Point and came in sight of Yorabay, in its natural cove at the foot of a wooded gorge. It was all exactly the same. The maple grove was heartache green. The rude log pier was crowded with weather-beaten boats, and a few old fishermen sat smoking on it. As the coast south of the village came in sight, Harg gave an exclamation of astonishment, and Jory turned to stare.

Near the rocky headland called The Jetties, smoke rose from a scar on the island's green shoulder. The skeletons of two new wooden buildings stood out starkly near the shore, swarming with workmen. A new pier rose half-finished from the water. And in the shallow bay, loftily overseeing all this activity, were anchored two boats: a Tornabay cargo vessel and a five-gun sloop from the Native Navy.

"Horns of Ashte!" Harg swore softly. "What are they doing here?"

"They're burning the rhododendron grove!" Jory cried out in an anguished tone. For generations the thicket of rhododendrons had been the special realm of Yoran children. Tunnels under the thick leaves had been castle halls for the games of Pirates or Ice King. In spring, the blooming hillside had been like a beacon for returning fishermen. Now a blackened wound marred the hillside.

Harg had intended to come in at the tumbledown old Yorabay dock, but now he set a course for the navy vessel instead. Soon they were alongside it, peering up at the markings that identified its origins. "It's one of Tiarch's," Harg said, meaning the squadron that had patrolled the north while the rest of the Native Navy fought in the war.

He steered over toward the unfinished pier. A group of workmen was erecting a scaffolding to drive the next log piling into the sandy bottom. The labourers were all Adaina—short, brown-skinned, curly-haired. "It's our own people at work there," Harg said. "Look, there's Bonn and Thole on the pier."

The people on the dock recognized them at the same moment, and one began to wave wildly. Harg brought the dinghy up beside the new dock and lowered the mainsail. Thole's shouts had gathered a crowd, and many hands reached out to help tie up.

"Jory! Harg!" Thole cried in a voice that had changed timbre since they had seen him last. The boy had wanted to go with them, Harg remembered, but they had told him he was too young.

As they climbed out onto the dock they were surrounded, barraged with embraces, welcomes, and questions—where had they been, what had they seen, what had they done. Before long the amazing news of Harg's rank came out, and he had to get out the box with his epaulette and cockade to show them, and try to list the names of the ships and battles they had been in. Jory looked on, a little tense and uneasy in the crowd.

"Jory, will Agath ever be glad to see you safe and sound!" Thole said enthusiastically. "She'd given you up for lost, I think."

As the others turned their attention to Jory, Harg drew aside Gill, one of the older men in the group, and said in a low tone, "Listen, you'll have to be careful with Jory. He took a shell in the head and hasn't been right since. He's a little dangerous, actually." He knew he only had to say it once. Soon the news would be all over the island.

"How are *you*, Harg?" Gill said carefully.

"I'm here," Harg said. "That's all that counts." He scanned the new buildings, the dock, the smoking hillside. "Ashwin above, what's going on?"

"You'll never believe this," said Gill. "They found a lead mine on the island."

Several people gathered round to fill in the story. Prospectors from the Inner Chain had arrived a month before, following tales of the Yoran lead that had once weighted the steadiest keels in the isles. Discounting all assurances that the lead was long mined out, the surveyors had set explosives in the rocks and bared a new vein that ran far out under the sea. Then, a week ago, the two ships had come, bringing machinery, tools, and Torna overseers to start construction on a smelting factory. The navy sloop was there to escort the mining boat and keep it safe from pirates.

"That's going to be the new smeltery," Gill said, pointing at one of the buildings. "The dock is for the boats to bring the coal and take away the lead."

"Have you ever seen a lead smelter?" Harg asked, a little appalled. He had seen one in Rothur. Not a plant had lived in a three-hundred-yard radius around it, from the poison fumes.

"We need the jobs," Gill said. "You can't imagine how bad trade has gotten. I know the pirates think they're doing the right thing, but when they hit the Torna merchants, the prices just go up for the rest of us, till we can't afford a lump of coal. We're caught between the pirates and the profiteers."

"I heard about that," Harg said, recalling his conversation with Admiral Talley. "I think it's about to change."

"These are good jobs, too," Thole said. "You won't believe how much they're paying us to work in the lead mine."

"Try me," said Harg. Thole named a number; it was only a little more than a common seaman made in the navy, but Harg pretended to be impressed.

"What about Yorabay?" he asked. "What's been going on?"

Everyone fell oddly silent, looking at each other to say something.

"Not much," Gill said at last. "Nothing's changed."

"Oh, come on. Somebody must have died, somebody must have been born."

"Gill and Wilne have two kids now," Bonn volunteered, since Gill didn't seem about to. "But nobody much has died."

So Yora really was the protected, idyllic place he had imagined. Trying to sound casual, Harg said, "Is Goth still here?"

"Oh yes," Gill said. "Though he's been gone for a couple weeks now. Who knows, maybe he's sick of us."

They were looking down, away, everywhere but at each other.

"He's got a girl now," Bonn finally said.

"A what?"

"A sexmate, for his pleasure. He made her just after you left."

Harg could hardly believe what he was hearing. "He *made* her?"

"Made her from his own flesh, they say," Gill said noncommittally. "He snared a soul from one of the other circles, one that suited him. He can do things like that, you know."

"I know he *can*," Harg said. "But I didn't think he *would*." They were all taking it so calmly; but then, they had had years to get used to it. To bring a soul to life for no reason other than his sexual pleasure—it seemed beyond the bounds of common decency. It would have been a scandal, if it had been anyone but Goth. Goth could get away with anything, Harg thought with a trace of the old bitterness.

He couldn't think about it now; it would dredge up too many unwelcome feelings. So he tried to make a joke of it. "And you say nothing ever happens in Yorabay."

They laughed, relieved he was so cool about it. After all, it could be argued that Goth had done much the same with him. The dhotamar was the man most responsible for Harg's existence, more so even than the father Harg had never known. But at least Goth had done that for better reasons.

"I want to go see the village," Harg said. "Anyone want to come?"

They all did, of course. "Yes! We'll have a cracking celebration tonight!" Thole said.

But someone near the edge of the crowd gave a whispered warning. "Not now. Emperor Crustup is coming. He won't want us to leave."

Down the beach from the smeltery was coming a powerfully built Torna overseer, followed by two marine soldiers. Crustup looked like a man at the end of his patience. "All right, fellows, what is it this time?" he said in a tone of strained geniality.

No one answered. "Well then, how about getting back to work?"

As the others moved reluctantly to return to their stations, the overseer spied Harg and Jory. "Who the fuck are you?" he asked.

Coolly, because of his tone, Harg said, "Captain Harg Ismol, Native Navy. And you?"

Clearly thinking the "Captain" part was an attempt to pull his leg, Crustup said, "I'm Admiral of the Ocean Sea. Are you from here?"

"Yes," Harg said.

"Want a job?"

"Depends," Harg said. "Who's making money from this mine?"

"You are, if you want to," Crustup said.

"No. I mean, who's paying you?"

The overseer recognized trouble then, and crossed his arms suspiciously. "You'd have to talk to management about that."

Having expected some such answer, Harg shrugged and started to leave.

"What about you?" Crustup turned to Jory. "You want a job?"

"Leave him alone," Harg said.

"What are you, his wife? Let him talk for himself."

"He's wounded. He can't work."

To Jory, Crustup said, "You look all right to me. What do you say? Want to earn some money?"

Suspicious, Jory looked from Harg to Crustup and back again. "Come on, Jory," Harg said. "I'll take you to your family."

Putting an arm around Jory's shoulders, Crustup started to lead him off toward the smeltery. "If you can lift a beam, we can use you."

"Stop it!" Harg yelled.

The sound of tension in Harg's voice was all it took. With an explosive force, Jory hurtled himself at the overseer, knocking him to the ground, and went for his throat with a cold, homicidal mania. Harg was on them in an instant, meaning to drag Jory off, but one of the marines was closer, and raised his truncheon to strike.

"No!" Harg cried out, but the marine brought the club down on Jory's shattered head.

The young man's body went stiff, and he fell to the ground. Then, as Harg knelt over him, Jory began to shake in the grip of a seizure. Looking up, Harg saw the marine raise his truncheon to strike again, and with a yell of rage, Harg launched himself at the man. His fist landed in the marine's face with a crunch, and the man flailed the air with his club, clutching a bloody nose with his other hand.

A gunshot went off, and in a moment of sheer instinct, Harg grabbed for his officer's pistol, an elegant flintlock which, as soon as he had it in his hand, he recalled was loaded but not primed. It didn't matter; the sight of the gun had the necessary effect. The marines both froze. On one knee over Jory's rigid, quivering body, Harg paused with the gun in his hand. Seeing an opportunity to calm the situation, he said in a commanding tone, "No one move, and we can work this out."

The soldiers both obeyed, but the instant Harg thought everything was under control, something barrelled into him from behind, knocking the gun from his hand and the breath from his body, laying him out on the ground. He had forgotten the overseer, twice his size and three times as angry.

The marines sprang to life again, laying into him with their truncheons, so that all he could do was try to shield his own head from the blows. As several more marines, summoned by the gunshot, came racing up, they wrenched Harg's arms behind him and tied them with some sort of twine to his ankles. Four men picked him up, and he saw the box with the epaulette fall from his jacket into the sand.

"Gill! Bonn! Take care of Jory!" he shouted at the Yorans, who stood frozen, appalled at the explosion of violence on their beach.

After that, Harg saw only the sands of Yora passing under him as they carried him off to the brig.

3
PRISONERS OF
THE PAST

The city of Tornabay was wedged into a crescent between the mountain and the sea. To a ship approaching from the east, it seemed to rise nearly vertical from the water, the conical peak of Mount Embo at its back.

It was a smoky, hodgepodge city that climbed the mountainside in an architectural tumult, clutching for toeholds on the steep slope. Neighbourhoods butted aggressively at each other; their boundaries looked like the results of fierce haggling sessions like the ones that went on in the markets by the waterfront.

Tornabay was a trading city, always in the market for something new. In its chameleon history it had incorporated every wave of migration that had washed over the isles. The smoke-darkened, geometric mass of its stone palace, built on a rocky spur that bisected the city, was proof that the Altans had once found something there worth guarding against, though what it was no one knew. When Alta fell in the time before history, the town became a sleepy Adaina settlement of timber, woodsmoke, and net reels, clustered along the bay. Then the industrious Torna had immigrated and transformed it into a busy, brick-and-beam emporium organized around a hundred markets. When the Innings conquered the isles, they spurned the ancient capital of Lashnish and made Tornabay their colonial headquarters. They cleared away whole tracts to impose an island of rational order on the mercantile hubbub.

It was just after dawn when an imperial frigate flying the red-and-white standard of Inning moved into the bay between the black, knife-edged headlands. It was a grand sight in the morning sun. Forty guns ranged on two decks, sails piled to the sky to catch the morning breeze, it walked the water with authority. As it cast anchor in the harbour, the only sounds that drifted to the piers were the faraway rattle of anchor cable and the occasional muffled bark of orders as the sails came down and the ship swung downwind of its mooring.

The captain had brought the ship in at dawn for a reason. His orders were to transport the prisoner into the city before many people were abroad. The vessel held only one passenger. The fewer who knew of his presence, the better Governor Tiarch would be pleased.

The captain and three marines escorted the passenger on deck. His grey Lashnura skin was gullied deep with wrinkles, and his hair was white; but he stood erect, taller than the stocky Tornas who guarded him. His face, lean with years of hardship, held an expression of unfathomable sadness. It was a face a little like the barren mountainside behind the city—rough and sheer, beyond control or comprehension.

A six-oared scow with an enclosed cloth awning in the stern bumped up against the ship's hull, and the men turned to it. Now the prisoner's head bowed again. One of the boatmen put out a respectful hand to help him step from the accommodation ladder into the rocking scow. Though the help was not needed, the old man murmured a word of thanks. The boatman, an Adaina, gave a gesture of respect and murmured, "Ehir." The Torna commander frowned at this. He ushered the old man under the awning, and pulled the curtains tight.

On the maps, Tornabay lay at the mouth of the river Em; but the river had long ago disappeared underneath the crowded buildings. Where it once had met the sea, Tornabay had extended long wooden fingers into the bay, spawning warehouses and shops over the water. By now a boat could sail far into the mazy waterways between buildings, and the sense of where the land ended and the sea began was hazy. As they pierced deeper into the watery lanes, the smells of the city changed: from the salt and seaweed of the harbour, to the fish and oily rope of the outer wharves, to the rancid tar and offal of the inner wharves, to fresh-baking bread and wood smoke as they neared the inner city.

They landed where a flight of slippery marble steps descended to the water from a broad plaza lined with the stately houses of Inning authority in the Forsakens. They crossed toward the centre of the grand colonnade that faced the bay. Seagulls and pigeons competed in the broad, empty square. The building dwarfed the five men as they climbed the wide steps and passed beneath the pillars. The great bronze doors stood open.

The captain did not recognize the Navy Office functionary who met them. "I was to report to Tiarch with the prisoner."

"Thank you, Captain," the official replied. "Commodore Joffrey will be taking charge from here."

"My orders came direct from the Governor."

"There is a new commander of the Fourth Fleet. You should have been informed."

There had been a letter, but the captain hadn't thought it would affect his mission, hatched in the utmost secrecy. It appeared that much had changed in Tornabay in his absence. Some Fluminos flunky no one had ever heard of thought he was taking over the reins from Tiarch. "Very well," he said, standing aside. Then, under his breath, "We'll see how long this lasts."

The official cast a curious look at the captive, but the old man was gazing off into the distance. He followed abstractedly as the official led the way through the broad, quiet corridors of the state house.

Commodore Joffrey was working in the bright, high-ceilinged room he had chosen as an office. The tall windows faced south into a courtyard where imported Inning plants bloomed in the brief Tornabay summer. The arms and trophies of war decorated the opposite wall, marshalled in columns. In the centre of the room, a mahogany table was set in gleaming silver for two. When the old man was shown in, Joffrey rose from his desk. He was a young Torna officer, so newly promoted that the ink was still wet on his commission. He had seized this situation away from Tiarch to prove a point about his authority; but in fact he had very little experience dealing with Grey Folk.

"Factor Goran," he greeted the prisoner. He had decided to use an Inning title to avoid acknowledging Goran's real station; but now that he heard it, it sounded absurd. To cover his unease, Joffrey spoke forcefully: "May I welcome you again to Tornabay." It sounded more like an order than a greeting.

The old man did not move from the doorway. Putting on a more urbane tone, Joffrey said, "I see they have already supplied you with proper clothing. Breakfast will be served shortly. If there is anything else we can provide, please ask."

Still the prisoner did not speak. His prolonged silence was beginning to seem disrespectful. Perhaps the old man did not realize he was in the presence of the commander of the Fourth Fleet's Northern Squadron; perhaps he did not care.

"Please come in and sit down," Joffrey said stiffly.

Goran turned his strange, silver eyes on Joffrey. "Why have I been brought back here?" His tone held none of the arrogance Joffrey had expected, only resignation.

"For your own protection, Factor Goran," Joffrey answered. "We feared that unscrupulous people would try to use you for bad causes."

"I have managed to prevent that for forty years," Goran pointed out wearily.

"In uneasy times, extra caution is needed."

"Is this an uneasy time?"

Was it possible, Joffrey wondered, that the man did not know of the impending Inning occupation of the outer chains? If so, best to keep him ignorant. "The isles are as quiet as always," he said. "We merely wish to keep them that way."

"I see," Goran said.

Joffrey was finding he had to prevent himself from falling back on the old superstitions he had learned from his mother. In spite of all his Inning education and years in the navy, Joffrey felt a secret fascination at facing a man who had been born to give his lifeblood for the isles. There was a more familiar excitement as well—the knowledge of political power in his control. In the Forsakens, this meek old man could create kingdoms.

He showed Goran to the table where a samovar of tea sat waiting. The servants entered with breakfast almost as soon as they sat down. There were five courses to the meal; Goran stared as the servants set them out in gleaming dishes, and Joffrey had to invite him to help himself. He did so awkwardly, picking up the linen napkin and the heavy silver utensils as if they were outlandish and strange. "Your pardon," he murmured to the Commodore's curious look. "I have not touched a fork in thirty years."

"Your exile must have been harsher than anyone intended," Joffrey said, helping himself to smoked mackerel and hot scones. "I'm sure they never meant you to leave behind civilization altogether."

"I didn't," Goran replied. "But I did leave forks behind."

As he reached out to set down a serving dish, Joffrey glimpsed his lean arm, covered with a patchwork of white scars from elbow to wrist. Joffrey caught himself staring.

The old man saw his gaze, but made no effort to hide his mutilated arm. Instead, he gazed at it, as if the sight transported him somewhere else. Joffrey, watching closely, realized the old man was struggling with some intense emotion.

He wondered in alarm if the stories might be true, and Lashnurai separated from their bandhotai could pine away to death.

When the meal was cleared away, they sat together over some rich imported tea. Goran awkwardly cradled the translucent porcelain cup in his large, hardened hands, his face still tense with the effort to keep his emotions under control. Joffrey realized now that his guest was not silent from artifice or pride, but because he could not trust himself to speak.

In a casual tone Joffrey said, "I thought the Heir of Gilgen did not need to perform ordinary dhota."

Goran seemed to be steeling himself to answer. "That is true. The Black Mask did not compel me. I chose to give dhota, of my own free will."

Chose it? Joffrey wondered at that. Who would choose pain and slavery?

"It was very foolish of me," Goran said. "But I never thought I would have to leave them. I never thought you would want to . . . protect me." There was a momentary note of irony in his tone, gone so swiftly Joffrey could not tell if it had truly been there.

"We did not wish you to be the victim of the first misguided demagogue who fancies himself leader of all the isles," Joffrey said.

Goran put down his cup. For an instant, a steely firmness glanced from his light eyes. "You did not need to worry. I do not grant dhota-nur merely to raise one leader or another to power. I grant it only if the balances are in danger, the cause is justified, and the leader is of the stature to restore harmony to the world."

In spite of himself, Joffrey felt a twinge of awe. And that, he told himself firmly, was where this man's political power originated. The leader to whom he gave dhota-nur attained a sanction that was nearly divine. "Yet your father gave dhota-nur for a hopeless and foolish cause," he said, "trying to prevent the Innings from governing the Forsakens."

"It was hopeless, I grant that. Perhaps foolish as well. Dhota-nur does not prevent foolishness, or it would prevent heroism as well. But if the Torna had not sided with the Innings, there would have been no invasion."

"If your kind hadn't stirred up the Adaina, there would have been no resistance," Joffrey said stiffly.

Goran shook his head as if the argument were not to his taste. "I cannot defend my father's choice, or condemn it either. I was only a child when Orin's War ended. They say I was captured at Sandhaven; I do not remember that. I do remember what happened after I was in the Innings' power. I was imprisoned for six months until the last of the Inner Chain surrendered. And then I was held for fifteen years. Here, in the palace at Tornabay. When I was twenty-four years old they told me to go and lose myself in the islands, and forget who I was. I obeyed them; I always have. But it seems I did not flee far enough. I forgot who I was, but others remembered for me."

"The Inning authority has known all along where you were. We traced you even when you fled to that flyspeck island in the South Chain."

"Yora," Goran said distantly.

"That's right."

"The eye of Tiarch sees far," Goran said.

"Factor Goran—" Joffrey started; but the old man held up a callused hand.

"Why do you call me Factor?" he asked. "I have never owned Inning property. If you must give me a title, then give me the right one."

"Onan?" Joffrey said stiffly. "That title has been abolished."

"I have not earned it anyway, not until I give dhota-nur. If I am simply a citizen, call me Goran. Or better yet, give me my real name, Goth Batra."

It made Joffrey uneasy to hear him speak of dhota-nur as if there were still a chance he might give it, since that was what he had been brought here to prevent. "I hope that you may be the first Heir of Gilgen in many centuries to avoid the curse of dhota-nur."

"At any rate, I will be the last." To Joffrey's cautious look, Goran said, "I have no children. I long ago decided I could not inflict on another human being the life of persecution I have led."

"So you intend your line to perish, after all these centuries?"

Joffrey watched him closely, wondering what was going on in his involuted Lashnura mind. At last the old man said, "There is a tradition that someday the Lashnura burden will be transferred to other shoulders. When that day comes, we will have paid our debt and at last we will be free."

He paused so long that Joffrey asked, "You think that day is coming?"

"I cannot tell," Goran shook his head. "After all, we have been hoping for six centuries now."

By the time the guards arrived to escort the prisoner up to the palace, Joffrey was relieved to relinquish charge of his guest. He had learned less than he had hoped. The old man's mind was a paradox, he told himself angrily as he poured a glass of wine to wash down breakfast. But the paradox that truly bothered him was in himself. Deep down, his mother's primitive reverence still persisted. It made him feel ashamed.

He sat down at his desk to resume the delicate task that had been interrupted by the prisoner's arrival—composing a letter to his commander, Admiral Talley. Joffrey had to strike just the right note: tell his superior enough about the curious situation in Tornabay to make him appreciate the skill it took to cope with it, but little enough that he didn't feel compelled to arrive on the scene.

The offer of promotion to Commodore of the Fourth Fleet, the new name for the Native Navy, had come as a surprise to Joffrey, because his background was not in field command. He had been in military intelligence. His job had been to spy on the officers of the Inning Navy for Admiral Talley, and report back on their opinions, their loyalties, and their competence. It had led Joffrey into the intricacies of Inning politics, a subject for which he now had a deep appreciation. It was not until he had arrived in Tornabay that he had understood why Talley wanted someone of his background in the post.

During the war, the Northern Squadron, stationed in Tornabay, had grown lax and corrupt. Far from the fighting, it had become a haven for Inning officers who enjoyed the easy life as aristocracy of a provincial capital, and it had served as a trough of patronage for the worthless sons-in-law of wealthy Torna merchants. Joffrey had arrived to find the payroll packed with people who barely worked, and had no loyalty to anyone but Tiarch, the governor who had gotten them their jobs. In fact, the Northern Squadron had ceased to function as a navy, and more closely resembled a thuggish private security force owned by the merchants and the governor, with a few indolent Innings enjoying the kickbacks. It was a cozy little private party—Innings, Tiarch, and the merchants all in bed together, and Joffrey had been sent to break it up.

Which he had no intention of doing.

And therein lay his dilemma. His previous job had given him a vivid appreciation of how thin was the ice upon which the Talley family walked, with their crowd-pleasing penchant for reform. They were riding high now all right, but it would not take much to make the wind shift, and when it did Joffrey wanted to be in a position to trim his sails a new way. He could not afford to make enemies of the Tornabay cabal. Accommodate, adapt, accept the situation: that was how he had gotten ahead in the Native Navy. And at the moment that meant keeping the Admiral far away and in the dark.

He was almost relieved when his adjutant looked in to announce another visitor. But when he heard the name, Provost Minicleer, he gave an inward groan and steeled himself for the encounter.

When Minicleer strolled into the room, he looked perfectly at ease—as he should, since this pleasant office had been his until two weeks ago. He was one of the Inning officers who had resigned their commissions rather than serve on an equal footing with islanders; but unlike the others, he had not gone away. Instead, he had pulled strings to secure himself a civilian appointment in Tornabay, though what a provost did was a mystery to Joffrey. It apparently involved attending parties, gambling, and sleeping with a great many merchants' daughters. No matter; Joffrey had to get along with the dissolute fellow, since there was nothing he could do about him.

"Joffrey, how are you?" Minicleer drawled pleasantly, looking down from his six-and-a-half-foot height at the compact Commodore. He had wavy, honey-coloured hair and a long face with prominent teeth and fleshy, sensual lips. Joffrey could not imagine what women saw in him; perhaps it was that he radiated an air of privilege.

"It is a pleasure to see you again, sir," Joffrey said, managing to sound both gracious and respectful.

Tossing his hat on the table and sinking into the chair that Goran had recently vacated, Minicleer regarded Joffrey with the kind of fondness another man might have reserved for his dog. "You outlanders live in a state of primitive bliss, did you know that?"

"Indeed?"

"Your conflicts are at such an elementary level. Race hatred is refreshingly primal to a person accustomed to the complexities of the Court."

"You must have received news from Fluminos," Joffrey said.

"Yes," Minicleer said, but then proceeded not to share it. "I have come to invite you to a celebration. There will be ladies present. It's really unseemly for you not to couple with them, Joffrey. You know the rumours that get started about men in ships."

"Give me a chance," Joffrey said with a tense smile. "I've not been here long. What are we celebrating?"

"A great victory. My team won the tournament."

"Congratulations, sir!" Joffrey said warmly. "Against some stiff opposition, too. And everyone said sacking the coach was the wrong move."

Joffrey had learned to follow Innings sports once he had realized that the teams were all sponsored by various factions of the old aristocracy, who avidly followed them in place of the real power they had once wielded, and still craved.

Minicleer, protesting modestly, allowed himself to be praised and congratulated for five minutes, until he grew bored.

"Who was the man with the peculiar complexion being escorted up to the palace when I came in?" Minicleer spoke with stylish indolence, but his eyes were sharp.

For a moment Joffrey hesitated. "He was a man we feared might cause trouble in the outlands during the occupation. The Governor ordered him brought in, and I concurred."

But Minicleer had caught the instant of hesitation, and it was enough to arouse his curiosity. "His name?"

"Goran," Joffrey said, gambling that the Inning would not recognize it.

"He did not look like a rebel commander. What is his significance?"

Technically, Joffrey would not have had to answer; but he was not about to resist a direct question from an Inning. "He is the son of Onan Listor, who was involved in the last rebellion."

This was something Minicleer could understand. "You think he would have made a bid for the crown of the Forsakens?"

The question was so impossibly wide of the mark that Joffrey could not think at first how to answer it. "There is no crown of the Forsakens," he said at last. "Goran's power lies . . . elsewhere."

Misreading Joffrey's hesitation, Minicleer said coldly, "I advise you not to withhold information from me."

A chill of tension passed down Joffrey's back at that tone, and he said, "The Heirs of Gilgen have a religious significance, sir. Ordinarily, there is no formal king or government. But in times of crisis, a leader will often arise. If the Heir of Gilgen endorses that leader's righteousness, then he or she becomes the Ison of the Isles. Any cause that Goran backed would become a holy crusade." It was a feeble way of describing it, but at least the Inning would understand.

"Well then," Minicleer smiled, "get him to endorse our cause."

"I am afraid he would not do that willingly."

"There are ways of getting men to do things, even against their wills." Minicleer's smile had turned into a cruel smirk.

"I am afraid torture would be counterproductive with a Lashnura."

"Perhaps you islanders are not as skilled at such things as we are. Or perhaps you fear supernatural vengeance. Is there a trace of superstition hiding even in you, Joffrey?"

Joffrey answered calmly, "No, sir. The man will do as we wish."

"Good." Minicleer strolled toward the east wall, where a mosaic map of the Inner Chain was inlaid in many-coloured woods. He looked as aimless as if he had never uttered a threat. "I never understood why the South Chain and Outer Chain were left off this wall. You will have to get them added." Taking a sharp knife from the table, he gouged a rough line in the wood where the missing islands should be placed.

"I will hazard a prediction, my friend," he continued. "Eyes in Fluminos will be turning north in the next few years. I think the Forsakens will be the place to achieve power and fortune in the years to come. And I intend to be here when the rewards are harvested."

Not if Corbin Talley can help it, Joffrey thought to himself. Aloud, he said, "I am glad to hear it."

"How is the occupation proceeding, by the way?" the Inning asked suddenly.

"We are moving a bit cautiously at first," Joffrey said. "I have sent out three ships to re-establish the old fort at Harbourdown, which appears to be a hotbed of piracy. Beyond that, we will have to wait for reinforcements from the Southern Squadron." *Well-trained, experienced reinforcements*, he thought. Men who knew what discipline was.

"I see no reason to wait," Minicleer said.

"We don't want to stir up resistance."

"Resistance?" the Inning asked sharply. "From Rothur?"

"Oh no, sir; from the islanders. The Adaina are a rebellious and intransigent race, you know. It does not take much to make them start talking of war. Nothing will ever civilize them, I sometimes think."

"Don't tell me about Adaina. I had to deal with the smelly little brownskins when I had your job. It was like commanding wild animals—barely even housebroken."

"Yes," Joffrey agreed ruefully. "Well, I have been ordered to promote some of them."

Minicleer gave a venomous sneer. "Just the sort of order a Talley would give. The navy as social engineering project. Damn it, I did the right thing by getting out." He fell silent, but the subject was still rankling. Joffrey knew that if he just waited, he would learn more. This was exactly the sort of thing he had been doing for the last four years.

"It's this doctrine of individualism," Minicleer went on. "It puts our most cherished institutions at risk, claiming the law applies to individuals without regard to race or class or family. The law shouldn't be poking into the personal realms of family and household, setting child against parent, hirelings against their employers, men against their officers, giving them 'rights' to quarrel with one another. There ought to be a sacred barrier protecting traditional institutions against the usurpations of the law."

"I know," Joffrey murmured. It was the great debate in Inning.

"But the individualists want to spread their doctrine across the world," Minicleer said. "These Talleys, you know, they aren't an old family. They're not even wealthy. All they've got is their wits."

Joffrey reflected on the mindset of a world in which this could be construed as an insult.

Minicleer went on, "The grandfather was a tradesman, the father has seized the highest post in the land, the sons are poised to become our emperors and tyrants. If we don't check them now, we'll all be living in a world they created."

"Mmm," Joffrey said. "Especially us islanders."

This had the desired effect. "You are a faithful friend, Joffrey," Minicleer said. "I wish that more of your race were like you."

It was not long before Minicleer left, and Joffrey could settle down again to his letter. The Provost's visits always left him in a foul mood. When his secretary brought in a pile of papers he shuffled morosely through them, complaining bitterly about the hours he had to keep. Among the papers was a handwritten note saying only, "No. 2 reports all is well and full information to come soon." Joffrey smiled grimly. Number 2 was the spy he had set on Minicleer. He hoped soon to know enough about the Inning to ruin him.

"Get a woodworker to see if that wall can be repaired," Joffrey snapped at the waiting secretary, and immediately felt better.

Harg was no stranger to ships' brigs. This one had the advantage of being empty of other occupants; it had the disadvantage of being overrun with cockroaches. Shortly after the marines dumped him into the dank and fetid hole, he discovered that if he stayed still the roaches would be on him in a ravenous swarm—crawling up his pants legs, down his collar, dropping into his hair. Once he managed to doze off, and woke up bitten all over, to find them feasting on his eyelashes.

Driven beyond endurance, he resorted to drastic measures. Focusing his disgust into an intense beacon, he sent out a prayer to any dark power listening.

Praying had never worked in Inning, but here the circles ruled by the Mundua and Ashwin lay closer to the surface, and the boundaries could be crossed. For hours he concentrated, and that night he had a dream that a pinprick hole opened into one of the other circles and sucked the whole godforsaken swarm down into what he sincerely hoped was perdition. The next morning he woke unbitten. Some day, he knew, he would pay for having incurred a debt to supernatural forces; but at the moment no price seemed too high.

Over the next two days he waited. His mind was racing and jumpy, endlessly playing over old memories. When he slept, his dreams were haunted by horrific images. Over and over he started awake, thinking his clothes were stiff with caked blood. But it was only his own sweat. It was no better when he woke, because then the memories came attached to shame and second-guessing. Why had he decided to leave the navy? At least they knew how to deal with people like him, damaged men with ugly things hiding in their skulls. The Innings were the ones who had created him; let them deal with the problem. He never should have inflicted himself on Yora.

And yet, in moments when his exhausted mind fell still enough to let him hear the quiet lapping of water against the hull, he felt that if ever he were to be cured, it would be on Yora. There was a healing power here to filter everything Inning out of him. Here, he could hope to finally feel clean, inside and out. He could be alone and at peace with himself.

The marines came to get him on the third day. They led him without explanation up onto the deck, where he blinked like a cave bat in the sunlight. Some sort of ceremony seemed to be in preparation; they had stretched an awning over the poop deck, and a large delegation of Yorans was gathered, sitting cross-legged in the waist of the ship. On the break of the quarterdeck a table was set out with three chairs behind it, two of them occupied by the captain and lieutenant of the ship, the third by a lanky young Inning civilian dressed soberly in black. Harg instantly decided he did not care for the symbolism—the Tornas and Inning in chairs on the dais, the Adainas on the floor below.

"What's this?" Harg asked the marine at his side.

"Shut up," the soldier explained.

The villagers had just noticed him, and turned to stare curiously at his filthy, bruised condition. It was so bitterly far from the homecoming Harg had dreamed of that it triggered a familiar mental switch. It wasn't himself the Innings were degrading; it was Captain Harg, and through him all Adainas who dared to rise above their stations. The thought gave him a burn of indignation that made it possible to seem defiant while his insides were withering with humiliation.

When the marine guard led Harg to a stool in the front of the assemblage, it dawned on him that perhaps he was going to be court-martialled—an unlikely thought, since he wasn't even in the navy any more. When Harg was seated, the Inning rose to address the crowd of Yorans. "We have brought you here today to witness a demonstration of Inning justice," he said. "We hope you will find it instructive. The purpose of this trial is to determine the guilt or innocence of this man—" he glanced down at a paper in his hand "—Harg Ismol, and to decide upon the penalties he should face. I am Justice Nathaway Talley, and my role here is—"

He embarked on a little speech about the role of a Justice of the Peace in trials where no attorneys had been retained. Harg heard it only vaguely. He was too busy wondering about the name, and whether there could be a connection. He knew for a fact that not all Innings were named Talley—very few of them, in fact. It was possible, he decided as he studied the young man. That blond hair and skinny build . . . if you took Corbin and ran the clock back fifteen or twenty years, then replaced his look of arctic control with one of bewildered self-consciousness, they could be brothers.

Harg's attention returned when Justice Talley asked the captain to read the charges. The Torna stood, resplendent in his uniform, and read from a paper.

"The charges are as follows, to wit: that you did disobey the lawful order of an officer in the pursuance of his duty; that you did commit assault upon an officer of the law, causing grievous bodily harm; that you did use a deadly weapon in the commission of said assault; that you did resist arrest; that you did commit theft upon the person of an Inning officer. The penalties for which, if all found true, shall be sale into slavery for a period of fifteen years, or loss of a limb." He looked up. "How do you plead?"

Harg was still trying to absorb the depth of the trouble he was in. And all from a brawl on the beach.

"You have to say whether you're guilty or not," Nathaway prompted.

"Not of *those* charges!" Harg declared. "I didn't disobey an order because he didn't give one; I didn't cause him grievous bodily harm; I tried to use the weapon to stop the assault, not to commit it; and as for theft—where the rotting hell did you get that idea?"

The guard behind him struck him on the ear. "Respect your betters, brown boy," he said.

The Inning rose to his feet in dismay. "You can't hit the defendant," he said.

"Nobody hits anyone else in court, all right? And no one uses curses or racial slurs. You've all got to respect the venue, or this won't work. Just try to pretend you don't all hate each other till we're out of here." He turned to Harg. "You'll have a chance to answer the charges. We've got to get through some preliminaries first."

The first preliminary was selection of a jury. Justice Talley gave a speech extolling the practice of trial by jury, the crowning glory of Inning jurisprudence. "The jury system gives you the power to decide for yourselves about what constitutes justice," he told them. "We don't want to impose our ideas on you. We want to give you the tools to enact your own ideas."

Harg wondered what the man thought he was doing at the moment, if not imposing Inning ideas. But Nathaway seemed unaware of the contradiction.

When the Inning called for someone to step forward to be empanelled, the Yorans all turned expectantly to the spot where the elders were gathered. Stiffly, Father Argen rose to his feet and came forward to face the Justice. It was astonishing how little he had changed in seven years: hair white as seafoam, face like weathered driftwood. And he looked as cantankerous as ever. The older the ginger the sharper the bite, Harg thought. He and Argen had never gotten along.

The Inning asked, "Do you know the defendant?"

"Oh, I know him all right, and I can tell you truly, he's been a problem since the day he was born. He was a kmora child, you know."

Harg winced, thinking that now the whole story was going to get paraded out.

"I beg your pardon?" the Inning said.

"A kmora child. In our custom, when a couple can't conceive, they follow our ancient way and go to a dhotamar. If the Grey Man consents to become bandhota to them both, then it is like a three-way bond, and the dhotamar is a vessel or conduit in the creation of the child. Then it is like the child has three parents. The only risk is that the babe might be born Lashnura. But this one wasn't."

He turned to survey Harg, who was trying stoically to pretend he wasn't there. "Five years later his natural parents both died in the same boating accident, and there was no one to take him in. It was then the trouble started. We tried to do our best, the powers know, but it was like trying to tame a raccoon; he just ran wild, and no one could do anything with him."

"This is fascinating, but not really relevant," the Justice said.

Irritated at the interruption, Argen said, "I'm getting to that part. It nearly broke Goth's heart, you see, since he felt responsible, having given of himself to create the child. But the only cure in his power was dhota, and that the boy would never consent to. So when Harg's heart turned so black and he lured Jory away to the war and all, why it nearly killed Goth. He brooded and wasted away for months. If he hadn't made that girl to solace him, he wouldn't be alive today."

"Thank you, I think you can step down now," Nathaway said to stop this recital.

"I'm just trying to tell you, the boy is bad, and whatever they say he did, he probably did it all right, and more to boot. And if Goth doesn't come back, that's probably his fault as well."

"Thank you, that will be all. Please return to your seat."

"I was to sit on the jury," Argen reminded him.

"I'm sorry, but we are looking for people who are impartial."

"I was there when it all happened," Argen said with defensive pride. "I'm more partial than anyone here."

"That's the problem, you see," Nathaway explained. "We need people who haven't formed an opinion."

"Well, you won't find anyone on Yora who doesn't have an opinion about *him*."

It took several more minutes to get Argen to vacate his spot. Then Strobe the shipwright stood up. He was a stocky, powerfully built man with close-cropped grey hair. His immense chest and square shoulders belied the fact that he was gentle as a kitten.

"Do *you* know the defendant?" the Inning asked.

"Yes, and I'd like to say something. Argen is a wise man and has his opinions, but there is another side to the story. Goth bears a lot of responsibility. After all, it *was* his kmora-child, but he would never take the boy in, never care for him, so instead Harg grew up in half a dozen foster homes, traded from place to place whenever he became inconvenient. Just a little human kindness from Goth is all it would have taken. A lot of people thought they hated each other, but that wasn't true. It was only because Harg and Goth loved each other so much that they were so good at hurting each other. And the most hurtful thing Harg could do, in the end, was to go away."

He turned then to address the Yorans. "But you know, I think it was like Goth's conscience left when Harg did. Harg was the only one who demanded more from the Grey Man, and wouldn't forgive him for everything. It was living up to Harg's expectations that drove Goth's life for a long time. Then when Harg left, Goth just gave up. You all know it; there are things that we all wish hadn't happened, and they happened because Harg *wasn't* here, not because he was. It was like Goth felt there was no point any more, so he might as well see what he could get away with."

Everyone was silent, shamed by the honesty of this testimony. No one ever said such things in public; but in a way, having strangers here made it possible.

The Inning cleared his throat. "Thank you, I think you may step down." He rustled some papers in front of him, then changed tactics. "Let me ask this. Is there anyone here who *doesn't* know the defendant?"

Harg scanned the group, hoping there was someone on Yora who was still neutral about him, but not a single hand went up. They all had formed opinions about who he was, or had been seven years ago.

"Well," said Justice Talley, a little perturbed by this turn of events, "there are provisions in the law for everything. In the rare case that an impartial jury cannot be found, the trial may be conducted by a judge. Would that be acceptable to the defendant?"

It took Harg several seconds to realize he was actually being asked. "It's your show, not mine," he said.

"Please answer yes or no. You have rights, you know."

"Yes. Go ahead. Whatever you want."

"Thank you." The Inning was clearly a little rattled by now. Harg would have enjoyed his discomfort more if the situation hadn't seemed likely to result in some actual consequences for him.

Justice Talley called for some witnesses. When Mother Tish the herbwoman stood up, he asked her if she had seen the incident; she acknowledged that she had not. "But I can still witness," she said stoutly. "I have something to say about Jory."

"Look, everyone," Justice Talley said. "We're trying him on the charges. We're not trying him for being born, or for leaving Yora, or any of the other things he's been accused of. The question is only, did he assault a marine guard?"

Finally they began to understand. Gill stood up, and under some patient prompting from the Inning, managed to give a cogent account of what had happened. He finished, "Jory's still having fits, and it's because of what that soldier did to him. If anyone should be tried, it's him."

Bonn then testified, giving much the same story; then Overseer Crustup gave his version, and the marine guard his. At last it came Harg's turn to speak. He rose to begin, but the Inning interrupted, "Please identify yourself to the court first."

"You don't know who I am?" Harg said.

"Just do as you're told."

"I'm Captain Harg Ismol, Native Navy."

"That's a lie," the captain of the ship spoke up suddenly. He leaned forward, as if this were the moment he had been waiting for. "There are no Adaina captains in the navy." He fairly radiated contempt.

"There aren't now," Harg said. "I've resigned."

"You realize we can add a charge of impersonating an officer."

"It's no impersonation. I've got the commission, the discharge papers, the insignia. Or I had, until you threw me in the brig."

"These insignia?" the captain said, holding up the wooden box Corbin Talley had given Harg. It had been sitting on the table in front of him. "How did you get these?"

"I earned them," Harg said. "Fighting in the war." *And I could have been your superior officer, you racist pig*, he wanted to say; but there was no point.

The captain looked smug. "You're too ignorant to even know that this is an Inning Navy epaulette, not a Native Navy one. Only an Inning could have owned these. How did you get them?"

So this was the origin of the accusation of theft. Harg should have known to leave those insignia sitting on the table in Admiral Talley's office. They were so far above his station, they would only bring him trouble. After seven years of beating the Tornas at their game, he was still no more to them than a brown boy.

"You wouldn't believe the truth if I told it," Harg said.

Nathaway Talley spoke up. "You have to tell the truth."

"Well then, they were given to me by Admiral Corbin Talley himself."

"Ha!" the Torna captain said, as if he had caught Harg in a transparent lie. He turned to Nathaway. "Is this true?"

"How the blazes should I know?" said Nathaway.

Watching Nathaway closely, Harg said, "He gave them to me on the night in Fluminos when there was a fireworks display in the harbour. The Chief Justice had sent a carriage to fetch him to a reception, but he made it wait till he had finished his business with me."

Nathaway looked arrested by this account. Seriously, he turned to the captain. "He could be telling the truth. I remember the night he means."

The captain looked unconvinced. Nathaway went on, "But regardless, if there is no one complaining of a theft, we can't try him for it. There has to be a victim, or proof a crime has been committed. We can't try him for what he might have done, or thought of doing, or anything but what we can prove. And the only objective fact in evidence is one bloody nose, for which he appears to have been amply penalized."

"We can't just dismiss the charge," the captain said, fingering the box. "He needs to forfeit these to someone in authority."

Nathaway appeared not to catch on, but Harg did. "Keep them, they're yours," he said to the captain. "All right?"

The captain gave an imperceptible nod. After a beat Nathaway realized that a bribe had just changed hands, and seemed about to object. Harg turned to him fiercely. "Don't cause me more grief. They're no good to me. They'll only bring me trouble." Like all the rest of my navy career, he thought bitterly.

Visibly grappling with his principles, Nathaway said, "If everyone is content, then . . ." He looked around for any objections, then stood. "The charge of theft is dismissed. As for the other charges, I sentence you to one month of probation, plus three days of community service working on the new dock, to be served within the next two weeks. This court is now adjourned."

Everyone started milling around, waiting for the boats to take them all back on shore. Feeling some urgency to get away before anyone changed their mind, Harg found Strobe, who always brought his own boat. "Can I go back with you?" he said. Strobe nodded.

When they were alone on the water, out of earshot from the rest, Harg said, "Thanks for what you said there, Strobe. It took a lot of courage to speak like you did."

"Well, I felt like I owed it to you," Strobe said.

"You don't owe me anything." Strobe was one who had always been fair and kind.

"We all do. A lot of people felt bad once you'd gone, and wished things had happened differently. But there's something you can do to repay me, if you want."

"What's that?"

Strobe brought the boat upwind so that the sail luffed and they stood still. "Go to Goth. Make it up with him, Harg. Not just for your own sake, for his sake and ours. Will you do that?"

"Sure. I can do that," Harg said.

I can start over, he thought as Strobe turned the tiller and the sail caught wind again. I can wipe the slate clean, no grudges or old business.

Strobe's house was smaller than Harg remembered, more weather-beaten and rude. When they entered the murky interior, a vigorous voice called out Harg's name and Tway came out of the kitchen, throwing her arms around him in an energetic bear hug. "Welcome back, Harg," she said. "Things sure do get more interesting when you're around. Why, we haven't had a trial in—well, forever. I guess they must have let you go."

"Yeah, the whole thing was supposed to be a demonstration of godlike Inning law," Harg said, "and in the end we still just settled it the old way."

The room was just as he remembered it. There squatted the ancient cast-iron stove imported from the Inner Chain. It had been the wonder and terror of his childhood, a demonic presence that belched fire and yet never burned. Now it seemed small and rusty. A wooden crate in the corner was heaped with old net; the glass floats peeped from the folds like wondering, bulbous eyes. Through the door into Strobe's lean-to workshop he could see a litter of lumber and translucent curls of shaved wood on the floor. The living room was cluttered with every manner of thing turned into something else: a barrel had become a stool, a spoon had become a stove lid lifter, a file had become a chisel. Everything was cramped, as if the dimensions of life at sea had been translated onto land. It smelled of wood smoke and cedar.

"Sit down," Tway said. "It's not a picture; you're really home."

He laughed a little; she could almost read his mind. "I thought you would be married by now," he said to her.

She paused so long he wondered if he'd said the wrong thing. But her tone was still light when she said, "Oh, I'm just waiting for him to settle down and ask me."

"Why wait? Nail the bastard to the wall."

"If he'd stand still long enough, I would. Here, what would you like? Some nog?"

"Sure, that's fine." He stood indecisively. It had been so long since he'd had nothing to do that he didn't know how to behave.

"Strobe," he said suddenly, "have you heard how Jory is?"

Strobe was quietly filling his pipe with some shag. He paused to light it, then shook his head. "Not good," he said.

"Damn, I'll have to go see him."

"Better leave it alone for a bit," Strobe advised. "Agath's taking it pretty hard. It's a bad time for Goth to be gone."

"She wouldn't—" Harg stopped himself, knowing suddenly that she would. "Listen, she can't claim dhota for him. What's wrong with Jory is more than dhota can heal."

Tway set the cup of nog on the table before him. She and Strobe exchanged a look, and Harg sensed they had already been talking about this.

"That's something you don't hear much around here any more," Tway said, "the idea that there's something dhota can't heal."

"What do you mean?"

"People have gotten used to running to the Grey Man about everything."

"Well, he's just got to say no."

Tway looked at Strobe ironically. "When was the last time Goth said no? Do *you* remember?"

Harg was just beginning to realize that this was something important when they were interrupted by a knock on the door. They all three turned to stare; no one ever knocked in Yorabay.

It was the Inning, Nathaway Talley. He stood awkwardly on the doorstep, holding his hat. "Harg? They told me you were here. Might I have a word?"

Tway went into a paroxysm of housewifely panic. "Come in, sir, come in. We were just having some nog. Can I offer you some? Please, sit down."

Nathaway entered, ducking under the low lintel, and peering around in the gloom. He took the chair Tway offered, automatically brushing off the seat before sitting. Harg forced himself to sit down as well, since it would have looked deferential not to; but he felt on edge. Tway set another cup of nog down in front of the Inning, and then disappeared; Strobe had vanished as well.

"I didn't get a chance to talk to you after the trial," Nathaway said. "I just wanted to ask whether you really knew my brother."

"I don't lie in court," Harg answered defensively.

"I didn't mean that. It's just . . ." He started speaking in a rush. "I remember that night you mentioned. Everyone thought Corbin was deliberately snubbing my father. Maybe he was. They got into a frightful row about it the next morning. Then I got my row just after." He shook his head as if to free it of the unpleasant memory.

Harg was startled by this candid glimpse into Talley family dynamics. He wondered if it had been offered up to him as a kind of exchange for having pried into his own private affairs.

Nathaway picked up the mug of nog, but absently set it down again without tasting it. "Listen, if you were in the navy, you could be really helpful to me. You know about Innings, and what we want. I could use some inside knowledge."

The wise move would have been to stay monosyllabic and sullen, but Harg was at the end of his rope. He rose out of his seat, glowering. "You have really got some nerve, Inning."

"What do you mean?" Nathaway looked lost.

"You've just let me rot in that hellish brig for two days, then tried me for half a dozen crimes, and now you want my *help*?"

"Oh, that," Nathaway said.

"Yes, that!"

"Captain Quintock would have kept you in prison forever, without so much as a charge, if I hadn't insisted on a trial. That was your way out. I had to *fight* for that trial." He paused. "Besides, it was perfectly obvious the Tornas were as much to blame as you."

"Now you tell me," Harg said, sinking back into his chair.

"So you really owe me some advice, you see. I'm having a hard time figuring this place out."

"What a surprise," Harg said.

"Don't be like that. I don't have any information. The Tornas are no use; they're such bigots about the Adaina, and so damned deferential to me they won't say a word if I've got something wrong. To my face, that is. They're probably laughing themselves sick behind my back."

He had that right at least, Harg reflected. He took a long drink of nog, feeling sick to death of Innings and longing to be done with them forever. But as he looked across the table, it occurred to him that Nathaway was about the same age he had been when he had first left home to find what the world was all about. More educated, but just as ignorant. He remembered what it was like to be in a strange land. If no one had helped him out . . .

"All you need to know about Yorabay is that we're like a big family, and families don't always get along," he said.

"I figured that out at the trial today," Nathaway said. "It didn't take a genius."

"Everyone pries, everyone thinks other people's business is their own."

"If it's any consolation, Fluminos is just the same," Nathaway said. "You can't sneeze there without it getting in the papers."

Harg reflected that he could have sneezed a thousand times in a row without it getting in the Fluminos papers. But his name wasn't Talley.

"The problem with your law is, it's all about arguing and confrontation," Harg continued. "The Tornas are fine with that, but we Adainas don't like to disagree in public. It's against our customs. I'm surprised you got them to speak up."

"I didn't do a thing," Nathaway said. "They just wanted to talk about you. Too much, in fact."

Way too much, Harg thought. As if he were some sort of public issue.

He was no longer comfortable with this conversation, so he fell silent. The Inning didn't notice.

"What I can't understand is the power structure here," Nathaway said. "Who's in charge?"

Against his better judgment, Harg answered. "You Innings say that as if it were one word: powerstructure. It's not. We've got power, but no structure. Innings love hierarchies and organization charts, everything defined and settled. That's not how we do things. We have alliances and factions, and every morning when we get up it has to get renegotiated." He was only exaggerating a little. "No one's in charge. We don't have permanent leaders like you do. Whatever person's best for the job, that's who's in authority. When the job changes, so does the person in charge. That goes for a fishing trip, and it's the same clear on up to the Ison of the Isles. They're all just the best available for the job."

"But there isn't an Ison any more," Nathaway pointed out.

"No, you Innings saw to that. Since you executed him, well, we just haven't needed one. We don't keep leaders around when we don't need them. They just make trouble."

"What about Goth?" Nathaway asked. "He seems to be some sort of respected leader."

Harg laughed drily. "Respected, yes, Leader, no. He's more like . . ." he cast about for some Inning equivalent, but could think only of a lame one. ". . . like a minister or a doctor, maybe. It's not like anything you have."

"But if he could endorse what I'm doing, maybe . . ."

His innocent, ignorant words sent a shock through Harg's system. "No!" he said, too forcefully. The Inning had no idea what he was talking about; best he should not know. "He wouldn't do that," he explained, trying to cover his first reaction. "The Grey Folk stay out of our business." Except on the rare occasions when they didn't, and then everything changed. The Lashnura were key to power in the isles; but that was a private, Adaina thing, like family business, and it was best no Inning know it.

His nog was gone, and Harg realized how sore and tired he was. "I don't want to be rude, but I haven't slept much, and the last bath I had was—" he tried to think. "Mundua know."

"Of course," Nathaway rose to leave. "Can I come back later?"

"I don't know who's going to stop you."

It was scarcely an open invitation, but Nathaway took as such. "Good. I've got a lot of questions."

When the Inning was gone, Tway crept back in, looking apprehensive. "Harg, what were you yelling at him about? We could all hear."

So half the village had probably been listening. He couldn't even imagine what that would do for his reputation. "What do you think? I was yelling because he locked me up and accused me of all those crimes."

"Are you crazy? You can't yell at an Inning. Next time, they'll cut your tongue out."

"Don't worry, we patched it up," Harg said. He was deadly tired, and wanted to shed his reeking clothes. "I'm just no good at this being conquered, Tway," he admitted.

"Well, you'd better get used to it," she said, "because that's what we are."

THE WIND
FROM THE SEA

Dear Rachel, Nathaway wrote. It was his fourth letter to her. He knew it would get passed around the family, but he still addressed it to her alone, since she was the only one who had been the slightest bit encouraging about his choice to come here. His family's tepid support still rankled.

> *I have now met members of all three of the races inhabiting the Forsakens. They are very distinct.*
>
> *The Tornas and Adainas are physically indistinguishable to my eyes—both small and compact, brown-skinned, with dark curly hair—but they claim to see a difference between themselves, and the Tornas never tire of pointing it out. The real difference lies in character and customs. The Tornas are avid, active, acquisitive, and above all opportunists. To my face, they are obsequious and ingratiating; behind my back, manipulative and untrustworthy—though when I confront them, they are masters of the plausible explanation.*
>
> *The Adainas are far more primitive. They live in perfect hovels, and are poor as dirt, you would really be shocked at the squalor. They are far harder to draw out. To me, they are sullen and uncommunicative, though in private their lives appear to have some simple gaieties. They are acutely aware of their status*

as a conquered people, and resentful because of it, but they will not confront me or speak honestly about their grievances. I have hopes that I am making some headway with them at last. I had the opportunity to befriend one of them recently, and it may give me an entry into their closed community.

The last race, rarest and most mysterious, is the Lashnura or Grey Folk. There is only one on this island. She is a fascinating creature. . . .

He paused, deliberating what to say. He had to mention her striking appearance, but somehow without suggesting her sexual allure, the way her creamy grey skin had made him itch to run his hand along her all-too-visible thigh, her little breasts dimpling the scanty cloth covering them, her indecent proposal that had shocked him because it had so perfectly mirrored what he had been thinking. . . .

These were not things his sister needed to know. After all, he had come here to uplift and protect these children of nature, not to take advantage of their innocence. Because there *had* been something childlike about her, something he felt a strong impulse to guard from harm, not to violate.

He skipped a space to insert a description of Spaeth at some time when he could think about it without getting heated.

She is the daughter of their local shaman, the mysterious Goth, whom I almost suspect of not really existing. However, the Adaina seem to be reluctant to admit their relationship, which they cover with a preposterous story about his having made her.

Puzzled, he looked up, thinking that there was a similar reluctance to admit plainly that Harg was Goth's son, which from the story Argen told seemed perfectly obvious. He shrugged. Perhaps a dhotamar was supposed to be celibate, and they were all studiously looking the other way. He would add it to the list of things to ask Harg—very delicately, in this case.

He stared out the window of the ship's cabin that was his home until something adequate could be constructed ashore. The view was always different, since the ship rode at a single anchor and so swung according to the prevailing wind. At the moment it showed the western view, where the sea was a steel-grey expanse and a storm front advanced across it from the southwest, trailing skirts of rain. The sea made him uneasy; it was so uncontrollable, so oblivious of all humans and their concerns. He would be glad to be ashore again, away from its infernal rocking motion—although the urgency of his desire to move had abated a bit since the cockroach situation on the ship had, quite inexplicably, improved.

Turning to his letter again, he wrote:

> Before coming here, I was led to believe that the Lashnura were kept in a state of bondage, obliged to perform their blood ritual for whoever commanded them; but the reality is somewhat different. The Lashnura claim to feel motivated by an altruistic ethic of self-sacrifice. They really believe their blood can cure, but consider it a joyful gift to their fellow man, a service they perform willingly, even at considerable cost to themselves. I cannot help but feel that putting an end to this practice, as we must, will eliminate something noble from the world, an expression of mercy and humanity.
>
> I hope you will forgive my writing at such length about the Yorans. To tell the truth, I find them more interesting than I expected. The Torna we shall need, but the Adaina and Lashnura should be the objects of our compassion and care.

At the moment Nathaway was signing his letter, Harg was on his way to Goth's cottage to keep his promise to Strobe. He suspected that his arrival might end the Grey Man's absence.

He felt apprehensive about seeing Goth after all these years, but it was something he had to do, or feel incomplete. So much of what he had accomplished in the Inning world had been an effort to prove something to Goth—stupidly at first, and with greater wisdom as the years progressed. He needed Goth to see him now, and acknowledge the change.

It was an unsettled day; the weather couldn't make up its mind what mood it wanted to be in. Outside Goth's house the trees were whispering to each other in the gusty wind. When Harg came into the yard he stopped. It looked like someone had just been here. There was a shiny new axe in the chopping block and a pile of wood waiting to be split. The tomato vines in the garden were staked up, and some chickens pecked in the dirt. Clearly, Goth had returned.

The door was closed. The sunlight beating on it brought out the texture of the unpainted wood. He touched it, and it swung open. There was no one inside. He stepped in with the familiar feeling that he was entering a sanctum. Then he saw the rumpled bed and suddenly remembered Goth's girl, the sex toy. Of course, she must be the one splitting the wood and caring for the chickens. She was the one whose breakfast dishes were still on the table.

He crossed to the fireplace and looked on the mantelpiece. Yes, it was still where he had seen Goth place it seven years ago. He picked it up: a small, round stone. It was the soulstone he had asked Goth to keep for him before he went away. If he had died far from Yora, this was where his soul would have come to be at home. He remembered how terrified he had been that Goth would say no.

Fingering the stone, Harg thought how unlike him it looked: wave-washed and grey. More like Goth himself. Harg wondered why he had picked this stone. Then he noticed that its surface was darkened from being handled. Someone had held it often enough for hand oils to soak in and polish it. With a pang, Harg thought: *He held the damned stone more often than he ever held me.*

He closed his eyes. In the utter silence he could almost feel Goth's hands closing over his own, over the stone.

The back door banged, snapping him out of his reverie. Blown in on a gust of wind, her silver hair in disarray, a young Lashnura woman stood before him, as surprised to find him there as he was to see her.

"Who are you?" she said.

Everything he had thought since hearing of her changed in an instant. This was no mere sex toy, no work of lust or need. She was an exquisite creation, born of mad inspiration. It looked like Goth had poured all the love and longing of a lifetime into her. If she had been a statue, she would have been a master work; but she was real, a glimpse of what happiness would look like if it breathed and walked.

And she was Goth's.

Why had he even looked at her? Why had he found out there were such possibilities in the world? Men like him were not allowed perfect beings; they just spent their lives watching and wanting.

She was studying him with a direct, unwavering gaze, completely unafraid, as if he were the most fascinating thing she had ever seen. "Who are you?" she said again.

He had to clear his throat before he could speak. "My name's Harg Ismol. Sorry, I—"

"*You're* Harg?" she said in astonishment.

71

"Has he spoken of me?" There was no need to say who; it was like Goth was in the room.

"All the time. Everyone does." She took a hesitant step forward, then stopped. "You have a very strong mora," she said. "I can feel it from here, like a furnace. I think if I touched you, I would get burned." She came forward another step, drawn by the tantalizing prospect of pain, as all Lashnurai were. Carefully, she reached out to touch him on the neck, near the pulse point. "You've been hurt," she said, just a whisper. Her eyes clouded like a tarnished sea on a moody day. "They told me about Jory, but not about you."

He took her hand and, simply because he couldn't resist, brought it to his lips. They were watching each other so closely the gesture felt more intimate than it was.

"Would you like to have sex with me?" she asked.

He was struck by the innocence of the question. It was like a child asking him to play. "Yes," he said, "very much. But there would be hell to pay if I did."

"Why?" she asked.

"He really has taught you nothing, has he?"

"Yes, he has," she said, more in Goth's defence than her own.

She was completely guileless, defenceless, without any survival instincts. Goth had created this exquisite innocent, then gone off and left her to make her own way. Just as he had done to another child long ago.

"Bastard," Harg said under his breath. "He did it again."

"Did what?" she asked.

He pressed her hand between his. The bones felt light as a bird's. "Listen—what's your name?"

"Spaeth."

"Spaeth. If you ever need something, or get in trouble, come to me. I'll help you, I promise."

"What kind of trouble?" she said with a slight frown.

"Any kind."

"Well, then, you can strike Agath dumb for me," she said lightly.

He frowned. "What's Agath after you about?"

"She wants me to cure Jory."

She said it as if it were a joke, but he knew better. "No!" he said forcefully. The thought revolted him. Jory's damage was such that it could kill or cripple any dhotamar who took it on, especially an inexperienced one. Harg could not bear to see her maimed, even for Jory.

"You must not go near Jory," he said seriously. "Especially don't touch him. It doesn't matter what Agath says, or anyone. Promise me."

Her smile told him how presumptuous his demands seemed. "Jory lives here now. I live here. I can't not go near him."

"Well then, don't let them lure you into—"

"I'm not giving dhota for him," she said positively.

"Good," he said.

"I want to choose, not be coerced."

"Good."

He wanted to touch her face, and was just reaching out when a suspicious voice behind him said, "What are you doing here?"

He whirled around, stepping away from Spaeth as guiltily as if he had been doing more than just holding her hand.

Mother Tish the herbwoman stood in the doorway, frowning at him.

"Nothing," he said.

"Then get on with your business, if you have any," she said, standing aside for him to leave. "And stay away from Spaeth."

Her vehemence made him defensive. "I'll cause her no harm," he said.

Mother Tish came into the cottage to take Spaeth by the arm, and draw her away from him protectively. "She's ours, not yours."

He saw then what was going on. The girl was their next dhotamar, and already they were crowding around to possess her. "You pack of parasites," he said to Tish. "You've bled Goth till he had to run from you, and now you're starting in on her. Can't you solve your own problems?"

"What would you know about it?" Tish snapped. "You're not his bandhota."

It was true; he was on the outside. There was something about their faces, this private clique of Goth's dependents. A strange blood-kinship. They protected Goth, revered him, loved him, and drank him dry.

"Get out!" Tish ordered. But instead of letting him leave, she said, "He could cure you of your hard heart if you gave him the chance. If you didn't love your anger so. The Ashwin alone know why he loves you."

That was their secret grudge. They thought Harg was their rival for Goth's love. "At least he's got a choice whether to love me," Harg fired back.

He left then, feeling shaken. When he came to a downed tree beside the pathway, he sat on its trunk, bending forward and pressing his knuckles into his forehead. Seven years away, and he was still right back in the middle of everything divisive and bitter about Yorabay. He had thought the Harg who had left all those years ago was dead and gone, but he still existed in the minds of Yorans, and they were constantly calling him back into being. It made Harg feel like a stranger in his own skin, to have their expectations controlling him. But perhaps the competent, respected Captain Harg of the Native Navy was really the creation of other people as well, and could be dismantled by others without his consent.

Now he thought back to his days in the navy with a paradoxical longing. He had had only one goal then: to survive in spite of everything they could do to him. There had been a purity about that struggle that had stripped layers of unnecessary complexity from life. He took the soulstone from his pocket, where he had put it. It felt small and hard as a lump in the throat. Once, death had lain in the palm of his hand, cold and hard, and he had learned to grasp it. Now, he needed to learn to do the same with life.

That night, a new wind blew over Yora. It was a wind with a tang of faraway lands and a chill of changing times. It stirred in the tiny, crowded cottages of Yorabay, straining to burst into wider spaces, to sweep across the waters to other shores.

Just after noon, the storm that had been threatening swept in from the southwest, sending the fishing boats scurrying to port. Late in the afternoon someone spotted a trader's vessel riding the dark seas west of Yorabay, trying to beat south into harbour. A little group gathered on the rain-swept quay, watching. Everyone had an opinion about what the sea was up to. Old man Gimp thought it was angry because the Innings were trying to tame it with their breakwater. Bonn held that the storm was more mischievous than malicious. Others smelled something melancholy in the air. They all agreed that Goth would have known what the trouble was. The Lashnurai, after all, knew the sea personally.

It turned out that the sea was just bluffing. The ketch made it safely into the cove. The Yorans on the dock cheered, for now they saw it was the *Ripplewill*, a familiar cargo boat out of Thimish. *Ripplewill* and her skipper, Torr, were legendary on Yora, and not just because Torr would carry any cargo, regardless of legality. Twenty years earlier, he had been fishing the outer banks of Spole when his nets had brought up a mirror that showed not the reflection of whoever looked into it, but a woman's face so beautiful that every one of Torr's crew pined for it, and longed to jump into the sea to find her. They tried to bring the mirror ashore, but it tarnished quickly in the air, and when it was polished up again, would show nothing at all.

Knowing this story, everyone thought it significant that Torr had never married, unless you counted *Ripplewill*.

Strobe invited the skipper to his home. As they trudged together up the wet dock, Torr never stopped talking for a moment. "By the horns! I told those empty-headed commissaries that the sea was testy today, and their damned mining machines were as likely to see the bottom of the Pont Sea as Yorabay's cove. But would they listen? Ha! There was a schedule to meet, and all the powers forbid a schedule should wait upon the weather. So it was up to old Torr to brave the worst the Panther could do, or lose his contract for shirking!"

Since he had brought groceries and dry goods for the Yorans as well as the mining machines, no one criticized him for his rashness.

Several of the men from the dock joined them to hear the news. When they all crowded into Strobe's warm cottage, they found Harg lounging by the hearth, drinking Tway's home-brewed beer and staring moodily into the fire. After a scurry to provide Torr with dry clothes and a warm drink, Tway installed him next to the fireplace, where he warmed his backside appreciatively. Rain drummed on the roof.

"Is there good news out of Thimish?" Bonn asked the guest with irony. It was an old Yoran proverb, *Good news never came out of Thimish.*

The trader shook his head. "The news is bad. Scarce a ship has stirred from Harbourdown all month because of the godforsaken customs regulations. No one knows what's going on. All they know is we can't be allowed to make a living without doing more tricks for the Innings than a trained dog."

The Yorans exchanged looks. Harbourdown's "traders" had been poor neighbours for a century. Twenty years ago the rest of the South Chain, fed up with piracy, had banded together to clean the brigands out of Thimish. Their success had been dearly bought and short-lived. Now the Innings were trying to succeed where the islanders had failed.

"It's hard to imagine a customs office on Thimish," Gill observed mildly.

"That's what we all said," Torr replied. "We didn't think they could be serious. Then a shipful of Tiarch's militia came and planted themselves in the old abandoned fortress above the town, and said they'd blow up any boat that tried to enter or leave the harbour without permission. They've got the guns and the idiocy to do it. Now we hear there's three more ships on the way to make us all toe their line. Then you'll find out what it's like."

"They won't do that here," Gill said. "Yora's not Thimish."

"Do you think they know that?" said Drum. He was known about Yorabay as a perpetual malcontent, but occasionally he voiced grievances that others just hadn't yet realized they cared about. "What do you think that Inning is here for, anyway, decoration? Pretty soon you'll have to be buying licenses from him yourself, Gill."

"I'm not a trader," Gill said.

"You don't have to be," said Torr. "They want you to have a license if you're going to own a boat or a gun, or sell beer, or go fishing. You have to get a license to be born, or to get married, or to die, or move away. Don't tell me you're not planning on doing any of those things."

"That's just crazy," Gill said.

"Welcome to the Inning empire."

As they were talking, Harg was thinking what idiots the Innings were. Everything he had told Talley not to do, they had done. Sent in the hated Northern Squadron to the very hotbed of discontent. Failed to promote Adaina officers. Then started to impose Inning law without any finesse or regard for older customs. It was almost as if they were *trying* to provoke rebellion.

"You're very quiet tonight, Harg," Strobe said, pouring him another beer.

"I'm listening," Harg said.

Torr had caught the name and now scanned Harg curiously. "You're not the same Captain Harg that won the battle of Drumlin, are you?"

Surprised that his reputation had traveled to Thimish, Harg said, "I didn't win it alone, but yes."

"I'd like to shake your hand," said Torr, genuinely impressed. "We've got a lot of men in Harbourdown who served in the Native Navy. They've come home now, and are mad as hornets to find they fought a war just to see their own people conquered. They keep saying, 'If only Captain Harg were here, he'd show them a thing or two.'"

The other Yorans were looking at Harg in bemusement. Strobe said, a little jokingly, "You're sure it's *our* Harg they mean?"

"There's only one of me," Harg said, "thank the Mundua."

"Fancy your being here, and me coming to this house just now," Torr said, appraising him.

After that, his tone changed, and the information he started to give showed that Torr knew about some activities that would have made the captain of the ship at The Jetties sit up and take note. Listening, Harg began to realize that the pirates he had been hearing of were not just the old pack of criminals preying on the weak and defenceless. They were boldly hitting only ships owned by Torna merchants of the type who supported Tiarch's regime; small Adaina shippers like Torr were safe. There was a low-level, slow-motion rebellion already under way.

"Who's behind all this?" Harg asked, but as soon as the words were out of his mouth he knew what an Inning question it was. As if the Adaina needed a hierarchy to tell them what to do.

"No one, really," Torr said. "We—that is, they, the pirates—just decided to take this tack. Of course, we couldn't be doing it without some people you may have heard of."

"Such as?"

It went against the grain for Torr to mention names, but at last he brought himself to say, "Have you ever heard of Holby Dorn?"

The Yorans stared. The name was almost a myth on Yora, the incarnation of the vicious foe of the Pirate Wars. Even now, twenty-three years later, Yoran mothers frightened their children by saying Holby Dorn would eat them if they misbehaved.

"He is involved?" Gill asked, awestruck.

"He must be sixty if he's a day," Harg mused.

"And all sixty years he's been growing craftier," Torr said.

"When he wasn't busy stealing Yoran shipping," Harg said. Holby Dorn might be a great man on Thimish, but there was no chance of him drawing support from other islands. And against the Native Navy, he wouldn't last ten minutes.

Harg said, "You pirates know, don't you, that the Innings are sending the Native Navy from Fluminos to put you down? I'm not talking about Tiarch's navy. I'm talking about the Southern Squadron that beat Rothur in the war. And they don't have in mind just a crackdown; it's to be a full-scale occupation, to make the outer chains safe for them to do business in. Admiral Talley himself is coming to the isles to direct the action. That's how serious they are."

There was such complete silence that the sound of rain on the roof seemed loud. "How do you know this?" Torr said at last.

Harg hesitated, fearing the truth would sound overblown. But seeing their eyes on him, he shrugged. "Because Admiral Talley offered me command of the operation," he said. "I turned him down."

In the pause that followed, Harg could feel their opinions of him changing. Torr gave a low whistle. "Then it must be true. We're knee-deep in shit."

"Not necessarily," Harg said. "The Native Navy is something to be feared, but it has its weaknesses. It can be beat."

"By us?" Torr said.

"Not by a bunch of free spirits acting alone, no. But by Adainas? Yes."

Watching him keenly, Torr said, "By you?"

"By anyone who understands them, and how they think. But you'd need arms, organization, and support. The most important part is what happens before the fighting starts."

"What we need is an Ison," said Torr.

This comment made Harg pause. Now Torr was talking about something bigger, a unification of the isles to fight again the war they had lost fifty years ago. He frowned and said, "No, we don't. Why should we have to wait for the Lashnura to pick someone to lead us? We're capable of leading ourselves without their say-so." He looked around the room. "Everyone here is capable of commanding a ship in battle. Tway included."

Strobe glanced up at his daughter, who was standing behind his chair, listening to their every word. "This talk scares me," he said. "We tried fighting the Innings once before, and all we got was bloodshed and defeat. We can't beat them."

"We don't need to beat them," Harg said. He was just talking off the top of his head now, but it came out as if he had been thinking about it all along. "That was our problem before, we thought it was all or nothing. What we really need to do is cause them enough trouble that they're willing to negotiate and make concessions."

"Negotiate!" Drum said sceptically. "Can you see them sitting down at a treaty table with a bunch of Adainas?"

Harg gave a sudden laugh of inspiration. "Well, if we wanted it, we've got the perfect hostage to get their attention, right here on Yora."

They stared at him blankly. "Don't you know who that Inning is? He's the son of their Chief Justice, the most powerful man in their land."

It was Strobe's turn to say, "Who told you that, Harg?"

"Well, I guessed, but he admitted it."

"Is that what you were talking about the other day?" Tway asked.

"Among other things."

"By the horns!" Torr said. "If you believed in coincidences, this would be one. It looks to me more like fate."

"Fate's just seeing your opportunities," said Harg.

Torr gave him an earnest look. "Harg, come with me to Harbourdown. Our navy men are right; if you arrived there with all your ideas and your knowledge, everything would change. We wouldn't have just a pack of pirates no one trusts; we could have us a real resistance."

Strobe was watching Harg with dread, the others with intense curiosity. Harg shook his head. "I don't know, Torr. I don't really want to get involved."

"It seems to me you're already involved," said Torr. "It's your own damn country, man."

"You're talking to someone who's worn out with fighting." And yet, being in his other persona had felt right. He had been Captain Harg again for a while, and liked it.

"Don't you see all the signs?" said Torr. "I was brought here for a reason. To set the balances straight again."

"Don't listen to him," said Strobe. "Right, Tway?"

But Tway was watching Harg with a curious expression, as if she had realized something unexpected. "No, Dad," she said, "I don't agree with you. I think he should go."

Harg and Strobe both turned to her, dumbstruck.

"I think Torr's right, there's more going on here than meets the eye," she said. "The invasion we see now may be only the beginning. I've thought this ever since Spaeth told me the Innings want to outlaw dhota."

There were exclamations of consternation from all the Yorans, but Torr only nodded. "Yes," he said, "it's another way they want to save us from our savagery. They haven't said yet how they're going to enforce it."

"They didn't do that in the Inner Chain," Gill said.

"They didn't have to," Torr said. "A lot of folks there, they just stopped believing in dhota. And about the same time, they stopped feeling the mora of their islands, and the circles of the Mundua and Ashwin stopped overlapping with ours. I tell you, where the Innings go, something dies. Something more important than just our right to go where we please without a licence."

"I think there's a bigger battle coming on," Tway said quietly. "These Innings aren't just invaders; they're a disease of the soul. And we're going to be called on to defend more than our freedoms. We're going to need to defend our world."

A glowing arch of coals settled into the grate and a plume of smoke rose from it into the silence. The patter of rain on the roof had almost stopped. Harg felt chilled to the bone by what Tway was saying. If it was true, there could be no compromise, and people would be called upon to make sacrifices greater than any of them could imagine.

He reached for the poker to wake up the fire. Once the flames had scattered the shadows he said, "Well, I'll think about your offer, Torr. I'm not saying yes or no tonight. Though I'll tell you truly, tonight the answer would be no."

"Then sleep on it," Torr said. "Who knows, maybe tomorrow will be different."

5
THE WHISPERING STONES

The last drops of rain were still pattering down from the tree leaves when Spaeth went out to look at the sky. High above, the wind was hustling the clouds along, bullying them like a herd dog, so that already the stars showed through in patches. She could hear the dim heartbeat of the sea.

It was the kind of night when she didn't want to be hemmed in by walls. Lightly, she grasped the corner post of the porch and climbed up onto the edge of the cistern, then from there to the porch roof, where she lay down on the damp shingles, looking up. Her body shivered, partly from the cold, partly from delicious anticipation.

She was thinking of Harg Ismol. Adaina men had always seemed familiar and uninteresting to her—pleasant, like the smell of woodsmoke and wet leaves. Harg was different. He was taut as a set trap, and she felt a delicious compulsion to touch the trigger and spring him, though she knew she might be caught painfully in the jaws. The sense of danger was horribly tantalizing.

When she had first seen him standing there in her house, she had mistaken him for Goth; and though a second glance showed that they looked nothing alike, she could still understand the first impression. There was the same complex knot of undigested pain inside them both, and she had felt the same hungry compulsion to cure that drew her back into Goth's arms again and again, though by now she knew it was impossible to rid him of it.

What an interesting place the world was, she thought, to have two such people in it.

Above her, a torn curtain of cloud blew back to reveal the deep, crystalline sky beyond. Constellations hung there, each star a possibility that she could pluck down like fruit. Invisible beyond the stars, a thousand potential universes were stacked, the realms of the Ashwin, and below her a thousand more, where the Mundua dwelt. She lay balanced at the fulcrum. This precious world, always at the brink of unbeing, bloomed with the beauty of all doomed things. It was the pivot point, where any flaw in symmetry could bring the whole structure crashing down. She raised a finger high, and it seemed as if the whole sky spun like a platter on it.

A step on the path below her made her sit up to look. A bent form carrying a lantern was approaching the cottage. When the visitor was almost underneath, Spaeth recognized her. "Mother Tish!"

Tish looked up, confused to hear a voice from the roof. "Spaeth," she said. "What are you doing up there?"

"Looking at the stars."

"Well, come down here. We need you."

Dutifully, Spaeth climbed down. "What is it?"

"The elders want to talk to you. Come with me."

The elders were gathered at Argen's house. It was an old-fashioned hut that lay back in the woods, a little separate from the others. As Spaeth followed Tish up the woody path, she had to shrug off a feeling of misgiving.

Inside, the walls were lined with bark, and in the orange firelight the room looked like the interior of some huge, hollow tree. The elders had gathered their chairs around the hearth; the faces that turned to her looked brown and seamed as wood. Lacking Goth, there were seven of them: five widows and two men. The sea claimed the men of Yora young, and left widows in their place.

Mother Tish sat next to the only empty place. She patted the seat and said, "Sit down, Spaeth."

It was where Goth should have sat. If she took his seat, it would be like taking his place—and that was like admitting he was not going to return. She saw an old trunk against the wall, on the edge of the firelight, and said, "I'll sit here."

Argen's eyes followed her, frowning. He had not missed any of the symbolism. "You're going to have to take his place some day, you know," he said.

Some of the women hushed him, but he only raised his voice. "Best she should be settling down with some bandhotai, instead of running wild and causing trouble."

"Oh, quit fussing, Argen," Tish said. "It's the way she was made."

"That's what I mean," Argen said. "Goth's a saint in his way, but he never gave her modesty or shame. It didn't suit his purposes. But he never thought we'd have strangers on the island who would be tempted by her."

"She's Lashnura!" Mother Greer said indulgently. "You can't stop them coupling, you know. Might as well try to stop the birds."

Argen wasn't mollified. "I don't care who she couples with, so long as it leads no farther. She's *our* dhotamar, not Harg Ismol's."

So that was what this was about. Spaeth forced down the indignant protest that rose in her throat. Argen made it sound as if they owned her.

"Harg's not exactly a stranger," Tish pointed out.

"No, we all know what he is, and for him to be hanging around her . . . well, it's unseemly."

At last Mother Pilt spoke up. Her voice was thin and piping as a bird's, but her air was one of authority. The others fell silent. "These are unsettled times. None of us quite know how to behave. First the Torna came, and while their wealth is welcome, it caused rivalry and dissent. Then that Inning started poking into people's affairs. Then Harg and Jory came back, and we've had nothing but problems ever since."

She paused. "But there are things more worrisome than any of this. Goth is gone, we don't know why. But there is reason to fear some grave imbalance in the world."

Seven wary faces turned to Spaeth.

"Spaeth," said Mother Tish, "let me see your hand."

An irrational reluctance seized her. She forced herself to hold out her hand. Tish motioned someone to give her an oil lamp, and she held it close to examine Spaeth's nails. She gave a soft click of the tongue and the others gathered round to see. It was only then that Spaeth saw the dark half-circles at the base of her nails.

"As I thought," Tish said, sitting back. "The Black Mask."

Frowning, Spaeth crossed her arms, hiding her hands away. "What do you mean?" she said.

"Has Goth never told you about this?"

She shook her head. They all exchanged significant looks.

Mother Tish leaned forward into the lamplight, her voice grave and urgent. "Spaeth, this is serious. You know that the world we live in is not a safe one. Since time began this circle has been a battlefield. The Mundua and the Ashwin have fought their shadowy war on our very shores, and mankind has survived only by tact and vigilance. We must maintain the balance of forces at all costs, or all we love will be destroyed."

"I know," Spaeth said.

"Pain is the inroad of imbalance into our minds. It makes us susceptible to the manipulations of the forces of disorder. That is why dhota exists: because unhealed people are a danger, not just to themselves, but to the world around them. They are cancers where imbalance breeds.

"When your ancestors by their terrible crime brought suffering into our world, they created you, the Grey Folk, to help set right what they had made wrong. They gave you the power to take on our pain so that the forces of imbalance would have no tools among us. But they could not give you that power without also giving you its sibling."

Her voice dropped very low. "Grey Folk were not given the choice to refuse dhota. Unless they do what they were created for, the Black Mask comes upon them. First the fingertips turn black, then if they still refuse, the hands and feet, and then the disease flows inward till all their blood is poison. Gradually, their limbs, then their whole bodies dissolve and turn to slime."

A moth had found the flame of one of the lamps and was throwing flickering shadows of its own death on the walls. Outside, a cricket began to chirp, loud and rhythmic in the hushed air. Spaeth sat rigid. Her mouth felt like sawdust.

Tish said, "If Goth were here, we would ask him to handle this. Since he is not, we must do it ourselves. Spaeth, you must fulfill your ancestors' covenant with our community. You must give dhota at once."

They wanted her safely bound to someone on Yora, so that she could never escape. They had begun to think that Goth would never return, and they did not want to lose her.

There was hunger in all their eyes. Spaeth looked around the circle of them, and they seemed to have changed. They were wizened shells, animated only by the desire that shone out through their eyes. Goth had given them dhota too many times. They were addicted to it.

She stood abruptly. "I'm not obliged to give dhota to you." In the flickering light they looked half maddened by their need. She had to get away.

"No," said Tish, also rising. "We know that. But there is someone who needs you more than we do. We have talked it over, Spaeth, and we wish to claim dhota on Jory's behalf."

Spaeth looked around, tense and suspicious. "I don't know Jory."

"Come and see him, Spaeth. He was such a handsome young man, so full of life and joy. Without you, he has no future. Your heart would go out to him, I know."

They had all risen now, and were standing in a circle around her. It was a trick, she thought; somehow they thought they could force her.

"Dhota must be freely given," she said. "Otherwise it will not work."

"We know that. Just come and see him. Then you can go home if you want, and make up your mind."

"I need to think it over."

"That's right. Just see his situation, and then you can take all the time you want."

"You promise?"

They all nodded. It seemed like a way out. She would just look at him to satisfy them, then escape.

They all set out down the path together. When they came near Agath's house, Spaeth could see through the trees that the lights were burning and the front door stood open. A loose group of people was waiting in the yard. When they saw her coming, one man went inside. She pushed past the gathering in the yard without a word to get into the safety of the house.

Inside, Agath's house was crowded full of friends and relatives. Every eye in the room turned to her in expectant silence. In a glance she saw that Goth's bowl and knife lay waiting on a table. Someone must have gone up to her cottage to fetch them so they would be here for her, so she would have no excuse to leave.

The people from the yard crowded in behind her and closed the door. Stiffly, Spaeth said, "Where is he?" Her words sounded muffled, as if all the listening ears had eaten them as they left her lips.

"Over here, Grey Lady," Tish said soberly.

The title made Spaeth feel like a stranger. Goth had slipped so effortlessly from symbol to person and back again, they all thought she could do the same.

Jory was sitting on the edge of a low cot in one corner, dressed only in shorts. Tish had been right, he was a handsome young man, well built and muscular; but every few seconds he twitched convulsively, his muscles contracting and head jerking to one side.

Spaeth could feel the eyes beating on her back as she approached him. "Jory?" she said softly.

He looked up at her. His face was drawn with exhaustion and frustration at the battle he was having to fight with a body that seemed possessed. His eyes pleaded with her. "Grey Lady," he whispered. "Can you help me?"

At the sight of his suffering, everything else fled from her mind. He was fighting so bravely even to sit up straight, it made her heart sore; she could not simply walk away. Impulsively, she reached out to take his face between her hands. The instant she touched him, she could feel the damage in his head. She ran her fingers through his curly hair, feeling the indentation in his skull. There was something underneath it, a dark place of clotted blood and scar, and a jagged shard of black metal still embedded. It was a horrible, savage wound that frightened her even to touch.

He was looking at her with desperation. "Can you?" he said.

"I don't know," she said. It wasn't an evasion, just the truth. She had never encountered an injury like this before. But she found she couldn't let go of his brave, tortured body. She felt a maddening urge to help him, no matter the consequences.

She closed her eyes and swallowed with an effort. This was why Goth had told her about the need for steely self-discipline, to control the delicious yearning that human pain would always wake in her, so she would not be a victim of blind instinct. But before she could gather her resistance, his muscles convulsed in her hands, and a keen desire pulsed through her body. In that instant, all her resolutions shattered. She had to do it.

"Give me the knife," she said. Her words sounded slurred. Tish placed the stone blade in her hand, and in a rational remnant of her mind Spaeth realized that the elders must have known this would happen, just as it always happened to Goth. But she had no time left for resentment; the yearning had grown too acute.

She had to breathe deeply for a moment, to get control of her shaking, sweaty hands. Carefully, reining in her sense of urgency, she found a vein in her arm and made a small cut. Never having done it before, she did not cut deep enough, and no blood came. Steeling herself, she cut again, deeper, and this time a trickle of wine-coloured blood ran down her arm. Tish held out the silver-lined bowl, and she let the blood fall into it. When there was enough, she dipped two fingers into it and touched it to Jory's forehead, then his temples, then his throat. Almost at once the blood lost its deep colour and turned clear as water, disappearing into the skin. As she touched the last of the blood to his chest, just above the heart, she could feel his mind stirring and waking inside hers.

"Look at me, Jory," she said.

For the first time in days, the quivering in his body stilled, his muscles relaxed, and he turned to her. His pupils contracted as if he looked into a bright light. "Who is it?" he whispered.

She wanted to caress him, to press her cheek against his. She held back; in a few moments they would share an intimacy far deeper than that.

"I am going to come into you," she said. "Don't resist. We're going to go together all through your body. When you find anything that doesn't belong, push it into me. With every breath, breathe out the evil. Let me take it from you."

She sank into him them. Every nerve in her body thrilled; she felt fuller than she had ever been. When she penetrated his mind there was a tremor of fear and he choked, his body instinctively trying to repel her. She stroked his chest, calming him till she had entered deep inside him. All his memories, his guilts, his passions and hurts, were hers as well.

The injury was like black rot in a fruit, reaching deep into his brain. She made him see it, so he could push it from his body. There was no way to be rid of it but to tear it out, pull it by the roots. He tried, then stopped, groaning with the pain.

"I know it hurts," she whispered. "But you have to do it. A little at a time."

He clenched his jaw and steeled himself to carve out the first patch of rot from his own flesh, gasping with the effort. When she turned him to the next one he held back, clutching at her. She stroked his forehead and whispered encouragement in his mind, waiting till he was ready. There would be no cure unless he did it himself.

Bit by bit Spaeth gathered the blackness into her own body. She could not yet feel its effect, only the intense pleasure of sharing Jory's pain. With every minute, the bond grew between them, like a strong, elastic cord from heart to heart. Already she felt a tenderness for him so intense it made tears start to her eyes.

Jory was exhausted with the effort at last; his weakened body could take no more. "You're very brave," she said. She felt an intoxicating love for him. She wanted to stay buried in his mind forever.

This was the most dangerous moment. She could not stay linked to him; against all instinct, she must sever the bond. Yet no effort of hers would be sufficient; there had to be some sudden shock, as of pain, to draw her out.

She groped for the knife; Tish pressed it into her hand. Far away behind her there was a stir in the crowd of onlookers. She said to Jory, "I have all your injury inside me now. I am going to take it away, and you must give it to me. Are you ready?" He nodded, gazing at her still and entranced.

She paused, steeling herself. The instant she withdrew, all his injuries would flood into her at once. They couldn't kill her, but they could make her far more ill than Jory.

There was a tumult behind her. "Stop this barbaric rubbish!" someone shouted. "It's stupid and useless!"

She swayed, distracted; the words flamed across her vision. For a moment she thought the knife had cracked in two; then she realized it was the bond with Jory that had snapped, recoiling into her face with stinging force. She spun around.

Three men were trying to restrain the Inning from striding forward and seizing the knife from her hand. His face was hot with indignation. He said loudly, "This man has had the best medical care in the world. No sacrifices or mutilation can do him any good."

Anger roared in Spaeth's ears. She wanted to bury the blade in his heart. Instead, she bared her arm and slashed deep across it, the cut that was supposed to seal the dhota bond.

The Inning gave a cry of horror.

"Get him out of here!" she commanded. Three men forced him from the cottage. Spaeth watched till he was gone, the precious blood dripping unheeded from her arm onto the floor. When she turned back to Jory, she knew with a glassy clarity that it had not worked. The bond had broken prematurely. The evil had flowed back into him, not into her.

She stood numbly as Mother Tish rubbed ashes into the cut to make it scar, then bandaged it tight. People were filtering out, thinking the drama was over. They did not know yet. They thought it had gone well. In all their years they had never known dhota to fail. Neither had Spaeth.

"You should lie down, Spaeth." It was Mother Tish, speaking in that voice she reserved for children, sick people, and dhotamars.

"I feel fine," Spaeth's voice grated. That was just the problem. By now she should be in the grip of Jory's injury. He had fallen back unconscious on the cot. She longed to press him close, to gather him back to her, but she fought for self-control. There was no bandhota bond between them; the Inning had broken it.

"Would you like to go home?" Tish asked.

"Yes," Spaeth said. "I need to be alone." She had to get away before they found out she had failed.

The night was cool outside, and the wind that touched her hot cheeks still had the smell of the departed rain. She walked home from Agath's house, listening to the trees sigh and rustle. Far off in the east, thunder growled hungrily. She did not see the shadowy form waiting on the porch of her cottage till she was almost upon it, and he rose to meet her.

"You!" she spat out, when she saw it was the Inning.

"Spaeth," he said, and reached out to touch her bandaged arm. "I came to—"

She pulled away. "Don't touch me."

"I can tell you're in pain," he said gently. "If you like, I can give you something for it."

Her pain had nothing to do with her arm. "You fool," she said. "You can't take pain away from a Lashnura. It's why we exist."

"That's exactly how these people manipulate you!" he said earnestly. "They play on this belief of yours. You don't need to suffer for them."

An hour ago, she might have listened. But her emotions were rubbed raw now, and it was his fault. "Listen, Inning," she said intensely, "pain is what balances the scales of nature. It has been woven into the fabric of this world since it was first created. You should be glad we are willing to take it on, or you would have more of it yourself."

"You're wrong!" he answered. "Pain is something we create ourselves, out of ignorance and malice. It's not natural or right. We should be working to drive it from this world."

She gave a bitter laugh. "If you did that, you would destroy all the joy as well." She tried to push past him into the house, but he stood in her way, confronting her.

"Maybe what you really mean is that there would be no glory left for you. You like it, don't you—their reverence, their awe. That's why you're willing to do this thing. It makes you better than they are."

Anger sang in her ears. A gust of wind blew past them, casting strands of silver hair in her face. She wanted to make him weep—and she knew how to do it. "Do you know what mora is, Inning?" she asked.

He frowned. "It's your word for magic, isn't it?"

It was far more than that; mora was the binding force that held the atoms and the stars together, and set them all in motion. But let him think he knew it all. "Our powers are not limited to dhota," Spaeth said. "Mora runs in our veins. If Goth Batra Namora were here, he could show you things that would cure you forever of denying what you cannot understand."

"Goth the shaman?" Nathaway said. "Never mind; I've seen charlatans before."

Now she knew he would not just weep. He would bleed, he would scream in terror. She would stake him to the hillside and call the Mundua to feast on his viscera. Ridwit would love her for giving them an Inning to devour. "You're a big brave man, here in the safety of the village," she taunted. "You wouldn't dare go to the Whispering Stones on the night of the full moon."

"Stop trying to scare me," he said. "I'm not like your Adaina."

"Then come with me, if you have the courage. I'll show you the way. To get back, you'll have to find your own way."

He hesitated a moment, then saw the challenge in her eyes. "All right, I will. We'll see who's convinced."

As if in reaction, the sky to the east boomed in laughter. Spaeth knelt and pressed her hands to the earth, trying to draw the island into alliance against the race that had harmed it. The sand flowed reassuringly through her fingers. Yora would stand by her.

She stood up. "Wait a moment, I have to fetch something," she said. Inside the house, she knew where Goth kept carefully hidden the leather bag of tools he used to pierce the barriers between the circles. In a few moments she had them in hand, and swept out the door past the Inning.

"Follow me," she said.

This was not the outcome Nathaway had expected.

It was pure luck that he had been ashore when the rumour came around that a dhota ceremony was about to commence in the village. The Tornas would have done nothing, and Captain Quintock had actually refused to send soldiers to break it up, claiming it was a private affair and none of their business. So Nathaway had been obliged to come alone.

He had expected opposition from the Adaina. But from Spaeth, he had expected, if not gratitude, at least acquiescence. Her furious reaction had taken him by surprise, and he had come to her house to patch things up. Now, it seemed, he had gotten himself in even deeper.

"Spaeth!" he called out, hurrying to catch up with her long strides.

She stopped. "Have you changed your mind already?" she said contemptuously.

"No," he said, "but what I really want is to talk to you. If I go with you, will you listen?"

"I have nothing to say," she answered. "I only have things to do. If you don't want to go with me, then good-bye." She turned and continued up the path. The shifting shadows quickly engulfed her.

He followed. She spoke not another word as they headed across the swelling hills toward the centre of the island. The thick-matted grass was spongy underfoot from the rain, and the blustery wind buffeted their backs. Above them the swollen moon dodged the wind-driven clouds. Behind them, the lights of the town were hidden by the hills.

Soon they were surrounded on all sides by rolling, silvery grassland. Nathaway found it hard to keep up with Spaeth, who darted silently across the treacherous ground while he blundered through tuffets of grass, straining to see the pools and potholes. For a long time their path approached a curious, rounded hillock that rose above all the others, so regular and hemispherical that Nathaway guessed it must be man-made. He had thought he knew the island well, but this earthen monument was strange to him. As they stopped at its foot, the wind ceased. Not a sound could be heard but Nathaway's laboured breathing.

"Is it a burial mound?" he whispered.

Spaeth gave him a strange look, and he thought for a moment she would not answer. But she spoke in a low voice that blended almost imperceptibly with the silence of the hills. "It is the skull of the Great Bear, whom Hannako slew."

From his books on Adaina myth, Nathaway knew that the Great Bear was part of their creation story. "The people on Rusk say the Great Bear's skull is on their island. There's another one on Vill. Is this the *real* one?" He had intended the remark jokingly, but something was caught in his throat, and the words came out in a hoarse whisper. He coughed.

"They are all the real one," Spaeth said. "They are all the same place."

She was gazing intently ahead of her, as if searching for something. At last she seemed to find what she wanted. "Follow me closely," she said. "If you can, put your feet where I put mine."

She started up the hill by a winding route, sometimes doubling back on her own path, sometimes circling up in spirals. When they finally got to the top, Nathaway found himself facing the circle of stones where he had first met Spaeth four days before.

"So this is where we are!" he exclaimed, puzzled at his own disorientation. "I should have recognized the spot."

"You saw it only by day," Spaeth answered, as if that should make any difference.

They were at the highest point of the island, and an unimpeded view opened up on all sides. Far past the grass hills he could see the glimmer of the moonlit sea, dwarfing the tiny spot of land they stood on. Not a light showed as far as vision reached, except from above.

After turning completely around once, Spaeth sat on the grass outside the ring of stones, facing south. She opened her leather bag and drew out a long wooden box. Inlaid on its cover were two intertwined ovals in opalescent mother-of pearl. Spaeth opened the lid and took out a long-stemmed pipe with a curiously carved stone bowl. She filled it from a cloth sack, then spread a piece of leather on the grass and laid out flint, steel, punk, and splints to light it. As she knelt to begin the process by striking a spark, Nathaway took a box of sulphur matches from his pocket and offered them to her. She hesitated a moment, then shrugged and took them.

She lit the pipe, took a few puffs, then gestured Nathaway to sit on the ground next to her. She handed him the pipe.

"You must smoke it too."

"Why?" he demanded suspiciously.

"It is an herb," she answered. "It brings out the mood."

Grudgingly following her instructions, Nathaway drew in the fragrant smoke. It had a calming but clarifying effect, and it was quite some time before either of them spoke again. Nathaway sat trying to think of a strategy to engage her in debate, but as he smoked the urgency faded. At last he said, "What sort of magic can you work? Make trees sprout from a box, or eggs appear in your hand?" He knew such tricks from the magicians who performed in Fluminos salons.

"I am going to try to catch the attention of the world."

"What?"

For a moment she seemed to consider whether to ignore him or go on. At last she said, "Back in the days of Alta, there was consciousness in everything. Even the stones were aware. Nowadays it's not so true. But there are still ways to wake the world. It is a matter of mood. You have to have a strong mood. We call it mora."

All he could think was that she intended a kind of séance. "Will you summon spirits?" he asked.

She stared at him a moment, then said, "Yes. That's what I'm going to do."

When he handed back the pipe she sat smoking it in short puffs. Slowly he realized she was angry. "What's the matter?" he asked.

Her tone was dark with enmity. "You come blundering in here as if the balances were not resting on a pinhead. You have no idea how fragile this world of ours is. There is a war going on! For centuries, we Lashnura have been saving the Isles from destruction through cleverness and sacrifice. We have given our lives and freedom to make sure neither side has the upper hand. Now, if you keep acting as you have, you will upset everything."

"Who is at war?" Nathaway asked.

"The Adaina call them the Mundua and the Ashwin."

He had read of them. "The spirits of the sea and the spirits of the air," he said.

"Some people call them the powers of imbalance. The powers of balance are what we Lashnura serve."

An inspiration struck him. "So do we! We call it justice. It's what all our law is based on. That is why we have come to the Forsakens—to right the balance. You see, we have a lot in common."

"I don't think we are talking of the same thing," she said.

Her tone silenced him a while. At last he said, "Do you have to shed blood to work your magic?"

"No," she said curtly. "This has nothing to do with dhota."

"But I thought—"

She cut him short. "It is almost time." She tapped the ashes out of the pipe and refilled it. "Finish this bowl of weed, and we will start."

They waited as Nathaway continued to smoke. Spaeth seemed totally unconscious of him now, staring away to the south. He took the opportunity to study her. She looked older than his first impression, less innocent and more commanding. She sat slim and straight, like a woman of silver condensed from the moonlight. Her skin shone soft. He wanted to touch it. He tried to marshal his thoughts, but only found himself remembering the invitation she had made four days ago, in this very place. Had she felt attracted to him? It gave him a heady feeling. She could not have wanted him for the sake of his status, like women in Fluminos. Out here, closed off from the world, there was no possibility of scandal or blackmail. No one would ever know. He wondered if she had entirely given up.

Presently she began a soft, low humming. As he listened idly, the tuneless chant crept into the cracks between his thoughts, becoming a background to them all, like the same frame repeated endlessly in a gallery of pictures. Without ever having listened, he knew her chant by heart. Two notes, pause, three notes, pause, two notes, repeat. He did not even notice when his own thoughts disappeared from his mind, leaving him open and unencumbered.

Suddenly the music stopped. Nathaway straightened and opened his eyes. He felt strangely rested, and wondered how much time had passed. He turned to ask Spaeth if he had been asleep; but she was looking at him with a strangely appraising smile. Somehow, he realized, she had gotten behind his guard, removed the defences of his mind, and for a short time controlled him. He felt indignant. Yet what could he accuse her of? Hypnotism? He did not even believe in what he felt she had done.

He looked away. She ought not to taunt a man when she was totally at his mercy, he thought. It would be so easy for him to reach out and pin her back on the grass, to press his tongue between her lips, to lower his body down on hers. . . .

Shocked at finding thoughts so unlike himself erupting from his brain, he stood up. He could no longer bear the thought of being so close to Spaeth.

"Stop!" she cried out. "Where are you going?"

"Away," he said unclearly, his mouth stiff and awkward. But before he could move, Spaeth had grasped his arm and pulled him down with a surprising strength. "Listen!" she whispered.

The scene before him had changed. Not a detail of the hillside was different, but the space seemed to have grown larger, as if viewed through a lens. His senses had become painfully acute: he could pick out every individual blade of grass down the hillside. He was keenly conscious of the unnatural stillness that had persisted ever since they had come to the hill. He felt suspended in a limbo world where there was neither movement, breath, nor death.

At his side, Spaeth began to sing again, but now there was an urgency to the four-note pattern, a summons. A chill trickled down his spine. He strained to hear over the persistent crooning of the song and the discordant pounding of his blood. At last, on the edge of hearing, he sensed the sympathetic notes of the sea far below them in the night. A soft, answering whisper from behind his back made his skin prickle.

"Don't look!" Spaeth warned. "Just listen."

The stones at his back were ringing, singing to the sea. Second by second the sound grew and blended with the wind, until he could recognize the very notes of Spaeth's song. A sense of terrible desolation shook him. The song was hollow, inhuman. He had no business hearing it.

"Speak, Inning!" Spaeth's voice lashed him with derision. He looked up as in a dream, to see that she was standing above him with a night-wild triumph. There were no longer any stars behind her head. "Go on," she taunted, "argue to me now about justice."

He opened his mouth to speak, but all he could do was sing the notes of the wind's song. His head was a bell of glass, a crystal ringing with the organ tones of the air around him.

"Go on, preach to the wind!" Spaeth's voice cut against the flow of the sound, scarring his consciousness. "Tell the night about reason and law!"

Her last syllable was drowned by a peal of wind tuned to the timbre of her voice. She looked up, her triumph drained in an instant. He realized she was afraid.

Mutely he reached out a hand toward her. She ignored him, preoccupied by something in the distance. He summoned all his strength and concentration to say her name.

She turned to him, her face waxy. "You took the risk in coming with me. I cannot help you any more."

Again the wind echoed her tone, and she flinched. She turned away, and for a moment he thought she was going to leave him alone. He gave a terrified, animal cry. She hesitated, then turned back with an angry exclamation and took his wrist, jerking him to his feet. It was easy to do, for he was light as a fish in a sea of sound. "Hide in the eye!" she shouted, and started up the hill.

He began to follow her, but stopped in confusion. He stood on a chalky white slope, grassless and smooth with wind and age. It curved away into a distance lost in the inky fog. With a shock he realized that what he had taken for a hillside was in reality a vast, undulating field of bone; and what he had taken for an island was the bleached skull of an enormous creature, lying slain in the sea. He looked to Spaeth in wonder, but she was already halfway up the slope to the eyehole that stared up into the blank heavens.

The bone was slick and clammy underfoot. The ridge before him seemed impossibly sheer. He tried to gain a toehold on the smooth surface, but his boot slipped and he fell back. Again he tried, only to slide farther down. He clutched with aching fingers at the bony slope, not daring to look down. Spaeth was far ahead, disappearing up the hill into the fog. He wanted to call her back, but could not make his voice work. Then it occurred to him that his boots were weighting him down. Frantically he tore them off and leaped forward on bare feet.

When he reached the edge of the eyepit, Spaeth was gone. The socket held a darkness dense as liquid. He could not bring himself to step over the edge. As he hesitated, a sucking wind pulled him back. He fell full-length on the bony ground, clutching the orbital ridge as the wind mouthed his body. Pulling against that terrible suction, he edged forward until he hung over the pit. Without allowing himself to think, he threw himself in.

What he landed on he never knew. He lay on his back staring up out of the cavity. The air was cold; he could see his breath. Beyond his hiding place rang the desolate song of the wind, and his bones responded. He struggled not to hear, pressing his hands over his ears and shouting to drown the sound out. He felt he must give way when suddenly the sound grew faint. He looked up to find Spaeth bending over him, her hands covering his ears. She had lent him the brief strength not to hear.

But her face was worn and pale. "Are there gods that protect Innings?" she asked.

"Some of us believe—" he began; but it was too much effort to speak.

"Then pray to them," she said.

Desperately he wanted to escape from this nightmare, to waken and find himself back in his own world; he saw in her eyes that she wished the same.

"What is happening?" he said.

"I don't know. We must wait to see if anything finds us here."

"What sort of thing?"

"Don't talk. Don't even think. They can smell thoughts. Just pray."

She drew away, and he felt part of him draw away with her. He was left attenuated, spun thin and fragile, as if he were all eye. She had stolen all but his power to witness.

As Spaeth stepped back, there was a cold breath of air, and on the edge of the pit above them appeared a condensation of blackness against the black sky. For a moment Nathaway thought it was a large block of stone; then he realized it was breathing. Spaeth flinched when she saw it. A heavy tread jarred the air, and a second shadow appeared on the lip of the pit. Then a third. They were trapped.

Spaeth crouched like an animal at bay. Panic rippled over Nathaway's skin, for he knew his safety depended on her. With a jolt, her last words came back to him. "Pray," she had said. He knew no prayers. He had never needed a god before. Now, haltingly, he began to say words, jumbled and desperate at first, a confession of his own smallness against the immensity of the world.

Subtly the scene before him changed. His sense of time was lost, but it seemed as if he could discern some movement. In slow flashes it came to him that Spaeth was dancing. He wanted to stop her, to cry out the urgency of the situation. But her dance had caught the attention of the dark watchers. As her movement took on a circular pattern, they began to follow her. In the flickering light, her shadow danced behind her against the walls of their refuge. Faster they all began to spin, until Nathaway was dizzy with watching them. A vortex began to form in the centre; the current tugged at his life-force, a black magnet attracting all energy to itself. Desperately he fought to keep his heart beating, his mind functioning against that gravitation of energy to the centre.

Suddenly an explosion that had once been a woman swooped into the vortex and erupted upward. The shadows above met it, and Nathaway was blinded by a detonation of the darkness. He had no time to turn away or shield himself. As he lost his hold and fell, his mind grasped onto the only conviction in reach: he still wanted to live.

FUGITIVES

Harg was deep asleep the next morning when the door crashed back against the wall so hard that dust filtered down from the rafters. Before he could quite struggle awake, four marines pushed into the house, armed for police duty: clubs, handcuffs, and pistols. They scanned the darkened room and saw Harg, then went straight for him. Two of them dragged him roughly from bed, then shoved him across the room and through the door, out into the cold morning air, wearing only the shorts he had been sleeping in.

Two of the marines held his arms, and another stood watch. Without any preamble, the fourth marine, the one whose nose Harg had bloodied, struck him in the mouth so hard that Harg's jaw nearly came unhinged. This was followed by a blow to the other side of his face that left white spots dancing before Harg's vision.

The third blow, to his stomach, buckled Harg's legs, and they let him sink to the ground. Gasping for breath, his mind still careening, he crouched on all fours in the dirt. He could make no sense of what was going on.

"Where is Justice Talley?" the marine demanded.

Harg gaped at him, speechless. One of the others raised his truncheon, so Harg yelled, "I don't know!"

"You threatened him the other day."

"What?" Harg said, sounding nearly as stupid as he felt.

"Come on, you piece of brown. He came here last night. What happened then?"

"I never saw him," Harg said. The marine behind him brought the truncheon down on his bare back. "I swear to you, I was here all night. He was never here."

The door behind them banged and Tway came flying out into the yard, an old coat wrapped hastily around her nightgown. Fearlessly, she thrust herself between the marines and knelt on the ground beside Harg, putting an arm around his shoulders. "Four against one?" she shouted at them. "Is that your idea of a fair fight?"

The marines stepped back. She went on furiously, "He was in the house all night. I was here. He did nothing but talk and sleep. We would have known."

All around the landing, the doors of other houses had started opening, and people were collecting to see what was going on. Strobe had come out of the house, and was frowning darkly, his massive arms crossed on his chest. Unwilling to continue with so many witnesses, the marine said to Harg, "If we find out you're lying . . ."

They marched off noisily in a thuggish clump. Harg's lip had started bleeding profusely, and Tway pressed a piece of cloth into his hand to stanch it. "Here, come inside. I'll give you something cold to put on that."

She led him back in while Strobe stayed outside to talk to the neighbours. Once he had a cold, wet cloth pressed to his face and the bleeding had slowed, Harg said, "What the bloody hell were they talking about?"

Grimly, Tway said, "You men were so wound up in your conspiracies last night, you didn't know what was going on outside. Probably everyone in the neighbourhood could have answered their question."

"So the asswipes decided to beat on the one person who didn't know a thing." He paused to spit some blood into an empty beer glass by his chair, then looked up at her. "Justice Talley? The Inning?"

In a low, tense voice, she said, "Last night, the elders asked Spaeth to give dhota for Jory."

This news sent a shock of alarm through Harg. He grasped Tway's arm hard. "She didn't do it, did she?" The thought of her, so beautiful and graceful, drooling and twitching with Jory's injury, was more painful than the beating.

"Well, they brought her to him, and of course you know what happened when she saw him. She wanted to do it."

"Oh gods," he groaned, "why didn't you tell me? I would have gone."

"There was no need. The Inning found out about it, and barged in. He interrupted the ceremony and Spaeth never finished."

For once, an Inning had done the right thing. For all the wrong reasons, of course, but at least he had prevented a tragedy. But now he was missing. "Did someone take it out on him?" Harg asked.

"Spaeth," said Tway significantly. "She was furious with him. The last anyone saw of them, she was leading him up the hill to the Whispering Stones. Later, they saw lights up on the hill. Everyone was too scared to interfere."

Harg felt queasy with the thought of what that might mean. "She wouldn't have—" He saw on Tway's face that they were thinking the same thing. He whispered, "She took an *Inning* into one of the other circles?"

He staggered to his feet to find his clothes.

"Where are you going?" Tway said.

"I've got to find out what happened. For one thing, if that Inning doesn't make it back, there's going to be a hue and cry from here to Fluminos. For another . . ." He had to find out if Spaeth was all right. He didn't say it, but Tway understood.

"Wait for me, I'm coming too," she said.

Ten minutes later, they were walking together up the path to the Whispering Stones. Even from the base of the hill they could see that something had happened there, for the grass was flattened in a circle, as if a whirlwind had stood there. When they reached the top, a dark mood seemed still to hang about it, dimming the morning light, and there was a smell of charring. Harg could not bring himself to cross the invisible circle traced by the stones. He waited while Tway checked inside. Laying his hand on one of the stones, he found it was icy cold.

"The grass in there is all black," Tway said when she came back out. "But there is no sign of anyone."

Harg scanned the landscape, and his eyes fell on a gully on the north side of the hill. "Let's check down there," he said.

They found Spaeth sitting with her head bowed on her knees. Nearby lay what looked like a pile of clothes, with a telltale shock of blond hair sticking out. As Tway scrambled down the steep bank toward Spaeth, Harg headed for the Inning.

Nathaway's face was the colour of a cadaver. Quelling his revulsion, Harg knelt and felt for a pulse behind the ear. The Inning's skin was cold and stiff. For an instant, Harg thought he felt a flutter under his fingers, but it was only his own pulse, racing.

"Don't be dead," he whispered to the lifeless body, pressing his hands over the heart as if to warm it with his own body heat. He could feel nothing. Then he picked up a hand, chafing it between his own. "Come back," he said; but it was useless. He let the Inning's hand drop.

"Is he dead?" Spaeth was looking at them in a glazed torpor.

Instead of answering, Harg picked up the glasses lying broken on the ground next to the body, folded them, and put them in the Inning's pocket. Then he stood up.

"What happened?" Tway said to Spaeth.

She looked as if it were taking all her strength to keep her head upright. Her voice was dull and lifeless. "I shot him off like an arrow into space. I thought he would fall to earth again two feet in front of me. He didn't. It was as if he had been practising with mora for ten years, and had never learned the first thing about it."

In silence, Tway and Harg looked at the lifeless Inning.

"I hated him." Now Spaeth's voice was thick with emotion. "He scoffed at me and at dhota. I wanted him to die in the wastes outside the world. I wanted the Mundua to feast on his liver. But in the end I couldn't do it. Oh, what an idiot I was!"

What she had done was dangerous beyond description—not just to herself, but to all of them. Calling up the Mundua and Ashwin was an unthinkable act, because once in this circle there was no sure way of getting them out. If it had gotten out of control, the delicate balance on which all the circles rested could have been shattered. They were unspeakably lucky that only one person's death had satisfied the forces of chaos.

But now . . . Harg sank to the grass, his hands over his face, overwhelmed with the repercussions this insane act would have.

"Harg?" Tway said.

"The Inning's dead," he said dully. "They're going to want someone to blame. You know who that's going to be." His back, his ribs, his bruised face all ached with the knowledge of who it would be. But next time it wouldn't be just a beating. They would have to make an example, provide a deterrent.

He turned to Tway. "I've got to get away from Yora."

She looked horrified. "If you run, they'll only suspect you the more."

"If I stay, I'm a dead man."

"What happened to your face?" Spaeth broke in. She had just focused on Harg for the first time, and she looked starved, spellbound at the sight. "You're hurt. I've got to help you." She started trying to undo the bandage on her arm.

"Stop that!" Harg ordered her. She paid no attention, but started tearing at the bandage with her teeth, so he caught her wrists and held them so she couldn't harm herself. For a moment they faced each other, kneeling in the grass, and he saw the raw, uncontrolled longing in her eyes. Then she lunged forward and kissed him on the mouth.

"Harg, let go of her!" Tway ordered. "Stop touching her, she's out of control."

He drew back, the sensation of her lips on his still vivid, and let Tway come between them. "Don't let her hurt herself," he said.

Tway shook the Grey Girl by the shoulders and said sternly, "Spaeth, control yourself."

Spaeth closed her eyes and grew absolutely still, sinking back on her heels in the grass. "I'm sorry," she said. Her voice was strained with the effort it took to check her instincts.

Harg and Tway looked at each other. "What are we going to do with her?" Tway whispered.

Letting out a long breath, he said, "We can't turn her over to Goth's bandhotai again. She'll never be safe with them; just look at her. We've got to get her off the island for a while."

It looked like a thousand objections were crowding to Tway's tongue, but she never uttered any of them. At last she nodded. "They'll go berserk, but you're right. Until this blows over."

Down in the harbour, Harg knew, the *Ripplewill* waited to take on cargo for the return run to Thimish. "We can't go back through the village," he said. "I don't want to run into those soldiers, and we can't let the elders see Spaeth leave. Tway, you've got to take a message to Torr. Tell him I'll join him, but he'll have to pick me up at Lone Tree Point. You can tell him about the Inning and the soldiers, but don't tell him about Spaeth yet."

"Can you manage her without me?" Tway said, glancing at Spaeth dubiously; but the Grey Girl looked calm again—so calm exhaustion seemed to be overtaking her.

"I think so," said Harg. "It's the only choice. When you're going through the village, stop at Goth's and pick up some of her things. Give them to Torr, but don't tell him what they are." For an instant he thought about telling her to get someone to tip the Tornas off about where to find their Inning. It seemed like the decent thing to do; but he quickly dismissed it. As soon as they found Nathaway, the scapegoat hunt would start; they might not even let *Ripplewill* leave.

"All right," Tway said, and rose to leave. Harg caught her hand.

"Tway. Thanks," he said.

She paused for a moment, looking down at him with an expression too complicated for him to parse. Then she quickly leaned forward and kissed him, just as Spaeth had, on the lips. She left without a word. He watched her go, wondering if he had been missing something about Tway all these years.

After Tway left, Harg settled down to wait. Spaeth had fallen asleep on the grass, and he didn't want to rouse her right away, since it could take hours for Torr to make the rendezvous. Watching her sleep, he could see Goth in every line of her face. She had that same paradoxical blend of power and innocence. The ardency and recklessness that Goth hid so well were right on the surface for all to see. For the second time in two days he wished he had never seen her, and yet couldn't take his eyes off her.

Three hours passed before the *Ripplewill* rounded the headland west of Lone Tree Point, edging forward on staysails. Harg and Spaeth were waiting on one of the sandstone ledges that angled down into the water from the mouths of the rocky caves on the point. He had roused her over an hour ago and walked her down to the shore half-asleep; but now she was beginning to wake. She saw the boat and glanced at him, then looked away, wincing at sight of his face.

"That bad, eh?" His lip and eye had begun to throb in earnest now; he could tell they were swollen.

"You'll have a black eye," she said, her back turned.

When the ketch came close enough, he whistled and waved. He saw a flash of sunlight on Torr's spyglass, and then the boat's anchor went down. The crew launched a small rowboat from the foredeck as efficiently as if they made clandestine pickups all the time.

Harg didn't know the woman in the rowboat, and they exchanged only cursory words as he and Spaeth climbed in and started back across the choppy waves to the *Ripplewill*. As they approached, Harg saw two people standing at the gunwale watching them approach, Torr and—

"Tway!" he shouted. "Blood and ashes, what are you doing here?"

"Did you think I was going to let you two go off to Thimish alone?" she shouted back. "I can't think of two people who need more looking after."

"Torr! Why did you let her come?"

"Have you ever tried to stop her?" Torr replied. He was looking curiously at the second passenger in the rowboat, the one he didn't yet know about. As they came alongside and the seawoman shipped the oars, Harg swung himself up onto the deck, then turned to grasp Spaeth's hand and help her on. Torr said,

"Wait a minute, Harg." His voice was hard and suspicious. "You're welcome, you know that. But her—" There was something almost superstitious in his look. "What is she, Yora's dhotamar?"

"No," Harg said, "and we mean to keep it that way." He pulled at her wrist and she stepped lightly up on deck, facing Torr.

"What are you getting me into?" Torr said, his eyes flicking from Harg to Spaeth and back again. "I'm already skating against Inning law by taking you. If I help her escape, all of Yora will want to nail my hide to a tree."

"Don't worry, it's me they'll blame," Harg said, a little bitterly.

In a low tone, Torr said, "Is she your bandhota?"

It was Spaeth who answered. "If he was, do you think I'd let him walk around looking like that?"

Torr was momentarily distracted by the sight of Harg's face. "They really worked you over, didn't they?"

"Not as much as they wanted to."

The skipper turned back to Spaeth. "Listen, lass, I don't know what this is about or why you're following him . . ."

"You have to take me, captain," she said with a quiet certainty. "There are larger things at stake here."

There was a pause. Torr looked at Harg again, as if his premonitions now extended to them both.

"Torr," hissed one of the crew. "We've been spotted."

As the others turned to look, Harg shoved Spaeth down into the cockpit. "Into the cabin," he hissed at her, and only then turned to look up. But it wasn't one of the Yorans, as he had feared. Far away on the hillside by the Whispering Stones, four men in uniform had stopped to look down at the boat so suspiciously at anchor where there was nothing to anchor for. Someone must have told them where to search for the Inning. It would only be a matter of minutes before they found him.

"Torr, we've got to get out of here!" Harg said urgently.

"Ashes!" Torr swore. "By the root, Harg, I hope I don't regret the day I met you. Cory, get the anchor. Galber, mainsail." Tway had already grabbed the oars from the boatwoman, and Harg leaped to help raise the rowboat on deck. For a few minutes the ship was a silent flurry of work as the mizzen sail went up and the jib billowed out in the breeze. Soon Harg felt the boat heel to starboard and gather way under him. The choppy rhythm of the inshore waves yielded to the slow roll of the ocean.

And suddenly, he was on his way to a destination he had never intended to seek. As recently as last night he had felt that his future lay on Yora; but here he was, as sure as if some unseen force had interceded to propel him. It was almost a giddy feeling to think of surrendering to it, and letting it blow him forward, to surf on a great grey wave of history.

❧

When Yora was just a low grey bump on the horizon, Spaeth came up on deck, feeling a little lightheaded from the strong odour of dreamweed in the hold. She stood looking back toward Yora. She had never seen it from this angle before. Never in her life had she been so far away from it. The thought made tears rise into her eyes. She was leaving the island that loved her, to go into a world where the land would not even know her name.

Exile seemed like an appropriate penance. She felt a biting regret about everything that had happened the previous day. There was nowhere her thoughts could turn without making her wince. Jory. Nathaway. Harg. Herself most of all. She had acted so badly, shame smothered her spirits. It was not a familiar feeling.

Tway poked her head out the companionway, and saw Spaeth. She held out a cloth bag. "I stopped by your cottage and picked up some things for you," she said. "I didn't know what you would want."

Taking the bag, Spaeth said, "Thanks." There was something hard and heavy in it, so she drew back the string and looked. Tway had put in Goth's bowl and knife, the instruments of dhota. The sight made Spaeth feel like a stranger to herself. They were not hers; they could never be hers. When she looked up again, she felt with a bitter ache that she was leaving her childhood behind on Yora. Ahead lay only the life of a Grey Lady, sacrifice and duty.

Wanting to get away, she went to the windward rail and sat, looking out at the dark waves rushing toward them from the west. They looked like they were in a hurry to get somewhere, impatient with the boat in their way. One of them crested and bared white fangs at her, then gathered its muscles and leaped onto the deck beside her, sitting down and beginning to dry its fur with its tongue. Spaeth glanced around in dismay, but none of the others on deck appeared to notice the horned panther beside her.

"Well? Are you satisfied?" she said to Ridwit in a low voice.

"Not really," said the cat.

"I gave you what you wanted. You asked for the Inning, and I brought him to you."

"And then you changed your mind," Ridwit said. "That was a very foolish thing to do."

Bitterly, Spaeth said, "But you took him anyway."

"No, I didn't." Her eyes glowed like amber lamps.

"You mean he's not dead?"

"No." Ridwit's tail flicked with frustration. "He didn't taste good."

From the tail, Spaeth knew the god was lying. For some reason, the Mundua hadn't been able to devour him. Spaeth felt a rush of relief. She hadn't killed him, then. She brushed water off Ridwit's back. Under the guard hairs, the cat was perfectly dry.

"It was more amusing to let him escape anyway," Ridwit said. "We'll eat him later, when he's aged." She was bluffing, as gods will do when thwarted. She went on, "I don't know why you wanted to save him. They are hateful creatures."

"He fought so hard to stay himself," Spaeth said thoughtfully. "Harder than I would have been able."

"That's what makes them dangerous. They believe more than anything that they are real. It's closing off the doors into other possibilities. And you thought *we* were a threat."

The panther looked away, sly and secretive once more. "Oh, well, it doesn't matter. Everything worked out anyway."

"What do you mean?" Spaeth asked suspiciously.

"We have better things to think of than you." She bared her fangs. It looked almost like she was laughing. A pang of alarm passed through Spaeth.

"What has happened?"

"We have found an ally," Ridwit drawled.

"A human ally? In this circle?"

"Yes."

This was chilling news. It was precisely what the Grey People had been created to guard against—the danger that a human being, corrupted by pain and power, would consent to be a tool of the forces of disorder in their perpetual war for control of this circle. Time and again over the centuries, the greatest of the Lashnura had had to sacrifice their own lives to cure such flawed humans, and make them whole again.

"Why are you telling me?" Spaeth said.

Ridwit turned to look at her with a taunting grin. "Because there is nothing you can do about it. You Grey Folk are degenerate. Once you ruled this circle, now you are all slaves to your bandhotai. Your Heir of Gilgen is a prisoner and a fool. Soon, even you are going to find someone whose pain appeals to you, and then you'll give in like all the rest. Now that we have an ally to do our work, we have nothing more to fear from you."

"Who is it?"

Ridwit looked at her with disgust. "You must think I am as much of a fool as you."

"Is it a man or a woman?" Spaeth said. "Adaina or Torna?"

Ridwit rose and laughed—a night-black, feral sound. "Find out yourself, if you care so much." She crouched, muscles rippling beneath glossy fur, then sprang into the sea. The wave passed on under the hull and was gone.

Spaeth sat staring out across the water. The cold wind seemed to pierce through her clothes now. She needed to find someone to tell, someone who would know what to do. It was news that called for the intervention of greater powers than she.

Ripplewill scudded forward across the waves, propelled by the tension between wind and sea, drawing power from the clashes born of the boundary. This whole world was the same, a boundary line, precariously poised on the edge of annihilation. Only humans had the power to tip it over the edge. She looked at the others on deck, suddenly suspecting them all. Her eyes rested longest on Harg where he stood at the bow, looking forward. But no, that would be too simple. Ridwit would not have risked telling her if he were the one.

She hated the panther's malicious humour then, for giving the warning to her, the least likely of any Lashnura to know what to do about it.

HERBS
AND POISONS

They were trying to kill him with contrasts, Goth thought as he stepped from the palace into the garden. A breeze fresh from the invisible sea stirred his clothing, still musty with sweat. Above him the birds were warbling promises they could never keep, and the trees rustled as if they were not, like everything else here, prisoners.

They had sent him straight from their Hospital of Justice to regain his peace of mind in a garden. He had been in the clean, sunlit hospital for ten minutes before he had realized that the gleaming instruments set out on white linen were not made for mending bodies, but for rending them. The cultivated Inning doctor who toured him around never used the word "torture." He called it "correctional science."

"It is a far more efficient and rational method of criminal justice than incarceration," the doctor said. "It is more effective as a deterrent, it operates faster, and it is far less costly. Lock a man up for ten years and he comes out as incorrigible as before. But a month here will break even the most defiant and courageous criminal, and make him abject and compliant. Pain has a remarkable transformative power. We have refined our methods to work efficiently on the mind, for that's the point, isn't it? Anyone can break a body. We want to modify the man."

Goth was not timid when it came to pain; he had known too much of it. Other people's pain, mostly. It had had a sanctity in his life, coming to him as it had in the intimate embrace of dhota. But here in Tornabay, it had lost its purity. It was not an act of love, but of control.

"Why are you showing me this?" Goth had asked.

"You will have to consult Commodore Joffrey," the doctor had said politely. "He asked me to give you the tour; that's all I know."

As the shady gravel path unfolded before him, Goth reflected that there were only two things they could want from him: to anoint a new Ison of the Isles, or not to. If the object were to prevent him, then threats served no purpose.

The problem was, they also served no purpose if the object were to gain his support.

What his captors evidently didn't know was that he was already in pain—the unending heart-pain of separation from his bandhotai. The Innings had already sliced away great parts of him, as sure as if they had used a razor. There was an aching pit inside him, where severed bonds hung dangling. In that cavity the universe was empty, a grey waste fit only for kindling.

He forced himself to walk on. The garden was placed in an angle where the palace walls met the sheer side of Mount Embo, so that on one side the gnarled black rock of an old lava flow formed the only wall, rising nearly vertical for forty feet. Down the cliff's knotted side a small mountain spring tumbled into a moss-edged pool. Goth sat on the bank and splashed some water on his hot face. A few yellow poplar leaves were drifting on the pool.

It was very beautiful, he thought, trying to keep his mind balanced away from thoughts he could not control. And yet the beauty was deliberate—as if the garden had been placed in the fortress just to create a mocking illusion of freedom. When he saw that the ivy climbed hopefully up the wall to the iron spikes set at the top, he shook his head at its useless optimism. It would never escape.

At first he did not notice the bottle bobbing in the water by his hand. When he saw it, he took it up with suspicion, for there was a message in it. He unfolded the scrap of paper, holding it well away from him. It was printed in a large, childlike hand. It said:

> *Heir of Gilgen, be of good heart. Your*
> *people know that Tiarch holds you. Believe*
> *in us, and we will make you free.*

He frowned, angry and frustrated. Evidently, some mad patriots had once more rallied against the rule of Inning, and now in their foolish zeal they had managed to compromise him with an incriminating letter. His first instinct was to shred it and scatter it on the water; but as he was about to act, a sound made him stop, certain he was watched. Not a movement stirred the holly bushes around him; a squirrel browsed nearby, oblivious of human presence.

It occurred to Goth then that the letter might be just one more contrivance of his captors—a test. How, after all, could rebels penetrate Tiarch's citadel to leave a message in a garden where Goth had never been before this moment, and where only the governor's staff could have known he was likely to be?

Putting the note in one of the tiny ornamental pockets of his Inning waistcoat, he rose to pace. Soon he heard again the sound that had startled him; it came from another part of the garden. He passed through an arbour and came to a place where the air was perfumed with herbs that grew in little terraces against the frowning mountain. In one of the plots a middle-aged woman was working with a trowel, planting seedlings in the black soil. She looked up for a moment on hearing his step, then turned back to her task. Goth stood and watched her, ridiculously pleased to see an ordinary person performing an ordinary task.

At length the gardener finished the row she was working on and sat back on her heels to survey her visitor. Her grey hair was tied back in a red scarf. Her high cheekbones and broad mouth revealed her Torna origins.

"Have some tea," she said in a voice that was both rough and pleasant.

Going to where she pointed, Goth took a hot teapot swathed in cloth from the lunch pail she had set under a bush. He poured the steaming liquid into a small pottery cup, tasted it, and nodded. The heat soothed the ache inside him.

"You like it?" the gardener asked, reaching out a knotted, mud-caked hand to take a taste. "It's a blend of four mints I mixed myself. They all came from this garden. The star mint here, rose mint here, the ruffled mint in the plot behind you, and white mint over by the wall." She sounded as if she were introducing him to friends.

"It looks like a mess, but all the plants are grouped so they will help one another grow," she explained. "One plant will attract the butterflies, while another keeps off the aphids. This plant enriches the soil with foods that plant takes away. I have been working for twenty years to balance them perfectly. The secret is variety. Always I need a greater variety to create a plot that will sustain itself."

"What are they used for?"

The gardener rose, brushing dirt off her skirt. "Some are used in the kitchens.

Others are for medicines. Some are never used. Those, for instance." She gestured to a nearby terrace. "They are mostly poisons, some of the deadliest native to the isles."

"If they are never used, why do you raise them?" Goth asked.

She shrugged noncommittally. "Many poisons have medicinal properties. It's all in the dosage, whether they cure or kill. This one is the only import." She paused by a waxen-leaved plant that had been covered against the cold of night. "In Rothur, where it grows wild, they call it achra, or delight. There they eat the root whole for the feeling of pleasure it gives. But the Innings have found a way of distilling the elements of the root, and creating a substance so strong that people who have tasted it can never again rest with ordinary pleasures. They say achra gives each person his heart's desire, for a time."

Goth said nothing.

"Everything else here is native," the gardener said. "Seeds and bulbs and grafts have been brought from every corner of every Chain. Here representatives from all the isles live and bloom in peace. How unlike the real world, eh?" She gave him a wry and knowing smile.

"Perhaps someday the people will learn from the plants," Goth replied.

"Not in your lifetime or mine."

It was the voice of an actress, Goth decided. It had a harsh, throaty quality that made it arresting even when she spoke the softest. For some reason—he could not tell why—Goth liked this chance companion. She did not have the cold officiousness of the Innings, or the wiliness of the servants of Tiarch. On an impulse he took the piece of paper from his pocket and showed it to her.

"What do you think of this?" he asked.

Her face grew very grave as she read it. At last she handed it back to him. "Where did you get it?"

"In a bottle in the pool over there," he said. "Is it genuine, do you think?"

"Oh yes, it's genuine enough." She had an air of resignation. "How they smuggled it in here, I can't say. There may be a spy on the staff."

"Who sent it?"

Instead of answering, she strolled on down the path to where a big, gnarled boulder jutted out of the grass. She settled down on its sun-baked back and regarded him sharply, her black eyes glittering with a thousand thoughts.

"I can't tell you," she said. "A band of zealots hiding somewhere in the city, I suppose. You had better tell Commodore Joffrey."

Goth was silent. Somehow, he had expected a more compassionate, less official answer from her. She read his emotions with the skill of a fortune-teller.

"Disappointed?" she said roughly.

Her tone provoked him to honesty despite his better judgment. "You answer like a minion of Tiarch's."

"That's not surprising," she said, "considering that I *am* Tiarch."

For a moment he thought she was joking; but the set of her jaw convinced him otherwise. He struggled with confusion then, unwilling to believe he was at last facing the Innings' viceroy in the isles, the politician who had ridden Inning power to dominion.

"Surprised?" she demanded. "What did you expect me to be like?"

Goth's long years among the Adaina had left him unskilled at navigating with words. He did not have the agility to come about into this wind. So he drew his dignity about him and was silent.

"You," said Tiarch, "are exactly as I expected: a man concealing his heritage under rustic ways, using age as a veil to hide his strength. It's so, isn't it?"

"I have nothing to hide from you," he murmured.

"I am glad to hear that. If it's true, you are the only person in Tornabay who can say as much. They all have something to hide from me. Even my 'minions.' Especially my minions. But that is the way with rulers, isn't it?" She looked to him for confirmation.

"I don't know," Goth said. "I have never been a ruler."

"Would you like to try?" she gave a wry, sandpaper chuckle. "I'll give you my kingdom for a day."

"You could not bribe me to take it."

"Wise man. So you think I've been unjust in bringing you here?"

He groped for the right answer. Justice was an Inning word, an Inning idea. Impatient at his slowness, she said, "Come along. You told Joffrey as much."

"Yes," he forced the word out. "It was unjust. I have done nothing to merit being taken from my bandhotai."

His voice faltered on the word. For an instant he thought he was going to break down right in front of her. With an effort of will, he kept control. Slowly he went on, "It was also unwise."

"How so?"

"Where I was, not a soul knew me. Here, they not only know me; they rally around me against my will." He touched the paper in his pocket. "There, I would have lived out my life in peace, surrounded by my bandhotai. Here, you are making me a desperate man."

112

She was thoughtful at this, regarding him keenly. "Tell me," she said, "what could I do to make you content?"

"Free me," he answered. "Let me go back."

"I think you do not appreciate what a dangerous man you are," she mused.

He protested, "I have never opposed you or the Innings. Who rules in the isles is of no concern to me. All I have ever cared for is to rule myself."

"Who rules in the isles is supposed to be your concern," she said. "The Heir of Gilgen is supposed to keep himself free of dhota, so he *can* care about who rules." She paused to let him answer; when he didn't, she said, "Why did you do it? Why give dhota when you didn't have to?"

How could he answer? He had done it because union with the human soul had filled his need to lose himself in something higher. He had thought that by giving himself away to all, he might come close to touching the divine. But it hadn't been that easy. Love had a way of becoming personal, fixed on the individual rather than the universal.

"I was a terrible fool," he said.

Frowning, she said, "But it doesn't disqualify you, true? If someone were to come to you now, claiming to be the next Ison, you could still confirm or deny him?"

As she said it, Goth felt a deep rumbling in his bones, and the earth quivered under him. The Mundua were restless under the mountain—far more restless than they had been in his youth. Then, Embo had slumbered; now it only dozed.

"It is not that simple," he said.

"Then enlighten me."

If he had been facing her in one of the long, echoing marble conference chambers, as he had expected, he would have found it easy not to answer with the truth. But here the very aspen and willow disarmed him. He settled down on the boulder next to her. "We Lashnura were created to guard the balance between the forces of chaos. The Adaina call them the Mundua and Ashwin. It doesn't matter what you call them. In this world, the horrors of disorder are waiting everywhere, every moment, to break through. When people are in pain, they are vulnerable to that. Dhotamars take on the pain of others so humans will not be weakened by it and ally themselves with chaos, allowing those powers to gain a foothold in our world.

"But when there is some need in the isles for a person with more than ordinary influence, someone who can unite and lead, it is essential to know that that person is not acting in alliance with powers that will bring suffering to our world. We must be vigilant, and suspicious of anyone who seeks power, unless we know his motives are disinterested and pure. That is why dhota-nur exists. It is a deep cure. It cleanses a person of all scars that might give imbalance a foothold in his soul. Before anyone can be Ison of the Isles, I must enter every corner of his being, explore every wound, examine him to make sure no taint exists. And whatever I find, I must take upon myself, a lifetime of pain. Dhota-nur has been known to kill. If it does not, it is the most profound bond two people can share."

Tiarch had been listening carefully. Her face was stern. "So, in your view, you actually create a new person. A better one."

The words the Inning doctor had used to describe his job sprang unexpectedly into Goth's mind: to modify the man. Horrified, he tried to banish the notion from his mind. It was not the same, surely, even though both processes involved a passage through pain.

"A wiser person, I hope," he said. "Better able to resist the corruption of power."

"And do you find that saints make good leaders?" Tiarch asked.

"Not always," Goth murmured, looking at the grass. "So many of those who rise to leadership are propelled by past pain. It is the fuel on which they draw to act. Usually, great men are hiding great scars."

"You keep saying 'men.' Must it be a man?"

Goth looked at her directly, thinking that at last she might have revealed her purpose. "No, of course not. A woman is just as capable of being Ison."

"And must it be an Adaina?" she said.

"No. A Torna could be Ison. Even an Inning."

She glanced at him sharply. "I would advise you not to mention that," she said.

He pondered that response. It had been so quick and instinctive.

"Has Joffrey threatened to torture you?" she asked abruptly. Goth answered with his eyes. Tiarch smiled at him disarmingly. "Don't worry; he won't. He was bred up licking the boots of the Innings, and he is still terrified at the thought of making you suffer unjustly. But the Innings aren't like Joffrey. Especially Provost Minicleer. You need to be careful of him."

"What do you all want from me?" Goth asked. "Just tell me, and I'll give it if I can."

She was gazing off into the arbour. Pointing down the leafy aisle, she asked, "Do you think that apple tree needs trimming?"

"No," he answered sullenly.

"You're wrong," she said decisively; "it does."

There was a silence as Goth tried to control his frustration. At last Tiarch turned to look at him, assessing. "You ask what we all want, as if we all wanted the same thing."

"Then I will ask what *you* want, Tiarch."

Her smile was sad and ironic. "What do I want?" She mused over the words, as if she had never asked herself the question before.

The temptation to touch her was strong, since it would sharpen his vision. Like everyone, she was a pattern of old scars—a complex pattern, since she had had a long and eventful life. But she was a controlled and closed-off person. He could not see deeply enough to know what drove her without some physical contact.

"I'll tell you what I want," she said at last. "Before I die, I would like to see the isles united."

Goth laughed. "Surely you have already united the isles—under Inning."

"If you call it unity to all pay taxes to the same despised invader," Tiarch answered.

"You rule more isles now than any Ison for five centuries past."

"Yes," she said, "but from time to time I think of being loved."

So what the tyrant of the isles wanted was not so different from what everyone else did. Goth had spent a lifetime trying to meet that need in people, that urgent, demanding need for love. Sometimes it had scalded him with its heat. But even that had been preferable to the vacant isolation he felt now. His hand moved of its own accord to hover over hers. She noticed it, and looked at him. He swallowed hard, and forced himself to pull back.

"I'm sorry," he murmured.

Somewhere off in one of the palace towers, a clock began to strike the hour. Tiarch rose. "I must go," she said. "Will you dine with me tonight?" He nodded, though her question scarcely needed asking; he would dine where her guards took him.

On the verge of leaving, she paused. "Give that note to Joffrey. Don't say you showed it to me; it will make him think he's found something, and keep him busy. Young men need to be busy." Goth had risen to take leave of her, but she waved him abruptly off and hurried down the path toward the palace.

As he watched her go, Goth felt a twinge of regret that he could not befriend this small, determined woman who was the fabled tyrant. He could not afford to think as an actor in these affairs, neither ally nor adversary. Repeating to himself the Lashnura proverb, *surrender is victory*, he infused his thoughts with submission. By the time the guards came to fetch him, he was as gentle and resigned as they had ever seen him.

℞

It was twilight on a rain-slick evening before the *Ripplewill*'s passengers went ashore. Torr had brought the boat in at one of the filthiest wharves in Harbourdown, far from the bustling town centre and its new customs house. From the near-derelict dock, Harg eyed the line of dark buildings that teetered on the brink of the oily water, their slimy lime foundations crumbling into the sea. There was a strong smell of sewage and rotting fish.

They had waited till dark because Harg didn't want many people to know he was here. "I've got to keep my head down," he had said.

"Don't worry," Torr had responded. "People here know all about disappearing."

Harg felt a misgiving as he watched Spaeth step onto the dock, looking at her surroundings with wide grey eyes. He hadn't wanted her to come tonight, but she had insisted, and Torr had backed her up. There was something of Yora's innocence about her that Harg didn't want to see destroyed, especially not in the brutal way it had been destroyed in him.

They set out down the dock with Torr in the lead, Harg and Tway on either side of Spaeth. Soon the skipper plunged into a narrow alleyway whose entrance was almost blocked by a pile of refuse, and they had to go single file. They passed an emaciated woman sitting on a doorstep with a man too drunk to sit up. She ran a hand over her greasy black hair and eyed them hungrily. A man with a hare lip pushed roughly past them, headed in the other direction.

"It's so strange," Spaeth said in a whisper.

"What's strange?" Harg said.

"They're all in pain."

Torr gave a short laugh. "That's *normal*, Grey Lady. It's Yora that's strange."

Deep in the warren of alleyways, they came to a ramshackle doorway with a green-shaded lantern hanging over it. A beefy man lounged by the door, his complexion sickly in the jaundiced light.

"Evening, Bole," Torr said. "I've got three guests here."

Bole nodded, looking close as if to memorize their faces. Torr jerked the swollen door open, and gestured them inside.

The tap room they entered was a large space lit by lanterns, and simply packed with loudly talking people. They paused just inside the door as Torr scanned the crowd. At last he spied someone at the bar. "Hey, Barko!" he bellowed across the room. "Look who I brought."

A man paused in his conversation and looked their way. Harg recognized him instantly: Barko Durban, ugly as sin, with a sharp, feral-looking face and thinning black hair pulled back in a ponytail. He looked every inch the pirate. He was one of the men Harg would have promoted to captain, if he had ever gotten the chance.

Barko recognized Harg just as quickly, and yelled across the room, "Harg Ismol, by the root! Hey, Cobb, Birk, look who's here!" He started pushing his way through the crowd toward them.

So much for staying inconspicuous, Harg thought.

He was soon surrounded by four or five men he only vaguely recognized, but who seemed to know him like a brother. Alert to his surroundings, he was aware that the din of conversation had lost some volume as people looked to see what the commotion was about. Then, as he was touching hands, the background noise suddenly dropped to near-silence. Spaeth had stepped to his side. Barko's left eyebrow rose at sight of her, and he glanced sharply at Harg. Instinctively, Harg put a hand on Spaeth's shoulder to reassure her; but when he glanced over, she was looking around with the wide, wondering expression of someone too young to know what danger was.

"Is there a table we could sit at?" Harg asked.

"Sure," said Barko, shaking himself out of the paralysis the sight of Spaeth had induced in everyone. He started off through the crowd, which parted before them.

"Don't they have Grey Folk here?" Spaeth whispered to Harg as they followed.

"Sure they do," he said. "They just don't show up in bars very much." Inwardly, he was cursing. Nothing could have made him more conspicuous.

Barko evicted a group of people from a secluded table by the back wall, and the newcomers settled down, eyed curiously by their neighbours. Tway whispered to Harg, "If they stare any harder, we'll be picking eyeballs off the floor."

The young woman who sauntered forward to wait on them was vigorously attractive. She crossed her strong, tanned arms in front of her chest and stood staring at Harg and Spaeth in a tough, appraising way. At last, tossing a strand of light brown hair behind her shoulder, she said, "What can I bring you folks?"

"I'll buy a round of beer, Calpe," Torr said.

With a last, lingering look, Calpe turned and walked with a swaying gait back toward the bar. Harg only realized he was staring, mesmerized by her ass, when Barko waved a hand before his face and said, "Harg. She's married." Everyone laughed.

They spent some time catching up. Barko and the other Navy men had been back for several weeks, and their simmering discontent at the situation they had found was palpable.

Eventually, Barko eyed Harg over the rim of his beer mug. "So are you here just for a visit?"

Harg shifted uncomfortably. "I had to get away from Yora. I got into some trouble there."

"Does this have anything to do with the fact that someone tried to rearrange your face?"

"Something. Four of Tiarch's marines gave me this."

"It took four of them, eh?" Barko said, grinning evilly.

"Yeah." Harg willed Tway not to say anything about how little fighting back he had done. She didn't. "Actually, Barko, I need to keep my head down for a while. They'll probably come looking for me."

"Assholes," Barko said. "They ought to be buying you drinks. These Tiarch's-men don't really believe the war happened; it's just a set of stories to them."

So Harg told them how he'd been accused of theft for having an officer's insignia in his possession. Though he tried to laugh about it, the outrage of the others made the bitterness come back. Every Adaina in the fleet had known about Harg's captaincy. To have it denied was a personal insult to them all.

"Well, if you feel like getting a bit of Adaina justice to offset the Inning type, let me know," Barko said.

"I'm not looking for trouble," Harg said. "I came here to get *out* of trouble."

Torr spoke up. "I thought we should introduce him to Holby Dorn."

"Good idea," Barko said.

"He has some ideas Dorn needs to hear."

"I bet he does."

Harg just stared at his beer. He actually had half a hundred questions about the supposed resistance—how organized it was, how widespread, what resources they had, what plans. But he wasn't about to ask them here. "Maybe we can get together some time, and you can fill me in," he said.

"Sure," said Barko. "We've got a little problem now that's right down your alley. Three of—"

He was interrupted by a hubbub at the doorway. A new person had entered—a huge, white-bearded man, dressed in gaudy silks, with a king's ransom of gold chains hung around his neck. He swept in, surrounded by half a dozen bodyguards. Instead of making way, the crowd surged toward him, yelling out "Dorn! Dorn!" so that the bodyguards had to push and shove roughly to make their way through. Halfway into the room the pirate stopped and tossed a handful of silver coins into the crowd. People fell to their knees, scrambling to pick them up. In the distraction, the pirate and his beefy retinue made it to a door in the back and disappeared through. Two guards took up stances on either side of the door.

"That was colourful," Harg remarked as the room returned more or less to normal. The Thimishmen were smiling, he wasn't sure why. The whole performance had seemed tawdry to him.

"Yeah, Holby Dorn's a character all right," Barko said. He had caught Harg's reaction, and was assessing it.

Torr said to Barko, "What do you think, should we wait till Dorn's drunk?"

"I think it's too late," Barko said.

"What's his power base?" Harg asked.

"You saw it," said Torr, rubbing two fingers together.

"Money?" Harg said. "That's it?"

"That's all there needs to be," said Torr. "He gets payments from the merchants in town, and in return he keeps a lid on all his rivals. He keeps things quiet, at least, and that's all most businessmen want—especially now that he's running raids farther from home."

"How many men does he command? How many ships?"

The Thimishmen exchanged glances that Harg found inscrutable. Barko said, "It's not like a navy, Harg. Dorn's got a boat, *Vagabond*, and he's got his guys. Other people with their own boats come along when they think there's profit to be had. They follow him because he passes out spoils. All in all, if everyone came, maybe twenty, twenty-five boats. Between them—what do you think, Torr, how many guns?"

"Counting small arms?"

"No, just ordinance."

Torr tipped back his chair, rubbing his hair. "Oh, maybe forty, fifty." He looked at Harg. "Little guns, five-pounders and such. These aren't big boats."

"You guys are in deep shit," Harg said.

There was a short silence as they all took drinks of beer. At last Barko said,

"Yeah, we know that. That's why there's a big argument going on about the three warships coming here from Tornabay, and what we ought to do about it. Some people say it'll only provoke them if we take them on, so we ought to lay low and wait. Other people are saying there's never going to be a better chance, and we ought to strike before they can establish themselves."

"What side are you on?" Harg looked at Barko. He respected the man's judgment.

"I'm waiting to hear what you say," Barko said.

"Me? I don't know a damn thing about it."

"Not yet."

"I told you, I can't get involved."

"You can give us your opinion. You owe us that much." Barko rose. "Come and meet Dorn."

As Harg rose, everyone at the table followed suit. He turned to Spaeth and Tway. "You ought to stay," he said.

"No, let them come along," said Barko. "You, too," he said to the other navy men.

When they all came to the door into Holby Dorn's private room, Barko signalled them to wait. He talked quietly to one of the guards, who let him through. After a few minutes the door cracked open again, and Barko waved them in. Everyone gestured Harg to go through first. When they followed him in, it looked like he had his own troop of bodyguards.

Holby Dorn and several of his men were sitting at a large table spread with food, eating. Calpe, the woman who had served their beer, was replenishing cups and clearing away plates as Harg's group entered. Dorn didn't rise, or even look up, until Harg stood directly in front of him. Then he set down his beer mug and gave a deliberative belch.

Up close, the old pirate's face was a patchwork of scars scabbed over with belligerence. One jagged old cut ran up the side of his face, barely missing his right eye. He regarded Harg suspiciously from under bristling, steel-grey brows.

Barko said, "Dorn, this is the man I was telling you about, Harg Ismol."

"I hear you're some kind of hero," the pirate said, picking his teeth with a fingernail. "Won the Battle of Drumstick or something."

"Drumlin," Harg said, not getting angry, since Dorn so obviously wanted it.

"Ismol," Holby Dorn mused. "Any relation to Immet Ismol?"

Surprised, Harg said, "His son." People almost never asked about his father.

"I knew him," Dorn said. With surprising quickness for such a large man, he stood up and held out his arm as if to touch hands. Harg reached out, then saw that where Dorn's left hand should have been was only a stump. Dorn held up the truncated arm, smiling grimly. "I owe this to your father."

There was a long, tense silence. It was Holby Dorn who broke it at last, with a low, grating chuckle. "By the root, I never want to meet his like again. When his boat went down I figured the Mundua must love me. I never knew he had a son."

Harg's voice was low and controlled. "Then maybe you can tell me something about the . . . accident that killed him." There was a persistent rumour on Yora that it had been no accident.

Dorn eyed him keenly, combing his wiry beard with his good hand. At last he shook his head. "No, I don't remember. It was too long ago."

Some of Dorn's men shifted, and one cleared his throat.

"What's your business here?" Dorn broke the silence roughly.

Torr jumped in. "I brought him, Dorn. We were talking on Yora, and he has information you need to know."

"Information, eh?" Dorn looked at Harg. "I hope it's not 'The Innings are coming.'" He said it in a mincing falsetto. "I'm sick of hearing that."

Harg crossed his arms. "That doesn't make it less true. And when the Native Navy arrives from Fluminos, your little boats and pop-guns are going to be so much flotsam, unless you start planning now."

"Stop, you're scaring me," Dorn said mockingly.

"You don't know what you're up against," Harg said. "It takes different tactics to fight them. You need to listen to some of these guys who know how Innings think."

"So what do you bring us?" Dorn demanded. "You have a boat and crew?"

Taken aback, Harg said, "No."

"You have money? Guns?"

"No."

"Then what do you expect us to do? Split our profits because of your name?"

"I'm not here for profits," Harg said. "I'm here . . ." He stopped, uncertain why he *was* here. Then, words he had been swallowing for days started coming into his mouth of their own accord. "Because I realized that if no one stands up and tells the Innings they've got to respect us, they're going to trample us down and shove us aside while they help themselves to our islands. They don't respect us, they don't respect the Grey Folk, they don't respect anything but power and profit. I lived for seven years in their world, and I don't want to any more. So *that's* why I'm here."

Dorn's men were all staring at him, and he realized he had spoken with some passion. The pirate was frowning, first at him, and then at the people behind him. Softly, he said, "Big brave words out of a little man. But the fact is, you've got nothing but words to offer. Bring me a boat, and I'll talk to you. Till then, I don't want to hear your name again."

Before Harg could react, Dorn shifted his gaze. "On the other hand, *you* are welcome, Grey Lady. If you'd like us to get rid of him for you, we will."

It was only then Harg realized that Spaeth was standing at his side. She was facing the menacing men before them without the slightest fear.

"You ought to listen to him," she said, her voice cutting cleanly through all the rivalry and bravado. "It's the Innings who are the enemy. They are coming here to ban dhota and spread their law-power where mora used to be. You don't know how dangerous they are. The balances are cracking, and you are quarrelling amongst yourselves."

No one spoke. Harg felt a cold premonition, as if it weren't just Spaeth beside him, but someone else, someone ancient as Alta. The thought made him queasy. He wanted nothing to do with such matters.

But then she looked at him, and it was Spaeth again, all of Goth's dreams made human. He took her hand. "Come on, let's go," he said quietly. He had nothing more to say to the pirates of Thimish.

He led the way out. Barko, Torr, and the others followed, grim-faced. When they emerged into the tap room, Harg headed for the door, but before he could get there a voice called out behind them, saying, "Stop! Wait!"

It was Calpe. She had followed them from the back room, and now pushed through the crowd to catch up. She faced Harg with a searching, intense look. "He can't order you out of here like that," she said. "This isn't his place; it's mine, and I want you to stay. There's a room upstairs where you can talk, all of you. I'll send up some food. Don't worry, it's on the house."

"That's mighty nice of you, Calpe," Torr said.

Calpe looked at Spaeth. "This isn't a good place for you, Grey Lady. I know a dhotamar in town who could take you in. Would you like to go there?"

"A Lashnura?" Spaeth asked, interested.

"Yes. His name is Anit. I'll take you."

Wanting Spaeth safe but reluctant to let her go, Harg looked around for Tway. She was already at his side. "I'll go with her," she said.

"Thanks, Tway." He was still holding Spaeth's hand. He forced himself to let go. "Be careful," he warned. Spaeth had been perfectly magnificent in there, facing down Holby Dorn, but far too incautious. Her sense of invulnerability could get her in trouble.

Calpe gave a piercing whistle, and a man came out from behind the bar, drying his hands on a towel. Calpe gave him a series of curt orders, and he nodded, glancing curiously at Harg. Then she said, "Follow Noll," and turned to shepherd Spaeth and Tway toward the door.

঩

For Spaeth, leaving the Green Lantern was like escaping a furnace. She had not realized how the presence of so many uncured souls had overtaxed her senses till she breathed in the cool night air outside. She stood, gratefully relaxing her mind, as Calpe gave some instructions to the burly man by the doorway.

She felt much farther than a day's journey from Yora. From her first glance of Thimish's pine-covered hills, she had known it would not be a friendly island. It eyed her from under its cloak of forest, old and crafty, wearing Harbourdown like a tawdry bangle. She remembered how Mother Tish had always said that people were not meant to go from island to island, because they might get tricked into trusting one that wasn't theirs.

Coming to the Green Lantern had been repellent and mesmerizing. She had never encountered so many people in various sorts of pain, psychic and physical. They were damaged in ways she had never seen, and could barely understand. She had felt the tantalizing tug of it from all sides. It was like smelling a hundred spices competing for her attention, waking her desires. There was a complexity, a depth of adversity in these people; each one was a landscape of wounds that would take months or years to explore. She could dive into the souls here and never surface.

"Are you all right, Grey Lady?" Calpe asked.

Shaking herself out of the memory, Spaeth said, "Yes."

The noise of pirate revelry died away behind them as they went down the alley. A gusty wind awakened a hollow rattle of rigging from the moored boats in the harbour. The streets were very dark, and the lantern Calpe carried cast a sickly light. As they began to climb uphill, buildings closed in on either side— silent, crowding shapes of brick and timber.

After a time they reached an open square. Against the northern stars ahead, Spaeth could see the symmetrical outline of the ancient fort that dominated the town. It lay atop a steep ridge of stone, its five bastions spread out like a reaching hand. She could see pinpricks of light where a late caravan climbed the switchback road to the citadel.

Calpe fell back by Spaeth's side. "That is the Redoubt," she said. "Perhaps you have heard of it."

When Spaeth shook her head, Calpe said in a low tone, "It was built in the time when the great lords of Alta ruled. No one knows what use they made of it. Now and then our young men would try to stay the night, but they said it didn't want them there."

"It looks inhabited now."

Calpe nodded darkly. "The Innings stationed soldiers there."

Spaeth peered up at the ancient pile. "It doesn't look ruined."

"It isn't. The Altans built it in such a way that no piece of it decays. They say the whole thing would shatter into slivers at a single blow well aimed, but until that blow comes, no part of it will break."

They crossed the square and began to thread their way up a cobbled alley aromatic with trampled spices and rotting fruit. Now the buildings of brick and wood gave way to ponderous stone. The grim, dilapidated masonry still had an air of magnificence; the houses soared three stories, taller than Spaeth had ever seen.

It was strange being near so many people, and yet alone. Beyond each wall, Spaeth could tell, people swarmed like ants: talking, smoking, loving, swearing, dying. Yet outside the boxes of their houses, the street was like a desert.

They stopped at last before a tall, shuttered house with gaping, empty upper windows. A rustling came from a garbage bin across the way. When Calpe rapped vigorously on the door, a cloud of bats issued chittering from the second-story window.

Presently they heard the rattle of bolts being drawn inside, and a tiny crack of light appeared. Calpe raised the lantern to her face, and the woman inside gave an exclamation of alarm.

"He is ill, Calpe!" she said. "He can't help you tonight." She tried to close the door, but Calpe's foot was wedged in the crack.

"It's your help I want this time, Lorin," she said.

"Mine? Why? I'm not one of them—"

Calpe drew Spaeth into the lamplight. "We have a new dhotamar," she said.

The eyes inside the door caught at Spaeth with a look of fearful hope. "Ehir," the woman breathed. The door fell open, and Calpe pushed Spaeth through.

The room inside was snug and wood panelled. As Lorin lit the lamps, Spaeth caught her breath in wonder. The room was a fantasia of ivory carvings. Ivory fish sported among the rafters, owls perched on the cabinets, lizards lurked behind the spice-jars, mice peeked out from beneath the hearth-broom. A wreath of snow-white holly hung above the fireplace, and by the shuttered window a pot of ivory asters bloomed. The room was crowded with life, frozen into motionless immortality.

"This is the home of Anit the Bonecrafter," Calpe explained. "He is my bandhota. Lorin is his daughter."

Now that Lorin stood in the light, Spaeth was surprised to see that she was Adaina. Her brown face was framed with dark, curly hair; her body would have seemed small if she had not been many months pregnant. She greeted Spaeth and Tway with respect, clasping her hands together with the index fingertips touching. "You honour our house, Grey Lady."

An old man's voice called out from the next room, and Lorin turned like a shy, wild thing to the doorway. "Calpe has brought us a guest, Father," she called. "A dhotamar from another isle."

There was a thump and some shuffling steps, then Anit appeared at the doorway, dressed in his nightshirt and walking with a cane. His grey face was entirely circled with a bush of white hair that hid his ears and chin but left his round cheeks to glow like apples of ivory. "Why Calpe, my dear!" he said, taking her hand and giving her a lingering kiss on the cheek. "Sit down, sit down," Anit gestured them to some chairs by the fireplace. On the calico cushion of one of them an ivory cat was curled. "Here, don't sit on Tassie," Anit warned, and picked the cat up. "We'll just put her by the window; she loves to look out on the street." He placed the cat on the windowsill and shuffled back to hang a shining copper teakettle over the fire.

"Some people claim that Anit's creatures come to life at night, like the statues in the song of Ison Omer," Calpe said.

"Why," Anit's grey eyes twinkled, "don't they look alive to you now?" Without waiting for an answer, he began to introduce Spaeth and Tway to his menagerie of friends. All of them had names, from the ivory goldfinch perched on a teacup to the ivory beetle under the woodpile.

"Where is Gamin, Anit?" Calpe asked when he seemed to have finished his introductions.

"Why, that Torna trader bought him," Anit said.

"I hope you made him pay dearly," Calpe muttered darkly.

The bonecrafter only gave a laugh like apple cider being poured into a glass. "He came here two days since, all eager to dicker his copper pots and fishhooks for my carvings. Imagine!" He ran his finger thoughtfully along the curved back of a leaping fish. "He thought he could buy the wind with a fishhook, and sea-spray with a pail. I let him have what he wanted. He said he would take them off to a fine Inning lady at Fluminos, who would put them in a glass case. It made me sad to think of her and her glass cases. They say the Innings have lost their past, you know. I think that would be a terrible thing."

For the first time since leaving Yora, Spaeth felt perfectly safe. She laid her head back against the chair cushion, breathing out the collected tension.

"You've been out in the town?" Anit said, eyeing her keenly. Spaeth nodded. "It's hard to go out there," he said softly. "So many hungry people. If you did all that was needed, you'd have no blood left. I stay close to home these days. We all do; to go out would be tempting madness."

"Are there many Grey Folk here?" Spaeth asked.

"No, not many; there aren't many anywhere any more. We've lost our taste for keeping the race alive, I think. I know I did. Would you want to bring a child into this world only to inherit the kind of life we lead? It's a cruelty I could not commit."

Tway was looking at Lorin, puzzled. "I thought—"

"Ah, but you see her mother was Adaina," Anit said, taking Lorin's hand fondly. "The half-Lashnura don't always inherit the disease, or the gift, or whatever it is."

Spaeth said, "Goth always said the isles were full of half-Grey children, but they were only born Lashnura if their parents truly wanted it."

Anit chuckled. "Goth, whoever he was, was only telling half the story. Can you ever say, with perfect certainty, what it is you truly want? Eh?"

The kettle was boiling. Lorin went to the hearth to pour some tea, and Calpe moved silently to Anit's side. He looked at her with a radiant, doting smile.

"I can't stay," she said softly.

Anit shook his head in disappointment. Calpe put her palm on his cheek and turned his head to her, then kissed him slowly, open-mouthed. Their bodies pressed together, a picture of inflamed desire.

Lorin had frozen, watching them, with the kettle in one hand. Then she banged it loudly down on its wrought-iron stand.

Anit and Calpe broke apart. Calpe squeezed his hand, then turned to leave. The old man's gaze followed her longingly; when the door had closed behind her he turned to Spaeth. "My daughter's a prude," he said in a loud whisper.

"She preys on him," Lorin said to Spaeth, as if her father weren't in the room. "Every week, sometimes twice. He can't deny her; he's besotted. It will kill him one of these days."

Lorin's helpless rage was achingly attractive.

"We have one like that on Yora," Tway said.

Lorin handed Spaeth a cup of tea with a look of yearning. "But now you are here," she said. "If you stay, you can take some of the burden off him."

"Oh, for shame, Lorin, to put such an obligation on a guest," said Anit. "Pay no attention to her."

To Spaeth's relief, Lorin turned away then and began fetching blankets to make up beds for the guests. Spaeth sat wondering if there were any place where she could escape the desperate needs of humans.

After Calpe departed the Green Lantern with Spaeth and Tway, the men trooped up the stairs at the heels of the bartender, Noll. He showed them to a small room under the eaves, and left with the promise that their dinners would be up soon.

Torr said, "Holy crap, that's some magic you've got, Harg. Calpe *never* gives away food."

"I thought she was just the barmaid," Harg said.

"No, she owns this place, and runs it like a Torna drill sergeant."

Harg filed away that useful information in his head. It made him realize that, mentally, he was already recruiting. He frowned, trying to stop himself from thinking that way.

Barko said, "I'm sorry about Holby Dorn, Harg. I didn't know you and he had a history."

"Neither did I," said Harg.

They settled down around the small table. Harg could see from their faces that they were wondering how angry he would be. He decided to dismiss what had happened and skip ahead. "Why don't you tell me about your situation?" he said.

They crowded round to fill him in. It turned out there were already two of

Tiarch's ships in Harbourdown: a frigate guarding the harbour and an unarmed troop transport that had brought the soldiers and arms to re-man the fort on the hill. The three additional warships en route from the Inner Chain were due to arrive in about three days. The Thimishmen had good intelligence on them: the largest was a two-decker with forty guns, the others had twenty and sixteen. Once they arrived, the pirates would be outgunned more than two to one.

"Which route are they using?" Harg asked.

"The northern one," Barko said significantly.

"So they'll have to go through Rockmeet Straits."

"Right. It's the obvious place for an ambush, but some of the pirates think it's too risky."

"Fuck the pirates," Harg said, momentarily revealing that he wasn't as dispassionate as he seemed. "Who else do you have?"

The others started discussing names. At last Barko said, "We could probably put together two dozen navy guys from Thimish and Romm. But we don't have ships or guns. That's why we need the pirates."

And even if the pirates were trustworthy, their boats would look like mosquitoes next to the warships. It seemed perfectly hopeless on the surface. But Harg was unwilling to let the problem go. "What about the fort? How many men in the garrison?"

"At the moment only forty, and at least ten of them are usually stationed around town. There will be twice as many once the ships arrive. But it doesn't take many to defend the Redoubt. Wait until you see it, Harg. It's impregnable. You couldn't take it without siege weapons."

"And what about the frigate?"

"We could take the frigate," Barko said, "if it weren't for the fort. They've got guns up there covering the harbour. They could blow us to smithereens."

It was all an interlocked puzzle, and you just needed to find the key to make it fall apart. Harg couldn't yet see the key, but he was sure it must be there. People were always fallible; they left some loose end hanging. There were only three days to find it. Once the ships were here, the military options would be even more limited.

He had fallen into an intense, focused silence that the men who had served with him recognized, and knew better than to interrupt. But before he could emerge from it, the food arrived, and all of them set to demolishing it.

They were still eating when Calpe came in to check on them. Harg said, "Everything okay?"

Calpe nodded. "She's safe, don't worry."

When the food was just a remnant of its former self, Barko leaned back and said, "So what do you think, Harg? Are we screwed?"

"I don't know yet," Harg said. "I need to look it over myself, in the morning. But it depends some on what you want to accomplish."

The man named Cobb said, "What do you mean?"

"Well, do you just want to get their attention? Do you want to turn the boats back? Or do you want to actually capture them?"

They all looked at each other. Finally Barko said, "I'd settle for any of those."

"Okay," Harg said. "Say the object is to get their attention—that's most realistic. Then you've got to ask yourselves why we don't have their attention already. Seems to me there's two reasons, and only one is solvable by military means. First, they think we've got no power. Second, they think we don't have anything to say. We've got to show them they're wrong on both counts."

Barko gave a slow grin. It made him look like a banshee. "You just stopped saying 'you' and started saying 'we.'"

Irritated, Harg said, "It was a slip. I told you, I can't get involved." It was sounding less convincing every time he said it.

Barko poured him some more beer. "Okay, then just theoretically. If you *were* involved."

"You need to pull together some demands—things the Innings could imagine themselves doing. Something short of 'Get the hell out.'"

"Like what?" Cobb said.

"I don't know. Giving us an Adaina governor with power equal to Tiarch's. Appointing Adaina officers. Giving us full citizenship rights. Whatever you want."

They were all frowning at the prospect of coexistence that Harg's examples seemed to imply. "They wouldn't do those things," Torr said.

"How do you know unless you ask?"

There was a sceptical silence. This was the larger problem, Harg thought: they had gotten so used to being conquered that they couldn't think any other way. The Adaina could only think as far as rebelling, not as far as ruling. They needed people who could plan, and talk, and organize. People who could communicate with Innings. What they needed was Torna help.

"Barko," he asked, "are there any Tornas in Harbourdown who might support you?"

"Are you crazy, man?" Barko said. "They're all for law and order. They support anyone who will control the pirates."

"But we're not pirates. We're people sticking up for the rights of the South Chain."

"I don't want Tornas involved," Cobb said. "They'd just take over. This is about us, the Adaina." There was a murmur of assent from the others.

Harg stared off into the darkness beyond the candles on the table. Calpe was still sitting there, in the shadows by the wall, listening. He said slowly, "Didn't you hear what Spaeth said down there? This *isn't* just about us. It's about mora, and the balances. That means we've got a duty not to lose."

They were staring at him gravely, and he felt a qualm for having brought the Lashnura into it. He could feel the tangible power of reverence in the room, changing the whole tone.

Barko said, "There are some Torna navy men, discharged just like us, and not too happy with the way things are going."

"I do shipping for some local Torna shopkeepers," Torr said. "Some of them are saying the Innings are giving all the contracts to the big Tornabay merchants, Tiarch's cronies, and leaving them out."

"You ought to talk to them," Harg said. "Sound them out."

"*You* ought to talk to them," Barko said seriously. "You're the one who knows what the Grey Folk want."

That remark gave Harg a feeling that he had gone too far. He said quickly, "I don't know what they want. No more than you."

The vehemence of his tone made them fall silent. Then Calpe spoke up out of the darkness. "You might not know what the Grey Folk want, Harg," she said, "but it sure looks like they know what they want from you."

"It might look like that," he said. "It's not true."

He got up, so uncomfortable with this turn of the conversation that he couldn't sit still. All evening he'd been thinking guiltily that he was leading Spaeth into danger, and now he realized it was the other way around. He wished he had never mentioned Spaeth, never gotten mixed up with her, never been seen in her presence.

They were all watching him, but no one said anything. To change the subject he said, "Calpe, do you have a room I could stay in? I can pay you—not tonight, but soon."

"Sure," said Calpe. "I'll put it on a tab. You want to see the room now?"

"Yes." He had to get away and think.

The tone changed back to normal as the party broke up and they all made plans for the next day. As Harg stepped out into the hall and heard the hum of conversation from downstairs, the feeling came back to him that he was straddling a crack—but this time it was a four-way crack. Torna, Lashnura, Adaina, Inning. He was going to have to dance fast to keep on his feet.

TRUE SHAPES

At a fundamental level of his being, Nathaway Talley had always believed that the universe was an orderly place. Despite the random cruelties and blunders of human beings there was a transcendent pattern of fairness and rationality underlying all of Nature.

Now, his faith had been uprooted.

He lay in his bunk on the ship, where he had spent most of the two days since the Tornas had fetched him back from the hillside. He stared at the wooden beams above his head through the cracked lens of his glasses, which made it look like there was a seam in the world.

His memories of the night at the Whispering Stones were jumbled and sore, like an unhealed bruise. He could not piece them together in sequence; it was as if the night had been more a succession of moods than events. He had considered dismissing the whole experience as a hallucination. It would have been easy to conclude that Spaeth had fed him a hypnotic drug. There were only two things wrong with this scenario. First, it meant that the horrors he had experienced had sprung from a buried level of his own mind and were still there. The second problem was that he didn't believe it.

Deeply, instinctively, he felt that something real had been revealed to him that night. He had glimpsed a more fundamental layer of reality—a terrifying landscape that dwarfed him and all the artifice he had used to hide from it up to now. Everything that had seemed to make sense about the world—law, civilization, learning—was just a set of paper screens erected to hide what lay outside.

It made him feel empty, like a hollow bowl reamed out with an adze. All that had ever filled him was gone. He wanted to weep, or die, but he no longer felt any power to act. There was just no traction in the universe, no way to gain a purchase to pull himself out.

A knock on the cabin door made Nathaway realize that he had been hearing, and ignoring, activity out on the deck for some time. In a monotone he said, "Come in," and a sailor leaned in with an envelope addressed in a firm, neat hand. "Mail for you," the sailor said.

It was from Rachel. Nathaway sat up with a sharp ache of homesickness. The envelope seemed to come from another world, a world where everything made sense. He tore it open eagerly, but it was too dark to read in the cabin, so he pulled himself out of bed and mounted the companionway steps into the sunlight.

The letter was a chatty one, full of family news and political gossip.

> The navy reforms have become hugely controversial, now that people begin to see their larger purpose. It has occurred to the Communitarians that the mass resignation of officers was exactly what Corbin was aiming for. Now that he is rid of the old officers, and replacing them with his own people, even some of our friends are growing alarmed at the prospect of a unified military, backing a single leader whose ambitions they are unsure of. To have a military genius off conquering new lands seems like a fine thing—but having an actual one underfoot, building a power base, is altogether different. Everyone but the public is beginning to wish he would go off to the Forsakens and be heroic somewhere else. The public still adore him. You should see the women throwing themselves at him—poor things, I wish them luck. Domestication is not on his agenda just now.

But the passage that struck Nathaway most strongly came near the end.

> Your letters cheer us all, Nat, and make us confident that you will be sensible and not reckless. The only thing I'm still afraid of is that you will come back changed. Please don't change, Nat—at

least, not without my permission. It is very lonely here without
you, and I long to talk and hear how things are really going.

He longed to talk to her, as well. He needed someone to confide in, to help him figure out what he was feeling. The Torna seamen who were even now glancing at him with suggestive grins were no help. They had made no secret of what they thought he had been doing alone in the hills with a lovely, ardent Lashnura woman; and his subsequent moodiness had only made the snickering innuendoes more unbearable.

He stood up, looking for someone in charge. The boatswain was the only one on deck, so he said to him, "I need to go ashore. Have someone bring round the boat."

"Yes, sir," the man said, but looked hesitant. "Going into the village?"

"Yes."

"Let me fetch someone to escort you."

"No!" Nathaway said peremptorily. "I'm going alone."

"Yes, sir."

When his long strides had taken him into Yorabay, Nathaway began to understand why the boatswain had made the offer. There was a change in the atmosphere. People had regarded him with curiosity or indifference before; now he attracted glances of pure hostility. He didn't feel unsafe, exactly—just unwelcome. He walked faster and avoided eye contact as he mounted the path to Spaeth's cottage.

His estimation of Spaeth had done a complete turnaround. On that night, in her own sphere, she had not seemed like the innocent, childlike being he had taken her for. As Nathaway had shrunk into helpless insignificance, she had grown into a majestic figure, terrifying and wise. She had turned his world inside out, and now he needed her to explain.

Her cottage was deserted. Frustrated, he returned to the path, unsure whether to look for her in the village or in the hills. A woman was standing where the path branched off to a nearby house, watching him with arms crossed. He recognized Agath, who had hosted the barbarous healing ceremony that had precipitated everything, and he turned uphill to avoid her. But she called out something to him, so he dutifully turned back and said, "I beg your pardon?"

"I asked if you were satisfied now," she said.

Approaching her cautiously, Nathaway saw that she looked half crazed with anger and grief. He tried to speak calmly. "I don't know what you mean."

"You've driven her away," Agath said, tilting her head at Spaeth's house. "Just like Goth before her. You've brought death back to Yora. Are you happy now?"

"She's gone?" Nathaway said. "Where?"

"I thought you Innings knew everything," Agath said contemptuously. "But maybe all you know is how to maim and kill."

"Look, I'm very sorry about your son. But he—" He was about to launch into an explanation of medical procedures when something told him to leave it be. "He fought bravely to uphold justice," he finished, acutely aware of how clichéd it sounded.

Her face crumpled. "That is so much slop," she said. "He fought for nothing. If you think it's so noble what he did, then why weren't you fighting with him?"

Nathaway had no answer to this question. He mumbled "I'm sorry" again and set off down the path, his shoulders hunched defensively.

The encounter had unsettled him. He walked blindly toward the harbour, the cool wind grating against his skin. A thousand questions were crowding his head—what was he doing here, how had it all gone so wrong, what could he have done any differently—but above all, where was she?

When he reached the shipwright's house, Strobe was in his workroom, rhythmically planing a board. The older man looked up and frowned when Nathaway entered. "I'm looking for Harg," Nathaway said.

Strobe set his plane aside and brushed off the board. "He's not here."

"Where is he?"

"He left Yora."

It felt like everything was falling apart. "Why?" Nathaway said blankly.

"Your goons came and beat him up," Strobe said. "It was pretty clear they weren't going to leave him alone."

The Tornas had never breathed a word of this. "I never authorized that!" Nathaway exclaimed, outraged. Strobe only shrugged fatalistically and began to rummage on a shelf for some varnish.

"Where has he gone?" Nathaway demanded.

Strobe didn't answer.

An inspiration struck Nathaway. "He took Spaeth, didn't he?"

Strobe gave him a suspicious glance, then shrugged again. "I don't know."

This only made Nathaway more certain he was right. It made sense. They shared the bond of their common parentage. Surely they would stick together.

"Can you take me to Thimish?" he blurted out. It was the obvious place for them to have gone. Leaving Yora was against his instructions, but at that moment it seemed like a course of action that might drag him out of his morass.

Strobe found some imaginary flaw in the board and started smoothing it with a pumice stone. Frustrated, Nathaway turned to leave, but then turned back. "Is he in trouble?"

"No. But he thinks he is."

"Look, I know I'm not the person Harg wants most to see—"

"Actually, you might be wrong about that." The shipwright brushed off the board, then said, "I can take you there. As long as you don't tell Tiarch's men it was me."

"I won't say a word if you don't," Nathaway said. "Wait here. I have to fetch some things from the boat. I'll be back shortly."

As he hurried down the beach, Nathaway felt not exactly optimism, but a sense of purpose.

"Impregnable, my ass!" Harg said to Barko. "You can't have been serious."

"I wasn't looking at it from this angle," Barko said in his own defence.

Just like a pirate, Harg thought, to think if a fort couldn't be attacked by sea, it couldn't be attacked at all.

They were standing in the high meadows behind Harbourdown, looking down at the Redoubt. From this perspective they could see the whole town sprouting like a growth of kaleidoscopic lichen between the harbour and the hill. It was a mongrel town, half rude fishing village and half emporium of a far-flung pirate network. "Everything is for sale in Harbourdown," so the saying went. As Harg and Barko had passed along the streets that morning, bangled women and keen-eyed artisans had beckoned to them from street-side displays of bright carpets, glassware, brass, and ivory. Now and then shuttered windows showed where a shop had dealt in weapons or fortune-telling or dreamweed before Inning regulations had come to Thimish. Not that the Inning presence had truly halted Harbourdown's age-old traffic. By mutual agreement, every shop that dealt in black market goods had hung out a wind chime, and the streets were now musical with outlawed solicitation.

When Harg had looked up at the Redoubt from the town, it had made his heart sink, for its dark, seamless walls rose atop a ninety-foot sandstone cliff with only a narrow switchback road for access. But as they had circled round behind it, climbing the bluff behind the town, the fort had dwindled. Now they stood looking down into the small, pentacle-shaped courtyard. The Redoubt was all grand façade, and nothing behind.

"I'll wager it was never even intended as a fort," Harg said. "If it was, the Altans didn't fear attack by land. They put all their strength toward the harbour and left their backs exposed. Get an army on top of this hill, and with a couple of ten-pounders you could blast them into the sea."

"But we don't have any ten-pounders," Barko pointed out.

To this, Harg said nothing. Lying down in the long grass, out of sight of any sentinels, he raised the Inning spyglass he had borrowed from Torr. There were only two gates. The main one on the southern, seaward side stood open for the almost continuous arrival of donkey carts, wagons, and visitors who had business with the military. The small north postern closer to them was shut at the moment, but was clearly used for access to a level, grassy parade ground behind the fort.

"What do they use that field for?" Harg asked.

"It looks like they've been grazing their mules out there."

"How many mules?"

"Two teams. They used them to get the big guns up the hill."

Harg located the placement of the guns. They were all aimed toward the harbour, and still mounted on the carriages that had brought them up here. He swung the spyglass around to study the frigate they were protecting, anchored below. A small vendor's boat was pulled alongside it, the proprietor dickering with some sailors for his wares.

He collapsed the spy-glass with a click. "No, we don't have any ten-pounders," he said. "We'll have to think of something else."

"Harg, the fort may be weak, but we can't attack it with pitchforks and fillet knives."

"I wasn't thinking of pitchforks," Harg said. "I was thinking of catball rackets."

He got to his feet and started off across the hills toward the west, leaving Barko scrambling to catch up. Harg felt totally focused; he loved the sheer intellectual challenge of the problem before him. Coming up here, he had only intended to see if any portion of the puzzle were soluble, but now the pattern was falling into place in a chain reaction, and the whole thing was lying open before him. As they walked, he peppered Barko with questions: How far to Rockmeet Straits by boat? By land? Was there a road? How many people could Barko recruit? What skills did they have? Any boats?

After walking over grass hills for ten minutes, they plunged into a pine forest.

Around them, scaly trunks towered to the sky, ancient presences whose majestic silence made them lower their voices. Underfoot, a carpet of needles cushioned their steps, and the wind whished eerily in the treetops far overhead. There was little undergrowth; it was like a hall of pillars. They walked for forty minutes and only had to cross a single ravine before they heard the sea ahead and came out atop a high stone cliff. Across the narrow strait lay the sand flats of Ekra.

"How deep are the shoals over there?" Harg asked.

"Oh, it varies a lot. They're like rolling sand hills under water. Pilots try to stay as close to the east side of the channel as possible."

So the warships would be hugging the cliffs as they came through. Not perfect, but manageable. Scouting along the cliff, Harg chose a spot and started piling some loose rocks in a cairn.

"What are you doing?" Barko asked.

"Marking gun emplacements," Harg said.

"For what guns?"

"Don't worry, we'll have guns. Sharpshooters as well."

"Harg, would you mind explaining?"

So Harg laid it out, in all its crazy inspiration. By the end Barko was shaking his head. "I don't know," he said.

"What don't you know?"

"Whether we can pull it off. If we do . . ."

"If we do, we'll give the Northern Squadron a taste of real South Chain hospitality," said Harg with a grim smile.

Spaeth sat on the threadbare carpet of Anit the Bonecrafter's home, staring at her nails. They looked black and bruised, as if hit by a hammer. The tips of her fingers were beginning to darken; when she pressed them she could feel nothing.

It was the morning after her first restless night there. Around midnight she had roused with a sense that the darkened room was full of the eyes of small, scurrying things. The fire had settled into a bed of ashes that gave some heat but little light. She had lain awake listening to tiny scrabblings and footfalls, and now and then the flutter of a wing. It had been a long time before she could fall asleep again.

The lump of blankets that was Tway stirred on the floor beside her. No longer fearing to disturb her, Spaeth rose and went over to make a new fire in the grate.

A soft footfall made her look over her shoulder. Anit was standing in the doorway, leaning on his gnarled stick.

"Did you sleep well?" he said.

Spaeth glanced at Tway. She looked as tousled and sleepless as Spaeth felt. Tway pushed her hair back out of her face, then got up and went to the back door, which opened onto the yard where the pump and outhouse stood.

Anit came over to his chair. He looked hesitant and fragile. Spaeth was about to sit down in one of the chairs facing his when Anit warned, "Take care you don't sit on Tassie." Spaeth looked down to see the ivory cat curled on the cushion, looking content and well-fed. She picked it up and placed it on the windowsill, distinctly remembering that Anit had done the same the night before.

"Your carvings—" she said.

"Ah yes," Anit chuckled. "They aren't really mine, you know. I just find them and set them free." He reached out to pick up an ivory mouse from the side table. His hand shook slightly. "They are imprisoned in the ivory, you see. My creatures are much like people that way: when you first look at them, they seem to be only a block of raw stuff; but that is because so much dross surrounds their true nature. Once the excess is removed, what beautiful shapes we find! But sometimes a single piece is not complete in itself; it needs another to reveal its true shape." To demonstrate, he picked up two shapeless sticks of driftwood from the kindling bin, held them together, and suddenly there was a sandpiper in his hands, hesitating before it sprang forward across the beach. "That's like people, too," he said.

"How did you do that?" Spaeth said, astonished.

The bonecrafter regarded her with a look of wan mischief. "Matter mimics matter, as your namorai say. Lightning is the shape of a tree root, a seashell is like the whirlpool, waves are found in grass as well as water. Sea, tree, and bird are all the same underneath. It would be amazing if there were no similarities."

"You must be a namora yourself," Spaeth said.

Anit waved a hand dismissively. "Oh, no. My uncle tried to make a namora out of me, once. It was useless. I have no sense of balance. Why, your true namora can take the *essences* of two pieces of driftwood, put them together, and create the essence of a bird—one that can fly away before your eyes. My uncle said all it took was to see things right. Once you could see the shapes, putting them together was simple. I still couldn't do it."

Lorin came into the room, tying a freshly washed kerchief over her hair. She set to work heating the kettle and mixing up a batch of biscuits for breakfast. Tway came back in and helped her build a fire under the brick oven.

Over the morning meal, the visitors learned that Lorin had come to live with Anit only a few months before, when her baby's father had been drowned in a fishing accident in the Pont Sea. When Anit mentioned the fact, Lorin looked away and would not speak for a while. Spaeth could feel grief radiating from her, and had to edge away.

"It will soon be time for me to follow him," Anit mused. "An old man must think of seeking out his soulstone and preparing to leave the islands." Lorin looked at him darkly. He smiled patiently, as if they had argued over the point before.

"I dreamed of my soulstone last night," he continued, to Spaeth. "Would you like to see it?"

He rose and went into the other room, where they could hear him rummaging inside a chest. When he came back he carried a small leather pouch. He placed it in Spaeth's hands and sat down again.

The leather was old and very soft. Long ago, someone had embroidered geometric designs in dyed deer hair on the cured hide. She drew back the laces and shook out a stone, grey and smooth-polished by waves, shaped like a still drop of water.

"It is very like you," Spaeth said. It was a conventional thing to say, but she meant it.

"I only found it last week. I have been a very lazy old man not to have sought one before."

"I think no one seeks a soulstone without some reason," Spaeth said. She had begun to wonder why the conversation had taken this turn.

"Do you mean to say you have none for yourself?" Anit chided her. "Just like my daughter. Young folk!"

"You're a fine one to talk!" The slight sharpness in Lorin's tone betrayed how much the topic pained her. "You just admitted you only found yours the other day. Where was your great foresight when you were our age?"

"I was never a young woman facing childbirth. Nor a dhotamar in such dangerous times as these. When I was young, the ills we faced were like ripples in your teacup: a barren ewe, a sickly child, a marriage in need of mending. In those days, women did not die of childbed fever, and people did not seek out dhotamars to set the whole world on its hinges again."

Anit's eyes and Spaeth's met across the table, and she had an intuition that he was trying to send her a message. She wanted to speak with him in private.

They had to wait until Tway and Lorin had cleared away the breakfast dishes and gone together out into the yard to wash them. Spaeth helped Anit back into his chair. She could not help noticing that his arms were a patchwork of scars, just like Goth's. The sight made her feel restless. It was like looking at her own future. She became aware that the bandage on her own arm was itching, so she began to take it off. Anit watched silently till she tossed the bandage into the fire; then he said quietly, "What happened to you?"

"What do you mean?" she said.

"You have the scar," he said, "but you have not given dhota. How can that be?"

"There was an Inning," she said. "He stopped me before I could finish."

Anit winced at the thought. "That is cruel," he said.

"No," she said. "He was right. If I had finished, I would be in bondage today. I should have been grateful to him."

Anit was silent, looking at her hands. Self-consciously, she crossed her arms to hide her darkened nails.

"It is a dangerous risk you are taking, resisting dhota," Anit said. "No Inning can save you from the Black Mask."

He delivered the fatal diagnosis so gently, it barely seemed real. "So it's true," she said. "There really is such a thing."

"Did you doubt it?" Anit said.

"I thought they were telling me tales to scare me into doing as they wished."

Slowly, Anit shook his head. "It is no tale. It starts in the fingertips and toes. If nothing is done, they will eventually decay and dissolve. But long before that happens, the disease flows inward and wakes a hunger, but not a healthy one like dhota. Nothing can satisfy it. In such a state of unmet longing, a Grey Person is terribly vulnerable, and can easily become a tool of the powers of unbalance."

Spaeth hugged her arms to herself.

"But there is a simple cure," he said.

Bitterly, she said, "Dhota?"

"Yes. You must give yourself to someone. Soon."

Restlessly, she looked around the room, as if to find some escape. "All I want is to be free, like I used to be," she said.

Anit shook his head. "There is no freedom, by any route. Not for us. Except one way."

"What way?"

Anit pointed a trembling finger at his own chest. "Inside us, in our hearts. If we choose to do what we will be compelled to do anyway, then that is freedom."

"No, it's not. It's giving in."

He smiled sadly. "You won't say that once you have done it."

For a long time Spaeth was silent, thinking. At last, hesitantly, she said, "Anit, if you knew there was someone who had become a tool of the Mundua and Ashwin, but you didn't know who it was, what would you do?"

The bonecrafter had a look of grave dismay. "Such a person must be hunted down," he said. "Hunted down, destroyed, or cured at the cost of another life."

"But how?"

"That is why we have an Heir of Gilgen."

"Who *is* the Heir of Gilgen?"

"Today? I do not know. Years ago, it was Onan Listor. He had a son, Goran. If Goran is still alive today, he would be the Heir. But where he is, I have no idea."

A prisoner, Ridwit had said. "I have to find him," Spaeth said softly. "I need to warn him."

"You know this thing surely?" Anit said, frowning.

"Yes. I don't want to know. I don't know what to do."

Anit paused, thinking. "You have brought a world of troubles to my doorstep," he said. "I know nothing about the balances. You speak of powers I have never encountered."

"Then who can I ask?" she said, a little desperately.

"We live in a world where the great leaders have abandoned us. Perhaps in such an age, ordinary people must do what the great did in former times."

"Not me!" Spaeth said. "I'm less than ordinary."

"Perhaps," said Anit, "you are like one of those sticks of driftwood, incomplete without the other part. Find your bandhota, and you will find your true shape. It is the only answer I can give you."

It was not until Nathaway stepped onto the dock in Harbourdown that he realized he had no real plan for finding Harg and Spaeth. It was a smallish town, but a town nevertheless, with a thousand places for people to disappear.

As he circled the crowded market square opposite the wharf, trying to get his bearings, he composed in his mind how he would describe the exotic scene to Rachel. It was a raucous bazaar where broad-faced shopkeepers flaunted finery and foods set out on unsanitary open counters. Colourful homespun awnings flapped in the sea breeze, and a cacophony of wind chimes jangled everywhere he turned.

At last he spotted an island of order: a tall stone building with "customs house" inscribed over the lintel. Relieved to find an Inning authority to appeal to, he sprinted up the steps and entered.

Inside, the building was a mayhem of construction. Workmen swarmed everywhere; the hall was nearly blocked with piles of lumber, bricks, and unmixed plaster. Nathaway picked his way in and peered into the first room he came to. A line of Torna clerks sat working, their desks all shoved over to one side while painters worked on a wall. There was an Inning overseer in charge; with a feeling of relief, Nathaway said to him, "Excuse me, could you direct me to the person in charge?"

"Who are you?" the man said, frowning. When Nathaway gave his name, the man eyed him suspiciously, but only said, "Proctor Fullabeau is in the back."

Dodging plasterers, Nathaway picked his way down the hall to the back room. Here, a tall, cultured Inning with an erect, almost military bearing, was berating a foreman over some deviation from a set of plans. Nathaway waited patiently until they had hashed out the problem, when Proctor Fullabeau turned and surveyed him with autocratic disdain.

"And you would be . . .?" was all Fullabeau said.

When Nathaway gave his name again, he felt the same chill of scepticism. Fullabeau said, "You are supposed to be on Yora."

Startled that the official, whom he had never met, knew about his assignment, Nathaway said, "I . . . I know. I'm looking for two Yorans who came here in the past two days. It's important that I find them."

"Has there been an infringement of the law?"

"Oh, no. Not by them, at any rate."

"The islanders are free to move about, you know," the proctor said. "We can't exactly stop them."

"I know that. But I'm concerned for the woman's safety. She's—well, she's Lashnura."

"And what do you expect me to do about it?"

Nathaway was taken aback by the man's attitude. From a fellow Inning, out here where there were so few of them, he had expected camaraderie, cooperation, even fellowship. Not this frosty obstructionism. He said, "I thought perhaps you might have some knowledge of the people under your authority, and be able to tell me where to look."

Fullabeau reacted to this as if it were a sword-thrust of criticism. "Look," he said, "I've got seven or eight thousand uncounted, undocumented, unwashed natives out there, and the only difference between them is that some wait till our backs are turned to break the law, while the others do it in front of our faces. I don't yet have enough men or arms to police them, and barely enough to keep them from outright rebellion. So when you come to me looking for one of their ritual prostitutes—"

"She's not that!" Nathaway blurted out. Fullabeau paused in mid-rant, and Nathaway felt his face going red. Then he blushed because he was blushing.

"You did say she was Lashnura," Fullabeau said, scrutinizing him.

"I know. It's just that . . . you see, I'm trying to protect her."

Fullabeau gave a slight sigh. "Very well. I'll have the patrols keep an eye out for her. It's all I can do. In the meantime, I advise you not to walk the streets unescorted. It's simply not safe."

"What *should* I do?" Nathaway said. It wasn't as if he could hire bodyguards, or stay hidden in a hotel.

"Go back to Yora," Fullabeau said. "If I find her I'll send word."

Thoroughly nettled by this brush-off, Nathaway managed to force out a semi-civil "Thank you" before he turned and left.

Outside, he stood on the steps of the customs house till his temper cooled so that he could think of what to do next. It was clear that if he were going to find Spaeth, he would have to do it on his own. Grimly determined, he set out across the square, determined to canvass every street if that was what it took.

The streets around the square had a prosperous, mercantile character, and he guessed that this was the Torna neighbourhood, an unlikely place to search for two Adaina refugees. So he headed uphill, where the buildings were older and more dilapidated. He walked randomly, searching for some clue, indifferent to every face but one: a haunting, grey face with mother-of-pearl eyes.

And then he saw a face from Yora. Not her, but Strobe's blowzy daughter, who had no conceivable business here in Harbourdown unless she was somehow complicit in the whole affair. She was walking purposefully downhill, and did not see Nathaway, so he followed her at a distance.

She headed toward a poor section near the harbour. He tracked her through crowded, winding alleys. Though he was several lengths behind, his head rose above the stocky Adainas around him, making it easy to spot her. At last she flitted through the green door of a grimy, ill-kept tavern. Arriving moments later, Nathaway ducked his head under the low lintel. A burly man just inside the door lurched to his feet, but Nathaway paid him no heed, and barrelled on into the room.

A crowd of men was gathered around a table, listening intently. On one end of the table was a heap of antique firearms. But none of this registered as it should have. All Nathaway saw was that the man speaking to them was Harg Ismol.

"Harg!" he said, terribly pleased to have found him.

Harg looked up, and a shock of recognition crossed his face; then his eyes shifted to something behind Nathaway, and he shouted, "No! Don't hurt him!" just as something came smashing down on Nathaway's skull from behind, and the world exploded into fiery splinters. The floor crashed into his face.

There was a crowd. Noise. Men arguing. Harg kneeling over him, saying, "He's worth his weight in gold alive." Then Nathaway was fleetingly aware of being carried up some stairs. He was lying on his back when an overwhelming urge to vomit woke him, and he struggled to turn over, to get up, then threw up violently on the floor. His head hurt ferociously, and he groaned.

"Go fetch him, Calpe," Harg said.

When Nathaway next drifted into consciousness, his stomach was in spasms again, and he retched till his muscles ached without anything but bile coming up.

An old man with a soothing manner sat down on the bed beside him, placing a hand on his sweaty forehead. There was something cool and calming about his touch, and Nathaway relaxed, feeling he was in competent hands.

"Yes," the old man said, "I can help him, if he is willing. It's a nasty blow, but not mortal."

Harg was hovering beside the bed, looking down at Nathaway in an agony of anxiety. "I can't risk him dying again," he said. "Did you bring the knife and bowl?"

Only then did Nathaway realize that the old man touching him was grey-skinned, and they were about to perform one of their barbarous healing rites on him.

"No," he said weakly. Then, summoning all his resolve, "No!"

The old man said to him gently, "I can take away the pain."

There was nothing Nathaway wanted more than to be rid of this skull-splitting pain. But not at this price. "No," he said.

"Please. I want to," the Grey Man said.

"No," Nathaway repeated, then sank into oblivion.

THE BATTLE
OF THIMISH

The gaily dressed picnickers who gathered on the windswept hill above Harbourdown's Redoubt were in high spirits as they spread their blankets on the grass. They had collected gradually, having climbed the hill in little groups, lugging their wicker hampers of food, with their catball rackets on their shoulders in canvas bags. There were about forty of them, thirty men and ten women—enough to make up two catball teams with a few left over to cheer and run after the ball when it went out of bounds. The level parade ground behind the fort made a perfect playing field, while the hill behind it formed a natural amphitheatre for viewers to sit and watch.

Harg sat in the grass watching, with his three team leaders—Calpe, Cobb, and Birk—on either side. He felt itchily nervous. It had all been thrown together so fast, with no time for training or dry runs, and it was a plan that depended entirely on timing. If they struck too early, the approaching warships would be tipped off and would never fall into the trap. Strike too late, and there would not be enough time to carry out the plan. He listened over the shouts of the catball players, hoping not to hear the signal from the lookout they had posted on the north shore of the island. Two shots in quick succession would mean the ships had been sighted. He didn't want it to happen till after noon.

On the field below, the play was vigorous and the wind was brisk, a combination that often sent the ball out of bounds. At last, as one team made a particularly daring goal attempt, the catball went flying out of control right over the walls of the fort and into the enclosure beyond. A groan went up from the onlookers.

One of the players, a girl with bouncing brown curls and an open, sunny face, raced up to the small postern door and pounded on it with her fists, calling for someone to let her in. The face of a Torna guard appeared over the wall, looking down at her with amusement.

"Will you let me in to get our ball?" she asked.

"What's your name, darling?" the guard asked, grinning. Harg had seen him watching the game from the guardhouse window; if he knew soldiers, they probably had wagers riding on the outcome.

"Essie," she answered with a little toss of her head.

"Well, Essie," the guard answered, "I'll give you your ball if you give me something in return."

Pertly, she blew him a kiss.

"She's overplaying it," Harg said through clenched teeth.

"No, she's not," said Calpe. "You don't know how they think about Adaina women. Their brains turn off."

Calpe was right. The guard said, "Wait there. I'll be right down."

He only opened the door a crack, but Essie squirmed through past him. She snatched up the ball where it lay in the open gravel courtyard inside, agilely dodged the guard, and slipped out again. The watching soldiers hooted at their comrade for his lack of prowess.

In the course of the game the playing field had shifted closer to the fort, so it was no surprise when the ball went sailing over the walls a second time. By now the game had a small audience inside the fort, and they laughed in anticipation when Essie and a young man came running up to the gate.

"Who are you, her younger brother?" the guard called down to the young man.

"I'm her fiancé," he answered hotly.

"Oh no! You have a jealous lover on your hands!" a soldier called to the guard. "Better watch your step."

This time when the guard opened the gate, he didn't let Essie get away from him. As her companion searched for the ball, the guard pinned her against the wall and pressed his mouth against hers. When he slipped a hand into her shirt she wriggled from his grasp and dashed red-faced out the gate. Returning, the young man gave the guard a poisonous look. The soldier wiped his lips and grinned.

This time the guard did not even bother to bar the gate, but left it ajar, and leaned against the jamb. When the ball went over the walls a third time and he saw Essie heading toward him, he grinned in anticipation.

Without a sound or signal, the players all turned in unison and rushed at the gate. Metal flashed, and the astonished guard fell, clutching at Essie's throwing-knife in his throat. The gate fell open and armed warriors poured into the fort. Harg and the other onlookers seized up the arms hidden in the picnic baskets and raced in after, tossing weapons to anyone who lacked them.

The four team leaders split up as soon as they got inside, heading for prearranged targets. Birk's team stormed up the steps toward the guardhouse. Cobb's headed for the powder magazine. Calpe's went for the barracks. Harg shouted for his team to follow him toward the front walls to secure the cannons.

Taken by surprise, the soldiers on duty scattered. Some of them dashed toward the safety of the armoury, but were headed off by Cobb's band, and a fierce hand-to-hand battle broke out. The great front gates slammed shut, a futile precaution that only prevented escape.

There were fewer in Harg's team than there should have been; people had gotten confused in the rush. With only five others behind him, he headed for the seaward walls. As they reached the base of the steps, two young soldiers came to the top, muskets at the ready. Rather than lose momentum, Harg shouted, "Rush them!" He stood back to take aim with his pistol, but never had to fire. At sight of the shrieking pirates racing up the steps with cutlasses, the two soldiers fell back to take cover behind one of the cannons. "Helpful idiots," Harg said grimly. They might have held the stairs a long time if they had tried.

When he reached the top of the wall, the two soldiers had surrendered, and the pirates had disarmed them and bound them with their own belts. "You guys would scare the Mundua," Harg told his team appreciatively. "Here, take those muskets and two of you get back to the top of the steps. Hold them against anyone who tries to come up. The rest of you—"

A peppering of shot thudded into the stonework around them, and they all dived for the pavement. From behind the low parapet on the inward side of the wall, Harg peered out, trying to locate the source of the fire.

It was coming from across the courtyard behind them. Some soldiers had locked themselves inside the postern gatehouse where they could pick off the invaders in safety. Harg gestured for three of his troop to join him. They came crawling over on their bellies as a hail of buckshot ricocheted over their heads. One of them, a strapping woman with heavy eyebrows, was bleeding where a shot had grazed her temple.

"We need to turn this cannon round and aim it at the gatehouse," Harg said. He turned to the woman, whose name he didn't even know. "Go find Cobb, see if he's secured the magazine. Bring back some powder cartridges and fuse cord. Keep your head down." She crawled away.

The courtyard below them, which had been a scene of mayhem only moments before, had cleared of people. The snipers in the gatehouse were keeping everyone pinned inside. Birk's troop was nowhere to be seen. Harg crawled over to the two men with the muskets. "Try to keep them busy," he said. "Shoot whenever they show their faces. Don't let them fire." He then turned back to the last two. "Ready?" They nodded. "Okay, now. Let's turn the cannon round."

Three shoulders straining against the gun carriage, they wrestled it round till it was trained directly at the gatehouse. They had to dive for the floor then, as a volley of musket fire zinged around them. From the other side of the cannon, Harg heard a man swear. "You okay?" he said, not daring to lift his own head. A musket ball hit the cannon barrel, making it ring.

"I'll live," the man said, sounding more angry than hurt. "But Harg, look at the watchtower."

Harg twisted round to peer at the tower that rose like a protruding tooth above the fort walls. "Bloody hell," he said.

A thin column of black smoke was beginning to thread its way into the sky from the top of the beacon tower. One of the defenders had managed to climb the tower and kindle a fire there, to signal the warships. And at the moment there was nothing they could do about it.

"Keep firing," Harg hissed at the two men with the muskets, and crawled forward on his elbows to add what help he could with his pistol.

It seemed like an age passed as they waited for the woman pirate to return with the powder, and Harg was starting to think they might have to storm the gatehouse, or be pinned down all morning, when he saw her coming back, dragging a burlap bag. Swallowing his impatience, he shouted, "Good job!" at her, and gestured her to hurry.

She had brought three felt-wrapped gun cartridges and a couple of feet of fuse cord. "It was all I could get," she apologized.

"It'll do," said Harg. I hope, he thought silently. With his knife he cut a length of fuse, then stopped. "A match," he said. "Who's got a match?"

No one did. "Use the flint and steel from your pistol," said a lean man with big ears. "We'll load the gun."

"Be careful," Harg said. He poured some of the contents of his powder flask onto the stone, ripped a strip of cloth from his bandana, then snapped the pistol flint against the frizzen till a spark fell on the pile of powder and ignited it. He then lit the cloth. "Ready?" he said.

They were just ramming the ball down the cannon's gullet. "Ready," the big-eared man said. Harg lit the length of fuse, then scrambled over to the gun, pierced the cartridge with the spike, and rammed the fuse down through the touchhole. He rolled away, fingers in his ears.

The cannon went off with a bone-shaking force, recoiling against the outer parapet. They had barely aimed it, but at such close range it didn't matter. The ball crashed through the wall of the gatehouse, bringing beams and stone down, and sending up a cloud of dust and smoke. There was a moment of silence, then a dust-covered soldier came climbing out through the wreckage, his hands raised. Harg heard a cheer from below him as Birk's crew came pouring back into the courtyard, racing up the steps to take the prisoners.

Harg met Birk in the courtyard. "Is that it?" he asked. "Anyone else still fighting?"

"Not that I know. I think we're in control."

"Not quite," Harg said, turning to the tower where the warning smoke still rose. As he did so, he heard, from far away across the island, two shots in quick succession. "Ashes!" he swore. It wasn't quite noon. The ships were here too soon. "Birk, get Cobb up here quick to aim those guns. Tell him he needs to place a ball close to that frigate in the harbour. Don't hit it! Only aim for the ship if it tries to escape." Cobb had been a gunner in the navy, legendary for his accuracy. If anyone could send a cast-iron message to the frigate's captain, it was Cobb.

Meanwhile, Harg turned to the beacon tower, which had just become the most pressing problem. He beckoned the only unoccupied man of his team to follow, and headed for the door at the tower's base. It swung open onto a narrow stair that spiralled up through the thickness of the outside wall, dimly lit by small slit windows.

"We're going to need something to put out the fire." Harg looked around, and spied a cistern barrel under the downspout of a nearby building. "Go soak your coat in the water and bring it along—what's your name?"

"Gibbon, Captain."

"Be quick." As Gibbon peeled off his coat and headed toward the cistern, Harg leaped up the stairs two at a time.

Fifty steps later, he emerged into a small room set like a box on the flat top of the tower, apparently the light-tender's shelter. A small door stood open onto the top of the tower, where a windswept fire now smouldered in a shallow pit, billowing clouds of damning black smoke. There was no sign of whoever had set it. Harg checked to right and left, then pushed on through the door, intending to kick the fire apart.

He had forgotten to look up. He was barely out when heavy boots landed on him from behind, and he crashed to the stone floor, the breath knocked out of him. He heard an ominous click and looked up straight into the barrel of a pistol held by a tall, aristocratic Inning. The weapon was levelled to blow his brains out.

His arm flailed out wildly to knock it aside. The gun exploded in his face, blasting him back into a sulphurous darkness. Choking on smoke, he tore at the blackness, striking out in a blind fury. His fist hit something solid and he felt stone under his hands. The world swam greyly into focus. He was kneeling on the floor. The Inning stood three feet in front of him with another pistol that Harg recognized as his own.

"Brown bastard!" the Inning spat. Harg watched, dazed, as the Inning levelled the gun at his face and pulled the trigger.

The pistol clicked harmlessly and the Inning swore, for Harg had forgotten to reload it. An instant later, Harg dived for the Inning's legs and knocked him sprawling on the pavement. They wrestled in silence then, muscle straining against muscle. Harg managed to ram a knee into the man's stomach. The Inning doubled up, and Harg reached for a burning billet of wood from the fire to club him senseless. Before he could bring it down the man rolled free and lunged again.

They grappled, and the Inning forced Harg backward step by step till they were at the edge of the tower, with no parapet or rail between them and the sheer drop to the rocks below. The Inning brought a fist up under Harg's jaw, snapping his head back, then threw him down with bone-jarring force on the pavement. With a desperate energy Harg grabbed at the boot raised to shove him over the edge, and squirmed round to kick with both feet at the other boot. Then the stone edge was under his shoulder. One arm flailed in the air; the windy drop gaped below him. He clutched for some handhold on the smooth pavement, his bruised fingers scrabbling on stone.

A hand grasped his wrist and a strong tug brought him back from the brink. He fell gasping onto the solid stone at Gibbon's feet. The Inning was nowhere to be seen.

The wind whistled past the edge of the tower. Harg looked up at Gibbon's face, then at the precipice he had almost gone over.

"You pushed him over?" Harg said numbly.

Gibbon shook his head. "You did," he said. "You pulled his foot out from under him, and he fell."

A little queasy, Harg crawled on hands and knees to the tower's edge and looked over. The Inning's body was only a small patch of white on the tumbled rocks below.

"I killed him," he said in a tone of strained disbelief. "I killed an Inning."

It didn't feel like it. He hadn't thought it out, or really even intended it.

Gibbon was staring at him gravely. Harg touched his head where there was a tight feeling, and his hand came away smeared with blood and soot. Then he remembered.

"Get that fire out!" he said.

As Gibbon headed toward the fire pit with his wet coat, Harg wadded up his bandanna to sop up the blood where the pistol ball had grazed his scalp. He had started shaking in delayed nervous reaction, and didn't quite trust himself to stand yet. As he sat, there was a cannon blast from the walls below, and he saw a ball arcing out into the sky, over the town, into the harbour. It landed thirty feet from the bow of the frigate.

"Oh, good shot, Cobb!" Harg said.

At this signal from the fort, a horde of small boats set out from the docks, heading for the warship, whose decks were suddenly swarming like an anthill. Harg wanted to sit and watch the outcome, but there was no time. The rest of the plan had to be set in motion.

When he reached the courtyard again, some of Calpe's team were already leading the mules out of the stables and harnessing them in preparation for hauling the guns across the country to Rockmeet Straits. Harg met her at the stable door. "Are the prisoners secure?" he asked.

"Yes. Birk's sweeping for stragglers. Harg, what happened to you?"

"A little disagreement with an Inning," he said. "It was stupid of me."

"Sit down and let me clean it off."

Still a little shaky, he sat on a barrel and let her wash his scalp with a wet handkerchief. "I've got to get down to the harbour to join Barko," he said. "Can you spare one of those mules?"

"Even better," she said as she worked. "There's a horse in there. The Innings must have used it to get to and fro."

"Have somebody saddle it," he said. He had barely touched a horse in his life, but reasoned that if Innings could ride them, so could he.

As two women were leading the horse out into the courtyard to saddle it, Harg went over to the walls to talk to Cobb. "There might not be time to get the guns to Rockmeet before the ships arrive," he said. "If not, just give it up and abandon them. But get your troop over there with muskets to line the cliffs; it'll be just as good. Be sure to let the ships go by before you fire. Wait for our signal if you can; if we don't make it, fire anyway."

"Right, captain," Cobb nodded. "Are you okay?"

"I'm fine. Hurry, the ships were sighted forty minutes ago."

The horse turned out to have ideas of its own about the proper speed to carry its rider down the hill to town, which was considerably faster than Harg would have chosen. He had little choice but to hang indecorously onto the pommel. When he reached the town, the streets were crowded with people, either craning up at the fort or watching the harbour, where there was now sporadic small arms fire. They scattered before the horse, and Harbourdown swept by in a blur of buildings, handcarts, and astonished faces.

A four-oared dinghy was waiting for him at the dock. He turned the horse loose without regret and climbed into the familiar sanctuary of the rocking boat. "What's happening?" he asked the oarsmen.

"Can't tell from here," one of them replied, "but the firing's stopped."

As they pulled out from between the boats moored at dockside, Harg could see the frigate still lying at anchor out in the bay, with a dozen small boats clustered round it, like puppies attached to the mother dog. There was almost no one on deck; the fighting, if it was still going on, had gone below.

A watchman on the poop deck spotted their rowboat approaching, and for a moment Harg was poised to duck if the man levelled his gun at them. But instead he waved and went to alert someone below. As Harg's boat came to the frigate's side, Barko Durban came to the rail, his head tied in a bright red bandanna, grinning maniacally. Harg called out, "Permission to come aboard, Captain Durban?"

"Granted!" Barko called back.

Harg clambered up on deck and turned around to survey their prize. It was a neat little ship, not new but solidly built. The recent conflict had left some disarray on deck, but little damage. "What's going on?" he asked.

"We're getting the prisoners under control," Barko said. "The Adaina seamen wouldn't fight us; only the Tornas resisted. The captain's a complete asshole. After that shot from the fort, he couldn't decide whether to leave or defend the ship, and so they didn't do either very well."

"That's the Northern Squadron for you," Harg said. "Listen, Barko, we need to get under way. The warships were sighted—" he glanced at the sun, longing for his lost watch "—over an hour ago. They'll be close to Rockmeet by now. Let's leave the prisoners in the hold and get going."

Barko disappeared down the companionway to redeploy his men, and Harg started loosening grappling hooks and mooring lines to detach the attack boats, aided by the men in the rowboat below. Soon, pirates started pouring back on deck to get the ship ready to sail. It was far from navy discipline or precision; everywhere he looked Harg saw things that made him wince. But he held his tongue; it would have to do, for now.

The anchor rattled aboard, the topsails billowed out, and soon the frigate was gathering way, heading for the harbour mouth. Beyond, the choppy sea that had been a brilliant blue all morning had turned grey under a sudden overcast. Harg looked up at the fort, then down at the town, barely believing they had gotten so far. He turned to Barko, who was standing next to the steersman, looking entirely in command. It was hard to believe it was the same person he had met three nights ago in the Green Lantern.

Before his eyes, Harg could almost see half a century of defeat and pessimism blowing away like mist. All the Adaina needed was a victory, and they were transformed.

Captain Slavens of the warship *Industry* stood on the slippery forecastle deck, peering into the chilly gloom before him. The air was blanketed with silence; a creak of rope and a tap of metal against wood sounded eerily close, yet distant in the grey limbo of mist. To larboard rose the slate cliffs of Thimish, topped with the ghostly shapes of pine trees. To starboard, lost somewhere beyond sight, lay the hills of Ekra.

All day the wind had been brisk as they had coasted down the north shore of Thimish. But as they had neared the strait that would take them to the south shore, a solid bank of fog had hung on the water as if placed there on purpose to form a barrier across Rockmeet Straits.

It was a frustrating turn of the weather. They had been behind schedule since leaving Tornabay, and today Captain Slavens had been trying to make up the time. His orders from the new man, Commodore Joffrey, had been to get to Harbourdown as soon as possible, and he could have been there two days ago, but for the Inning passengers. There were four of them, friends of Provost Minicleer, ostensibly bound for the South Chain to take up administrative posts. They were treating the journey as a sightseeing tour. For a whole day the ships had waited while the Innings had sampled the local wines at Larbot; and at Croom Light they had insisted on being put ashore so they could hunt birds with their fancy engraved shotguns. Captain Slavens was certain his new Commodore, who seemed to be a by-the-book young man, would not have approved of his giving in; but the Commodore was far away in Tornabay, and the Innings were here. Long experience in the Northern Squadron had taught Slavens that one catered to the Innings, no matter how absurd their demands. It was one reason he was a captain.

Beside him stood the navigator and the sullen Adaina guide they had taken aboard at Croom Light to see them through the straits. When Slavens turned, it was to the navigator he spoke, for the Croomman communicated only in surly monosyllables. "It's damned strange," he said. "The weather's fine everywhere else." His voice fell dead on the blank air.

The navigator was nervous. "We'd better wait."

"We could tow her with the cutter."

"Why? It's sure to break before too long."

Behind them, Captain Slavens heard the opening of the aftercastle door that led to the Innings' suite of cabins. He had thought the pack of them were stowed for the day, playing cards, but now apparently they were getting restless.

Proctor Gamiel sauntered across the deck toward them. As he came up, Slavens could smell the expensive tobacco the man had been smoking.

"Where are we?" Gamiel said.

"North shore of Thimish," Captain Slavens answered. "That's Rockmeet Straits ahead."

"How far to Harbourdown?"

"Five, six miles." And it might as well be a hundred, with this fog, he wanted to say.

"Will we still get there this afternoon?"

Now he was in a hurry. "It all depends on the weather."

The Inning seemed as if he resented not being able to order the weather to oblige him. "Could you put us ashore, and let us walk?"

"No," said the captain. "There's no road. You couldn't get through." He had no idea if it was true; he just wanted the Innings delivered safely, so he could wash his hands of them.

The proctor turned and paced fretfully aft. The Croomman had been oblivious to the exchange; he was facing westward into the mist, sniffing the air like a dog. Some of these Adaina had senses normal people lacked; they were closer to the elements, and had an affinity to them. "What is it?" Slavens said.

It took the guide a long time to respond. "It's not natural," he said at last. "The Ashwin are here."

The captain rolled his eyes. If there were any demons about, he knew where they were: in the after-cabin, smoking and playing cards. He glanced up, and saw a hopeful sign: the pennant at the top of the mainmast was stirring, and torn fragments of mist were swirling uneasily around the topgallant yards.

"I think it's breaking," he said to the navigator.

Sure enough, as they watched, over the next fifteen minutes a breeze thinned the fog above them, though it still hung on close to the water. At last Captain Slavens passed the word for the boatswain. "We'll proceed under topsails," he said. "The *Industry* first, *Pimpernel* next, then *Assurance*." He glanced at the guide. "Peel your eyes, now. If you let us run on a rock, you'll pay for it."

The boatswain's whistle tore shrilly through the silence and the sailors gathered from below to man the sails. Soon the *Industry*'s ponderous bow swung round and the great ship edged forward through the entrance of Rockmeet Straits. Under the shadow of the cliffs, Captain Slavens felt the air grow chill. The fog hid the channel beyond twenty or thirty yards ahead. Astern, the *Pimpernel* followed, ghostlike. An occasional call from the navigator, conning, pierced the thick air.

They had proceeded almost a mile when the lookout high in the masthead called down, "Ship in the channel, dead ahead."

Captain Slavens peered through the fog, but could see nothing. "What sort of ship?" he called.

"I can only see their masts—three of them. They must be aground; they're crosswise in the channel."

"Back the sails," Captain Slavens ordered. "Ready the anchor. Pass the word to the *Pimpernel*." This was just what he needed, some tomfool blocking the channel in a fog. It had to be a merchant ship, and now he'd have to give it aid. He called up, "Are they flying a flag?"

"No," the lookout said.

The *Industry* was still edging forward. A gust of humid breeze stirred the fog, and the captain glimpsed the shape of a dark hull ahead. A current of alarm passed through him. It was the shape of a navy frigate, and all its gunports were raised.

It was impossible. There were no hostile warships here in the Forsakens; Rothur was hundreds of miles away, and the war was over. In the instant he hesitated to issue the call to arms, the fog ahead lit up a ghastly orange colour, and a thunderous broadside crashed straight into the *Industry*'s bow. Seconds later, an answering thunder came from behind them, where the *Assurance* and *Pimpernel* were under fire from the cliffs.

"Man the guns! Hard to starboard!" Captain Slavens roared, intending to bring his guns to bear on the enemy while his ship still had some way on her; but they had caught him in the narrowest part of the channel, and the *Industry* shuddered down her whole length as the bow ran onto a sand shoal, leaving her helplessly aground.

A gust of wind swept the wall of fog aside, and Captain Slavens saw clearly for the first time. It was a navy frigate, their own ship, firing on them. The second broadside raked the decks to kill as many defenders as possible without damaging the ship itself. Still the *Industry* had not gotten a single shot off. "Issue the hand arms and cutlasses," Captain Slavens ordered. "Prepare for boarding."

The enemy ship had raised its anchors and now was making for the *Industry*'s stern, its gunwales lined with fierce-looking ruffians, its yardarms thick with snipers even now levelling their guns to pick off the navy men gathering on the *Industry*'s deck to defend her. Captain Slavens looked back and saw that the *Assurance* and *Pimpernel* were beyond coming to his aid; they were surrounded by a swarm of small pirate boats that had followed them down the channel from the north, and were now attacking from behind. Pinned in the narrow channel, fired on from above, unable to manoeuvre in order to fire their guns, the warships were nothing but enormous targets.

When the grappling hooks bit into the *Industry*'s after-rail and the first volley of fire raked through his men, Captain Slavens knew it was hopeless. A chilling shriek went up from the attackers as they swarmed aboard, cutlasses flashing. His own men were driven back; some turned to flee below.

"Surrender!" the captain ordered. "Lay down your arms!" For all he knew it was suicidal, since these savages might not know how to take prisoners, or anything but butchery and mayhem; but it was the only hope.

For the second time that day he was taken by surprise when a young Adaina warrior yelled out an order to desist, and the ruffians actually obeyed. With two henchmen at his side, the native leader strode across the deck to where the captain stood. He had an incongruously military bearing.

"Your sword, please, Captain," he ordered authoritatively.

Bitterly, Captain Slavens handed over his sword. "Who are you?" he said.

"Captain Harg Ismol," the Adaina said.

"Captain?" Slavens said. "Of what?"

There was an instant of hesitation, then Harg Ismol said, "Of the Independent Nation of the South Chain."

A stir passed through the listening attackers, growing as it gathered into a cheer. Looking around, Slavens saw a mad elation in their eyes.

Harg turned around, holding up a hand. "Disarm them, get them secured below," he said, and his followers turned to the job with a remarkably practiced air.

Across the water, the *Assurance* was already overrun by pirates, and the *Pimpernel* had floated onto the rocks at the base of the cliff. A second boat was approaching the *Industry*, like a scavenger come to see if there were any spoils to be had. On its deck was a massive white-haired man decked out in gold chains. Seeing the boat drawing near, Harg Ismol went to the huge warship's gunwale, leaned over it, and yelled out, "Hey, Dorn! I brought you a boat! Satisfied?"

The men around him broke out laughing.

NIGHT OF
THE BONFIRE

When Nathaway's wits returned to him, it was morning. He was lying in a room with a slanted ceiling, like an attic, and some sparse, battered furniture. Over by a dormer window sat a plain, solidly built Adaina woman, working at a small table. He squinted to see what she was doing. She took a cloth bag from a pile and put it on the table. From a wooden keg next to her she carefully measured three cups of sand into the bag, then started to sew it up with a needle and thread. Unable to make sense of this activity, Nathaway groped for his glasses on the floor beside his bed, where he always put them. They weren't there.

His movement attracted the woman's attention and she came over to his side. He realized it was Strobe's daughter.

"I ought to know your name," he said.

"It's Tway," she answered. She had a competent, take-charge air, like a nurse or a teacher.

"You're from Yora," he said.

"That's right."

"But we're on Thimish now."

"Right again. Your brains seem to have survived. I guess you Innings must be as thick-headed as we always thought."

She sat beside him on the bed, took a cloth from his forehead, rinsed it in a bowl of water on the nightstand, and put it back. It smelled of herbs. Her hands were gentle. It reminded him—

"That Grey Man," he said. Then, uncertainly, "Was there a Grey Man here?"

"Yes," she said.

"Did he . . . do anything?"

"No," she said. "You made it pretty clear you didn't want him to, before you passed out. He said he could still help you, even unconscious, but Harg wouldn't let him. He said it would be like rape. Harg's strange on the subject. But then, so are you."

Once again Nathaway found himself grateful for Harg's exposure to civilization.

"Where are my glasses?" he asked.

"I don't know," Tway said. "Lost."

"I couldn't see what you're doing."

She glanced back at the table, stacked with finished cloth bags. "Oh. I'm sewing up cannon cartridges."

"You mean that's gunpowder?"

"Yes."

There was enough of it in this small room to level a building. "Don't you know how dangerous that is?" Nathaway said.

She shrugged. "I needed something useful to do, and you weren't throwing off many sparks."

He wanted to sit up, but was afraid to move and make the pain in his head come back.

"Hungry? Thirsty?" Tway said.

"Yes," he admitted.

She went to the door and knocked on it. There was a rattle of a key in the lock, and someone opened it from outside. They exchanged some words, then the door closed again. The bolt shot home.

Frowning, Nathaway said, "Why is the door locked?"

Tway regarded him with crossed arms. "You're a prisoner."

This time he did sit up, despite the wave of aching dizziness, feeling like the situation demanded some action. From earliest childhood he had known that he could be a target of kidnappers. His mother had always said, "Don't be afraid, just prudent." He had spent his life alert, and nothing had ever happened. But since coming out here, where no one had the slightest idea who he was, he had let his guard down.

He said, "That's a really bad idea. You don't know what you're messing with. As soon as Proctor Fullabeau finds out, you're going to wish you never saw me. I'm serious, it could get bad for you."

She just said, "Well, you'll have to take it up with Harg."

"Fine. Let me talk to him."

"He's busy."

Through the day that followed, he was unable to get any more satisfactory response. After he had eaten, Tway picked up her gunpowder and left, and he was alone with the furniture and walls. The combination of anxiety and idleness was corrosive. He stared out the garret window at the wall of the building next door, he paced the floor, he examined every inch of the room. Toward noon, he heard the sound of distant gunfire and pounded on the door to find out what was going on, but no one answered.

He slept part of the afternoon, and fretted the rest. Late in the day he started to hear gunfire again, this time seemingly in the streets outside, and he imagined a phalanx of policemen come to rescue him. He pounded on the door and shouted to attract attention till a rough Adaina man unlocked the door and leaned in to say, "If you don't shut up I'm going to chain you to the bed."

"I want to talk to Harg," Nathaway said, unable to keep an imperious tone from his voice.

"So do a lot of people," the man said, and started to close the door.

"Stop!" Nathaway said. "What's the firing about?"

"Oh, they're just celebrating."

"Celebrating what?"

A slow, gloating grin grew on the man's face as he regarded his prisoner. "Independence," he said. "Harbourdown's no longer under Inning rule."

Nathaway stared at him, unable to imagine what he could mean.

The jailor appeared to be enjoying his reaction. "You'll probably be joining the rest of the Inning captives up in the fort before long. It won't be as comfortable up there, I promise you."

"Inning captives?" Nathaway repeated incredulously. "Is Proctor Fullabeau . . .?"

"Fullabeau's dead," the man said.

"Dead!"

"Yes. We captured the fort and four warships. You Innings are done here."

It was not until then that the true horror of his position struck Nathaway. This wasn't about ransom, as he had thought. He was being held by rebels with blood on their hands, uncontrolled by law or mercy. They not only didn't know who he was, they didn't care. He was just another prisoner of war.

"Oh my god," he said.

The man started to close the door. "Stop!" Nathaway cried out again. "Harg's not involved, is he? I have to talk to him."

The jailor only laughed and locked the door.

Sick with apprehension, Nathaway paced the narrow room. Nothing in his life had prepared him for this unthinkable situation. Chilling scenarios chased through his mind: abuse, beatings, lynchings, they had all happened in times of insurrection. As the minutes crawled past, he could hear through the door a celebrating crowd gathered somewhere below. Under normal circumstances it would have been a convivial sound; now it was nerve-racking evidence of an unpredictable mob who wished him ill simply because of his race. Never had he felt so anonymous, or so vulnerable.

The sound of footsteps and men's voices approaching up the steps sent alarm chasing through his nerves, and he braced himself to appear courageous.

When the door opened he exclaimed in relief, "Harg! Thank god it's you."

"They say you've been *demanding* to see me," Harg said. He came into the room and sank into the chair, looking bone-weary. There was a powder burn on his forehead, a purple bruise on one eye, and a two-day stubble on his chin. He would have looked desperately sinister if Nathaway hadn't known him.

"Is it true, what they told me?" Nathaway asked anxiously. "That the fort has fallen, and Proctor Fullabeau is dead?"

"Oh, was that his name?" Harg said vaguely. "Yes, it's true."

"This is a disaster. You weren't involved, were you?"

Harg looked at him with such a bemused expression that Nathaway realized it had been a rather stupid question, given the evidence.

"What were you thinking, Harg?" Nathaway said. "Don't you realize this is treason? The courts can't ignore this. I could have helped you if you hadn't taken up arms. Now, there's nothing I can do."

Harg was watching him as if he had stepped off a boat from another reality. "I'm touched that you're so worried for me," he said.

"I didn't even know you had grievances. There are ways to address grievances without blowing up warships. Why didn't you ask?"

"Calm down," Harg said.

Nathaway realized that there had been a hysterical edge in his voice. He forced himself to sit down on the bed and seem collected. "I'm just worried you don't realize how serious rebellion is, or how futile."

With a faint, ironic smile, Harg said, "Thanks for the lecture, but I do realize."

"Then what did you do it for?" Nathaway pleaded.

Harg didn't answer at once. He stared at the floor through a haze of weariness. When he spoke, it was as if to himself. "Honestly? I never thought it would get this far. I thought someone, or something, would stop us halfway. The soldiers would be more competent, or the timing would go wrong, or the weather would turn bad, or people wouldn't do what they were supposed to. I've never been in a battle where everything went right, or nearly right, like it did today."

He looked around the little room like a man struck on the head, half stunned. "This morning we were shit disturbers trying to get attention. Tonight, four warships and all of Harbourdown have fallen in my lap. I haven't thought it through yet. I don't know where we're going, or where we'll end up. It's like I set down a beer mug and it caused an earthquake."

It struck Nathaway that he had been right about Harg the first time. He wasn't vicious, or a fanatic. He *did* realize his position—both how serious and how futile it was. And in that fact, there was hope—not just for Nathaway, but for the whole situation.

"My father calls it the piled-up wardrobe phenomenon," Nathaway said.

"What?"

"You know how you keep stuffing things into a wardrobe till they're all piled up, then you go to take one thing out and it all comes crashing down. What he means is, in public affairs things can get away from you. Political situations are so complex and unpredictable you can set off cascades of consequences you can't foresee. We're always just one wrong move away from chaos."

"I'm glad to know he feels that way." Harg seemed to find some sort of wry humour in the thought.

"But this is the point, Harg: that's why we have laws. The law prevents us from accidentally setting off disorder. It gives us guidance to regulate our actions. It will always tell you what to do."

Harg shook his head slowly. "Your Inning laws have nothing to say to me."

"Oh, you're wrong there," Nathaway protested earnestly. "They have something to say to everyone. The law is universal. It doesn't ask whether you're Adaina or Torna or Inning. It doesn't ask if you're a Yoran or a Thimishman. It only asks if you're a human being."

"Odd then, how Adainas always end up getting pissed on by the law."

"That's just because you don't understand it," Nathaway said. He searched in his inner coat pocket, and brought out a slim, leather-bound volume. "Have you ever seen the law? This is it."

"You carry it around with you?" Harg said, mildly incredulous.

"Sure." Nathaway held out the volume. "Here, take it. It's very simple, a set of codes handed down to us from ancient times. There are less than a hundred laws. They give us a framework and guidance. Then the courts make them relevant to the present by reinterpreting them. So it's an organic, living system that can be adapted to any people, any place. Today we read it differently than we did a hundred years ago. Your own courts, when you have them, will probably read it differently than ours. That's what makes it work."

Harg was paging through the little volume, glancing at the closely printed pages. He closed it and held it out.

"No, keep it," Nathaway said. "You might need it. I can get another copy."

"Read me a few of them," Harg suggested.

After a moment of hesitation, Nathaway took the book back and opened it to the beginning. As he started to read aloud the words he had known by heart since childhood, he felt himself relaxing into their familiar spell. The rhythmic poetry of the ancient phrases, their simplicity, their truth, touched him with the certainty of another realm where order and justice prevailed. All his life he had wanted to enter that realm. It hovered somewhere, unreachable, above the disappointing world he lived in, and these words were the closest link he had ever found. He loved them, and revered them, and believed in them.

When he finally looked up, Harg's head was laid back against the chair and his eyes were closed. He looked asleep. But when Nathaway's voice fell silent he opened his eyes and said, "I'm listening."

"Do you want me to go on?"

Harg sighed and said, "No. I've got to go. I'll come back to hear the rest some other time."

As Harg stood to leave, Nathaway realized he hadn't said any of the thousand things he had intended, or needed, to say. "I didn't ask—I should have been pleading for my life or something," he said.

Smiling quizzically, Harg said, "I'd begun to think you didn't realize you were in danger."

Nathaway hadn't wanted his fears confirmed quite so openly. He looked down at the book in his hands and found his throat constricting so that he couldn't talk. Then Harg put a hand on his shoulder—a simple gesture that anchored Nathaway to hope in human goodness.

Looking up, Nathaway said, "Could I have paper and pen to write my family? I want to let them know I'm . . ." He had been about to say "I'm all right," but in fact he didn't know if it was true.

"Sure," said Harg. "I'll leave word." He paused. "Don't worry," he said, and left.

Nathaway felt much more balanced, more in touch with what was true and permanent. Looking around his prison room, he thought to himself that this was all temporary. It didn't touch what was really important. With that thought, he was able to lie back on his bed, the book pressed to his heart, and accept his situation.

ℂ

Harg hadn't really wanted to talk to Nathaway Talley. He had come upstairs solely to get away from the crowd and their incessant demands on his attention. But the conversation had been enlightening, if decidedly odd. He hadn't expected to find his prisoner quite so . . . evangelical. Stress and head injuries brought out strange things in people.

He paused at the head of the stairs, where there was a guard posted, as much to keep people out as the prisoner in. "Find him a pen and paper, will you?" he said. "But bring me anything he writes."

"Aye, Captain," the man said.

Harg paused, thinking. "Let's not move him up to the fort tomorrow. I don't want him talking to the other Innings." It was just a hunch, or perhaps curiosity to see what effect isolation and indoctrination might have on such an impressionable mind. At any rate, he wanted to continue the experiment.

As he descended the stairs, the hubbub in the tavern below rose up to engulf him. The instant he stepped into the taproom, he was surrounded by people who had been waiting impatiently for his return, needing answers, decisions, and orders.

There was a host of problems relating to the prisoners. The acquisition of over three hundred captives who needed to be incarcerated and fed had put a severe strain on resources. Then there was the security of the sacks of gold they had found in the aft cabin of the *Industry*, a discovery Harg wanted wrapped in the strictest secrecy. But worst was the combustible state of the town itself. Holby Dorn's pirate fleet had looted the two warships they had captured—Harg had given up thought of ever getting all the guns back—and returned to town, brazen with their victory and all too aware that civil authority had collapsed.

Now, three Torna merchants from the prosperous wharf-side neighbourhood were facing him as if he were the only thing standing between them and ruin. "There are pirates roaming the streets in bands out there," said their spokesperson, a middle-aged woman named Majlis Callow. "We have warehouses, shops, homes. The Innings at least protected us from looters and riot. You have to control these lawless men."

Harg felt a sense of despair at how instinctively they turned to him for authority. He didn't have a police force. He hardly had anything; the forces he had commanded that day were either guarding prisoners or stinking drunk by now. There was no discipline, no organization—it had all been cobbled together, spur of the moment.

"Barko!" he shouted over the din of the crowd. Barko came over, looking flushed with drink. Harg envied him; he hadn't had a chance to eat, much less drink, since coming back to town. "Where the fuck is Holby Dorn?" he asked.

"Up in the Redoubt," Barko said.

"What's he doing up there?"

Barko only shrugged.

"Well, send somebody up there and tell him to get his ass down here to control his men," Harg said angrily.

"You've got to be kidding," Barko said. He was looking at Harg in incredulity at the thought that Holby Dorn could, or would, stop anyone from looting.

The Tornas looked panic-stricken at Barko's response. Majlis turned to Harg. "Captain Ismol, you've got to do something. We're begging you."

He needed the Torna. If the pirates started a riot, it would turn racial, and then the Mundua alone knew what would happen. Harg thought of the piled-up wardrobe. By morning, he could be standing in wreckage and smouldering ruins.

He put a reassuring hand on the woman's shoulder. "Don't worry, I'll do something." What, he had no idea. "Barko, do you know the situation out there?"

Barko turned and beckoned over some new arrivals. "You guys see what was going on?" he yelled.

"They've built a big bonfire down in the Market Square, and they're shooting off guns and stuff," one man said.

"Any disorder?" Harg asked.

They laughed. "Sure, they're breaking some windows. I heard that some Torna shopkeeper shot a guy in the leg."

Harg didn't find it humourous. There was a window of opportunity to stop this before it got out of control. He couldn't use force, so it had to be persuasion, bribery, or flimflam, possibly all three. He said to Barko, "We need a distraction. Go get a couple of kegs from Calpe's basement, but for Mundua's sake water it down. Then bring it along to Market Square. I'll try to get the pirates there."

He looked around for Tway. Before he had gone upstairs she had been tending bar while Calpe tended prisoners up in the Redoubt. He spotted her, and pushed through the crowd, leaning across the bar to talk privately. "Go get Spaeth," he said. "Bring her down to Market Square."

"Are you sure?" Tway said seriously.

"No. But do it anyway." He needed the insurance.

He climbed up on a table then, and waved his arms for silence. When the din had sunk to an uproar, he shouted, "I'm buying a round!" There was a deafening cheer; he held up his hands for silence. "Not here! Come on down to the bonfire at Market Square, and the first hundred people that show up get a drink on me. Go out and make sure all the pirates know. Bring them along, and we'll have a *real* party."

He jumped down and headed for the door then, with a high-spirited mob pressing behind him. It was a risk, putting more people into the streets. Witnesses might be a deterrent, or just more fuel for the fire. As they passed through the streets of Harbourdown, Harg hailed everyone he saw, inviting them to the Market Square.

The bonfire turned out to be built from the contents of the half-renovated customs house, which had been stripped clean. There was already a crowd there, and a street fiddler entertaining them for tips. When Harg joined them, he saw that they were feeding the fire with all the licenses, passports, certificates, and registrations that the Innings had imposed on them. A fierce old woman came forward with a fistful of permits to toss contemptuously on the fire, and Harg laughed aloud to see the paper shackles of the invaders go up in flames.

It took some time for everyone to assemble, and Harg spent it going through the crowd shaking hands and congratulating people, telling them not to leave. He could tell when the pirates started arriving, because the tone became more rowdy and rough, the crowd laced with belligerent young men looking for trouble. When Barko finally rode into the square with a cartful of liquor, there was no time to lose. Harg sprinted to the top of the customs house steps and held up his arms. The fiddle fell silent, and so did the crowd.

"Did anyone ever say that Thimishmen didn't know how to stand up for their rights?" Harg shouted out over the square.

"No!" the people in the front of the crowd roared back.

"Well, if they ever did, you've proved them wrong today."

There were cheers and raucous shouts.

"Do you remember how those Innings were lording it over you yesterday?"

"Yes!" the crowd responded.

"Well, where are they now?"

There were catcalls and a few obscenities.

"I love you guys," Harg shouted.

There were cries of "We love you too."

"Today you've proved what islanders can do." He paused for the cheering to die down. "Pretty soon they'll be talking about you in Tornabay, saying, 'We'd better not mess with Thimish.' But they'll also be talking about you on Ekra and Pont and Romm. And you know what they'll be saying? 'Those Thimishmen stood up for me, too. We weren't able to do it ourselves, but Thimish did what we should have done, and we owe them.' Your names are going to travel all over the South Chain, because you had the courage to do what was right. Your names are going to travel to the Inner Chain, and even the Tornas are going to say, 'They stood up for us, too.' Because it's true."

There were a few hoots at this, but most of the crowd was listening, arrested by this new view of themselves. Looking out over their faces, Harg could feel a presence, a power, in their collective mood. It was like music; the square throbbed with energy, an invisible force that had sprung into being from their synchronized attention, and he suddenly knew he could shape it into something beautiful, or something deadly.

"What you did today is bigger than just Thimish," he said, his voice echoing from the buildings in the silence. "It's bigger than Adaina or Torna. It's bigger than all the South Chain. You stood up for regular people everywhere. Tonight, Harbourdown is your town, your home, but it's more than that, because everyone will be looking at you and saying, 'I wish I could be a Thimishman, too.' We're all in this together, rich and poor, man and woman, elder and child. Let's celebrate together, and show the world we're just ordinary, peaceful folks who aren't going to let empires shove us around."

They erupted in applause, and Harg felt the volume and force of their emotion lifting him, washing over him. They had a radiance, a greatness, that made him love them; he wanted to embrace them, to become their instrument, till he glowed with their invisible power.

The fiddler came up onto the steps beside him, and waved for silence. "I've got a song," he shouted out. "It's called the Ballad of the Battle of Thimish."

He struck some notes on his fiddle, and before long he had the whole crowd singing the chorus. Harg watched in wonder. The mood had completely changed. Good will and fellowship were flowing through the town in irresistible waves. By the time Barko broke out the booze, it was almost unnecessary; everyone was drunk on good feeling.

As he started down the steps, he caught the sight, over to his right, of silver hair and pearly grey skin. Spaeth was standing there watching him, fully visible to the rest of the crowd, and he hadn't even seen her. For a moment he froze, feeling a qualm at the implications. No wonder they had all listened to him. They had seen her, and thought her presence meant more than it did.

He went over to her. "Thank you for coming," he said. "I'm sorry, I shouldn't have involved you in this. I thought—"

She didn't let him finish. "Harg, I haven't seen mora so powerful, or someone who worked it so well, since . . ." She stopped, as if warned by instinct not to compare him to Goth.

Her eyes were the colour of moonlight, and they were looking at him with an expression that made his heart skip a beat. He had never thought that anyone would look at him that way. He put a hand on her cheek; she looked intoxicated with his closeness.

"You're in pain," she said, and reached up to touch his hair where it was matted with blood from the scalp wound the Inning had given him.

"I deserve it," he said. "I did something really stupid, trying to be a hero."

She ran light fingers across his forehead, down his cheek. Her touch felt cool and soothing, like wintergreen. Before he had time to think, his own fingers were running through her hair. It looked like moonlit water flowing over his hands.

"Let me help you," she whispered. "I want to. I need to."

"You don't want to be my bandhota," he said softly.

"I have to be someone's."

She was almost pleading. This was his chance, he thought. He could have her, body and soul. How ardent she looked, half mad with compassion. They could spend a night like he had never dreamed of having.

And in the morning she would wake with all her freedom gone. She would be his slave, and he would be her master forever.

With a pang of thwarted desire, he realized he couldn't do it. No matter how his body yearned for it. He took her hands in his, and kissed them softly. "I can't let you waste yourself on me," he said. "Save your dhota for someone who deserves it."

He turned away then. Behind him, she drew in a breath that was nearly a sob. Sternly he forced himself on. As he descended the steps, he wondered if he had gone insane. Any other man would have done it.

No one spoke to him as he crossed the square, engrossed in his thoughts. When he came up to Barko, the pirate raised a speculative eyebrow, and Harg knew then that everyone had been watching.

"I need to find a horse," Harg said. "I have to go up to the Redoubt and check out what Holby Dorn is up to."

"I'll come with you," Barko said.

"You think things are under control here?"

Barko scanned the square, where people had started dancing to the fiddle music. "Yeah," he said. "We're okay now."

The dark streets away from the square were deserted. Barko led the way to a stable, and Harg pounded on the door. A shutter next to him rattled open a crack, and the muzzle of a shotgun poked through. Harg backed away, his hands in the air. "Hold on," he said, "I just want to hire a horse."

Barko stepped between him and the gun. "Don't you know who this is?" he demanded angrily. "This is Captain Ismol. You owe him your freedom and your safety."

The shotgun lowered, and someone muttered an excuse. Then the bolt on the door shot back, and the proprietor gestured them inside.

They got two horses. Retracing the road he had ridden down only that morning, Harg was visited with a sense of unreality at all that had happened. Before passing through the fort gates he turned around to look down on the town, on the four warships riding in the harbour, the bonfire by the wharf.

"It's all ours again," Barko said with a quiet satisfaction.

Inside the Redoubt, they found Birk's squad still firmly in control of the guns, and Calpe's of the prisoners. "It was a little tense here for a while," Birk told them. "I think Dorn and his guys came up intending to start something, but when we wouldn't back down they decided to help themselves to the Innings' cognac instead."

"Good for you, Birk," Harg said.

"Well it was *our* fort," Birk said, with righteous indignation. "Those pirates never captured a fort in their lives. You going to kick him out?"

"No," Harg said. "I just want to talk to him."

"We'll stay close in case you need us."

They found Holby Dorn installed in the room that had been Proctor Fullabeau's office. It was lavishly furnished with Inning symbols of dominion. The light from a bright coal fire danced over the crystal decanters arrayed on the walnut side table, the brocade upholstery of the furniture, the polished brass fender. Things of age, beauty, and value: they were the symbols Innings used to stake out the gradations of rank and race, to show who ruled whom. Now the mahogany desk was littered with empty bottles, and two of Dorn's men were slumped on the settee, snoring drunkenly.

Holby Dorn was either not drunk or not showing it. When Barko and Harg entered, he was looking out the window between the wine-coloured draperies, massive as a snow-capped mountain. He turned, ponderous yet charged, and his small, bright eyes fixed on Harg's face.

"You, eh?" he grunted.

Harg crossed his arms. "I just had to stop your pirates from sacking the town, Dorn. Since you wouldn't control them, somebody else had to. Now don't complain to me if you've lost authority."

Dorn's face was hard as glacier-scarred granite. He said, "You think you're pretty damn smart, don't you?"

"Yes, since you mention it. And I am."

Their gazes met square on, and for a while their eyes contested silently. "You don't have the slightest idea what you stirred up today." Dorn said slowly. "Taking the fort and assassinating the commandant aren't acts of piracy. They're full-blown acts of war."

"I know," Harg said. "It was the only way to get the Innings to take us seriously."

"Well, congratulations. Now you've got their attention, they're going to send out half the fleet to hunt you down."

"I'll be disappointed if it's only half." It was bravado, and they both knew it. But Harg was still riding the surge of power from the Market Square, and he wasn't in the mood for humility. Deliberately, he sat down on one of the gold brocade armchairs, aware that he profaned an icon. "That's why we can't go around looting our neighbours. We're going to need them."

Holby Dorn placed a muddy boot on the edge of the polished fender. "My guys wouldn't have touched Adainas," he said.

"What the hell does that matter? We're going to need the Tornas, too. Especially them."

"Speak for yourself," Dorn said. "I've never sucked up to Tornas, and I never will."

"You'll never get them on your side, either."

"You think you've got them on your side? Well, check your back—there's already a target painted on it. Those mongrels turn to treachery as naturally as they breathe. They have nothing to gain by supporting you. All their wealth, all their power, comes from the Innings. For sixty years they've played the obedient dogs so they could become the masters. And it's paid off. Now they control the navy, the government, the commerce, the shipping. They'll be running souvenir stands at your execution."

Harg knew he was seeing the reverse side of the prejudice he had endured from Tornas for years. And Dorn wasn't the only one who thought this way.

"This is why we could never beat the Innings," Harg said. "Because we're so glad to fight each other. If we're going to win this, we need to pull together."

Dorn ran a hand through his dishevelled white hair. "Win? You really are mad, aren't you?" he said. "The gunpowder has frizzled your brains. This isn't some little band of islanders you've stirred up. This is the Inning Empire. They can wipe the South Chain from the face of the earth without even breaking a sweat."

"Don't talk as if you're not in this too, Dorn. Like it or not, you are. All of Thimish is. There's no backing out now."

"Rot you," the pirate growled. "You think I don't know that?" He began to pace. Despite his immense bulk he moved with an animal's silence, and like an animal seemed ready to jump in any direction. "What chance do you think Thimish has of holding out against the Empire?"

"Thimish alone? None at all. But Thimish won't *be* alone. There will be Romm and Spole, and Pont and Vill. It will be the entire South Chain against Inning."

"You're very sure all those islands will forget their grievances against the pirates of Thimish and join us."

It was Barko who spoke up then. "You should have been down in the town square tonight, Dorn. If you'd seen what went on there, you wouldn't be doubting now."

There was a long silence. The fire crackled in the grate, and the sound of the guard changing filtered in faintly from outside. At last Dorn said, "I know men who have spent their lives waiting for an Ison to rise and unite us, lead us back to the greatness of olden days. I've always said they were daft. It won't happen in our lives."

"Well, at last we agree on something," Harg said. "There isn't any magic hero who's going to appear and save us. It's up to us. If plain folk like you and me won't work to save the isles, it won't get done. We have to do it our way—the straight, honest, Adaina way. No Inning riches, no Lashnura power. Just us." He got up and went over to Dorn then, close enough that they could touch hands. "Dorn, we shouldn't be enemies. We're on the same damn side."

Dorn regarded him with a mix of suspicion, fear, and memory. "Do you know what the Innings do to rebels? They won't be so polite as to hang you, the way they did Ison Orin. He wasn't an Inning subject; you are. Their punishment for treason is impaling. They're going to ram a wooden stake up your ass and raise you up in the town square to die by inches, hanging there baking in the sun."

For an instant Harg had a vivid premonition that Dorn's words were prophetic. It lasted only a moment, but left him feeling drained, tired, and beaten. The tide of certainty on which he had been surfing all night receded, fast and fantastic as a swallow on the wind.

"I can't argue any more," Harg said, turning away.

When he and Barko had closed the commandant's door behind them and were facing the dark parade ground of the fort, Harg felt as if he had walked into a wall. All at once the day caught up with him and he couldn't think, he couldn't move. All he could do was sink down on the steps in exhaustion.

Barko sat down beside him. "Don't let Dorn make you doubt yourself, Harg," he said.

"What if he's right? What if we made a terrible mistake today?"

"You didn't. Maybe you can't see what's going on, but the rest of us can, clear as day. There is a force bigger than any of us at work here. There is a pattern unfolding in the isles. I don't know where it will lead. It'll probably demand a lot from us, you especially. But this I do know: if we miss the chance that's being offered us, if we waste our time with doubts, the pattern will sweep right on past. We're riding a wild wind, Harg. There is no giving up, no going back."

Harg couldn't answer. There wasn't a speck of energy left in his body, not even enough to open his mouth. He became vaguely aware that Barko had called out, "Hey Calpe! Is there an extra bed in this place? We've got to get this guy to sleep."

Then Calpe was on one side of him, Barko on the other, and they were leading him somewhere. There was a bed, the most welcome sight on earth. Calpe was taking off his boots and jacket. Her eyes were full of fierce loyalty. Ah, Calpe—so fit, so lovely, so married. What energy she would have. How tired he was.

He fell asleep almost before his head touched the pillow. But it wasn't Calpe he dreamed of. He dreamed he was standing in a shower of cool silver hair, washing in a lake of unquestioning Lashnura love.

After Harg had left her, Spaeth stood for a moment alone on the steps of the customs house, then turned to find a refuge inside the gutted building where no one could see her. Her whole body trembled with rejection. Never had she felt so inflamed with the desire; now it burned in her, unfulfilled. What a fool she had been, to think that her free sacrifice would be honoured, or her selflessness would be valued. She looked down at her hands. In the darkness it seemed as if the fingertips had grown blacker in just the last few minutes. She clenched them desperately.

The cure had seemed so close, so obvious. Watching Harg speak to the crowd in that charged moment of mora, she had felt a sharp urge to drink in his power, to let his will flow through and possess her. With his life-force animating her, she would have been full in a way she had never been before. Now, deprived of him against all her expectations, she felt hungry and vengeful.

The light from the bonfire outside cast odd shadows across the empty, ruined rooms of the building. Spaeth mounted a darkened staircase to the second floor and picked her way through smashed furniture to the front, where she could look out onto the square. The stone buildings that ringed the courtyard seemed to be frowning from under their dark lintels, and from time to time the firelight snagged on a glint of glass like a watching eye. The dancers below seemed unaware of it. A couple was sitting on the steps where she had stood, their bodies pressed so intimately close it made Spaeth ache to look. The woman was laughing. No thought for the sacrifices that knit the world together and kept them safe. The Lashnura and all their tragic love were of no consequence here.

Spaeth turned away and wandered through empty rooms till she found another staircase, this one narrow and steep, leading up to a trap door. When she pushed it open she found herself in the open cupola on top of the building, with a view on all sides. She leaned against the sill, feeling a deep bitterness in her blood. Was there a finite amount of happiness in the world, so that it could only be purchased by stealing it from someone else?

"Now you see," a voice hissed in her ear, black as night.

"We are used, Ridwit," Spaeth said. "The Adaina don't care for us. They trap us into loving them so they don't have to be responsible for their own folly."

"Yes," Ridwit said.

"They don't deserve our dhota."

"Especially not yours," Ridwit purred, stirring the hair behind Spaeth's ear.

"It's unjust that we should be forced to give what they don't value."

"There may be another way," Ridwit said, "if you have the courage to pursue it."

A chill wind blew past. Spaeth felt poised on the threshold of a domain beyond responsibility, and it gave her a forbidden thrill. She looked down on all the puny little humans making much of themselves around the bonfire below. Harg's name was on all their lips. The thought of him made her desire and rage flare up so bright she thought it would light the courtyard. She wanted to conquer him, to make him beg for her dhota.

A claw pierced her flesh. Her mouth opened in a soundless cry, half of pain, half of pleasure, as she felt it bury itself deeper and deeper into her body. It penetrated the place of her humiliation and transformed it into something red and steely. She gasped with the flood of power.

The night was no longer dark. She saw everything in sharp outline, as through the night vision of a cat. When she laughed, a feral snarl echoed back to her from the night wind.

11

A PERSONAL WAR

The vaulted ballroom of the Sorrell mansion was all aglow with winking currents of finery and faction, coquetry and manoeuvre. Commodore Joffrey, distinguished in his dress uniform, scanned the room. An eddy of merchants' sons and daughters swirled past him, inviting stares with their imported Inning fashions. It seemed that "savage chic" was all the rage this season. Feather headdresses bobbed above the ladies' elaborately braided hair, and their dresses swished and clicked with shell beads. The most stylish young men wore elegantly fitted versions of the Adaina leather knee-boot, blousy shirts, and sealskin hats. Joffrey wondered what the Innings made of these islanders imitating the Innings imitating them.

The Innings were scattered around the room in clumps, conspicuously taller than the rest of the crowd, many of them splendid in bullion and braid. Most of the newly arrived officers were surrounded by soberly dressed merchants, Tornabay's commercial elite, who were attracted to power like ants to sugar. Joffrey could tell instantly where the guest of honour, Admiral Talley, was standing—and not just because the largest swarm of merchants was around him. All of the navy officers were instinctively oriented so they could see the admiral, monitor his mood, and check where his attention was directed. They all looked tense and wary. None of them had spoken to Joffrey since he had entered the room—nor would they, so long as the admiral could see them.

As a group of merchants' wives swept past, Joffrey forced himself to concentrate on smiling. He was not in a mood to party. For one thing, he had already noticed several disturbing security lapses for which he was ultimately responsible. For another, he had just survived one of the most unpleasant days of his life.

That afternoon, he had had to brief his icy commander and the senior staff on the debacle in the South Chain. The news had only arrived the day before, hard on the heels of Admiral Talley's arrival, and new details were still filtering in. There was no way to paint it over pleasantly. The Fourth Fleet, the Navy, the whole Inning nation had been humiliated by a pack of savages. The admiral was furious, and someone was going to be held accountable. From the vacant space around him, Joffrey knew who everyone thought it was going to be.

The only one who appeared unaffected by the general tension was Corbin Talley himself. Joffrey watched him across the room, standing erect and elegant in his uniform. He had the charm turned on tonight. He was gracious, attentive, even witty. Though he was never exactly warm, tonight it gave him a tantalizing air of detachment. He made people feel honoured to have been noticed. Worden Sorrell, the host of this long-anticipated banquet, was standing next to the admiral, basking in his presence. What none of them knew was how abruptly Talley's charm could turn off.

"Looking for Livvie?"

Joffrey snapped out of his reverie to find that Tiarch had had the courage to approach him. He simulated a smile. "Yes, I haven't seen her yet tonight."

"I think she is waiting to make an entrance."

Joffrey's rather public courtship of Livvie Sorrell, openly encouraged by her parents, had been keeping the Tornabay rumour mills alive. The Innings, despite their power, were not seen as good matrimonial prospects, since they were apt to court, then leave. Joffrey, being an islander, had been a better prospect to stay and wield influence for years to come. From the bevy of young women who had been paraded before him, he had picked not so much Livvie as her father, rumoured to be the richest man in Tornabay. Of Livvie herself, he cared only that she was not repulsive. But he made a gallant effort to pretend he was smitten.

Despite her conversation opener, Tiarch knew perfectly well where Joffrey's attention had been directed, and now her gaze turned the same way. "They ought to back off and let him enjoy the scenery," she said.

"The women, you mean? He wouldn't notice them," Joffrey said.

"Really? What *does* our admiral enjoy?"

"Winning wars," Joffrey said.

"Nothing besides? Wine? Gambling?"

She wanted to know his vices. Joffrey had no encouragement for her. "He's an ascetic."

"I expect he has to be careful to avoid scandal. There must be suspicions that he achieved his position by nepotism."

"At one time there were. At first, it may have been true. No one says it any longer."

"You're very loyal," Tiarch observed.

With a thin smile, Joffrey said, "He has been very good to me."

Of all people in the room, Tiarch ought to know best what he meant. Neither of them had been born to prominent families; they had both used the Innings to claw their way upward, into the kind of exalted company they inhabited tonight.

Tiarch had been at the meeting that day. She had played the scene like an expert: grave and concerned, never breathing a word of criticism, but fairly radiating a message of "that will teach you to put anyone but me in charge." Joffrey couldn't afford to let himself resent it; in her place, he would have done the same. Besides, Tiarch was one he understood. She was a wily survivor who would play along with any faction, or all of them at once, till it became clear who was likely to win. Then she would strike, or betray.

Yes, he could work with Tiarch.

"Commodore?" A young ensign was at his side. "Captain Dorris is here, and would like to speak to you."

"Excuse me, Governor, I need to attend to this," Joffrey said. Inside, his stomach tightened with tension. This meant that more news had arrived from the South Chain.

When he returned to the party half an hour later, the guests were assembling by the door to the banquet hall. Livvie materialized by his side, iridescent in abalone and pearl. "Where were you?" she said. Evidently, he had missed her entrance.

"I was called away by my duties," he said. "You look splendid, Miss Sorrell."

His eyes strayed from her to locate the admiral. He felt doomed.

"What's the matter?" she said.

"Some bad news," he said. "It's a worried time just now."

"Those brutes on Thimish, you mean? I hate them."

Not nearly as much as I do, Joffrey thought.

The musicians struck up a stirring, patriotic march and the tall doors to the banquet hall swung open. The guests began to parade inside. When he reached the door with Livvie on his arm, Joffrey was disturbed to see that one whole side of the banquet hall was a wall of windows, now dark. The long, glittering table ran parallel to the windows. Automatically, he looked around to locate the admiral. Talley and Tiarch were hanging back by the doorway, conversing, both instinctively reluctant to appear before lit windows at night. He knew how Tiarch had come by that instinct; she had survived three assassination attempts. How Admiral Talley had acquired it, he didn't know—probably at his mother's knee.

"I've got to find your father," Joffrey said to Livvie, and then left her without even showing her to her seat. When he got to Worden Sorrell, he whispered, "Sir, are there curtains for the windows?"

"There is nothing outside but the garden," the merchant said.

"Still, it is a security risk. I'm afraid I must insist you draw them."

The servants, who had been poised to serve the first course, were redeployed to draw the heavy curtains over the windows. As Talley was finally strolling to his seat, Joffrey intercepted him and whispered, "Sir, when you have a chance, I need to speak to you."

"What is it?" the admiral said, his unnerving blue eyes on Joffrey's face.

"Some more news from Thimish." He strove to make his voice signal non-urgency, and willed the man to sit and enjoy his dinner first; after all, there was nothing they could do tonight.

But instead, Talley went over to their host and apologized for having to withdraw. Sorrell, by now concerned at the unsettled tone, suggested they use the scriptorium, and showed them the door. A watchful silence settled over the banquet hall as Joffrey led off the guest of honour.

The scriptorium was a long, board-floored room with two rows of clerks' desks running down the middle. The walls were lined to the ceiling with the merchant's letter books and records. Joffrey lit two lamps on the desks nearest the door.

"Who is handling security tonight?" Talley said in a deceptively conversational tone.

"Dorris, sir," Joffrey said. "He won't be doing it again."

"That's just as well."

There was a pause as Joffrey tried to think how to frame the news in the least damaging way. "We are getting some specifics now, and names," he said. "It wasn't the same band of brigands we knew about; they appear to have some new ringleaders. The chief insurgent is some character named Harg Ismol—"

"What?" Talley interrupted sharply.

Joffrey paused. He was quite sure he had never heard the name before. "Harg Ismol. You know him?"

"Yes." Talley looked like a thousand bitter thoughts were racing through his head. "He was Native Navy. A man I believed to have some loyalty towards me."

Joffrey realized that the admiral's tone reflected a real sense of personal betrayal. It was an aspect of Talley's personality he knew well. The man feared and despised betrayal above all things. He was always expecting it, and was almost always right.

Talley turned away, thinking. "This explains a great deal. I have much more sympathy for Captain Slavens now. He was up against a man—" He cut off his thought in mid-sentence. "Damn the ungrateful viper! We taught him everything he knows. We raised him up from nothing. He could have been . . . and this is our reward."

Joffrey waited silently, vowing to find out what had gone on between the two of them.

"This is going to change our plans," Talley said, and now his voice had a ruthless edge. "We're not dealing with criminals or agitators, as we thought. We're up against what amounts to a mutinous faction of the Native Navy. We have to expect them to fight us the way they fought the Rothurs. This is not going to be pleasant, Joffrey."

"No, sir."

"Was that all?"

"No, sir. There is a story that worries me, knowing the superstitions of the Adaina, and how impressionable they are." He told the story then, as it had been told to him, of how Harg Ismol had prevented the sacking of Harbourdown.

When he finished, Talley was silent a moment. "And for this he gets credit?"

"Yes, sir. Credit, and even reverence."

"So he is praised for preventing anarchy, when it was he who provoked it. We had been preventing looting right along, but do we get praised for it?" His tone was irritated beyond bearing.

He hadn't understood the point of the story, Joffrey reflected. It was not that Harg had prevented looting; it was the way he did it, with Lashnura backing. But it was impossible to explain to an Inning how dangerous that was.

"There is one more thing, sir." Joffrey drew a deep breath. "They have a number of Inning hostages, as we knew. What we didn't know was that one of the hostages is . . . well, they've captured your brother Nathaway, sir."

This time the admiral's reaction was totally silent, but not impassive. His jaw was clenched tight. He drew in a long breath. When he spoke, it was with coldly controlled anger. "Is there one single, solitary thing that has not been completely fucked up?" He pinned Joffrey down with those blued-steel eyes. "Well, Joffrey? Tell me there is one way Harg Ismol has not run circles around you."

There was nothing Joffrey could say. To open his mouth would sound defensive, an implicit confession of guilt.

"I will expect your resignation to be on my desk in the morning," Talley said.

"Yes, sir."

It was a sentence of exile. Joffrey would never be able to show his face in Tornabay again. He would have to move away, back to Fluminos. It was the only other place where he knew anyone. Mostly, he knew enemies of Corbin Talley who might find such a man as he useful to have in their employ.

The admiral had asked him a question. He had to say, "Sorry, sir?"

"I said, who the bloody hell sent Nathaway to Thimish?"

"No one. He was supposed to be on another island where there was a small force to look after him. Apparently, he left of his own accord, before they could prevent him." He hesitated, wondering how much compromising detail to go into, but decided he had nothing to lose. "There seems to have been a woman involved."

"The fool," Talley said under his breath. He gave Joffrey a piercing look. "Was *that* all?"

"Yes, sir. That's all."

"Very well."

Joffrey turned stiffly to leave, but the admiral said, "Joffrey."

"Yes, sir?"

"I've changed my mind. I have another assignment for you."

He paused so long that Joffrey said, "Sir?"

"Come back and see me in the morning, when I've worked it out. In the meantime, go enjoy the banquet."

"Yes, sir." He didn't say thank you. A commander couldn't sack someone, then take it back, and expect everything to continue on as before. The bond of trust had been broken.

The banquet was sheer torture after that. He had been seated next to Livvie, and she tried gamely to flirt him out of his morose silence. But every time he overheard Corbin Talley engaging in pleasantries with his dinner companions several seats away, his bitterness grew.

At one point, the conversation down the table turned to the subject of charity for the poor. Admiral Talley said, loud enough for Joffrey to hear, "Personally, I've found that altruism is a risky investment, as likely to end in disappointment or betrayal as in rewards. Debts cut both ways, it seems. Be careful who you help."

Joffrey could feel the eyes of the Inning officers on him. They had been waiting for him to fail so the admiral would come to his senses.

At the earliest possible moment Joffrey excused himself, pleaded the press of duty, and left. He emerged from the Sorrell mansion into a light rain that fell silently on the walled garden that surrounded the house. When he reached the front gate, a liveried footman intercepted him. "Commodore Joffrey? If you please, sir, the governor has sent word that she would like to meet with you. If you wouldn't mind waiting in her carriage . . ."

Joffrey glanced around, but no one was watching him. The invitation was balm to his smarting pride, proof that he was not yet out of the game. He crossed the walk to the plain black carriage waiting in the street. The footman opened the door for him, and he climbed inside.

He didn't have to wait long. Within ten minutes the carriage began to move, then turned into the gate of the Sorrell compound to pick up the governor at the door. Joffrey waited in the darkness of the curtained interior till Tiarch climbed in. She didn't acknowledge his presence till the door was closed; then she said, "I'm glad you're here."

"How could I decline such a mysterious invitation?" Joffrey said.

"Sorry if it seemed theatrical."

"Not at all."

The horses set off at a sedate walk. Once they were on the street again, Tiarch pushed back the curtains. There was no light in the carriage; they saw each other only by the occasional streetlamp.

"You're not a Tornabay native, are you?" Tiarch said conversationally. "Where's your family from?"

"Rusk," Joffrey answered.

"Merchants?"

"Shopkeepers." He didn't often admit it, but he knew the governor's father had been a butcher.

"They must be proud of you."

He gave a humourless laugh. Tonight, there wasn't much to feel proud of.

"Don't undervalue yourself," Tiarch said, a ray of light from the street outside glinting from her eyes. "*Never* undervalue yourself. That's advice from an expert."

He couldn't help reflecting on how much she must love the rebels on Thimish for demonstrating to the Innings how valuable she had been to them all these years.

"I was born in Tornabay," Tiarch said. "It's been home all my life, and I know it like my own hand. This neighbourhood we're in now is the oldest part of town."

Looking out the window, Joffrey saw they were passing one of the many angular little parks where pieces of forgotten statuary stood. The neighbourhood was a hodgepodge of old and new. All down the street, no two structures were the same height or style. It was as if they sprouted from the rubble whenever an old giant fell, as if the buildings fed on the remains of their own kind.

"The last decade has been good to Tornabay," Tiarch said. "We've had peace and prosperity, and the Innings took their tithes but left us to manage our own affairs. Fifteen years ago, the Inner Chain was a conquered satrapy. Now it is a profitable, self-sufficient territory. That kind of change doesn't happen by accident."

She spoke with an air of personal pride. Joffrey stayed silent, waiting to see where this was leading.

"And now it is all in jeopardy. You saw those Inning officers today: young, ambitious men, restless for command. These poor, doomed Adainas on Thimish have given them just the excuse they need. We're on the brink of a war—a ruinous and cruel war that will shatter our prosperity and take our independence with it."

Joffrey knew that she spoke for most of the merchants who had been at the banquet tonight. He was sitting at the junction of two sorts of power: the power of wealth and the power of force.

"Have you spoken to Admiral Talley?" he asked.

She shook her head. "I don't know him yet. I've just begun to know you."

It was important that she had turned to him. What he could do for her was less clear. "We can't ignore the challenge to Inning authority," he said. "We have to respond."

"Of course," she said. "But we don't have to over-respond. The event on Thimish is a flash in the pan, or would be if the Innings knew their islanders. The Adaina can't unite. They have nothing in common but their quarrels."

"They have united in the past," Joffrey pointed out.

"When they had an Ison and an Onan. But they can't have that while we have their Heir of Gilgen."

Joffrey said, "Does the name Harg Ismol mean anything to you?"

"No. Should it?"

"He's the ringleader of the rebels on Thimish. They are not entirely without leadership now."

The slow steps of the horses had carried them into the Gallowmarket, one of the many open squares that formed the commercial hubs of Tornabay. It was deserted except for a lone soldier patrolling. One side of the square was formed by the towering palace wall, and against it stood the wooden platform where criminals were executed. A row of six sharpened stakes stood there, symbols of justice. In the shadow of the stakes was the gate through which condemned prisoners passed from captivity to death. Ringing the square, the buildings looked down like witnesses, their faces blackened by the immortal soot of fires that had died generations ago.

Tiarch rapped on the ceiling of the carriage, and the driver brought it to a halt, parked in view of the execution stand. She sat looking out. "That's not bad news, actually," she said. "If it were just a general insurgency, putting it down would be like swatting mosquitoes. If they have a leader, at least there is someone to blame, someone to negotiate with, someone to defeat and execute."

"Admiral Talley will not negotiate," Joffrey said. He knew that with absolute certainty.

"Even for the hostages?" Tiarch asked.

Ordinarily, Joffrey would have said no. But knowing what he did, he hesitated. "Their policy is not to bargain," he said. "But he is in a bad spot. The rebels are holding his brother."

Tiarch gave a soft exclamation. "Damn them! How did they manage that?"

"I don't know."

"We've got to get the Adainas to stop this suicide. By hook or by net, we've got to make the problem go away."

Joffrey thought her use of "we" was interesting. But she was right; it was in his interest, as well. "Do you have a plan?" he said.

She smiled at him slowly, and he saw the iron woman her opponents spoke of. "Why, Joffrey, we need to bait a dainty hook."

By the time they finished talking, the rain had stopped. The night air was cool and misty when Joffrey left the carriage, and he stood watching it pull away and cross the rain-slick paving stones to enter the palace by the massive Gallowgate. He didn't think he was going to report the conversation to Admiral Talley. There were some things the Innings were better off not knowing.

❧

Dear Rachel, (Nathaway wrote)

I've received nothing from you in four weeks, so I don't know whether my letters are reaching you. Please write—you can't imagine how it would lift my spirits to hear from you.

You can tell Mother and everyone else that I am perfectly safe, in good hands, and no one ought to be the least bit worried about me.

His hand jerked and smeared the ink as if it were rebelling at being forced to write such a blatant lie. The truth was, he was racked with uncertainty about his situation. The enforced inactivity was bad enough; the boredom was sheer torture; but worst was having no control, no way of altering anything. For the first time in his life he felt utterly insignificant.

I am comfortably lodged in an inn in Harbourdown—a different one than where they kept me at first, more centrally located. They tell me I am in better quarters than the other prisoners at the Redoubt, but truth to tell I would gladly give up some comforts in exchange for company. I am alone almost all the time, and even when people do come by to give me food and so forth, they have no interest in conversing. The only exception is Harg Ismol, who visits from time to time for a chat, and I have really grown to look forward to our conversations, since they are the only relief from the tedium.

I wish I could inform you about what is going on, but I really have no idea, since they are very secretive. By the time you receive this, you may well know more about it than I.

A thump and raised voices interrupted him from somewhere downstairs, and he strained to make out the words, with no luck. This went on all day: footsteps, orders, muffled conversations. Things were going on all around him, and he didn't know what they were. He spent his time trying to string them together and form theories about what they meant. Now, he forced himself to return to his letter.

At every opportunity I advise them to bring this episode to a swift and peaceful conclusion. I think I have had some influence— at least on Harg, who listens carefully to what I have to say, and who seems to enjoy some credibility with these rough people. At least, they consult him on all matters concerning me.

I believe I've written about him before. Now I think I underestimated him at first, and assumed he was more unsophisticated than he is. It's true, he is totally uneducated—can barely read a simple text. But he has a sharp, enquiring mind, and grasps a concept faster than most law students I know. He is quite curious about Inning custom and law, and I have now read him the whole of the law twice over, with commentary.

It has given me a little uneasiness, whether I ought to be informing him, or whether it could be construed as collaboration. But in thinking it over, I have decided that this is exactly why I was sent to the Forsakens: to instruct the Adaina about Inning law, and encourage them to solve their differences through peaceful and constructive means. The circumstances are unanticipated, but the obligation remains the same. Besides, it makes the time go faster.

Harg has been quite eloquent to me about the perceived injustices that have led to this revolt. It may surprise you to learn that they don't, in fact, wish to throw off Inning rule; they simply wish to be accepted into our commonwealth with the same rights and autonomy that we have granted other territories. They wish to be independent from the Inner Chain, not ruled by the government in Tornabay. As soon as he understood that we are a government of laws, not of men, Harg asked why the Adaina could not have their own courts. It was an interesting question.

Nathaway stared at the wall, remembering the scene. Harg had been pacing restlessly, as if he found the small room intolerably claustrophobic. "You want to impose your law as if you could do our thinking for us," he argued. "We want to work it out for ourselves. How can we do that unless you let us have Adaina courts, Adaina judges?"

"You intention's admirable," Nathaway had said, "but there can't be separate courts for separate races. It undermines the whole concept, and isn't even to your advantage."

"Why not?" Harg said.

"If you define yourself as a separate group before the law, then you give others permission to define you that way as well, and to give you a different kind of treatment because of it. You must always think not 'What is just for Adainas,' but 'What is just for everyone, including Adainas.' Don't settle for anything less than universal justice. That is the only way to achieve a world where we're not cutting each other's throats."

At last Harg came to a halt, looking demandingly at Nathaway. "If we asked, would they grant us perfect equality under the law?"

"I don't know. But you won't get it if you *don't* ask."

Nathaway didn't put that in his letter. When Harg was in the room, he found it hard not to see the situation from their perspective; as soon as he was alone, he always wondered if he had crossed the line.

He resumed writing.

> In short, there is very little in their demands that could not be worked out if only some negotiations could be undertaken. There is a great deal about our system they simply don't understand, but assume the worst from having experienced only the roughest side of it, administered by arrogant and self-interested parties. If we approached them with a spirit of enlightened compromise, and offered amnesty in exchange for a cessation of hostilities and release of prisoners, then I think this crisis would be short-lived.

There, he thought, perhaps that would do some good, considering who was sure to read it. At least it couldn't do any harm. He was running out of paper, so he added some greetings to family and signed it. If Harg was as good as his word, it would get posted to Fluminos by the next available boat.

At that moment, Harg was sitting in the room directly below Nathaway's, trying to keep himself from speaking up.

The twenty-odd people around the long table in the private meeting room of Rosenry's tavern were supposed to be hammering out a set of demands for a delegation to present to the Innings in Tornabay. Out of necessity, most of the people in the room were Tornas. It wasn't the Adaina way to debate or make demands, and few of them were willing to sit and wrangle with a tableful of Tornas. So the politics of this rebellion was going to be a Torna creation, and therefore accommodationist.

Up to now, Harg had not been taking part in the discussions. But the demands were taking so long he was losing patience, so he had decided to stop in and see what the problem was.

Now he knew. They had spent the entire morning arguing over a demand he considered a complete side issue, the release of the Heir of Gilgen. Until the last week, Harg hadn't even known there was a living inheritor of that ancient title. Now, news of the man's captivity was distracting everyone from more important issues. The discussion today hadn't even touched on the demand Harg considered most critical, independent courts. The Tornas just couldn't see the importance of it. But then, they hadn't had the pleasure of being indoctrinated by the legal zealot in the upstairs bedroom.

The debate was lagging now. When Harg shifted restlessly in his seat, half a dozen people looked at him, hoping for something to energize the meeting.

Majlis Callow, the practical, middle-aged woman who usually spoke for the Torna merchants, said, "Harg, you're the only one who hasn't said anything. What's the matter, do you think this won't affect you?"

"It's not my decision," he forced himself to say. "You're the ones doing the demands."

"But we're asking your opinion."

He stared hard at the tabletop, then finally decided to give it to them, consequences be damned. "Well then, I say forget the Heir of Gilgen. Let them have him. We don't need him."

There was a silence. He had just confounded all their expectations; it was the Adainas who were supposed to care most about the traditional ways. At last Majlis said, "We can't have an Ison without the Heir of Gilgen."

"Then we won't have an Ison," Harg said. "We'll do fine without. Why should we want a leader chosen and controlled by the Grey Folk, anyway? We don't need the Lashnura meddling in our affairs."

When the Adainas learned what he had said, they would be scandalized, he thought. Well, so be it. He stood up. "I've got to get some fresh air," he said. "Go ahead, don't wait for me."

He passed out through the smoky common room of the tavern, which faced onto the Market Square. Out on the porch he paused, sheltered from the slow drizzle. He checked the harbour; Barko had not yet returned from his training run with the renamed *Industry*, now the *Ison Orin*. Harg wished he had gone with them in the *Pimpernel*. Out on the sea, it was just himself and his crew. The instant he stepped on shore, he was surrounded by expectations.

There was a story taking hold of everyone's minds. They all thought they knew where events were leading: upward to glory and the recapture of ancient power and unity. They had all forgotten the last time they had followed that story, to conquest and execution.

We need a new story, Harg thought. We need to break out of this old one, and do something unexpected.

He became aware of a commotion in one of the side streets. Shouts and catcalls echoed from between the buildings. As he watched, a rowdy mob of pirates erupted into the square, dragging a protesting figure toward the dock. They had wrapped a noose around their victim's neck, and were propelling him on at dagger point. They looked like they intended to string him up from the yard arm of one of the boats.

Exasperated, Harg left the shelter of the porch and set out after them. When he called out, they stopped. Harg had never seen the man they were harassing; he looked Torna, and his face was blanched with terror. His hands were tied behind him.

"What the fuck are you hoodlums doing?" Harg demanded.

"Executing a spy," said the ringleader of the mob. The man holding the noose gave it a jerk, making the victim stumble.

"Stop that!" Harg ordered. "How do you know he's a spy?"

"He came on a boat from Tornabay last night. He's been nosing around ever since, asking questions. He was asking about you, Harg."

On hearing Harg's name, the Torna turned to him with a desperate look of hope. "I'm not a spy!" he cried. "Yes, I'm from Tornabay. I never denied it. If you're Harg Ismol, I came here looking for you. But I'm not a Tiarch's-man, I'll swear it!"

"Give me that," Harg said to the man holding the rope. He took the cord and loosened the noose, lifting it from around the man's neck. "What are you, a pack of barbarians? Are you going to hang every foreigner who comes here? Blessed backside of Ashte, use your brains."

Seizing the Torna by the arm, he propelled him forcefully across the square toward the customs house, away from the mob.

"Thank you, sir, thank you!" the man babbled in relief.

"Shut up," Harg said. He didn't think the pirates would follow them, but he wanted to get inside before it occurred to them.

They mounted the customs house steps and got through the door without further incident. Harg shoved the captive into the room he had been using as a headquarters and closed the door. It was sparsely furnished with a few chairs. He left the Torna standing with his hands still tied, and sat in a chair facing him. "Now convince me I didn't just waste my time," he said.

The stranger was utterly forgettable: small and pale, with a head of curly black hair and a little moustache. Harg watched as the realization crossed the man's face that he wasn't yet out of trouble. He looked around the room, a little jittery, and cleared his throat. "My name is Jobin Dugall. I came on the merchant cog *Fairweather Friend*, from Tornabay. It was two weeks ago we first heard what happened here—the attack on the warships and the fort, the capture of Inning prisoners. I work for a merchant firm that has interests in the South Chain—"

"Which one?" Harg interrupted.

"Sorrell and Sons. Mr. Sorrell sent me here to see if a mutually advantageous arrangement might be possible."

Sorrell was well known as an importer of arms and munitions. Harg watched Jobin through narrowed eyes. "Your company would risk the Innings' justice by dealing with us?" he said.

Nervously, Jobin wet his lips. "No," he said. "The bargain we have in mind is to the Innings' advantage; it's just one they can't approach you about themselves, at least not directly. We are acting in the capacity of an intermediary."

"Do the Innings know you're here?"

Hesitantly, Jobin replied, "Not yet."

"All right," Harg said. "What's your offer?"

Jobin glanced at his bound hands. "Would you mind untying me?"

"Maybe. Tell me first how you knew my name."

"It's in all the reports, Harg Ismol is leader of the revolt."

Not terribly pleased to hear this, Harg nevertheless got up and untied the man's hands. Jobin rubbed his wrists and wriggled his fingers to restore the circulation. "Thank you," he said. "They said you were more civilized than the rest."

"Don't bank on it," Harg said.

Jobin looked up, studying him closely, so he turned his back and strolled behind his chair, finally turning around and leaning on its back. "Well?"

Drawing himself up straight, Jobin said, "You have some Inning prisoners."

"I know that."

"You have one in particular that I am authorized to offer a ransom for."

"What sort of ransom?" Harg didn't need to ask which prisoner; he could guess that.

Jobin named a handsome sum in money, but Harg was unimpressed, and showed it. "I have a limited range in which to negotiate," Jobin warned him.

"What makes you think we want money for him?" Harg said.

Taken aback, Jobin said, "What *do* you want?" Then, apprehensively, "Arms? That's a bigger risk for us."

"We have some demands," Harg said.

After a momentary pause, Jobin said, "The Innings won't negotiate political demands."

"I'm not talking to an Inning. Or am I?" He frowned at Jobin's studiously blank look. "You know, I believe you, that you're not a Tiarch's-man."

"It's true," said Jobin.

"Because I think you're Native Navy. You're working for Admiral Talley, aren't you?"

Jobin looked like he was poised to leap, but couldn't decide which direction. He was watching Harg's face for some clue. At last he looked down. "You're right, in a way," he said. "I *was* in the navy. I resigned a few weeks ago, and went to work for Mr. Sorrell."

"Why did you resign?" Harg asked.

Jobin's face flushed; it was obviously a sore point. Reluctantly, he said, "I was . . . encouraged to. Otherwise, I'd be demoted for something that wasn't my fault. The Tornabay command is in total turmoil. Everyone knows the occupation's being mishandled, and it's not always the right heads rolling for it."

"Is Talley there yet?"

"Yes," Jobin said with a mix of fear and resentment that rang true.

"The Southern Squadron?"

"Not all of it, yet. Only three ships."

"Who's in charge of it?"

"An Inning, Commodore Tenniel."

"I thought the admiral was going to nativize the officer corps."

"It was all just talk," Jobin said bitterly. "There was a Torna named Joffrey in charge of the Northern Squadron for a little while. Now he's out, and the admiral's in charge himself."

"I was wondering why they hadn't moved."

"Complete organizational breakdown, that's why," Jobin said.

"Some things never change," Harg said with a grim smile. "What do they know about us?"

"I wasn't in a position to know," Jobin said. "All I know is, the admiral's hot as a firesnake. He's taking it personally, they say."

Harg pondered this. He couldn't imagine Admiral Talley being less than professional. Perhaps his brother's captivity made things different. "Do you know the admiral?" he asked.

"No," Jobin said. "Don't you?"

Harg shook his head.

Jobin was watching him curiously. When their eyes met, Jobin said, "You *were* in the navy?"

"That doesn't mean I hobnobbed with the admiral," Harg said drily. "He didn't exactly invite us round for tea. I met him once, the day I resigned."

"Lucky you," Jobin said.

Harg wasn't yet sure whether Jobin was what he said. One thing he strongly suspected, though: if he spoke to Jobin, there would be ears listening on the other end, perhaps important ones. He had to take the risk—very, very cautiously.

"You said Mr. Sorrell was willing to act as go-between," he said.

"What do you have in mind?" Jobin said carefully.

"A peaceful resolution," Harg said, "if the Innings want it. But they'll have to listen to us."

The fact that Jobin didn't answer at once increased Harg's impression that the man was more than just a messenger. Messengers didn't have to think about their answers.

"There are people in Tornabay willing to listen to you," Jobin said at last, slowly. "War's not good for everyone's business."

"We want to send a delegation with a list of demands."

"What sort of demands?"

Harg didn't want to admit that they were still wrangling over the demands. He wanted Jobin to think they were firm and united. So he said, "We want to be an independent territory under the Empire, with full political rights. That means our own civilian governor, with power equal to Tiarch's. We want independent courts with Adaina judges. We want to be policed by our own squadron of the Native Navy, with Adaina officers. We want a promise of full citizenship rights. And we don't want to pay tariffs on our goods."

Jobin looked thoroughly taken aback. Harg said, "Why, what did you expect us to want—permission to go naked and pound drums?"

"They're ambitious demands," Jobin said at last.

"We're ambitious people."

"I can see that." He was obviously still trying to reconfigure his expectations. "And what about you? Where do you fit in this independent territory?"

The question was typical of the mindset of Tornabay, where corruption was the scaffolding on which everything was erected. Harg's first reaction was disgust at the implication that he was doing this for personal gain. But he caught himself before expressing it, because he was curious to know what Jobin would offer. "That's not up to me," he said.

"Who is it up to?" When Harg didn't answer at once, Jobin said, "The Heir of Gilgen?"

It was the closest anyone had come to asking point blank what his ambitions were. Scowling at Jobin, Harg said, "Did I say the word 'Ison'?"

"No, you said 'governor.' I was wondering if it was a euphemism."

The fact was, no one outside this room was saying "governor." They were all saying "Ison." It really *wasn't* up to Harg. That was his dilemma. What he wanted and what the Adaina wanted were not always the same.

"You know that Tiarch has the Heir of Gilgen?" Jobin said.

"We'd heard that," Harg said.

"You may not know that the Innings are going to take over custody of him. There has been talk of quietly getting rid of him for good."

Harg shook his head. "They'd be idiots to do that. There would be no surer way of making the Outer Chains explode into rebellion."

"From the Inning point of view, it would be eliminating one festering source of coalition."

Harg wasn't sure where Jobin was going with this, but he wasn't following.

"You're not concerned? Even as a fellow Yoran?" Jobin said.

"What do you mean?"

"Yora's not that big. You surely knew him."

"Knew who?"

"The Heir of Gilgen. Goran, son of Listor. He called himself Goth Batra, I think."

Harg felt like a shell had just detonated in his face. For a moment he was blinded, staring at Jobin without seeing him. "*Goth* is the Heir of Gilgen?" he said. His voice sounded distant, someone else's.

"You didn't know?" Jobin looked surprised in turn.

Goth was a prisoner of Tiarch. It was Goth's life that was a variable in the cruel political calculus of the Inning occupation. It was not the Heir of Gilgen, it was the person Harg cared for more than any human being alive.

Jobin had already seen how staggered he was by the news. Instinctively, Harg knew he had to get out before he gave anything else away, as he was sure to do. Without another word, he went to the door and left the room. Out in the hall, a Torna clerk who had been doing paperwork for him was passing by, but paused, arrested by Harg's expression.

"Go get someone to take charge of the man in this room," Harg said. "He's a spy, a dangerous one. I don't want him talking with anyone. Understand?"

"Yes, Captain," the clerk said.

Harg left the customs house by the back door. He didn't want anyone to see him or ask questions. The whole world had rearranged around him. He had to talk to someone from Yora.

He headed uphill fast, toward the dhotamar's house. When he knocked on the door, it was opened by the pretty, pregnant Adaina woman. "Captain Harg," she said, surprised. "Come in."

"Is Tway here?" he asked.

"Yes, I'll get her."

He stepped in warily, glad to see that Spaeth was nowhere in sight. He couldn't face her just yet. Before the woman could call out for Tway, she came into the room, drying her hands on a towel. "Harg!" she exclaimed. "What—"

"Is there a place we can talk? Privately?"

She gestured him to follow her out into the back yard. It was a snug little brick enclosure, entirely surrounded by walls, and shaded by a large oak tree. Once the back door was shut, Tway said in a low voice, "What is it? You look like someone stepped on your grave."

And so he told her. She was surprised all right, but nowhere near as blindsided as he had been. In fact, she shook her head and said, "This sure explains a lot."

"Where he was, for one thing," Harg said. "Tway, how could Tiarch's people walk in and carry him off without anyone in Yorabay noticing?"

"It must have been those lead prospectors," she said. "They weren't looking for lead at all, they were looking for him."

"And now Tiarch and Talley are quarrelling over who gets to execute him first."

"They wouldn't dare," Tway said firmly.

He tried to laugh at her certainty, but it came out sounding anguished. She put a hand on his arm, as if she had just worked out what this meant for him. "Harg, this means that you—"

"It means I have to figure out what to do," he said. He felt as if he were in a dream where he had to run and his legs wouldn't work.

"What's to figure out?" she said. "We've got to help him."

Maybe it was that simple, he thought. Maybe there really was no nuance in the situation. Whatever the risk, whatever the sacrifice, they just had to help him. "How?" he said.

"What do you mean, 'how'? You've got four warships, you've got prisoners, you've got half the South Chain behind you!"

And none of it would make the slightest difference, he knew. Not against an implacable empire that refused to bargain. Goth's only hope lay in ruse and subterfuge. He needed corruption, treachery, and a daring jailbreak. It couldn't be done from the South Chain. It could only be done from Tornabay. Harg shook his head. "I can't just abandon what I've started here and run off to do something personal."

"Harg, what makes you think this is personal? Everyone's been telling you to pay attention to this for a week."

He realized that she was thinking "Heir of Gilgen" while he was thinking "Goth." "It's personal because I wouldn't do it otherwise," he said. "I don't give a rip about the Heir of Gilgen. I give a whole lot of rips about Goth."

At that, she put her arms around him and hugged him close. He felt like she was infusing him with her strength. When she drew back he kept his hands on her shoulders. "Tway, do you think Spaeth knew?" he said.

She glanced back at the house. "Not unless she's a lot better liar than I think she is."

So Goth had deceived her, too. "How could he hide it from us?" Harg said. "This wasn't a little white lie, Tway. It was a great big lie."

"Harg, you don't know enough to blame him," Tway said. "Let it go. Just forgive him."

But can I forgive him? Harg wondered. He couldn't know until he could face him. Forgiveness was not something that could be done in the abstract, from a distance. It had to be reciprocal. Until they could face one another, there was going to be unfinished business between them.

He could think of nothing else till this was resolved. No longer was he fighting a war about occupation or independence. It had become personal.

SPIDERWEBS
OF IRON

Heir of Gilgen. Heir of Gilgen. The words pounded in Spaeth's brain as she sat staring out the rain-pebbled window of Anit's house.

During daylight hours, she had been spending time in the abandoned upstairs rooms of the building where Anit lived, for it suited her darkening mood. The windows there were mostly boarded over, so that very little light leaked in to illuminate the litter of broken beams and pigeon droppings. For the past week, direct sunlight had sent slivers of pain into her eyes and made her skin blister like poison ivy.

She had been up there when Harg had arrived, and the sound of his voice had drawn her irresistibly to the nearest empty window to listen while he spoke to Tway in the yard below. And so she had learned of Goth's location, and the identity he had hidden from her. But the most shocking thing she had learned from Harg was that it was possible to be angry at Goth. Now she felt, for the first time, a sense of separation from her creator. He had made her subject to the cruel compulsion of dhota, then gone off to Tornabay, abandoning her. She could feel Harg's resentment spreading like a dangerous contagion to her own heart.

There was not the slightest doubt in her mind what she had to do. She was only waiting till it was a bit darker to leave the house.

By the gloomy light, she examined her hands. The fingers were black as far as the second knuckle. Her palms had gone dark grey, and unwholesome streaks ran up her wrists. She pulled on the long gloves she had found to hide her hands—from her own sight as well as others'. When she looked up into a small mirror on the wall, she glimpsed behind her own reflection a catlike shadow, her constant companion.

"I have to find him," she said quietly.

"Yes," Ridwit said. "You are ready."

"Will you help me?"

"I will," the cat said. "Trust me."

Spaeth reached under the chair where she had secreted the bag holding Goth's bowl and knife, and a cloak the colour of storm clouds, stolen from Lorin's room. No one was there to see her leave; Anit was asleep, Lorin was out shopping, and Tway had disappeared somewhere after Harg's departure. Drawing the hood over her head, Spaeth slipped out the front door. The rain blew into her face, but she paid no attention. Gloomy as the waning day, she walked down the windswept street.

Heir of Gilgen, Heir of Gilgen, the breakers thrummed along the shore. She could not get it from her mind.

"You humans are so impatient," the panther said, padding soundless at her side. Her black coat glistened with rain.

"Have you seen my hands?" Spaeth said.

"You have plenty of time yet," Ridwit drawled. "It has to reach your heart, you know."

Ahead lay the pier where the cog *Fairweather Friend* was tied. The longshoremen were working in the rain, loading cargo for Tornabay. A man in a raincoat and broad-brimmed hat was supervising the work. Spaeth approached him.

He paid no attention till she came close enough that he could see the silver hair beneath her hood. Then, "Blessed guardians!" he exclaimed. His round face and moustache had a kindly look, but he was Torna, and obviously uncomfortable with her identity. Spaeth laid a hand on the panther's back, feeling the sharp shoulder bones beneath the fur. It gave her courage.

"Will you take a passenger, Captain?" she asked.

"That depends, lass. Where are you bound?"

"To Tornabay."

He frowned. "Not many of your kind there. Why do you want to go?"

"I won't ask your business if you don't ask mine."

He glanced uneasily up the wharf. "Don't you have a bandhota?"

"No," she said.

"Then who's going to pay your passage?"

It had not occurred to her that he would ask for payment. She had never paid for anything in her life. She didn't even know how people got money.

Reading her silence, the captain shifted closer and lowered his voice. "There's a way you could pay me."

Fearing he was going to ask for dhota, she said sharply, "What?"

"Don't be alarmed. All I want is a pint of your blood. The real article sells for a good price in Tornabay."

"Blood? It's worthless alone."

"Ah, but they don't know that, do they? It's been a generation since most of them saw a dhotamar."

There was something deeply distasteful about the bargain. Spaeth's hand fell to Ridwit's back, and clenched on the loose neck fur. Ridwit looked up at her assessingly. "Squeamish?" she said.

Spaeth drew a deep breath. If these were the dirty waters she would have to swim in, then better to dive than dabble. "All right," she said. "You can have your blood. Where's a knife?"

"No, no, give it to me when we arrive," he said. "It has to be fresh, you know."

A feeling of contempt for him, for herself, for the whole world pressed round her like a choking cloud. She stepped aboard the boat, dragging part of the dark with her. She glanced back at the captain before going below, and saw him looking after her with an expression of foreboding.

It gave her a surging sense of power.

"He feared me, Ridwit," she said when they were below deck. "He looked like a cold wind had blown through him."

The cat grinned. "Nice, isn't it?"

Spaeth knelt, so that her face was level with Ridwit's amber eyes.

"The Lashnura are flawed, Ridwit. We are not fit guardians for the isles."

"You're right," the panther said.

The lamp cast a sickly yellow glow across Goth's face, but he did not notice it. He lay with his eyes closed, longing for sleep.

He was losing his battle to stay out of the black pit. Hunger gnawed at him constantly, but food had turned sickening. His nerves were in a state of hyper-exhaustion. Everything hurt, even trivial things. Even staring at the wall, because he had to be inside himself.

It did no good to regret the foolishness that had brought him to this state. He had begun to give dhota too long ago, when he was sure of his ability to conquer himself. By steeping himself in many, he had thought no one could capture him. He could achieve compassion and detachment at once—detachment from the individual and commitment to the common essence of humanity. In that state of engaged disengagement, he had hoped to experience the seed of the divine in them all.

It had proved far different in practice. No matter how often he gave dhota, there were always individuals who had a special hold on him, who tempted him into particular rather than generic love. That weakness had trapped him into causing pain instead of curing it. And now he was paying the price.

The blackness inside his eyelids swirled and shifted, forming a scene, and he realized he had slipped through the fabric of reality without leaving his self behind. He stood at the top of Mount Embo and saw all the Forsakens below him, transformed. A mist from the east was covering the islands one by one, blotting out their colour, dulling the sparkle of the waves. The sea became a thick, reeking swamp, and the vapours that rose smelled of despair.

"You see what your world has become," a voice said.

It came from below him. He looked down at the cinders beneath his feet. He could see through them, into the bowels of the mountain. A light was there: a dazzling, dangerous glow that churned and slithered, chained by the waning power of mora. A narrow head rose from the lava nest, looking at him with jewelled eyes.

"You need us," the firesnake said. It was the only vivid thing left in the world. Goth stared, mesmerized by its beauty and danger, his pain momentarily gone.

"You need the Mundua," it said. "We can free you."

"No," Goth said, as he had been taught.

"If you free us," the firesnake said.

He saw the new world he could create: one that glistened with fire and gold, and roared with cleansing heat. The moral fetor that was Tornabay could be cauterized from the world.

"No," he said.

"Fool," the firesnake answered. "We will be free without you, then."

Something was shaking him. He forced his eyes open, onto the hatefully familiar little room in Tornabay palace. A soldier stood at his bedside.

"You are to come with us," the man said too loudly. He was uncomfortable with his task.

Goth sat up, blinking, trying to collect the scattered pieces of his mind and lock them up in his body again. As he rose, the ground quivered under his feet. He put a hand on the stone doorjamb and said, "Quiet." The rumbling faded.

The corridors of the palace were quiet; it was just past daybreak. The two soldiers escorting him set a fast pace, heading into a part of the building Goth had not entered up to now. It had been recently remodelled. The dark, musty corridors had been broadened, lightened, and furnished; the archaic Torna motifs had been stripped from the walls; the thick, stocky pillars had been replaced with shapely, fluted columns; all irregularities had been smoothed out and made symmetrical. It was a more Inning place now. Goth felt the lid of the safe box-world of logic close over him. Here, everything was shaped like a diagram. These straight lines and perfect circles would never admit a breath of duality or serendipity. Dream and luck were locked outside. Here, there was only one answer for every question.

They ushered him into a long, high-ceilinged room paneled in walnut. One of the walls was pierced by tall, arched windows looking out onto an open square. The main part of the room was filled with rows of empty wooden benches facing a raised dais with a towering lectern and adjoining seats. In the wall behind the altar-like stage was a circular window with leaded panes arranged so as to converge in the centre, like a spider's web.

The board floor made the soldiers' synchronized footsteps loud as they led Goth down the central aisle to a railing at the front of the room. A single Inning—a small, neat man in spectacles—was sitting there at a clerk's desk, reading some papers. One of the soldiers said, "Sir!" to attract his attention.

The Inning jotted a note on one of his papers, then looked up. Behind the glasses, his eyes were ice-blue. He said, "Wait outside, please." The soldiers saluted and left.

When the door had boomed shut at the other end of the room, the Inning said, "I am Admiral Corbin Talley."

"I am—" Goth paused for a second, uncertain who he was in this setting. "Goran son of Listor," he finished.

The admiral had noticed his hesitation. Looking at the man, Goth doubted there was much he didn't notice. The mora that radiated from him was of piercing intelligence and force of will. But there were complex undercurrents, intriguingly hidden. The feeling was almost tactile: here was an intense nature barricaded behind walls of frigid reserve.

"You had an Inning education, I am told," Talley said, still appraising him.

"Yes. Long ago."

"Then you know what this place is."

"Your temple of justice."

"Well put. This is the heart of Inning, and all our acts and institutions radiate out from here. We are a lexarchy: a government not of kings or parliaments, but of laws. In our land, courts are the ultimate authority. It is this system which will be our greatest gift to your people, when the proper time has come."

"A cruel gift," Goth said, looking at the spiderweb window.

"A demanding gift," Talley corrected. "A gift which frees men to be responsible for their own actions, their own destinies. Inning law recognizes no mysterious forces, no fates, no gods. The cleverest and most industrious create their own good fortune. The violent and heedless suffer the consequences. We ourselves make whatever meaning there is in our lives."

"And you find this freeing?" Goth asked. "What if the wind blows up and sinks your fleet tomorrow—where will you turn?"

"It will be my own fault for not having foreseen such an event. I will have no gods to blame, but I also will not have to rely upon gods to set it right. I have the power to rectify all wrongs."

"Then you have taken on a heavy burden." In the silence that followed, Goth felt the mountain coiled in impotent fury beneath his feet. It took more than law to bind some forces, and the people who became their tools.

Talley rose and turned around to face the judge's tall pulpit, his hands clasped behind him. "Of course," he said, "I speak of ideals. The reality is rather different."

He walked over to the railed-in box where witnesses stood to give testimony, and turned to face Goth. "You called this room a temple. You were right, of course. Here is where we have our priests and robes and ritual. We put our high shaman up there on that throne, and intone our liturgy. It's all a grand masque, a performance to fool the ignorant into awe. It's better than force at keeping the peace, and cheaper. But if I had my way, I would strip off all the rigmarole and bare it down to its abstract essence."

"What essence is that?" Goth asked.

"Justice. The provable, objective, empirical principle of justice."

His face was like a carving—severe, planar. "It is a principle, not a reality," he continued. "An ethical principle so demanding, so rigorous, that the corrupt humans on this earth can scarcely comprehend it, much less frame their lives by it."

"I do not believe we are all so corrupt," Goth said.

Talley gave him a searching look. "You do not know as much about the race as I, then."

Goth half-smiled at the hubris of this, but it was a bitter smile. Perhaps the man was right, and a long lifetime spent steeping himself in other humans had produced no knowledge at all. He said, "But if you are right, and we are all corrupt, then how can we presume to judge one another?"

"That," said Talley, "is the central lie all the trappings of law were created to hide. If I could find just one genuinely good man in this world, then I could rip down all this mummery, burn the very courts; they would no longer be necessary. But that day will not come. There are no good men. Many are called good, but they all have some taint of pride, or self-indulgence—elementary faults I even deny myself. They told me you were a good man."

He had come face to face with Goth, only the rail between them. His eyes held such a demanding expectation that Goth felt dwarfed. Talley went on, "You have been represented to me as a man who can create just kings and topple pretenders; who can see into hearts and declare who is fit to lead. You can sort the deserving from the merely ambitious, the false from the sincere. You can assay the gold in men's hearts, and refine them into saints."

Goth could no longer stand the look in those eyes, the sense that he was facing a hunger that almost matched his own. "I fear I must disappoint you," he said, looking away.

"Don't worry, I'm used to it," Talley said with a brittle, belittling humour.

Slowly, Goth said, "Your belief is in justice. Ours is in a thing called mora. Our teachings hold that in life, a person accumulates pain in his or her soul. Every harm we have suffered is still with us in some way. The scars make us stiff and unsupple; they cut off ways of moving and acting that we might otherwise be capable of."

"What does this have to do—"

"Let me finish. An unhealed person is a dangerous thing. The unhealed are susceptible to hatred and unreason; they are not truly free. The Adaina call the forces of imbalance the Mundua and Ashwin. However you think of them, they are real. They are always on the thresholds of our minds, waiting to seize control through the inroads of our pain and disappointment. That is why dhota exists: not just to cure, but to keep the forces of imbalance powerless, by robbing them of human collaborators.

"Ordinarily, an unhealed person is only a danger within his or her sphere. But a person with stature, someone fit to lead, affects us all. An unhealed leader becomes a terrible node of imbalance, a tool to destroy not just himself, but the world.

"That is why we believe leaders must pass through dhota-nur. Just as dhota erases present pains, so dhota-nur strips from a person's soul all the scars that could be inroads of imbalance. An Ison must be released from the bondage of pain. He or she must become a truly free being."

Talley studied him in silence for several moments. At last he said, "If what you say were true—if there were a magic ritual to free a leader from evil—then it would be a pernicious thing. A leader who cannot bear to do small evils in order to bring about great goods is impotent."

Frowning, Goth said, "That can be true. But acts are neutral things; they are never intrinsically wrong, in all cases. There are only acts driven by pain and those that are not."

With a slight, cold smile, Talley said, "Let me show you something." He opened the gate in the rail between them and gestured Goth to follow him to the window. Outside lay an open market square, deserted except for a few figures hurrying through the hazy air. "Down there," Talley pointed.

Below them lay a raised wooden platform. Goth's fingers tightened on the windowsill when he saw that two sharpened stakes stood upright on the execution stage, each with a naked human body impaled on it. The stakes had been thrust right through the men's bodies, up their spines. One of them hung limp and senseless, the tip of the stake protruding from the skin at his neck. But the other one was moving. As Goth watched, the victim's head rolled back, his mouth stretched open in unendurable agony.

"They are rebels," Talley said in a calm, detached voice. "They threw a bomb into a police station south of here, on Grora. We tried and spitted them yesterday, as an example. You can see, one is still alive. Our technicians can insert the stake in such a way that no vital organs are harmed. The poor devils can last for days."

Goth had never before witnessed such an extremity of pain, so deliberately inflicted. The compulsion to heal was so strong, his whole body shook with it.

His heart was racing. He pressed his hands against the window glass, longing to get through.

"It gives no one pleasure to see such a sight," Talley was saying at his side, "but justice must be done, and occasionally it must be cruel and degrading, so as to prevent the fools from idealizing martyrdom. It is one of those regrettable but necessary acts of leadership."

Goth scarcely heard him. All his attention was focused on the man below. Madly, he thought of breaking the window to get to him. But no. To give dhota to a dying man would be fatal. What a joyous death it would be. Unable to speak, he sank to the floor, eyes closed, hands over his ears, trying to blot out the sight. He wanted to sob with denied desire.

Whatever the admiral was saying, Goth heard none of it as he grappled with himself, trying to regain control. "Medic!" he heard Talley calling out, and soon another man was kneeling beside him. There was a sharp, phantom pain in his forearm, where the dhota knife would cut. The Innings would never give him a knife.

When he managed to look up again, the doctor was closing a leather case, and took his wrist to feel the pulse. Finding it satisfactory, the man nodded to the admiral and left. Talley was watching with a curious but remote expression. Goth stared back into those keen blue eyes with a dawning horror. "You are responsible for that," he said, gesturing to the window, not daring to look again. "To inflict such suffering puts a terrible burden on the soul."

With a mechanical smile, Talley said, "Then it's just as well that the nation has men whose souls are not overburdened with goodness." He looked out the window again; his refined features did not change at the sight. He looked like his heart had never warmed to compassion. "Inning law is even-handed but inexorable," he said. "If you drop a china dish, it will break. If you break the law, you will suffer. It is very simple."

What kind of man would perform the inner surgery it must have taken to make himself capable of such acts? The thought chilled Goth's spirits. Simultaneously, he had the curious realization that his own pain was gone from inside him. The air seemed clearer; the sun burned with a more piercing light. He felt giddy with relief.

"Your justice will not work here," he said.

"It works everywhere," Talley said.

"Threats of punishment are good only against people who are motivated by self-interest," Goth said.

"That includes everyone but deluded fanatics."

"What about people who simply believe in something more important than themselves?"

"As I said," Talley gave a cold smile, "deluded fanatics."

Perhaps it was the clear light, penetrating from truth to deeper truth. Goth gathered his legs under him and rose to face the Inning. He could hear a roaring in his ears, as of a powerful wind. He felt it swell inside him, and walked forward till he faced Talley like a cross-examiner. "You cannot dismiss me that easily," he said. "I challenge everything you think is true. You cannot explain me away, Admiral, nor mock me into insignificance. I defy your categories. That is why you have no power over me."

Talley's face was unyielding. "Only I *do* have power over you," he said softly. "Look at your arm."

Goth looked down and saw in his forearm a milky sliver, like a broad toothpick, just under the skin.

"You didn't even notice when the doctor inserted it, did you?" Talley said.

Wordless, Goth looked up from his arm to Talley's face.

"It is a drug," the admiral said. "I see it has taken effect."

Goth stepped back, his heart labouring. "What will it do to me?" he asked faintly.

"We call it achra. I cannot tell you what it will do. They say it gives each man his heart's desire. All I can tell you surely is that when you wake up tomorrow morning, you will want it again. You will want it more than anything you have ever wanted in life. And I will give it to you, again and again till you have no will left. You will do anything I ask of you."

He turned to the door and called for the guards. "These gentlemen will take you back to your quarters now. Enjoy yourself."

"How could you do this to me?" Goth whispered through a dry, constricting throat.

"I told you we were all corrupt," Talley said calmly. "It is your own fault for not believing me."

As the soldiers were leading Goth away down the aisle of the temple of justice, he looked back over his shoulder and saw that Talley had turned around to face the empty judge's bench, his hands clasped behind him like a prisoner's.

13
CITY OF CROOKED WAYS

Harg stood at the *Ripplewill*'s prow, scanning the eastern horizon. Out there somewhere was the *Fairweather Friend*, hidden by distance and the coming dusk. In a night and a day of skimming the trade lanes they had seen no sign of her. They had lost time stopping in Port Fair to ask after her, only to find that the cog had not been seen. But they had picked up rumours that an embargo was in the offing, and navy ships might already be patrolling to cut off trade to the South Chain. The news had forced them to alter their route, which would cost even more time. The chances of catching up with Spaeth were growing slimmer.

He couldn't let her go to Tornabay. The city would eat her alive. She would never survive. *Damn these Lashnurai*, he thought to himself. *How did I end up responsible for them?*

The two Grey Folk in his life had forced his hand. Spaeth's reckless flight from Harbourdown had thrown all his careful thinking into disarray, and forced him to set out before he was ready. He had wanted to have a plan to win Goth's freedom. He had wanted to make contact with an Adaina underground, or a corrupt official in Tiarch's notoriously bribable government, or even that old standby, a disgruntled worker ready to betray his employer for revenge and profit. Now he would just have to improvise on the spot.

Torr was sitting in the cockpit smoking a pipe when Harg came astern to join him. Behind them, the coppery sun was setting past Romm, the last island of the South Chain.

"*Ripplewill's* going as fast as she can," Torr said before Harg could ask. "Maybe you should try talking to the wind."

Harg settled down beside him. He had chosen the *Ripplewill* because she was a fast boat, and Torr knew how to be inconspicuous. It was important to sneak into Tornabay without so much as a wake. But it had severely limited the number of people he could bring. Barko had been needed in Harbourdown to train all the raw recruits. Instead, Harg had brought two Yorans he could trust—Tway, who would hunt for Spaeth like a bloodhound, and Gill, who had arrived on Thimish just the week before. He was a sensible, mature man, but inexperienced at fighting, if it should come to that. And then Calpe had volunteered, and Harg had said yes for all the wrong reasons. Now he wished he had brought one of his old navy comrades instead—not because he didn't trust Calpe, but because he didn't trust himself around her.

The last two people on board were their bargaining chips: Nathaway Talley and the Torna turncoat, Jobin Dugall. Jobin was the only Tornabay contact they had. There was no choice but to trust him until they could find a more savoury ally.

Tway emerged from the galley. "Your supper's ready, Torr. Want me to take the helm?"

Torr tapped out his pipe and rose to go below. Tway settled down on his seat. For a while she was silent, looking at the arch of evening sky above them. Then, quietly, she said, "I caught Jobin talking to your Inning."

"Did you hear what they were saying?"

"No, they broke off when they saw me."

The *Ripplewill* was too small to conveniently devote a cabin to keeping the hostage separate, so while they were still in the South Chain Harg had given him the run of the ship in exchange for a promise not to make a break for it. This was the consequence.

"Do you trust that Torna?" Tway asked.

"I trust him to act in his own best interest," Harg said.

"Yes, but what's that?"

Calpe emerged from below and walked toward the bow. Harg watched as she clasped her hands over her head and stretched, clean limbs flexing. When they had set out, her husband Torin had clapped Harg on the back and told him to look out for her. There had been a worried awareness in his eyes. Now she unpinned her hair and shook it, gleaming, in the wind. Her skin was a golden brown. At Harg's side, Tway tweaked the tiller, making *Ripplewill* tilt so that

Calpe lost her balance and had to grasp for a stay.

"I think I'll grow a beard," Harg said thoughtfully, running a hand over his chin.

Tway gave him an appraising look. "Good idea."

"Why, you think my face isn't good enough as it is?"

"No. I think your face might be dangerous to you as it is."

That night and all the next day they sailed on east, out of sight of land, far beyond the range of any Inning patrol boats. At some place in the wide sea—only Torr and the stars knew where—they turned almost due north. After a day, hills as gold as a cat's eye rose slowly before them, and they came to Rona, the garden isle. The fields were sown in strips and whorls, patch overlapping patch as far as the eye could see. "Look, they have drawn pictures on the land with plants!" Tway said. Torr knowingly explained that the patterns had to do with ownership rather than art.

The Inner Chain had been in Inning hands for sixty years, but it still seemed like the heart of the isles. They put in at Larbot for water and news, and gazed at the castle where Barrow had held a poisoned feast for his brother's followers. Then it was on to the tumbled rock cliffs of Tirol, covered with a shaggy growth of pine and maple. This was the wild, rocky isle where Larse had found the door to the land of death, and made a bargain with the king who dwelt inside. In the afternoon of the fifth day they rounded Tirol's shores and saw the low blue lines of Rusk in the west, and the bay of Sandhaven. They lined the deck to gaze at the site where Ison Orin's fleet had made its last stand against the Innings.

The next day they came to Tornabay. They knew where Mount Embo lay long before they drew near, for a towering, flat-topped cloud stood motionless over the mountain's peak. All morning the cone-shaped mountain rose higher. When they came into the strait between Embo and the jagged cliffs of Loth, they found a yellow haze hanging over the water, and the day darkened under the ashen cloud.

Their eyes smarted as they neared the great harbour. In the Outbay they passed three warships from the Southern Squadron. By now, their hostage was securely locked in the aft cabin. As they nosed into the crowded inner bay, thick with the shadowy shapes of other boats, Harg peered anxiously through the murk for any sign of *Fairweather Friend*.

Their plan was to stop at the dock long enough for a few of them to debark; then Torr would take the *Ripplewill* back to the Outbay to wait with the hostage till he saw a signal from his companions on shore. But as they neared one of the long-fingered docks, a rowboat drew up to them. An official-looking figure stood and summoned the *Ripplewill* to stop.

Leaning over the gunwale, Torr blinked to see who spoke. The oarsmen had cloths tied over their faces. Even the Torna in charge held a linen handkerchief to his nose.

"Customs!" the man called. "You cannot land until you have declared your cargo. I need to come on board."

"Let me land my passengers first," Torr said.

"If you have passengers, they must register with Immigrations."

"Since when?" Torr objected.

"It was always the law."

There was nothing they wanted less than a curious Torna bureaucrat on board, but Jobin whispered, "Don't argue!"

The customs man had sheaves of papers under his arm and a pocketful of pencils. The exertion of clambering across made him cough hoarsely.

"This normal weather here?" Torr asked.

The Torna shook his head. "The mountain has been smoking for a week," he said. "Can we go below?"

For an instant the captain hesitated, then led the way below to the main cabin. The official, a little disgruntled at not being shown to the privacy of the aft cabin, set himself up to write on the end of a cask.

"Ship's name?"

"*Ripplewill*."

"Commander's name?"

"Torr Bolgin."

"Port of origin?"

"Torbert of Grora."

"Purpose in coming here?"

"Trade."

Torr told his lies like a professional. The others listened silently. After endless questions about the origins and values of his lading, the Torna handed the paper over for a signature and said, "The landing tax is eight decamedes."

"That's robbery!" Torr protested.

"It's the law."

Torr said, "My strongbox is in the aft cabin. I'll go fetch it."

"Never mind, Torr, I have some money," Harg spoke up. The others took the hint and searched their pockets to put together the required sum. The official was counting the coins when he suddenly stopped to scrutinize one.

"A Rothur coin," he said, holding it up. "Where did you get this?"

Shrugging, Torr said, "They're common in the South Chain."

"Have you been doing business with the South Chain?"

"Of course. Everyone on Grora does."

"Know anything about the situation on Thimish?"

"I don't trade there. They're a pack of pirates," Torr said.

"It's that old outlaw, Holby Dorn, stirring things up again," Tway piped up. "The isles would be well rid of him."

The Torna gathered his papers into a neat pile. "Captain, I can't give you leave to dock until I have notified the military. They may want to interview you." He turned briskly to the companion way.

"A word with you, sir," Jobin said quickly, and followed him up onto deck. Harg watched them go, but didn't interfere; he thought he knew what Jobin was up to.

"What do we do now?" Tway whispered.

"Bluff it out," Torr said. "We're all from Grora, and we've been on a trading run to Lashnish. You four are here to purchase dry goods to take home. Answer only what they ask; don't volunteer any information."

The hatchway darkened as Jobin leaned back in. "It's all right," he said. "We can land now."

"Thanks, Jobin," said Harg. "How much do we owe you?"

"What? Oh, never mind. I was glad to take care of it."

As they neared the dock, Jobin drew close to Harg. "Staying out of the Innings' way is going to be harder than I thought. It will be best if you stay close to me. I can take you to a safe house."

"What's wrong with a room at a tavern?" Harg said.

"Tiarch's spies are everywhere. You're safer in a private place."

Harg would have declined if he had known of a better alternative. He didn't assume Jobin's motives coincided with his own, but he sensed that the man's goal was more complex than simple treachery. Jobin wanted something from them. Playing along was the only way to find out what it was.

Harg, Gill, Calpe, Tway, and Jobin debarked on a narrow wharf-side path. Jobin led the way down a twisted lane that issued into a clay-paved plaza. "Harbourmarket," he said in terse explanation. Tall brick-and-beam buildings jostled each other around the open square, none of them quite vertical. In the upper stories, ornately carved shutters were closed against the throat-stinging fog. Below, awnings spread like aprons from the buildings' waists, shading the street-level shops.

"We have to get your money changed before it gives you away again," Jobin said in an undertone. "Come with me."

He headed across the square. They passed windows crowded with ropes thick as a person's wrist, blocks, charts, and gleaming sextants. At last Jobin ducked into a store where barrels of salt pork, hominy, and meal were stacked to the ceiling. Nodding at the proprietor, he made them all empty their pockets and headed for the stairs to the upper floor. "Wait here," he said.

"Look at all this!" Tway said, staring at the shelves and bins of crackers, sausages, and cereals.

The shopkeeper was watching them. "Outlanders?" he asked.

Harg said, "From Grora. Is there a harbourmaster who keeps track of the arrivals?"

The shopkeeper said, "Try the customs office."

Tway's attention was still on the goods. "You must be a very rich man," she said to the shopkeeper.

He laughed. "Tell that to my landlord."

"But if you own all this—"

"Bless you, none of this is mine! Until I sell it, it's my banker's," he grinned.

Tway smiled politely back, but it was clear she didn't understand what was funny. She shook her head as if there were no accounting for Torna humour.

Jobin appeared again, and distributed shiny Inning coins among them. His mood seemed changed for the better, but he gave no explanation. "Follow me," he said.

As they climbed uphill away from the harbour, the lanes narrowed and grew crooked as old men. Flickering street lamps gleamed dully onto the pavement. The buildings' soot-blackened faces seemed patched and bandaged by the blankets in the broken windows and the grey laundry hanging from row upon row of rusty iron balconies. Lean-to hovels narrowed the street.

Soon the street ran into another open square, this one littered with handcarts and wagons selling vegetables, cloth, tinware, trinkets, boots and firewood. Few buyers were about. As the Yorans passed, vendors called out to them plaintively.

"Draymarket," Jobin said. "Don't come here unless you want to get cheated."

They left Draymarket by a broad avenue called Castlepath. Now the city changed around them again, like an actor donning yet another costume. The ramshackle brick buildings gave way to cut stone. The windows were high overhead, and grated with iron.

"Are these prisons?" Tway asked.

"No," Jobin answered impatiently. "These are the homes of the great folk of Tornabay. Those bars are not to keep them in. They're to keep you out."

While they had been walking, Harg had been aware of Tiarch's palace looming ahead on its spur of rock. Now the Castlepath carried them into a market that lay just under the shoulder of the palace walls. Here stood ponderous buildings whose doorways were framed with grim pillars and pediments.

"Gallowmarket," Jobin said. "Wait here while I fetch a key from a friend."

Harg stared at the forbidding wall of the palace. Somewhere beyond that wall was Goth. He longed for a troop of commandos to storm Tiarch's gate and batter down the doors. He wanted to see the Grey Man realize who his liberator was. All the years of mutual ambivalence and abandonment would be cancelled out by one desperate, heroic act.

The reality would have to be more devious and silent.

"Look over there," Calpe said tensely.

On a wooden platform across the square, two men were impaled on stakes. One was dead, his lips and eyes black with flies. The other still lived. His arms and legs gave little jerking motions, like a dying bug. His head was thrown back, and his face was frozen in a mask of agony.

The sight made Harg's legs feel weak. He had seen it before, in the Rothur city of Drumlin, when the Innings had held a public execution for some deserters. They had made the islanders line up and witness as the executioners had thrust the stakes through the men's bodies, then raised them, screaming, upright. They had stayed there in the town square, baking in the hot sun, till the smell had permeated everything. Harg had smelled it for weeks. He could still smell it.

He realized his hand was clutching Tway's shoulder hard, and she was looking at him. He forced himself to let go. "Sorry," he muttered, and turned away so he couldn't see the spectacle, and she couldn't see his face.

When Jobin appeared again from the shop where he had gone to fetch the key, he noticed where they were looking, and glanced at the sight. He seemed unmoved. "Insurgents," he explained. "Inspired by the news from Thimish. They threw a grenade into a barracks."

Harg had a crazy thought that Jobin had led them here deliberately, so they would see this sight. It was irrational; Jobin couldn't have known of the execution. "Let's get out of here," he said.

The Torna led them down one of the side streets that radiated off the Gallowmarket. He stopped before a towering wooden door studded with iron, and fitted a key into the lock. When he pushed, the great door swung inward without a sound. They entered a stone tunnel leading into a courtyard. Harg was aware of the trap doors above them and the dark arrow-slits on either side. When they reached the other end, he looked for an inner gate, and saw it, rusted open against the wall. Apparently the residents had not feared attack for a long time.

Their steps on the paved courtyard echoed up five stories of empty balconies. Jobin led the way up a switchback stair to the fourth floor, where he unlocked another door and showed them in.

It had once been a luxurious apartment, but had a look of long disuse. When Tway sat on the indigo brocade couch a little cloud of dust went up. Harg checked the window. They were too high for escape.

Jobin was locking the door. "I'll arrange to have some food sent up," he said. "It would be best if you ate up here. There are eyes everywhere; you should all stay out of sight. You especially, Harg."

Harg tossed his duffel bag on the daybed. "We didn't come here to hide," he said. "We need to locate Spaeth."

A momentary flash of irritation crossed Jobin's face. "I'll alert some people to look for her. But I also need to set up a meeting for you with Mr. Sorrell. You do still want to hear his proposal, don't you?"

"Yes," Harg said.

"Then don't go roaming off looking for lost waifs from Thimish. I don't know what time Mr. Sorrell will be free. I'll come back as soon as I know."

His authoritative tone struck memories in Harg's mind. He decided to let it pass. "All right, we'll stay here. Order us some beer while you're at it."

When Jobin turned to the door, Harg stopped him. "The key," he said. "Give it to me."

For a moment Jobin looked reluctant, but then gave him the key. When the Torna had disappeared into the twilight outside, Calpe turned to Harg and said, "Let's get out of here. We can slip away, find an inn, and he'll never know where we went."

"He just had half a dozen chances to betray us, if he was going to," Harg said.

"Maybe someone else is paying better than Tiarch," Calpe said darkly.

Harg shook his head. It wasn't that he trusted Jobin; he wanted more than ever to know who Jobin was working for. Here in the Tornas' native place there was no direct route from one spot to another—everything was indirection, implication, nuance. Looking at his companions, Harg felt how out of place they were. They had a fresh-breeze openness that didn't fit in this city of crooked ways.

"He's the best contact we've got. The only contact. It would be crazy to give that up before we find if it's useful." Harg didn't add what he suspected, that it would be harder than Calpe thought to give Jobin the slip. "Still, as soon as it's light tomorrow, we'll split up. Gill, Tway—you go out and see what news you can gather about Spaeth. Start at the docks. Someone must have noticed the *Fairweather Friend* come in. Calpe, I want you with me. We'll find out what Jobin's friends really have to offer us."

"Besides a sharp stick in the back?" Calpe said.

Harg said, "If we don't take a risk, we'll never know anything."

The *Fairweather Friend* had stopped to take on cargo in Torbert, and so it came into Tornabay a few hours after *Ripplewill*. Spaeth Dobrin stepped off onto a dock only yards from the one where Harg and his companions had landed.

The captain's pint of blood had proved to be a larger quantity than she had supposed, and its absence left her feeling lightheaded and odd. As soon as her foot touched ground she knew that Embo did not welcome her. There was a deep red anger in the ground, as if the island nursed an ancient grudge. Its hostility swirled around her ankles as she threaded uphill through the darkening streets.

The brick buildings leaned over, dark conspirators whispering to each other across the street. Passing boarded-up doorways, she felt an oppressive sense of pain—others' pain, not her own. The few people she met walked fast and kept to the other side of the street. She avoided them as well, afraid of seeing too much in their eyes.

She had set out toward the palace that brooded over the city from its rocky spur of mountain. But as she walked, the streets twisted under her feet, and buildings shoved forward to block her view. The sky was dark by the time she realized she was hopelessly lost. She stood on a corner, looking down littered streets that disappeared into night and sulphurous fog on every side. Under a nearby heap of old packing crates, something rustled. Spaeth whispered Ridwit's name, but there was no answer. She was alone. For the first time in her life there was no one in a hundred leagues who knew her name or wished her well. The thought made her eyes sting. She would have given anything to hear the voice of Mother Tish saying her name. But no, that was another Spaeth, someone she had left far behind.

Instead she heard booted footsteps approaching through the mist to her right. Quickly she dodged down another street clogged with refuse, past gap-walled tenements. Shattered windows gaped on either side. She saw light ahead, turned toward it, and burst into a broad square.

It was a tawdry market, lit by bonfires and iron cressets that made the mist glow yellow. There were people all around, selling cheap wares from tents and makeshift booths. Spaeth walked forward, her senses battling the unfamiliar confusion of noises, sights, and smells.

Under an awning hung with lanterns, a bangled woman vending brass was staring at her. Quickly Spaeth raised her hood to hide her hair, but the woman was already calling out to her in a strange, wordless moan. She stretched out her hands in supplication and pointed to her mouth. With a rush of mixed horror and desire, Spaeth realized the woman's tongue was only a black stump. Spaeth turned her back and the woman's voice blended with the sound of a wheezing old accordion. The music came from ahead, where a ragged blanket was spread on the pavement. As Spaeth came up she shied away again, for the old accordionist was blind.

They were everywhere, the uncured. Spaeth felt trapped, surrounded. Of course they had had no dhotamars for ages here; what Lashnura could survive the ills of a whole city?

Ahead, where a booth was selling nog, a crowd of men laughed noisily. She turned away from them toward the middle of the square, where a stone fountain stood, now dry. Its broad basin had become a dumping-ground for fruit rinds, soiled hay, and old shoe soles. She sat on its stone base.

She was in a symphony of suffering, tantalizing one moment, repulsive the next. She hugged herself, feeling a hollow sense of strangeness, of not being fully herself. Around her, people moved and shifted in the yellow cloud of pain; but they were without the currents of consonant purpose created whenever people gather to some end. All these people were moving, not going.

So this was the fate of the isles, when Inning had finished with them. Once, people had cared enough to raise this great forest of buildings; once, life-giving water had flowed from the stone fountain. Now the city was stained and trashy; disfigured, but not through any purpose or any need. It was only that people had ceased to care. The city was not their place any more. No one here had a place.

"Outland girl," someone said at her shoulder. She spun around to find a Torna man looking at her. He seemed out of place, for he was well dressed in a blue wool coat with an Inning cut. His shoes were polished. "You look like you need a friend," he said.

"I have friends," she answered, rising and turning away. He caught her arm in a gloved hand. She pulled away, and her hood fell back.

"By the rock, a Grey Lady!" he exclaimed, staring. "What are you doing here?"

"I am free to go where I like," Spaeth said.

"Free, yes; but not wise," he said. "Don't you know the risk you run here? This is not a place for the likes of you."

Spaeth did not answer. She knew it was true, but she had no other place to go.

"Put up your hood again," the man said, glancing around. When Spaeth obeyed, he held out his hand. "My name is Tolliby."

Hesitantly, Spaeth touched his hand, glove against glove.

Tolliby's eyes searched her face. He was middle-aged; he had receding black hair, and his left earlobe had once been pierced. "Let me give you some advice, child. You are in the city now. It's not like the outlands. You must follow the rules of this place. I know. I was once new in the city, too."

Spaeth knew how true his words were. Whatever she had been in the South Chain, she was no longer. She was not even an individual any more, only part of the drifting cloud of humanity under the angry mountain.

"I can show you to a safe place," Tolliby said.

"All right," she answered.

Putting an arm around her shoulders, he led the way across the square to the west, where the buildings backed up against a cliff of rock. Stairs had been cut into the cliff face, each flight becoming narrower and more step-worn than the one before. At last they emerged onto a cliff side street that looked down on the market over the tops of the buildings below. Ramshackle wooden shops clung precariously to the steep hillside. To one of these shops, where a hand-lettered sign in the dusty window advertised food and drink, Tolliby headed. A dead cat lay nearly in the door; he kicked it aside and entered.

Inside the shop, men sat on stools before a wooden counter running lengthwise down the room. In a back room more men sat talking in booths lit only by dim oil lamps. And in the middle, behind the counter, was a figure that dominated the room like a glowering Mount Embo of flesh.

"That is Romble," Tolliby whispered. He approached the place where she sat enthroned—for it did not seem possible for her to move—watching over the shop like a cat gorged on vermin. She was swathed in yards upon yards of cotton frock, and her greasy hair fell in every direction; but her eyes took in every movement.

"Romble," Tolliby said, "I have something for the Provost."

She looked at him in mountainous silence. Not a muscle of her face moved, though a fly had landed on her cheek and was scaling down the pale foothills of her chin. She turned to scrutinize Spaeth. Tolliby tugged back her hood to reveal her face.

Romble's small green eyes lit with a ferocious glee. "Lashnura," she said. "And young. Where did you find her?"

"Down in the Fountainmarket. I told her we would protect her."

"Oh, yes," Romble said. "No one will get at her." She gave a snort that passed for laughter, then turned and took a key from a hook behind her. She gave a shrill whistle, then turned and riveted her gaze on a young man who was trying to sneak out without paying. He slunk forward with his money.

An emaciated child of twelve or thirteen emerged from the back of the shop, wiping her hands on her apron. Spaeth felt her mouth go dry at sight of the bruise on the child's face. She tried to block it out.

"Grackle, show the Grey Lady upstairs," Romble said, tossing the key in the child's direction.

Spaeth looked at Tolliby. He said, "I will be down here. Don't worry, you'll be safe."

Without a word, Spaeth followed the child up a steep wooden stairway into a long hall with closed doors on either side. Grackle hesitated, looking at the key. "Did she want you to go with the other Grey Lady?"

For a moment Spaeth was so preoccupied stifling the desire to touch the child that she did not hear the question. When it penetrated, she said, "There is another Grey Lady?"

Grackle nodded solemnly. "Is that where you are to go?"

"Yes. I want to see her."

Grackle led her to the end of the hallway and unlocked a plain wood door.

When Spaeth stepped into the room, the child immediately pulled the door shut behind her and locked it. Spaeth tried the knob, but it spun loose.

At first glance, the room looked empty. There was a rope bed on one side, and a tall, battered wardrobe on the other. On the dressing table a candle burned before a mirror, surrounded by a gleaming forest of bottles, vials, and pipkins. Some were empty, but others glowed with a deep wine colour that Spaeth recognized. They were full of blood—dark Lashnura blood.

She heard a sound and turned to see, sunk into an oversize chair, what looked like the skeleton of a woman. Delicate stick ankles rose from loose shoes and disappeared into a dress that sagged over a wasted frame. Her skin was the colour of bleached driftwood.

"Who is it?" the woman asked in a voice like rustling leaves.

Spaeth stepped forward into the light. "Ah," the woman said. Her hollow eyes were dull. "Not one of my bandhotai."

Sinking onto the bed beside the woman's chair, Spaeth said, "Ehir. What are you doing here?"

"Why, leading my life, as we all do," the woman said. She gave a small, dry cough, but there seemed too little energy left in her for even that.

"Are you a prisoner here?" Spaeth asked.

"No, of course not. Oh, they lock the door, but there is no need. I would never leave this room."

"But you are—"

"Dying? Yes, I know. Leaving would not cure that. What is outside for me? Only the city. I could not survive in the city. It would drive me mad. I have lived in this room for twenty years."

She said it without resentment. Spaeth looked around at the close walls, and imagined how many times you could touch the same spot in twenty years.

"I thought there were no Lashnurai in Tornabay," Spaeth said.

"I may be the only one," the woman said with a light sigh. "They pay high prices to be with me, Romble says. If there were many of us, it would not be so."

"They *pay*?"

"Oh, yes. Romble sends them to me. Some are sick, others merely curious. I cure them all. One every night for many years. Everyone has something they want to give up to me, some hurt to heal. The only problem is—" Her voice caught; for a moment Spaeth thought she had choked, and was leaning forward to make sure, when she saw the tear running down the bony cheek. "They do not feel it the way we do," the woman said in a breathy voice. "Oh, at first they do. They can barely stay away at first. I see them again and again. But they always run out of money, and have to stay away. Then it fades."

"What fades?" Spaeth said.

"The bandhota bond."

Spaeth said nothing.

"But not for me." The woman's voice was barely a whisper. "It never fades for me." She raised a trembling hand to her mouth, and Spaeth saw that the tips of three of the fingers were missing. Carefully, barely daring to breathe, she took the woman's hand to touch the stumps, though under the gloves her fingers had lost all sensation. It was just as well. To give dhota to such a person would be death.

"Yes," the woman sighed, as if noticing her hand for the first time. "I do not heal the way I used to."

"Why not?" Spaeth asked.

"Who knows? A little bit of you dies every time a bandhota fails to return. After a while, your hope and faith start bleeding away. First a little, then faster and faster. In the end, nothing grows back."

Remembering the bottles of blood on the nightstand, Spaeth turned to look at them. "Are those yours?" she said.

"Yes," the woman said. "It is silly. Romble sells the blood as a cordial to cure all ills. It is amazing what people will pay great sums for. It does no good at all, of course. Not without the person who gave it."

Spaeth felt a coal of anger glowing inside her. Was this what Tolliby meant by safe? "Romble has a lot to answer for," she said.

Waving her hand lightly, the woman said, "Oh, no. It is not her fault. She has been kind enough. All this was inevitable as soon as I set foot in the city. Nothing else could have happened."

They could hear voices on the street outside, and the door below them opening. "Is there no mora here?" Spaeth said darkly.

"No, I suppose not," the woman said. "There is only law."

Only compulsion from without, not compassion within. The Lashnura were a quaint anachronism here.

"This will not happen to me," Spaeth said fiercely.

The woman looked at her with a childlike smile. "Why, it is nothing to be feared. I have been lucky. Look at how many people I have loved. I can remember each one, for each one left a part of himself in me. I have it still. Sometimes I dream that they have come back—all of them at once. The room is full to bursting with them, and my heart can hardly stand the joy."

Her eyes gazed off into a summery vision. For a moment, her face looked candle-bright.

Small footsteps came racing down the hall, and the key rattled in the lock. Almost before she had the door open, Grackle was saying, "You must come! You must come! Romble wants you downstairs."

Spaeth rose slowly. She knew what was going on now. Lashnura gifts were vended here like wares. She felt rage inside, and with it, power.

When she came down the stairs, the shop had filled with customers. Flushed faces and loud voices assaulted her senses. Romble had moved to one of the booths in the back room. Tolliby and another man sat with her, absorbed in a low-toned conversation that broke off as Spaeth approached. She saw with surprise that the third man was an Inning.

"God's piss!" he said when he saw Spaeth. "You're dealing in high-quality goods now, Romble." He spoke with an indolent, dismissive tone, but his eyes on her gleamed.

Romble's voice was wheedling. "Nothing but the best for you, sir."

Tolliby rose to take Spaeth's arm respectfully. "Do you know what she is, Provost?" he asked.

"Lashnura, unless you've painted her," the Inning said, taking a sip of wine. He was already slightly drunk.

"Oh, she's the real thing, straight from the Outlands," Tolliby said. "You may have heard of the Grey Folk."

"I've not only heard, I've seen one already. Tell me, is it true that if you let them pierce their veins, the sex is unbelievable?"

"Not only that," Tolliby said. "Once you couple with them, they become your slave for life. You can do anything to them, and they still worship you."

The Inning looked at Spaeth with a possessive interest. "Do they really rut with anything that moves?"

Spaeth had opened her mouth to give a barbed retort, but was arrested by his face. The fair skin was flushed with pursuit of oblivion, but the shadowed eyes showed he had not achieved it. His long, dark lashes gave his face a sensuous look. As she watched, his mouth curled up in a smile so bitter it looked half mad. She hated that face, and could not take her eyes off it. It masked a kind of pain she had never seen before. She wanted, with a deep instinct, to plumb it.

"Why, I think she fancies me," the Inning said.

"You are evil," Spaeth forced her mouth to say.

He laughed and rose to come closer. "I'm evil and you want me," he said. "Don't you?"

She bit her lip to keep control. He was a twisted thing; to cure him would be a dangerous bliss. Her body yearned one moment, repulsed the next.

"By God, this will be a treat," he said, and his fingers touched her face. She wanted to pull away, and couldn't. "You have done well, Tolliby," he said, his breath hot on her cheek.

Suddenly, Tolliby was between them. "You know the price, sir," he said.

The Inning's face turned hard. "Torna flesh-vendor," he said with contempt. Tolliby only shrugged. The Inning turned back to the seat where he had left a parcel sitting, and took from it a small blue bottle. He handed it to Tolliby. "This had better be worth it."

"It will," Tolliby said. "You have never had a woman anything like her." He took the glass stopper from the bottle and shook out some milky white slivers onto his palm, counting them.

Romble had a ravenous look. "Give me some," she said. "You owe me, Tolliby."

He hesitated a moment, then picked a sliver out of the pile and gave it to her. "Another," she said.

"You will kill yourself," Tolliby said.

"No. One isn't enough any more. I want two."

He handed her another one. They all watched silently as she bared her arm and pushed the sharp slivers just under the skin.

"That's the way," the Inning said.

A group of onlookers had gathered around them. Romble sat perfectly still, her eyes switching to and fro like a cat's tail. A little hum of conversation started up around them. Then silence fell, and all eyes were again on Romble.

She had stiffened, and her eyes stared motionless ahead of her. Her skin looked pasty in the dim light. She gave a shiver, and beads of sweat glistened on her face. A convulsion passed through her body, and she slumped senseless onto the floor.

Spaeth's instinct made her start forward; but Tolliby held her back, hissing in her ear, "Don't touch her! Don't interfere!"

"What is wrong with her?" Spaeth asked.

"Nothing is wrong. Everything is right, very right. She has taken achra."

A strange, bubbling cry of pleasure came from Romble's throat. Her body twitched and shivered; then an unbearable wave of ecstasy seemed to pass through her. Her back arched, her face contorted into a mad mask of delight. Scarcely had the first spasm passed when a second came. Her flesh rippled and she groaned in the clutch of frenzy.

The circle of men watched in awestruck silence. One of them moaned in sympathy.

Before long, sweat had drenched Romble's hair, and her skin gleamed wetly. The contortions of her body had worked her dress up to her vast, quivering thighs. She was crooning like an animal, and her arms flapped loosely on the floor. The Inning came forward to stand over her, his face suffused with desire. He lifted his foot and placed it lightly on the great, rounded mass of Romble's belly. She gave a shriek of delight, twitching helplessly.

"Touch her," he said to the gathered crowd. "You can only increase her pleasure."

They crowded forward, eager to participate. Their faces looked strangely alike. Watching, Spaeth felt her horror blend into a blazing rage at the Inning and his gifts. It seemed to come from the very ground below her, flowing up through her body, burning away all inside her with a pure, hot flame.

The Inning looked up over the heads of the crowd, his face feverish. His eyes found Spaeth, and he said, "Now for you."

He took her by the wrist and headed for the door. A leering mass of faces blocked her way. Hands reached out to touch her, but the Inning swore at them and they fell back.

Outside, a restless wind gusted down the street, scattering refuse before it. The fog was breaking up. She could see down into the Fountainmarket, where the cressets and lamps still lit the nightly commerce. She loathed everything she saw. Nothing here was balanced or pure. Even Lashnura compassion partook of its pollution. The thought of dhota repulsed her now. Far better, here, to be a thing of night. Whoever was not predator would be prey.

"Where are you taking me?" she demanded as the Inning set a fast pace toward the steps.

"To the palace," he said. "I'm not about to have you in that piss-hole."

She saw then that she had been led to him, or he to her, for precisely this reason, so that she could enter the palace. "Good," she said, laughing.

Under her feet the mountain rumbled; she felt its ravenous force, coiled but unable to burst free. Its fire was inside her, yearning to burn this fetid growth from its slopes, held back by the merest thread.

"Good," she said again, as they hurried down the night-wrapped street.

TREASON

When Jobin arrived early the next morning, Gill and Tway were already gone. Harg and Calpe were sitting on the carpet eating the remains of their dinner for breakfast. During the night a wind had blown away the fumes and now a wan sun shone in the dusty windows. Harg did not trust it to last; the morning had a dishonest smell.

Jobin spoke in a brisk, businesslike tone. "I've arranged a meeting for you this morning. We have to set out soon."

"Where is it?" Harg asked.

"A neutral place that won't implicate us. You have to understand the risk we're taking."

"My sympathies."

Jobin heard the sarcasm, but acknowledged it only with a nervous frown.

"Well, we'd better go then," Harg said, rising and brushing off his fingers. Calpe rose, too.

"Not you," Jobin said sharply. "My contact will only meet with one of you, for safety's sake. Harg must come alone."

"Will Sorrell be alone?" Harg asked.

"I can't dictate that."

Harg exchanged a glance with Calpe. She sank back down.

"Lead the way," Harg said.

Outside the gate, Jobin turned right down the narrow street, walking quickly away from the palace. Harg glanced over his shoulder several times, but could detect no sign of anyone following them. That was good. It meant Calpe was being careful.

Jobin took a tangled route uphill toward the Adaina section, a sprawling eyesore that slumped against the mountainside above the city. They finally emerged into one of Tornabay's ubiquitous markets. Tents and booths cluttered the square, selling a hundred commodities with only two things in common: they were shabby and overpriced. In the centre of the plaza was a grand structure of marble that had once been a fountain, and was now a dumping-ground for refuse. After circling the raucous maze of the market, Jobin came to sit on the stone base of the fountain. "We have to wait," he said.

Harg sat. It looked like an unpromising place for a war profiteer to carry on business. There was an air of hopeless poverty about the filthy square. The flies droned everywhere, as if they had scented the carrion odour of soul-death.

A middle-aged matron with a shopping basket settled down heavily on the fountain base a little way from Harg. She took off her shoe to massage her foot, complaining about steep streets and tight shoes. As Harg said nothing, she edged closer and began talking in a whining voice about a bloodroot poultice her mother had once used for blisters; the ingredients were impossible to get any more.

"So where is this friend of yours?" Harg said in an undertone to Jobin. The Torna shook his head, scanning the crowd.

"Ah, waiting for a lady friend, are you?" the woman at his side said. "You young fellows from the Outlands need to be careful, running around with Tornabay girls. Here, I've got a potion the young men use—"

Harg wanted to throttle her. How had she spotted him for an outlander? He rose abruptly. "I am sorry, Mother, but we have errands to attend to." He motioned for Jobin to follow him. But Jobin was staring across the square as if at a signal. He got up and said, "Over here."

They crossed quickly toward an unmarked stone warehouse with barred windows. Jobin dodged into a narrow passage leading around to the back of the building. In the alley, they climbed a set of steps to a sturdy door where Jobin knocked four times.

Presently they heard the rumble of a board being raised inside, then latches and bolts being shot, and finally the door opened a crack. An ancient watchman peered out, recognized Jobin, and let them in. Jobin gave him a small coin.

Their boots echoed on the thick board floor. Dusty sunlight filtered through cracks in the heavy shutters, revealing the dim shapes of field artillery crouched like black insects on either side. Slowly Harg walked forward, Jobin just behind him. The guns stretched abreast in lines down the warehouse bays till they seemed countless. Against the outer walls were stacked crates of muskets. There were barrels of flints, stacks of iron balls, mortars, grenades, and chain shot. The building was a war waiting to happen.

Tantalized by the sight of so many arms, Harg did not notice until he was halfway down the aisle that there was a lot of dust in the air for such a deserted place. He looked at Jobin. "Where's your friend?"

"Now, isn't this an impatient young man!" a querulous voice said. Harg turned around to see the meddling old gossip from the square sitting on a crate. "He walks off when I've scarcely even said good morrow to him!" Her voice dropped an octave and took on a steely edge. "Welcome to Tornabay, Harg Ismol. Please don't move."

There was a footstep behind him, and he whirled around to see two uniformed guards step from behind the thick wood beams. Harg snatched the pistol from his belt, but a hard kick in the small of his back sent him stumbling forward onto one knee. A shape came at him from one side; as he turned to meet it, a rifle butt cracked down on his wrist, sending the pistol flying.

"Cuff him," a man's voice ordered. Hands seized him from either side, and his arms were jerked around behind him. He kicked backward viciously, then felt the cold pressure of a gun barrel at the base of his skull. "Stop fighting, Harg," Jobin said calmly.

"You piece of filth," Harg's voice grated.

"Keep hold of him," Jobin instructed the guard as he stepped around to look at Harg's face, the gun still trained on him. "I haven't betrayed you, Harg," he said seriously. "I couldn't tell you the truth. If you had known who really wanted to talk to you, you never would have come."

They jerked him around to face the old woman. She had shed her dowdy disguise and was dressed all in black. There was an expression of sardonic amusement on her face as she looked Harg up and down. "So," she said, "this is the reckless young man who has unsettled us all. You're sure you have the right one, Joffrey?"

Joffrey. Harg was sure he had heard the name, but couldn't place it. As he saw them standing together, he realized who the woman had to be. The knowledge sent a surge to his head, half fear and half exhilaration. He was facing the most powerful native in the isles.

"My apologies for the precautions," Tiarch said to him, her eyes hard and black. "I did warn you not to move. Perhaps next time you will listen when I say something. Now, if you will give your word of honour not to do anything violent, I will have them release you."

"Yes," Harg said. "You have my word."

The guards let go of Harg's arms, and the key rattled against the manacles. Freed, Harg stood warily, rubbing his wrists. He felt thrown off balance by Tiarch's sudden mercy. He thought of making a run for his life, but the guard was too close.

"The truth is, I did not bring you here to arrest you," Tiarch said. "I brought you here to talk." She paused, looking to the guard. "Wait outside the door." Jobin—Joffrey—stirred restlessly, as if he disagreed, but the guards turned to obey.

Once the three of them were alone, the governor walked over into a beam of sunlight and jerked her head for Harg to follow. "Come where I can see you," she said. Harg came, watching her warily. She was utterly unlike the tyrant he had imagined. There was no haughty grandeur here. She didn't need it; she was too perfectly in control, too certain of where she stood. He had seen that certainty before, in good commanders.

"Joffrey's still got a gun on you in case you try anything foolish," she said.

And with any luck, Calpe might have a gun on Joffrey, Harg thought. He hoped she wouldn't try anything. "I won't," he said.

"Good. Because if I give you your life, I will need your cooperation." Tiarch looked down to collect her thoughts, then faced him forthrightly. "Joffrey brought you here because he thought you were the one most able to affect events in the South Chain. I needed to show you, for your own sake, what hopeless odds you face."

Her face was grave. "You don't know what you have started. The Innings were only waiting for a pretext to harden their grip on us, and you have played into their hands. If you continue as you have started, the best outcome I can see is the Adainas' brightest leaders handed over to the executioners. The worst I see is families torn apart, towns burnt, beaches red with blood. I cannot sit back when this land is poised on the edge of a savage war. The isles are dear to me, and while there is breath in my body I will not let them be destroyed."

She seemed sincere, but he knew she had been deceiving people since before he was born. He felt miles out of his depth. "What do you want?" he asked.

"There is another way," she said. "A political way. You would have to set aside courage and daring for the moment and learn instead patience and discretion. It takes courage to leap into the abyss, but only the madman does it. The wise man builds a bridge across the gulf and saves his courage for tomorrow. I do not want to see you die bravely for a desperate cause, when you might live bravely for a victorious one."

There was a kind of earthy charm about her. Fearing to seem either slow or taken in, Harg said, "Are you offering negotiations? A hearing with the Innings?"

"I am offering," she said, "under certain conditions, to act as a broker, a go-between."

His face must have betrayed his suspicion, because she held up a hand. "I know, I know, you don't trust me. Well, I don't really trust you, either, Captain Harg. The fact is, opponents in war never trust each other, for good reason. And yet peace happens. It's done by working out a set of penalties and rewards that would guarantee our bargains. We don't need trust if we can punish each other for betrayal, and reward each other for good faith." She regarded him appraisingly. "I'll set the stage by pledging not to turn you over to the Innings."

"It wouldn't do you any good if you did," he answered. "The war would go on just the same without me."

"I think not," she said. "It would not be the same, it would be much worse. The Adaina would fragment into a thousand warring factions—pirates here, clan chiefs there, traditionalists over yon—and the extremists would come to the fore. With you, we're fighting one war; without you, we'd be fighting a hundred different wars, and we'd be fighting them for decades."

She had an exaggerated notion of his importance, but that fact gave him power. "Then it's in your interest to bargain with me," he said.

"Precisely. Now, I know that and you know that, but the Innings are a little slower. To get them to the table, I need to bring them something, some inducement that would get their attention."

"What do you have in mind?"

"Offer me something," she said.

He had dealt with Tornas enough to know never to fall for that tactic. "No," he said. "Tell me what you want."

She smiled, as if he had passed some kind of test. "All right. You have some things we want. Hostages. Ships. Forts. We have some things you want. Amnesty. Negotiations. Peace. We need to figure out how to exchange the one for the other."

He felt like they were back in the square outside, where charlatans were busy cheating their customers. "I can't do this," he said, shaking his head. "I can't dicker about my country's future as if it were so many pots and pans. Do you know what *I* see when I look ahead, Tiarch? I see the isles bled dry to feed Inning appetites. I see children withered young by Inning contempt. I see our souls bought and sold with our land, our mora faded, our world dull with despair. The isles are dear to me, too."

Tiarch was looking at him with an expression of alarm. "May the gods deliver us from patriots!" she swore. "Don't you know how desperate your situation is? The Innings are preparing to sail against you. They have the means to crush the South Chain, and the cruelty to do it. Just look around if you doubt me." She gestured at the rows upon rows of guns, all Inning. "You must give me a chance to save you. It may be your last chance."

Harg crossed his arms and faced her stonily. "I know what the Innings are capable of. I served under them. Why do you think I am willing to risk everything to fight them off?"

"But you cannot win. You must know that."

He knew it very well, but was not about to concede it to her. He felt as if she had backed him into a cul-de-sac, and his instinct was to counterattack. He said, "What do *you* get from serving the Innings?"

"I beg your pardon?"

"They are not good masters. They have no gratitude. The longer you rule, the more power you have, and the greater threat you are to them. They probably fear and hate you, Tiarch. They want nothing more than to see you overthrown."

"Why, Captain Harg," she said with a steely sweetness. "Are you trying to get me to betray the Innings?"

"They would betray you," he said.

She turned abruptly and walked away from him down the aisle of dusty arms. With a sense of wonder, he realized that his random shot had hit its mark. At last she turned back; her face was hidden by the shadows.

"You are clever, Captain Harg. A clever fanatic. I am sorry we must be enemies."

He was about to answer, but she held up a hand. "Joffrey," she said, "please leave us."

"No, Governor!" Joffrey protested. "It is too dangerous."

"Give me the pistol, then. Wait outside. If I need help, I'll call."

"But Governor—"

"Do it!" she ordered.

With a black look at Harg, Joffrey obeyed. Tiarch watched him go, waiting till she was sure he was out of earshot. Then she turned to Harg. "I want to speak frankly. I want to speak about the future."

She paced away from him toward the window, her hands clasped behind her back. Once or twice she seemed about to speak, but stopped, as if what she was about to say came hard. At last she turned halfway and said, "For twenty years I have been working to keep the Innings out of our affairs. It's been a slow process, convincing them the Forsakens would run smoothly without them. I've cultivated allies among them, shared the rewards of leaving us alone. All of it was for one purpose: to get them to grant us status as a self-governing province. It would mean political independence, legal independence, commercial independence. I was so close I could taste it. And then you came along with your ruinous luck at beating them, and the freedom I have worked twenty years to achieve is swaying in the balance."

Her low voice was scratchy as she went on: "But I have not survived all these years without knowing how to see the opportunity in a setback. The Innings are not united, you know. There are parties in Fluminos who don't want to see this war go forward because of what it could mean for them at home. I might still find support for negotiations leading to independence, if it were in my power to offer them peace."

Harg felt like she had cracked open a window through which he could glimpse a complex and shadowy sea of power reaching beyond what he had ever known or speculated. She had been there. She knew its currents and winds. And if she were telling the truth, they were on the same side.

But he still didn't trust her. Slowly, he said, "You need us to lay down our arms so you can persuade the Innings to let you rule us?"

"Do I look that stupid?" she said sharply. "I know the outer chains would never accept me as their ruler. Particularly not when they still have hope of an Ison. It's not me that wants to fight against the currents of custom, it's the Innings. I say, go with the wind."

She came very close to him then, her eyes disconcertingly fixed on his face. "Since you object to bargaining, I'll give you my real offer, the last one you'll hear. Go along with my plan for a political solution. Pledge to work with me toward a goal of peace and freedom for the isles. Convince me you will support a unified nation independent of the Empire, and I'll release the Heir of Gilgen to you as a pledge of my good faith."

Hope surged painfully through him. The goal that had seemed so remote and impossible this morning was actually in his grasp.

"Why would you do that?" he asked, studying her.

"To give you the power to speak for the Adaina," she said. "To prevent what I spoke about, a devolution into insurgency. The Adaina need a voice—not a voice of aimless fury, but one of plan and purpose. It has to be someone they revere and trust, someone who can make commitments for their benefit that they might not accept from a lesser leader. When you can speak for them, you can put it in my power to speak to the Innings."

Alarms were ringing in his mind. "Wait," he said. "You think *I* would claim dhota-nur? You think I would be Ison of the Isles?"

"Why, yes," she said, surprised at the question. "Of course. In fact, it would be a condition of Goran's release."

He thought he understood then: she wanted to be kingmaker. She wanted to choose the Ison, and for the Ison to owe her his position. But she was very much mistaken about him. "You know nothing about me," he said.

"On the contrary," she said, "I know a great deal about you. I see you have underestimated Joffrey. People often do, and that's what makes him so good at clandestine work. I have your entire military record, with all your commanders' evaluations of you. I know what job you were offered before you resigned from the navy. I know what you eat for breakfast, your weakness for drink, and the name of the young lady you were sleeping with on the boat coming here. I also know whose son you are. As a result of knowing all this, I am perfectly aware that I couldn't control you, and if I attempted to I would regret it. But I flatter myself that I am a reasonable judge of character, and I think we could work together."

"You're serious," he said, shaking his head in disbelief.

"It's not my custom to joke about such matters."

He understood the bargain he had been offered then, and it wasn't with Tiarch. He could win Goth's freedom, prevent a bloody war, become the leader of his people, and achieve independence for his nation. And all he had to do was cease to be himself.

For that was it, the price of dhota-nur. The real bargain was with Goth, or the shadowy powers Goth represented. To buy freedom, Harg would have to surrender every experience, every memory, that had ever caused him pain—all those jagged shards in his personality that made him who he was. He would have to allow his own self to blend with Goth's until they became indistinguishable—twin saints, kindred souls, dependents, lovers.

Every instinct in him rebelled at the thought.

"Find someone else," he said raggedly. "I'm not Ison material."

"You can't be serious. Your record is practically shouting it. You're the one the Adaina want. Even the Innings would accept you. More to the point, *I* want you. Sacred fires, you're practically an Heir of Gilgen yourself, though why you haven't let that fact out is beyond me."

Harg thought: *Is she trying to corrupt me? Yes. Is it in the best interest of the isles? Yes.* And he still couldn't imagine doing it.

Tiarch was watching him carefully. "By the Rock, you're not just being coy. You really don't want it."

He shook his head.

"Well," she said, sitting down abruptly on the cannon opposite him. "I didn't expect this to be the sticking point. I'd drop it, if it weren't for the danger of someone worse arising. Let me put it to you this way. You owe this to your homeland."

He couldn't sort it out. "I can't make this decision alone," he said. "I have to talk to some others."

For the first time, Tiarch looked a little nervous, as if she were juggling too many balls. "I would give you time if it were in my power," she said, "but other events are pressing hard. I need your answer soon."

He frowned at her. She said, "Think it over today, talk to your friends. Then come to the Gallowgate at sundown, and we will work out some terms and conditions, safeguards and guarantees."

"Will you release the Heir of Gilgen then?" he asked.

"No. But I will let you see him, for as long as you like."

The offer sent a painful wave of emotion through him; he had to look away so she wouldn't see it. He had enough presence of mind left to say, "Let me see him first, before we meet."

She regarded him with a look that was almost akin to compassion. "I suppose I can't deny you that," she said at last.

"And I'll need some sort of guarantee that your commitments are truly yours to make, and won't be countermanded by the Innings."

"Don't you worry about the Innings," she said. "I know how to handle them."

"Nevertheless," he said stubbornly.

"What sort of guarantee do you want? You know it would be against their orders to talk to you."

"I need to know they will honour your promises."

"Very well, I'll have something for you," Tiarch said.

She rose. The bargain had been struck, their business was over. Still, there was something he couldn't help but ask her. "How is he?"

She paused before answering. "Honestly, not good. You ought to be prepared to see a change in him. Captivity has been hard on his health."

This news made him so anxious that she put a reassuring hand on his arm. "Don't worry, he'll still be there tonight. Physically, at least." She turned to leave, then turned back. "It is to your credit that you are so concerned for him," she said brusquely. "I wish I could be sure my own sons were so loyal."

She left then. For a long time he sat with his thoughts swirling. Then he got up and went to search for his gun. He found it on the floor where the guards had left it. Returning it to his belt, he went to the door. Outside, there was no sign that Tiarch or Joffrey had ever been there. He stood alone on the steps, hearing the caretaker re-bolt and bar the door behind him.

There was a footstep at the end of the alley, and he saw Calpe rounding the corner of the building.

"Where were you?" he demanded.

"I couldn't get inside," she said. "I finally found a window with a crack between the shutters. I could see you talking to that old woman. Was she the arms dealer?"

So she hadn't overheard. Harg felt a furtive relief. "That," he said, "was Tiarch."

"Blessed Ashte!" Calpe whispered, looking at him with an expression of awe. "What did she say?"

"I'll tell you later. Let's get out of here."

The signal from the harbour came that afternoon. Nathaway had carefully followed the instructions Joffrey had given him before their arrival in Tornabay. He had obeyed his captors quietly, hidden the key Joffrey had smuggled to him, and watched the harbour every afternoon for the rescue party's signal.

The sun was almost resting on the mountain's shoulder when it came. Two slow flashes of light, three quick ones. Anyone watching might have mistaken it for a chance reflection—and not noticed the sun was in the wrong position.

Praying that Torr and his deckhands had not been alerted by it, Nathaway prepared for his escape.

He could hear voices and movement in the galley just forward from the cabin where they had him locked. Torr was loading coal into the stove as the rowboat drew up to the starboard side. Quietly undoing the padlock that secured the casement window, Nathaway wormed his way feet first through the tiny opening, his buttons catching on the sill. Moments later, hands were helping him into the rocking skiff. No one spoke as they drew away from the *Ripplewill*, heading for the harbour.

When they were out of earshot, one of his rescuers introduced himself as a captain in Tiarch's militia. "Have you been harmed, sir?" he asked.

"No, I'm fine," Nathaway said.

He felt giddy with relief to be safely back in Inning custody. He had to suppress an urge to laugh wildly. Soon he would have a real meal, decent clothes, a bath, and a bed. He would talk to Innings again. Above all, he would not be locked in a room. He looked longingly at the city, rising up the mountain's base like moss up the trunk of a tree. He was impatient to be in it, to visit an optician and a bookseller, to drink coffee, just to go wherever he pleased.

"Is my brother, the admiral, still here?" Nathaway asked.

"Oh, yes," the captain answered.

"I'd like to see him."

"You will, sir."

When they came to the dock, a group of marines was waiting with a closed carriage. Nathaway had to force back an irrational feeling of imprisonment as they ushered him into the vehicle and secured the door. One soldier got in with him; four more rode on the outside. He tried to see where they were going as the carriage rattled through the streets. The palace gate opened before them and closed again, cutting off the city outside. The carriage rolled to a stop in a gravel courtyard, at the foot of a set of steps. When Nathaway climbed out, a smiling major domo came forward to meet him. "Welcome, Justice Talley. We are all very relieved to see you safe. I trust you have met with no accidents or injuries?"

"No, I'm perfectly all right."

"We have prepared rooms for you," the man said, gesturing Nathaway to follow. "Your bath and meal are waiting."

The accommodations turned out to be luxurious by the standards he had become used to. They had given him a suite with a study, bedchamber, and private bath. When he arrived, the bath was, as promised, waiting, and he soaked in scented water till all the sweat and fear was gone. After that, he found a very acceptable meal laid out in the study. He sat down to eat in his bathrobe. When he had finished, he strolled into the bedchamber with his coffee, to find that a new and very stylish set of clothes had been laid out for him.

All this while he had barely exchanged a word with anyone, and it was preying on his mind. He longed to talk about what he had been through, to share his observations, to learn what was going on. When he was dressed in his new clothes, he went to the door. It was locked.

The discovery sent a bolt of panic through him, and he pounded on the door till he heard someone come to the other side and fit a key in the lock. He stepped back, trying to quiet his racing heart, a little embarrassed at having created a scene. But when the door opened, the sight did not reassure him. A uniformed soldier stood in the hall, the key in his hand.

"What's going on?" Nathaway demanded. "Why is my door locked?"

"Are you ready to see the admiral, sir?" the soldier asked.

"Yes. Yes, please."

"I'll find out if he is free," the soldier said, then closed the door and locked it again.

Nathaway stood staring at the lock, absorbing the knowledge that he was still a prisoner.

He spent the next half hour pacing, full of nervous energy, unable to keep still. At last he heard booted footsteps approaching, and was waiting at the door when it opened. It was two soldiers this time. "The admiral can see you now," one of them said.

They fell in on either side of him, directing him respectfully through the halls. When they entered the antechamber to Admiral Talley's office, the place was a hive of activity. A line of officers waited on one side; on the other, two secretaries were busy writing out orders. As Nathaway entered, a group of four grim-faced Inning officers emerged from the door into the admiral's private chamber, and two more shuttled in. There was not a word of conversation; everything was running with clockwork efficiency.

A lieutenant leaped to his feet on seeing Nathaway, and offered him a chair. "I will inform the admiral that you are here," he said.

Nathaway sat, fidgeting, as the lieutenant carefully eased the door open and slipped inside. No one in the crowded room uttered a word. Nathaway caught two of the officers studying him curiously, but they averted their eyes when he looked at them. At last the door cracked open and the lieutenant gestured Nathaway quietly to enter.

Corbin was sitting behind a desk with two officers at attention before him. He broke off speaking when Nathaway entered. His eyes, cold behind their gold-rimmed glasses, pinned Nathaway to the wall. With a brittle formality, he gestured in the direction of a chair, then turned back to the two officers, giving directions in a clipped, rapid voice. The secretary taking notes at his side was sweating with effort.

It was not until this moment that Nathaway paused to reflect that he barely knew his brother. There were fourteen years and six siblings between them. By the time Nathaway had come along, his eldest brother had already been in the navy. They had seen each other only during brief holidays and leaves, surrounded by other family, and the relationship had never been affectionate. For all Nathaway knew, they had nothing in common but a name.

At last the admiral finished his instructions, handed the officers some sealed orders, and dismissed them. They saluted and left, the secretary behind them. Then Corbin turned to Nathaway.

"I am glad to see they have plucked you away from the savages," he said. "It was beginning to be an embarrassment."

The chilly tone of this welcome made Nathaway stiffen in his seat.

The admiral went on, "I gave orders for them to prepare suitable rooms for you. Did they do it?"

"Yes," Nathaway said. "It's all perfectly fine, except . . ."

"Yes?"

"Why am I still a prisoner?"

"Ah, yes. Well, you see, in the navy it is our custom to restrict the freedom of those whose loyalty we cannot be sure of."

"Loyalty?" Nathaway repeated, bewildered. "Loyalty to whom?"

"To our nation."

Corbin's expression was so severe that Nathaway wilted inside, even though he knew himself to be perfectly innocent. "What are you talking about?" he said. "I've never—"

"Your short career as advocate for the enemy is over," Corbin said. "You will find that your collaboration has made things a great deal worse for them, and for you."

"Collaboration?" Nathaway protested. "I wasn't collaborating. I was a prisoner!"

"A very busy prisoner," Corbin said. There was a stack of newspapers on his desk. He now rose and brought them over to Nathaway. The first thing Nathaway saw, when the front page of the *Fluminos Intelligencer* fell open before him, was "Dear Rachel . . ." circled with a red pencil.

"Oh my god," he said, transfixed to see his own words, his private words to his sister, emblazoned on the front page of the largest-circulation daily in the land. "She *published* my letters?"

"Either she, or some enemy of the Court."

Nathaway scanned the paper in his hands to see if she had at least edited out the personal parts; but no, it was all there. A burning embarrassment was rising from his neck to his face. It took a moment for him to process what Corbin had said. Then he looked up, his thoughts racing. "There's nothing in my letters against the Court."

"No, just advocacy calculated to inflame public opinion in favour of the rebels." Corbin was standing over him, clearly furious, though his voice stayed tightly controlled. "For god's sake, did it never occur to you that Harg Ismol was manipulating you?"

"I . . . yes, of course it occurred to me. That's why I took care only to write the truth."

"Then you don't even have the excuse of naïveté."

It was very difficult to face the intensity of Corbin's anger. It made Nathaway want to flee the room, or take cover. But he had long practice dealing with forceful personalities, and it gave him an unwise courage. He tried to keep his voice calm and reasonable.

"Look, I didn't say anything but what I really believe, that we ought to negotiate with them. I was saying the same thing to Harg, that he needed to settle his differences through legal means."

"It is not your government's position that we should negotiate with insurrectionists," Corbin said coldly. "It is your duty to support that."

"I'm entitled to disagree with my government if I think they're mistaken."

"Not while we are at war. Not while our citizens are being killed and captured, our ships seized, our cities occupied. By god, if you weren't politically connected I'd have you tried for treason here and now."

Nathaway was suddenly very afraid of what he had done, and very afraid of this implacable man who was his brother. There was a long silence while Corbin stared at him like a searchlight, and he stared anywhere but at Corbin's face.

"Good," the admiral said at last, his tone businesslike again. "You will be leaving for Fluminos tomorrow, on the next available boat. What they do with you is up to the Court."

"No!" Nathaway looked up, dismayed. "Please don't send me back, Corbin. Really, I could be useful to you here."

"Useful." Corbin said the word in disbelief.

"Yes, I learned a lot about the Adaina while I was among them. You've got to know how they think, why they're acting as they are. They're not like us. You have to set aside our standards—"

"Have you no idea how immeasurably difficult you have already made my job here?" Corbin's irritation was not just aimed at him now; it was broader. "If this were just a military problem, the solution would be simple: they are going to lose. My problem is getting to a spot where I can even use a military solution. This sort of thing—" he gestured at the newspapers "—makes that even more difficult."

"But that's just what I mean," Nathaway pleaded. "I can help you avoid a military confrontation. This whole dispute can be pursued in the courts—"

"The time for that has passed," Corbin cut him off, and turned back to his desk as if to terminate the conversation.

"No, it hasn't," Nathaway argued. "We could still persuade them to sue instead of shoot."

"I said, that avenue is no longer open. The courts have been suspended. The Forsakens are now under martial law."

Nathaway was shocked into speechlessness. The courts were the ultimate arbiters of civil society. To close them was like revoking civilization itself. "You can't do that," he stammered.

Corbin had seated himself behind the desk again, and now he smiled arctically across it, his hands folded. "Fluminos has made it known to me that they want this situation resolved quickly, by whatever means. The civilian authority was becoming an obstacle, so I suspended it."

"But . . . you don't have the power! No one does. The courts are where all power originates."

"All the lawsuits in the world don't add up to one bullet," Corbin replied.

Nathaway was chilled to the bone by this answer.

There was a knock on the door and the lieutenant looked in. Corbin's attention was instantly fixed on him. "Yes?" he said sharply.

"Sir, it seems we have a problem."

"What is it?"

"Tiarch's militia, sir. They're refusing their orders."

Corbin rose. "Send in Tennial." He gestured at Nathaway. "And take this man away. Confine him to his quarters."

The lieutenant held the door open for Nathaway. This time, he met Nathaway's eyes with a look of grim commiseration.

As the two Torna guards stepped forward to conduct Nathaway back to his room, the sound of a distant explosion rumbled through the thick walls of the palace, and the ground slipped treacherously sideways underfoot. Furniture tottered and swayed, the foundations of the great edifice groaned. One of the soldiers reached out to steady Nathaway on his feet. "Don't worry, sir," he said. "It's just the crack, opening a little wider."

"The crack?"

"The crack under the mountain that will someday swallow us all."

15
THE HEIR
OF GILGEN

It was half an hour before sunset, and Harg still sat in the taproom of a coarse back-alley tavern, drinking more than he should. Tway was beside him, and Gill sat at the bar. Calpe stood near the door. She had a tense, bodyguard posture, her eyes everywhere. Though there was no sign of the pistol she carried, she looked armed.

The bartender looked in Harg's direction, hoping to sell another pint. Tway motioned him away. She had a vigilant air, just like Calpe; but where Calpe was looking for external enemies, Tway seemed determined to protect Harg from himself. She was right, he admitted to himself; he needed to be able to think. And yet thinking was precisely what he didn't want to do.

The road branched before him, but as he tried to travel each way in his mind, the footing became rutted and treacherous. Down each route he met different versions of himself, all people he might become. None of them seemed like him.

The most alluring false self was the one he had seen in Calpe's eyes the instant he had told his friends about the meeting with Tiarch. Calpe was in the grip of a kind of hypnosis, a conviction that they were being guided by mythic destinies. In her mind, Ison Harg already existed. Whenever her eyes were on him, Harg felt ennobled; and when she looked away he felt deeply fraudulent.

"Calpe's going to be disappointed when she finds out what I'm really like," Harg mused in an undertone to Tway.

"Then she's a damn fool," Tway said.

He didn't pursue the subject. It was just masochism, trying to imagine what would happen when Calpe found out Ison Harg didn't exist and never would.

If he went to the palace tonight, he would be going under false pretences, because he knew he would never carry through with Tiarch's plan for him, not as long as it required dhota-nur. For better or worse, he was built of old wounds. It would all be for nothing if he let Goth take it away.

Then the other phantom selves rose before him. The prospect of alliance with Tiarch completely transformed the situation. If she were in earnest, they would no longer be engaged in a hopeless, lawless rebellion, but in a movement with stature and backing. The far-fetched notion of bringing the Innings to the table became suddenly plausible. And for himself, there was the prospect of an apprenticeship in real power. Tiarch could be his pilot on a voyage of exploration like no Adaina had ever made, into the secret provinces of imperial authority.

And yet, the avid attraction he felt for leapfrogging over his people's heads into Tiarch's world was like his desire for another drink—something that made him mistrust his own motives. It was too easy to imagine himself, solid with a buttery middle age, an expert at manoeuvre, colluding in the profitable enslavement of his people, all the while pretending to speak for them.

But not to enlist Tiarch might be even worse. Looking down that road, he was stopped by a phantasm of carnage. Through the smoke of burning villages he glimpsed the hills lined with a bristling picket of stakes. And all of it was due to him.

"There aren't any good choices," he said to Tway. "Just bad ones and worse ones."

Tway said nothing. She was the only one whose opinion he really wanted, and she had not offered it.

"Maybe I should just walk away, back to the South Chain."

She studied him. "And leave Goth here?"

Another bad choice. He felt like a prisoner of his own success. Now that he had come so close, it seemed like treachery not to go on. He longed and dreaded to see Goth. The Grey Man was part of a purer, simpler world—not this cobweb tangle of Inning cruelty and Torna treachery. Goth had been born to be protected, a treasured victim, and the Innings would use that against him, against them all.

"Damn him!" Harg said under his breath.

The one self he couldn't picture clearly was the one Goth would see, now that they both knew the truth that had been hidden for so many years. It was still an effort not to feel a sting of resentment at the fact that Goth had not trusted him to know.

Tway said, "Harg, you're not really angry enough at him to walk away?"

For a moment he wanted to shock her, to show her how unworthy he was; but that wasn't like him, either. "No," he said.

Across the room, Calpe had tired of waiting, and now came over to join them. "It's time," she said. "We need to go."

Harg went to the bar to pay their bill. As he was putting down his money there was a boom, like distant artillery, that shook the cracked window panes. "What's that?" he asked tensely.

The tavern keeper gave an oily grin. "Calm down, outlander. It's just the crack under the mountain."

When the four companions reached the street outside, they saw a black cloud rising into the sky from the mountain's peak above the city. Calpe eyed it darkly. "I wish we were well out of here."

As they headed toward the palace, the cloud rolled swiftly down the mountain slope, and soon the air was filthy with falling ash. Shopkeepers rushed to close their doors as an unnatural evening settled on the city.

Near the Gallowmarket the four friends split up, so they could come into the square from different routes. Soon Harg and Tway stood together at the easternmost entrance, where an ancient stone bastion arched over the street, remnant of some outgrown fortification. The ash was falling like a heavy snow; they paused to tie kerchiefs over their faces. The few lit streetlamps had eerie haloes around them.

Harg had wanted Tway to walk to the Gallowgate with him so they would look more like innocent pedestrians; but the market was deserted now. The ash had begun to mask the sharp edges of building and curb. He could barely make out the motionless shapes on the execution stand. As they set out across the empty pavement, their feet raised little clouds of dust at every step. Tway's brown hair was prematurely grey with ash.

The iron-studded gate was closed, but a light glowed in a guardhouse window. It went against instinct to boldly attract the attention of a palace guard, so Harg paused outside the guardhouse. A small window swung open and a Torna soldier peered out. "Yes?"

Tiarch had given him no password. Pulling down the kerchief so he wouldn't look so much like a brigand, Harg said, "I was told to come here for entry to the palace."

After a sharp look at his face, the guard said, "Right. One moment," and closed the window again. Harg saw him give a signal to someone else.

There was a small postern door next to the guardhouse, and as Harg waited nervously he heard someone unbolting it. But just as it swung open, a tumult broke out on the other side. There were shouts and running feet, and suddenly the great gate began to swing open.

Harg didn't wait to find out what was going on. He bolted for the nearest street out of the square, shoving Tway away from him to take another route and draw off any pursuit. Behind him, someone shouted an order; then a huge black carriage raced noisily across the square, raising an obscuring cloud of ash. Harg glanced over his shoulder to see a troop of soldiers who had emerged from the gate, lining up to fire after the carriage. But no guns went off. Instead, just as he was reaching the safety of a dark side-street, he heard a shout behind him: "Pursue that man! Over there!"

As he dove for the mouth of the alley, there was a gunshot and Calpe's voice shouted a pirate taunt. He spared no breath to praise her bravery, but ran.

The buildings whipped past in a blur. He flew down a steep staircase and through a crumbling arch where cressets guttered in the heavy air, past a glowering stonework tower with an iron-barred gate. At every turn he headed downhill and east, toward the harbour. His footfalls sounded muffled on the ashy pavement.

But the soldiers knew the city better than he. As he emerged into a cross-street he heard shouts and saw a troop rounding a corner, hot after him. He dodged back the way he had come. Through the murk he spotted a place where a cast-iron fence barred a narrow space between two buildings. With a leap and a scramble he was over the fence and into the garbage-strewn passage. Rats scattered into the street. Behind him the soldiers shouted; the vermin had given him away. He raced down the passage and broke through into a little garden surrounded on all sides by high brick walls. The place was filled with painted wooden whirligigs, all of them stunned into stillness by Harg's appearance. He clumped like a giant down a path lined by little soldiers with windmill arms. A miniature wooden fort stood in one corner, its battlements manned by clockwork dragonflies. Harg leaped onto its roof and jumped for the wall, dragging himself up. He was about to go over without looking when a snarl from the other side made him pull quickly back. He caught a glimpse of yellow teeth and slitted eyes. He crawled along the top of the wall till he came to the corner and dropped over into the alley.

There was shooting in the streets off to his left. He jolted to a stop as a troop of soldiers marching double-time in formation passed along a cross-street just in front of him. He dropped into a window well to avoid them, and found himself looking into a bare basement room. A grimy child looked up and pointed at him, but the woman in the room lay insensible against the wall, a bottle in her arms. Then the troop had passed and Harg slipped down the street after them.

He knew he had reached the harbour when he smelled tar and kelp. He paused in a cluster of barrels to catch his breath. Far up the hill, some sort of battle had broken out; a barrage of gunfire went off like a string of firecrackers. The city seemed to be teeming with soldiers; he would have to make his way to the *Ripplewill*, and trust his companions to follow on their own. He slipped out onto a dock, looking for a rowboat to steal. Too late, he heard footsteps behind him, then a shout. He dropped behind a bale and saw the soldiers, carrying torches, crowding onto the end of the dock in pursuit.

He brought out his pistol, but held his fire as he saw a tall figure step forward. "Surrender, Captain Ismol," the Inning called out. "We have you trapped."

Many words of defiance sprang to Harg's mind, but he used none of them. The commander paused for an answer, but hearing only silence he ordered, "Take him. Alive if you can, dead if you can't."

As the soldiers started down the dock, Harg took aim past them at the Inning. But as he pulled the trigger, a Torna soldier got in the way. He took the bullet in the rib cage, and his blood spattered on the commander's uniform.

The moment Harg's pistol was empty the soldiers broke into a run. Harg left his cover and dashed down the dock. As the end loomed near, he said an inward prayer, then jumped into the ash-scummed water.

The pursuit clattered up to the spot and scanned the surface for a sign of him. The Inning was close behind. "Shoot, damn you!" he ordered. "Don't let him come up again!" The whole troop lined up and fired a volley at the spot where Harg had disappeared, peppering the water with bullets. A plume of bubbles rose to the surface.

"Get some boats. Get a net," the Inning commanded. "The admiral wants proof this man is dead."

❧

Just before sunset, Spaeth stood at a window high in a southwest wall of Tornabay palace, looking out. The setting sun burned like a blister against the sky. She had been in Tornabay only a day, but it was enough to plumb the desolation that brooded over the mouth of the Em.

In the room behind her, Provost Minicleer's rangy body was laid out naked on the rumpled bed, insensible. It bore the marks of the previous night and day. His hair was matted with sweat, there were dark circles under his eyes, and a sallow cast to his face. His genitals looked bruised and swollen.

Spaeth felt no remorse at his condition. It had been a kind of experiment. She had been interested to find out whether sexual arousal could be intensified to such a pitch, and prolonged to such an extent, that it could become a kind of torture.

Her curiosity was now satisfied. In hindsight, she had almost certainly taken it too far; but it had been so amusing to play with him, especially at the end when he had begged and whimpered. Causing pain was a novel new experience for her; and there was little doubt that the pain had been excruciating by the end. Even now, in a stuporous sleep, his body flinched away from her touch as if to protect itself.

The episode, however entertaining, had diverted her from her true purpose. Looking out the window, she struggled to bring her errand back to mind. It had something to do with Goth. No, not Goth—the Heir of Gilgen. She had come to find him.

Outside, Mount Embo's bulk loomed against the sky. If she just reached out, she knew she could tap such destruction that Tornabay would never again raise its soiled head, but remain a smoking scar through the centuries. The balances were stretched to the limit, held only by a dwindling thread.

"Now," the mountain's growl reverberated in her skull. As she watched, a black cloud swelled from the peak, billowing skyward. A sound like thunder tumbled down the slope.

She turned to where she sensed the thread binding the Mundua and Ashwin was anchored—here in the palace somewhere, below her. Now was the time to act, now when her thoughts were clear and pitiless. She picked up the bag she had brought from Yora, and her hand closed over the hilt of the obsidian knife. It pulsed with blood-hunger. She slipped out the door as ash began falling against the window.

The palace was not one building but many, and where they connected, logic died. There were stairways to nowhere, mazy traps, and U-turn hallways that took her back to where she had started. With only instinct as a guide, Spaeth wandered blindly. At last, frustrated, she took out the knife and held it in her hand. It felt as if alive, tugging her down dimly lit corridors toward her goal. When she passed windows, she saw the ash collecting like snow on the panes. The halls were shadowy and quiet.

The quarters of the Heir of Gilgen were guarded, but she passed through like a shadow. The guard stirred uneasily, but saw nothing. She came into a long, unlit gallery with windows at the far end looking out on an ashen garden. Silhouetted against the windows was a tall, white-haired man.

She took a step forward, and he turned. His face was invisible in the grey light, but his voice was quiet: "I have been expecting you."

There was mora in him, Spaeth saw. She shifted the black knife in suddenly sweaty palms and took another step forward. The darkness condensed around her. Still her quarry just stood like an ordinary man, waiting for the thrust of her knife. She took another step, and the nearness of his mora prickled her face and raised the hairs on her forearm. It stirred a deep memory.

The windows suddenly blazed with lightning; the thunder crashed around them, hiding Spaeth's gasp as recognition flooded back into her. She stood staring at the face she had seen for the merest instant.

"Goth," she whispered. "I found you."

He looked at her as if his heart had stopped beating. "Spaeth?" he said. "My precious girl. Is it really you?" He took a step toward her, then stopped unsteadily. He was looking at the knife in her hand. "No," he said, "I am dreaming again. You are a tool of the Mundua."

The name of her allies flared on the air, sending cold fire through her veins. She held the knife up. "Yes, I am here by the power of the Mundua. You cannot stop me, Goth. I have come for the Heir of Gilgen."

"It *is* you," he breathed, shaken. "By all the gods, Spaeth, what sort of terrible bargain have you made?"

She could feel the Mundua in the ashy air, in the restless ground, in her own heartbeat, waiting for her to do their bidding.

"I can't do it!" she screamed. She tried to fling the knife away, but instead her arm raised it to attack. Her lips curled in a bitter snarl, and she heard her own voice say, "I *will* do it."

The white-hot rage that had filled her last night now surged to her head again.

She began to circle him, her knife ready. "You are no fit guardian," she taunted. "You have no passion for your land. You spent all those years on Yora, giving dhota to anyone who came by, while the isles cried out in pain."

He stood like a man stricken, though her knife had not yet touched him. "Spaeth, I had to serve another way."

He no longer seemed sure of his own words. He raised a shaking hand to his forehead. "Gods, if only I could *think!* It's not you talking; the Mundua have your mind. You must fight them, Spaeth. Be yourself again. Think of our times together. Please—you loved me once. Think of that."

What did he expect—that she would rush blindly into his arms and trust him to put everything right? He thought of her as a child, then. But she was not. She had learned about betrayal.

He held out his arms to her. "Let the Mundua go, Spaeth. Come to me."

A tiny voice inside her pleaded, *Help me, Goth! Stop me!*

She lowered the knife, hesitated, then stepped forward into the circle of his arms. Those same arms where she had once felt safe, invulnerable, wrapped in his all-encompassing love. Behind his back, her hands met over the hilt of the black knife. Slowly she turned the blade inward, toward him. *If only the blade were long enough*, she thought, *then I could pierce both of our hearts in one thrust.*

When Nathaway returned to his luxurious prison room, he lay on the bed in a state of nervous distraction. He could not shake the feeling that something truly awful was happening.

Corbin's suspension of the courts was deeply disturbing. Without courts, neither he nor anyone else had a defence against abuse of power. He felt a rebellious conviction that the navy had no *right* to suspend the courts. If anything, the opposite was true. Corbin might have the raw power, but he had no legitimacy.

But composing legal arguments in his mind, as he automatically started to do, was pointless. There was an urgent need for him to *do* something—but what or how, he didn't know. All he knew was that time was running out. In the morning he would be deported back to Fluminos, his attempt at independence ignominiously aborted. He would leave behind a host of people to whom he had made promises of impartial justice that would never, now, be fulfilled. His own country had betrayed him, made him into a liar.

There was a commotion out in the hallway. He sat up, listening. Footsteps hurried past; then a man's voice said, "What are you doing, soldier?"

"Guarding the admiral's brother, sir," said the man outside his door.

"Is the door locked?"

"Yes, sir."

"Then come with me. I need you for a moment."

As the footsteps of his guard receded down the hall, Nathaway went to the door and studied it. The room had never been meant as a prison. The door was intended to be locked from inside, since the iron box with the lock mechanism was on his side of the door. He scanned the room for some tool. The bedroom held nothing useful, so he wandered into the study. There, the attentive servants had laid out some pastries and butter for him to nibble on—and, luckily, a butter knife. He seized it up and took it back into the other room, then carefully used it to extract the screws holding the lock box together. Once the cover plate was removed, he reached in and shot back the bolt with his finger.

He paused with his hand on the knob. Ordinarily, Nathaway was a law-abiding person; but at the moment his feeling of injustice overcame his respect for authority. He was not being imprisoned by any legitimate power; quite the opposite. It was almost his social duty to disobey.

The hallway outside was empty. From the sound of it, all the activity seemed to be on the front side of the building, facing the courtyard where he had arrived. Carefully closing the door behind him, he turned the other way.

The method of taking whatever route seemed most deserted soon led him into an older part of the palace, where the lucid geometry of the Inning wing gave way to oblique pathways where there was no plan. He wandered randomly, searching for some exit. Coming to the top of a stair well, he glanced down to make sure no one was approaching and saw, on the flight below, a figure descending silently, ghostlike, in a grey cloak.

The windows were dark with dust, so the light was poor, but even so he felt a shock of recognition. It was something about the way she held herself, her flowing, almost feline motion. He watched until she rounded the corner and he glimpsed the silver braids coiled in snakes around her head. He didn't dare attract attention by calling out, so he followed her, walking as fast as silence would allow.

He had known that Spaeth would be in Tornabay; it had been a topic of worried conversation on the *Ripplewill*. How she came to be in the palace was beyond his imagination. But here she was, unless he was very mistaken. Her strange, trancelike demeanour made him suspect that all was not well with her.

She left the stairway when it opened onto a ground-floor hall. He followed her around a series of turns, drawing ever closer, still not attracting her attention. At last, focused almost entirely on the pursuit, he rounded a corner and had to pull hastily back, for there was a Torna soldier posted in the hallway outside a door, much as there had been outside his own. He waited, listening for the guard to challenge Spaeth; but there was only silence. At last Nathaway took the risk of peering around the corner. The guard was lounging at his post, staring off into space. Of Spaeth, there was no sign. She had vanished as if she had slipped through the doorway without the inattentive guard even noticing. As Nathaway weighed his options, he was interrupted by the sound of someone down the cross-corridor trying to attract the guard's attention. He flattened himself against the wall.

"Hey, Collum," a voice hissed urgently.

The guard answered, "Robey. Say, what's going on? What's all the shooting?"

"We're leaving. Come on."

"What? I can't leave. I'm on duty."

"No, you're not. Haven't you heard? The Innings tried to arrest the Gov."

"No! Are you serious?"

"We're to rendezvous in Croom."

"They tried to *arrest* Tiarch?"

"Accused her of conspiring with the enemy. Now they say she's not governor any more."

"Like hell."

"Right. Coming?"

"Who else will be there?"

"Everyone. The militia, M.P.s, whatever navy ships aren't in harbour. We're not going to take this lying down."

"Damn right. What do they think . . ."

His voice became inaudible as the two walked away down the corridor. Nathaway's main reaction to what he had just learned was that Corbin was going to have his hands full tonight, and that left Nathaway with time and some freedom to act. He rounded the corner and slipped into the room the soldier had just left unguarded.

He found himself in a long gallery with a wall of windows at the other end, now covered in ash. As his eyes adjusted to the gloom he saw framed against the window two figures. One he recognized instantly; she moved like a dancer as she circled the old man before her, graceful, taunting, deadly. She stopped as the man held out his arms toward her, then they came together in an embrace. Nathaway's heart lurched as he saw the shape of the black knife in her hand, poised to plunge into his back.

"Spaeth! No!" he shouted.

She whipped around to face him, half crouching. "You!" she hissed.

He crossed the room swiftly, reaching out to take her knife. She lunged at him with murder in her eyes. The knife sliced like a razor through his sleeve, and he pulled back, feeling its bite.

"You should have died," she said. Her eyes looked like an animal's.

"Put the knife down," he said, trying to sound reasonable.

She lunged again. This time he managed to catch her wrist, twist it around, and pin her against him. She fought him, snarling in rage, with such ferocity that he could barely keep her in control.

All this while the old man stood, watching as they struggled. "Do something, damn it!" Nathaway shouted.

"Spaeth," the old man said quietly.

Nathaway felt her stiffen against him. She became deathly still. In the silence he heard a drip, drip, and looked down, surprised to see it was his own blood.

"You must let me go," she said in an eerily quiet voice. "I have to kill him."

Nathaway tightened his hold. He could feel her shoulder blades against his chest, the tight muscles of her back. It was distractingly erotic.

The old man began to approach them slowly, his eyes on Spaeth. Nathaway stared, fascinated, at the grief and resolve in his face.

Spaeth stiffened as the old man drew near, step by ritual step. "Let me go," she said urgently. "He is going to kill me."

Something in her voice made Nathaway say, "Stop. Don't come any closer."

The old man stopped scarcely more than an arm's length away. He had no weapon, and there was no anger in his eyes. Before Nathaway could react, he reached out and touched her on the forehead. A shock passed through her body, knocking Nathaway a step back with its strength. Then she went limp.

Nathaway gave a strangled protest. Spaeth was a dead weight in his arms. He lowered her to the floor and felt for a pulse.

"I should have killed her." The old man was standing above them, looking drained.

"If you had, I'd have had the law on you," Nathaway snapped. He had found her pulse, sluggish and uncertain. He wanted to go fetch help, but didn't dare.

He took off his coat to cover her. She was still clutching the knife. He pried it from her grip and was about to put it in his belt when the old man stepped forward. "I will take it," he said.

Nathaway held it away, suspicious. "Who are you? What have you done to her?"

For a moment the old man seemed at a loss to answer. "I am her creator," he said at last. "I gave her life."

"Goth?" Nathaway said. He could hardly have been more astonished.

"Yes," the old man said, startled. "Who are you? How do you know my name?"

"I'm Nathaway Talley. I was on Yora. That's how—" He stopped. It was too complicated to explain.

"Talley?" Goth said sharply. A look of suspicion, then of dawning understanding, was in his face.

There was a low rumble, and the floor shifted under them like jelly. Goth looked to the window, alert with fear. "We cannot stay here," he said. "The Mundua are hunting tonight. Spaeth gave them substance. She was their messenger, and we have stopped her—for now. They are not happy." He turned to Nathaway. "Do me one more service, and then go back to your own world. Can you carry her?"

"Yes."

"Then follow me."

He led the way into a bedroom that adjoined the gallery. A fire smouldered in the grate, and the air was stifling warm. "Lay her there, by the hearth," Goth instructed, while he lit the lamps. As Nathaway laid her on the carpet, he noticed that his shirtsleeve was soaked in blood. Clumsily, he started to unbutton his cuff.

"Did she do that to you?"

Nathaway looked up. Goth's eyes were on him, keen and alarmed.

"It's nothing," Nathaway said.

"Let me see it." Kneeling, Goth tore away the blood-soaked sleeve with a few swift tugs, revealing an ugly diagonal slash across Nathaway's forearm, still oozing blood. The old man stared at it, transfixed; then his eyes rose to Nathaway's face, searching. That direct, unwavering gaze made Nathaway extraordinarily self-conscious; he suppressed the urge to fidget.

"You are bound up in this more tightly than I understand," Goth said.

There was another rumble from below. The lamp flames flickered, and a poker clattered over on the hearth. Goth clutched at the mantel to steady himself, and his face showed fear.

"They are close," he said. His gaze strayed toward a rosewood bureau by the door. On it stood a cobalt blue bottle on a silver tray. "They can smell my weakness," he whispered. "I am no longer a fit guardian, and they know it. Gods, what a mess I have made!" As he gazed at the bottle, his face lost all expression but inarticulate longing for oblivion.

The landscape of grief in the old man's face was fascinating to watch; it seemed like more than one life was mapped there. Nathaway had to drag his eyes away. Spaeth still lay insensible before him. There were long black gloves on her hands. He stripped one off and said in shock, "My God!"

Her arm was black to the elbows. Quickly he pushed back her sleeve; dark streaks ran up her arm to the shoulder, marks of the sepsis in her system. He picked up her hand; the fingers were icy cold. "We've got to get her to a doctor," he said. "I don't know what this is."

His exclamation had called back Goth's attention. The old man knelt down at Spaeth's side, his breath coming hard. "I know what it is," he said.

"What? I've never seen it."

"You wouldn't. It is a Lashnura disease. It has gotten very bad with her. No wonder the Mundua could take her." Gently he peeled back the other glove, handling her blackened hand so tenderly that Nathaway watched, entranced.

"What is the cure?" he said.

"There is none. Or rather, there is, but she is the only one who can administer it. All I can do is to drive the disease back for a short time."

Spaeth stirred, murmuring. Goth looked up urgently. "Where is the knife?"

Nathaway had stuck it in his belt; he shifted to put it farther from the old man's reach.

"I'm not going to use it on her!" Goth said.

"What do you want it for, then?" He suspected he already knew.

"It is how we cure, by sacrificing ourselves. Please give me the knife."

There was something so commanding in the Grey Man's voice that Nathaway hesitantly drew the knife from his belt, but he didn't hand it over. "I can't let you do this," he said. "She should see a doctor."

Goth didn't answer. He was staring at the knife. Nathaway looked to see what had attracted his attention. The blade was stained with blood, and the stone was milk-white.

"Is that blood yours?" Goth asked, his voice strained.

"Yes, I suppose. It must be."

Their eyes met across Spaeth's body. Nathaway felt he could enter those eyes and wander down corridors that never ended, into worlds he couldn't imagine. He felt disoriented, unsure of who he was or what he wanted to be.

"Tell me what your feelings are toward her," Goth said. His voice was soft, but demanded truth. "Please, I need to know."

Nathaway looked down at Spaeth. There were lines of strain around her eyes that hadn't been there before. He could see it clearly now: she was dangerous, incomprehensible in a way that nothing else in his life had ever been. It gave him a feeling of fearful attraction. "I . . . I wish her well," he managed to say.

"Then let me show you how to finish what you have started," Goth said gently.

He took Nathaway's arm in his hand and squeezed the cut till it bled again; then he dipped his fingers in the fresh blood and dabbed it first on Spaeth's forehead, then on Nathaway's, then his own. The spot where his finger had touched, just above the bridge of Nathaway's nose, felt cool and calming. Uncertainty receded from around it, replaced with a feeling of serene objectivity.

"Now give me the knife," Goth said.

Slowly he placed the knife's hilt in the Grey Man's hand. Goth took the sharp point and nicked a vein in his wrist. Wetting his finger with his own blood, he repeated his motions, touching first Spaeth, then Nathaway, then himself. Then he laid the knife on Spaeth's chest, where it rose and fell with her breathing. Her eyes were moving under half-open lids now. Goth leaned over her, saying, "Spaeth? Do you hear me? It is Goth."

"Goth!" she said, reaching out with a blackened hand. She was barely conscious, but there was a joy in her voice that reminded Nathaway sharply of the child he had at first taken her to be. He took her hand and held it. It was cold as a corpse's.

Goth clasped her other hand and said, "We are going to help you drive the Black Mask away, Spaeth. Are you ready?"

Dazedly, she nodded. Her eyes seemed to refocus on something far away, or far inside, and her body relaxed. Goth also looked like a man in a trance. A slight smile played across his face. He took Nathaway's hand and laid it on the knife blade where their blood was mingled, then put his own strong, grey hand over it. With the rhythm of Spaeth's breathing in his palm, Nathaway could almost feel his own personality dimming and growing indistinct about the edges. He felt a thrill of intimacy that it was his blood on her face.

Goth said, "You can feel the knife, Spaeth. Let the blackness flow into it. Let the disease leave your body until it is time for it to return. We will help you."

In the long silence that followed, the light in the room seemed to condense in a sphere around the three of them, leaving all darkness outside. Currents flowed through Nathaway's mind: the disease into the knife, the heat of his hand into hers, and Goth's strength into both of them, curing, restoring. Slowly, her flesh warmed in his grip.

At last Goth picked up the knife. It was opaque with blackness now. He held it before her eyes. "There it is," he said. "The disease is in the knife. Now I will take it home, into myself."

He bared his arm. The knife plunged down. All the blackness seemed to pour from it into the open vein, and Goth doubled over in pain. Nathaway seized the knife away from him, but the blade was so cold it burned his fingers and he dropped it to the carpet, where it lay smoking like dry ice. It was white once more.

Goth's face was twisted. "Ashes," he managed to say. Nathaway shook his head, uncomprehending. On hands and knees, Goth groped stiffly to the hearth and gathered a handful of powdery white ash. With shaking hands, he took Nathaway's wrist and began rubbing the ash into the cut on his forearm.

"What are you doing?" Nathaway protested, horrified. "It will get infected!"

"It will be all right," Goth said, his teeth clenched.

He then took a linen dresser scarf, handed it to Nathaway, and said, "Rip it into strips." When this was accomplished, Goth wrapped a strip tightly around Nathaway's arm, ashes and all. He then held out his own arm. "Help me," he said.

"I can't—" Nathaway started to say, but stopped as a spasm of pain wrung Goth's body like a rag. Now the old man was trembling with cold; his lips looked blue. Alarmed, Nathaway snatched up a handful of ashes and smeared them across the old man's wounded arm till his hand was a paste of blood and ash. He then bound it tight with the improvised bandage and jerked a blanket from the bed to wrap around the old man. Goth's body felt frail as a wisp.

"Come to the bed," he said.

Goth's eyes were glassy and brilliant with pain. He smiled at Nathaway. "This will pass," he said through clenched muscles. "Don't worry; we are easy to hurt, hard to kill."

Looking into his eyes, Nathaway felt a painful flare of empathy. In that moment, with the blood they had mixed still fresh on the knife, he felt giddy with an exhilaration of purpose. He wanted to participate in the uplifting surrender of the Lashnura, to give himself utterly away.

"I want to help you," he said, not expecting the old man to understand.

But Goth's eyes seemed to see everything. Softly, he said, "I accept your offer."

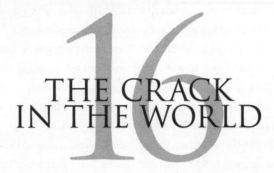

THE CRACK
IN THE WORLD

Goth's face was bright with euphoric pain. He began trying to unbutton his collar, but his hands were shaking. Already the tips of his fingers were darkening with the disease he had taken from Spaeth's body. "Hand me that bottle," he said.

Nathaway fetched the blue bottle from the bureau, and uncorked it. "Give me one sliver," Goth said.

"What is it?"

"Don't you know?"

Nathaway shook his head. "It's medicine," Goth said. "It will help me."

The bottle contained a dozen white, waxy slivers. Nathaway chose one and held it out, but Goth's palsied hands couldn't grasp it. The Grey Man held out his unbandaged forearm. "Under the skin," he said. "Just over the vein."

A little clumsy from fear of hurting him, Nathaway inserted the sharp sliver just under the skin. Goth clasped his hand over it and leaned back against the bed. Slowly, his trembling eased and his face relaxed. His head nodded, and for a moment Nathaway thought he was going to fall asleep; but, with a visible force of will, he dragged himself back. This time when he unbuttoned his collar, his hands were steady. From around his neck he took a stone pendant on a cord. He touched it tenderly, then held it out to Nathaway.

It was a rectangular slab of jade, inscribed with characters in an alphabet Nathaway didn't recognize. Its edges were worn smooth and round by the years, and its surface was unpolished. It looked ancient.

"Take it," Goth said. "I want you to have it."

It was still warm with the heat of Goth's body when Nathaway took it. "What is it?" he asked.

"It is my soulstone," Goth said. "As it was my father's before me, and his mother's, clear back to the beginning. All their souls are in it."

Immediately Nathaway assumed that Goth was giving him the family heirloom to hold in trust for Spaeth. He glanced down at her.

As if reading his thoughts, Goth said, "No, I am giving it to *you*. You must not give it away. Not to her, not to anyone, until your own soul is ready to enter it. Can I trust you?"

"If that is what you want," Nathaway said, uncertain that the old man's mind was sufficiently his own to make such a decision.

"It has nothing to do with me," Goth said. "It is necessary." He looked down at Spaeth, and his face was full of yearning. "Now you must wake her."

Kneeling at Spaeth's side, Nathaway gently shook her. He felt a precious tenderness for her now. They had shared something more intimate than ordinary life allowed. He knew her inside and out, as if he had explored every particle of her, looked out from her eyes, felt his own touch on her skin. He felt a sharp desire to experience that closeness again.

When her eyes flickered open and focused on his face, she looked dreamily entranced at first, as if she were just that moment discovering the most fascinating thing in the universe, and it was him. "Wake up, Spaeth," he said, wishing she didn't have to. She sat up, and her expression changed, but only to become a mirror of the sharp desire in his own. Then, on unpremeditated impulse, they were wrapped in each other's arms, their mouths pressed together. He wanted desperately to be inside her body, to be closer than skin would allow. The clothes they were wearing seemed like walls between them; he wanted to rip them off.

Spaeth's hands were already inside his shirt and he was fumbling at her belt when the fact that they weren't alone made him summon an enormous force of will and pull back. He had to swallow twice and bite his lip to get control. Every muscle in him was superheated. He drew a ragged breath, and saw Goth's face from the corner of his eye, looking at them with a mix of pain and tenderness.

"I had to be sure," Goth said. "I had to know the bandhota bond was true." He looked away then, as if the sight of them was more than he could bear.

"Goth," Spaeth breathed, as if seeing him for the first time. She tore one hand away from Nathaway's body to reach out to him. For an instant he seemed about to clasp it, then he drew away. A tremor passed through his body.

"No," he said, "Don't touch me, Spaeth. I can't trust myself. You must leave here now, the two of you."

"Leave?" she cried. "Without you?"

"Yes," he said. His eyes fixed on Nathaway's face, as if he couldn't bear to look at Spaeth's. "Get her out of here. Don't let her fall into the hands of her enemies. Especially not the Innings. To them, she would only be one more object to be warped and used."

"They won't touch her," Nathaway promised madly.

"Good. You must go to Lashnish, the two of you," Goth said. "Do you understand? You must find the Isonstone. Now, do you know this palace?"

Both of them shook their heads. "I do," Goth said bitterly. "I grew up here. The best way for you to escape is by the Gallowgate. If you cannot make it out that way, there is another way, but use it cautiously. This palace was built on a crack in the world. In the passages below us, the other circles ebb and flow into our own. When I last went that way it was a borderland. You must not stray into the realms of the Mundua, but keep to our circle." Moving painfully, he went to the hearth and sketched out a diagram in the ash there, explaining the route. "Do you understand?"

They both nodded.

With a swipe of his hand, Goth erased the map. "Then go."

Neither of them moved.

"Come with us," Nathaway said. "Please. You can show us."

Goth shook his head. "I would only draw the Innings to you. If they found I was missing, there would be a pursuit. But you can leave without suspicion, and they don't even know Spaeth is here." He paused. "You are her bandhota now. I know you will treasure her as I did. She needs to be free of me."

"But I don't *want* to be free of you!" Spaeth protested.

"Oh, my dear girl." His face was a map of thwarted desire. "What is worthy of love in me is present in all creatures. As long as your love is fixed on a particular object, a particular person, there is some taint of self-gain in it. You must learn to purge your love until all that is left is the essence. Obliterate all that is *you* in your love, and you will find that you have obliterated all that is *me* as well."

It seemed to Nathaway as if the Grey Man were speaking as much to himself as to Spaeth. She said in a small voice, "And what about you?"

"I will be all right," he said. Now his eyes were fixed on something far away, beyond them. "I have discovered a new road, a strange and backward one, but I think it may lead me—well, to my heart's desire." For a moment an ironic smile flickered across his face. Then he turned to them sternly. "Now, go. It is not safe for you to be here."

Nathaway rose, pulling Spaeth to her feet and toward the door. She reached out toward Goth one last time, but he turned away with a grim effort. The last sight Nathaway had of him, he was gazing into the fire like a statue of frozen misery.

As soon as they were out in the dark-windowed gallery, they pressed against each other and kissed again. Nathaway's desire was blazing so hot, his body was acting on its own; everything else was burned from his mind. This time, it was Spaeth who fought for control, pausing with both hands on his face. "We've got to get away," she said.

He couldn't understand what had come over him. He felt drunk, infatuated, unable to stop touching her. But, taking a deep breath, he put his arm around her waist and made for the door.

The building had a strangely awake air for so late at night. Though the corridors were dark, twice they had to stop when they heard a door closing ahead and swift, booted footsteps receding. They heard the hum of voices before they came to a doorway that opened onto the head of a broad ceremonial staircase leading down into a large hall, brightly lit and thronged with soldiers. Sharp orders cracked like pistols, and a company formed up to march out the great double door into a courtyard.

"That is the way to the Gallowgate," Nathaway said grimly as he and Spaeth peered down from behind a stone balustrade.

"We'll never get out this way," Spaeth said.

"Did you understand Goth's map?"

"No. Did you?"

He felt far from certain. "I think so. Down, then eastward."

They turned back into the empty corridor they had come from. Soon, coming around a corner, they saw ahead a servant woman carrying a lamp and a tray, walking away from them. Spaeth shrank back, but Nathaway boldly hailed the woman.

"Excuse me, what's the shortest way to the kitchen?"

The woman turned, her eyes widening as the light from her lamp revealed a dishevelled Inning with a Grey Lady at his side. "Well?" Nathaway said as if he always wandered halls at night in a ripped and bloodstained shirt.

The woman recollected herself. "That door leads to a stair, sir. Can I fetch you something?" Her eyes strayed again to Spaeth.

"Show us the way," he said.

"Follow me, sir," she said, turning to lead them.

The stair descended past four doorways and came out into a long, arched room of pitted, smoke-stained stone. Even at this hour, the depths of the palace were stirring. Across the way an opening glowed with the orange light of the roasting pits, and farther down the hall, fire-lit steam escaped from another cavern mouth. With a rattle of wooden wheels, a boy hurried past them, pushing a handcart piled high with tubers shaped like withered hands. Another trudged past, bent under a heavy sack of lentils.

"Which way is east?" Nathaway asked their guide. She looked momentarily uncertain, then pointed left down the hall.

"Say nothing," Spaeth told her gravely.

They passed by gnarled rock arches that opened into the bakery, glowing with the heat of brick ovens, its floor sanded with flour; and the slaughter room where carcasses hung over stone troughs, slowly draining of blood. Beyond this, the huge corridor grew dark. Nathaway paused to take a mirror-backed lamp down from a hook. Spaeth did the same, but blew her lamp out to save the oil.

The floor sloped down. More openings gaped on either side, barred with steel grates. In the dark beyond one cave mouth they could hear the rustle of movement; the smell told them that here lay the pens for the animals waiting in perpetual darkness for the slaughter room. As Nathaway's light passed the next cave mouth, storage bins full of turnips the size of children's skulls loomed from the dark.

At last the corridor ended in a rockfall where the great ceiling had caved in. On the left-hand side, half blocked by rubble, was a small doorway barred and locked with an iron grate. A chill wind blew out from it, smelling unpleasant.

Nathaway's lamp flickered as he shone it on the lock; it was rusted into a lump.

"Try it," Spaeth said.

Nathaway grasped the lock; it crumbled in his hand. He gave a jerk and the grill rained down in fragments. He kicked away the remainder and bent almost double to enter the low door. A flight of stone steps led down, and he followed them till they ended in oily black water.

As he turned back, he realized that Spaeth had not followed him down the steps. Panic shot through him, and he dashed back up, his heart racing wildly. She was standing at the top, just inside the grate. He pressed her close to him till the feeling of empty desolation subsided. "Don't do that to me," he said. "I thought I'd lost you."

She drew back, studying his face in the dim lamplight. "I don't understand," she said. "How can we be bandhotai? Did I give dhota for you?"

"No," he said. "Goth gave it for you. I . . ." He stopped, uncertain what he had done. Never had he felt this way before, nor acted so unlike himself. All he knew was that being parted from her was like having a limb severed. "I helped, I think," he said.

She touched his face with fingers that gave him an electric thrill. "Innings can't give dhota, can they?" she whispered.

"No," he said. "Not that I know. Of course, I don't know anyone who's ever tried. Why would we?"

"I don't even know what to call you," she said. "Talley, that's all I remember."

"Call me Nat. That's what my family does."

The island under them growled in a deep-buried throat. Crumbled mortar sifted down as bricks in the arched ceiling grated against each other like red teeth. Spaeth looked up, alarmed.

"What is it?" he said.

"The Mundua. They are very close, here. We need to get away. Sacred horns, they are angry at us!"

Once, he would have dismissed her words as quaint superstition. But the memory of the last time they had been together flashed strongly onto his mind. He glanced down the steps. "This passage just leads to the sewer. Should we search for another way?"

She stood paralyzed, obviously afraid to go on, but equally reluctant to go back. He took her hand. "We're going on," he said. "At least the soldiers will never follow us."

The water in the drain was only ankle-deep, but bone-chillingly cold. It was flowing sluggishly eastward, into an arched brickwork tunnel. Underfoot was a clammy muck that oozed into Nathaway's shoes. As they splashed on into the tunnel, invisible cobweb strands brushed his face.

At length his straining eyes made out a glimmer of light ahead, reflecting on the scummy water. As they came up, it turned out to be torchlight filtering down through a grate in the high ceiling, dimly lighting the slippery stream on the floor. A metal ladder led up to the grate. Nathaway had put his foot on the first rung when they heard tramping footsteps approaching. The light was briefly cut off as a troop of soldiers passed overhead, then on. They both flinched back into the darkness.

"Where are we?" Spaeth whispered.

"Beneath the plaza in front of the palace, I think." Shouted orders filtered down from above. "We can't go that way. The place is crawling with soldiers. We'd be seen in a second."

They both looked at the only alternative, the black tunnel ahead. Innings above, Mundua below. They were caught between mortar and pestle. There was a soft plop of something disturbed by their presence dropping into the water.

"Well, let's go on then," Spaeth said, gripping his hand hard.

The first stretch of tunnel seemed interminable. Nathaway went first with the lamp, lighting the slimy walls. The passage took several turns before they came to another overhead grate. This time, it was only a storm drain half clogged with refuse and far too narrow to squeeze through. As they went on there were others, connected to the main conduit by chutes like narrow chimneys. The city surface was drawing farther away above them.

The tunnel began to slant sharply downward, and the water picked up speed, gurgling past their legs. From time to time they passed a gap in the wall and a dank draft marking the opening of a tributary tunnel. The blackness pressed around them like a palpable substance. For a long time there had been no openings above. Glancing back to see if he could glimpse any light from the last one, Nathaway realized his eyes were playing tricks, for spots of light floated in the blackness, disappearing as soon as he tried to focus on them.

At last he came to a halt. "I don't know where this is leading us," he said, "but it's not toward the street."

A cold, steady wind was blowing past them. Spaeth was shivering with the chill, so he put his arm around her. "If we keep going down, we're sure to come to the harbour," she said.

"That's true."

They went on. The water grew knee-deep; it was hard to keep a footing in the current. From somewhere ahead, a steady rushing echoed down the tunnel, growing ever closer.

Nathaway felt space in front of him, and came to a sudden halt. Spaeth pitched into him from behind. He said, "Watch out!" The words echoed till they dissolved into a sound like hollow laughter.

Cautiously, he held out the lantern as far as his arm would reach. They stood at the brink of a waterfall where the conduit emptied into a cavern. From the echoes, it sounded like a vast underground lake before them. No, not a lake—a river. "The River Em," he said softly. Once, the city had stood along the banks of the Em. But successive generations had bricked the river over. It hadn't seen the light of day in two centuries.

"The river must run down to the harbour," Spaeth said. "All we would have to do is follow it."

Nathaway gave a strained laugh. "You jump first."

Spaeth pried loose a piece of masonry and tossed it down, but the sound of the waterfall drowned out everything else. There was no judging how high the fall was.

"Go back?" she said.

"We can't go forward," Nathaway answered.

As they headed upstream again, Nathaway prayed that they could find their way back to the one grate they could have escaped by. The branchings of the tunnel had been numerous, the way far. If they became lost, they might wander down here for a long time.

A phantom light was floating before his eyes again. He blinked to make it disappear, but it didn't. It seemed far down the tunnel. He stopped, shielding the lamp. "Do you see that?" he asked.

"What?"

Without answering, he turned down the lamp wick till it barely glowed. As their eyes adjusted, they could see the walls of the passage ahead. The tunnel was no longer made of brick here, but of a chalky stone. Every ten feet or so there was a ridge in the wall, dividing the tunnel into segments.

He said, "Maybe it's getting light outside, and we passed an opening without seeing it."

He started toward the light. On the third step he realized the tug of water against his legs was gone. Looking down, he found himself standing on a dry tunnel floor. He dropped to one knee and felt it to make sure. The floor was smooth and white. As the grey light grew around them, he realized they were walking on bone.

Ahead, the tunnel curved away into the distance, the ridges in the wall standing out like ribs. No, they *were* ribs, curving up to meet overhead at a gigantic spine. Before either of them could move, a creak of bone on bone echoed down the tunnel, and a massive jaw began to close ahead of them. Sabre-shaped teeth clashed together like a gate, barring their way.

Nathaway's first instinct was denial. It had to be an illusion: the world was not a place where corresponding things could transmute into one another. This time, he was going to fight back with all his knowledge. Resolute in disbelief, he started to walk forward, and saw a doorway he had not seen a second before, framed by grey stone pillars and a triangular pediment. Spaeth caught at him, trying to hold him back.

"Not there," she said.

"Yes, this way!" he insisted, and dragged her forward, across the threshold into a circle unknown even to the Mundua.

They stood on the outer perimeter of a rotunda in a great building long ago entombed by an eruption of Mount Embo. It looked strangely familiar to Nathaway. The architecture, miraculously undamaged by the cataclysm that had buried it, had a serene geometry of proportion. The domed ceiling rising to a starburst skylight, the inlaid onyx underfoot, the railing surrounding a central well—all provoked a haunting sense of déjà vu.

Spaeth looked back toward the dark door they had emerged from. But there was no sound of pursuit. There was no sound of anything. There hadn't been for centuries, here.

Nathaway walked slowly forward, his footsteps echoing loud in the great vault. He wondered if anyone else knew of this buried monument under the city. Only yards above, people slept thick in their tenements; but here all was serene. The room was a huge circle, lit—strangely, he had not noticed it before—by a grey light filtering through a layer of dust on the glass skylight. He took out his pocket watch to check the time. It was after midnight. It could not be daylight—or if it was, it was the light of a long-gone day that had been caught by the volcano and entombed along with the building. No, he caught himself. That was ridiculous.

In the centre of the room, a balustrade ran around a large, square opening to the floor below. When he came to the edge, he stepped back with a twinge of vertigo. He stood on the lip of a square well that plunged down floor upon floor until lost to his eyes in dust and darkness. On each floor a railed balcony overlooked the drop on all four sides. A staircase connected the floors, each flight on a different side of the square, so that it spiralled clockwise around the well.

Spaeth came to his side. "What is this place?" she asked in a whisper.

"How should I know?" Nathaway said.

"You brought us here. It must be a place that has to do with the Innings."

This made no sense; the Innings had only been in the Forsakens for sixty years.

"You mean our ancient past?" he said.

"Or your future."

He shook off the feeling that gave him. "This has to be the ruin of some great civilization, far back in history. A civilization much like ours—our ancestors, perhaps."

Spaeth glanced apprehensively back at the door they had entered by. "We shouldn't stay here," she said. "The Mundua have sharp noses. We should be moving on."

"On to where?" he said.

"I don't know. Not back, that's all I care."

They circled the room then, looking for an exit. There were many doors, but one by one they all turned out to be false panels that opened on brickwork, or trompe l'oeil illusions of inlaid stone. There was only one real entry—the one they had come from—and one exit, by the stairs.

Spaeth leaned over the banister. She looked unsettled at the thought of going down. "We are trapped," she said.

"Perhaps there is a way out on the floor below," Nathaway said.

It was the only choice, so hand in hand they descended the first flight of stairs.

On the floor below, the walls were set back from the edge of the well by a wide hall. At the centre of each wall was a double door standing open, one on each side of the square. Going to the nearest one, Nathaway turned up the wick on his lamp and held the light high to see inside.

It was the entry into a huge library. Parallel rows of shelves marched away into shadow as far as his light reached, all of them packed with books. Entranced, Nathaway walked down the centre aisle. The rows of books to either side seemed endless. Turning right, he passed between towering shelves, his light picking out the soft glint of gold lettering on calfskin bindings and ornate clasps on vellum covers. There was a soft litter of crumbled paper underfoot. The first book he picked off the shelf was in an alphabet he had never seen. The second was written all in straight hash marks tilted right and left at various angles. The third was all neat rows of fingerprints, arranged in a way that suggested meaning without communicating it.

Far away, someone was calling him. Returning to the centre aisle, he looked back and saw that he had come much farther from the door than he had intended. The entry was only a dwindling point of light down an endless corridor of books. Silhouetted against it he could see Spaeth. It took a wrenching effort to turn back. On either side were mysteries begging him to stop and study, to admire their illuminated pages or feel the soft leather between his hands. There was a civilization's worth of knowledge here, all undiscovered. Spaeth called urgently as he slowed at sight of a volume with a strange map traced on its cover. It took all his will to ignore it and continue on.

When he came out into the stairwell again, Spaeth grasped his shoulders, looking pale and anxious. "You must not go in there again," she said. He realized belatedly that he had frightened her.

"There's nothing to fear," he said, wanting her to understand. "It's a treasure trove. Think of all the knowledge preserved here! This is a priceless collection. The world needs to know about this."

"Promise me you won't go past these doorways again," she said severely.

"Why not?"

"Because this place has power over you."

Of course it did. He looked to right and left at the doors on the other sides of the square. If each of them opened into a room as large as the one he had just emerged from, then the library held acres of shelves, running far into the rock on every side, and more below.

She shook him urgently to call his mind back to her. "I'm sorry," he said. "I won't leave you alone again." He gestured with the lamp. "Let's go on."

They descended the next flight down in silence. The layout here was identical to the floor above, but when Nathaway held up his lamp to see what lay inside the doorway, he discovered that the books on this level were enormous tomes with spines half as tall as he was; it looked like it would take two people to wrestle them off the shelf. On the floor below that, the books were tiny, the size of little jewellery boxes. After that came the books in red covers, then books bound in metal.

Down flight after flight they passed. After a dozen floors the shelves were filled with tall stacks of scrolls. Then came levels of hinged wooden panels carved with symbols, books that opened like fans, spools of ornately knotted strings, and books shaped like vases. On one level, the doorway was blocked by an impenetrable mass of spiderwebs. Through it, Nathaway could dimly see where collapsed shelves had spilled boxes of etched slates onto the floor. As they went ever farther down, the air grew stale, as if it, like the dust, had lain undisturbed for centuries. It pressed close and stifling, and their footsteps sounded muffled.

At last they stopped to rest on a floor where the shelves were filled with white rhomboids. Nathaway leaned over the railing to see how far they had come. The well towered above them, the skylight only a tiny spot at the top. He peered down then, to see how close they were to the bottom. A draft of stale, wet air blew up past his face. As far as the light could reach, the flights of steps descended. And beyond that, somewhere down in darkness, a dim speck of light was moving on invisible stairs. It was the greenish colour of phosphor.

Nathaway beckoned Spaeth over. "Look, we're not alone," he said.

She looked uneasy. "I never thought we were."

"Who is it?"

"Bone-lights," she said. "We don't want to get near them."

"Are they the Mundua?"

"No. There are some circles even the Mundua and Ashwin shun. This may be one of them."

They went on.

Deeper, they came on floors of statues with strange, elongated features. There was a floor of masks staring blankly out, and one full of plaster casts of hands. Then came floors of everything triangular, then feathers in gilt frames. Once, as he stood looking at rows and rows of braided hair, Nathaway thought he saw far down the aisle a moving light. For some reason his gorge rose at the sight; the light looked unwholesome, the colour of something rotting.

The grand scale of the place still stirred him; it was a marvellous achievement of architecture and collection. Here was all their history, all their belief, all their art, classified and categorized. It must have taken centuries of effort. There was something a little insane about it.

They began to pass bricked-up doorways. The ones left open led into cavernous spaces where rusting machines squatted in rows: silent, towering cylinders, castles of gears and pistons with ladders leading up their sides to catwalks for the operators. The architecture had begun to change, too. Now the stones were huge and rough-cut, the doorways' low arches supported on squat pillars carved in spirals. From time to time the sound of dripping water echoed out into the stairwell.

It had grown very dark by the time Spaeth came to a halt, holding her finger to her lips for silence. As the sound of their footsteps faded, Nathaway became aware of a soft babbling and cooing from somewhere ahead. He leaned over the banister to look down, and saw a swift, dark shape wing out from the balcony several floors below. As if attracted by the light, it veered in midair and swooped past Nathaway's head. He ducked. It came to roost on the ceiling overhead. Gingerly, Nathaway held up the lamp. Black batwings unfolded to reveal a baby's face, moonlike and cherubic, staring at him with the blank innocence of a china doll. Its mouth opened to coo, and he saw needle-like teeth.

"Light my lamp," Spaeth said, holding it out.

"Perhaps we shouldn't go on," Nathaway said. "What if there is no way out?"

"Look up," was all Spaeth said. He looked out at the way they had come, and saw a light descending slowly behind them, many floors above.

When they rounded the square and came to the level under the one where they had stopped, they found that the ceiling was a crawling mass of black wings and round-eyed faces, and the floor was deep with droppings.

"Walk slowly," Spaeth said. "Perhaps they won't bother us."

But the bats discovered them while they were still on the steps. An eerie squealing of baby voices went up, and suddenly there was a cloud of them in the air. Spaeth and Nathaway both broke into a run. Black wings battered at his face, claws tore at his clothing. He felt needle-teeth pierce a vein at the back of his knee. He reached down to rip the bat away, and two more sank teeth into his wrist. Every moment he was heavier with the weight of them hanging on his clothes, fluttering, trying to find flesh. Desperately he plunged around the corner, past the cave mouth that vibrated with their shrilling, and down the next flight. They were in his eyes, but he kept on by feel, ignoring the prick of teeth. When he reached the next level, he rolled on the stone floor, feeling the crunch of little bones underneath him. A thin shrieking arose as the rest of the swarm fled. Panting and smeared with his own blood, he knelt and looked up. Thousands of them were pouring out and upward like billowing smoke. The cloud thinned as the bats scattered to each of the doors they had passed on the way down, each of the hundreds of levels.

Spaeth was bending over him, checking him over. She looked relatively unharmed. "They didn't like my blood," she said. He winced, rubbing his neck where it prickled with puncture wounds. "I can help you later," Spaeth said, "but not now. Can you walk?"

He staggered to his feet, wondering if his dizziness was from loss of blood or some poison. He wanted to rest. But when he looked out he saw what made Spaeth's voice so tense. On the stairway above them, a myriad of lights had appeared, moving slowly downward. At the sight, a heavy clot of nausea rose in his throat; his mouth filled with saliva, and he swallowed it down, almost choking. He could see now the rustling, ash-coloured figures, holding up torches of burning bone. The light felt clammy and unclean on his eyes.

Nathaway and Spaeth fled downward. The walls were slick with seepage and black moss. Soon the railing ended and the steps became an irregular jumble, carved into craggy stone. They hugged the wall, afraid of slipping into the pit. Around and around they went, as all semblance of architecture disappeared from the cave walls around them.

The light of their lamps was growing weak against the pressing darkness. Nathaway could barely see the steps before him. He turned up the wick of his lamp again, but it was only a dim, glowing coal. He groped on, unsure what would meet his foot at each step. His blind pace was agonizingly slow. He refused to look back.

It was pitch black when the stairs ended. Arm outstretched, he edged forward till his foot met the brink of a ledge. A dislodged pebble plopped into water. The echoes spread in rings, cold and deep. It was a dead end after all.

All that long time ago, when they had crossed the world's boundaries together on Yora, she had been so heroic. He said, "Spaeth, isn't there something you can do?"

"I don't know this circle," she whispered. "You brought us here. Only you can get us out."

A shaft of bone-light crawled past, casting a twisted shadow. Nathaway turned away, but felt its clammy touch on his back, worming down his collar. Whatever it lit on looked gangrenous and corrupt. Even the stone underfoot was growing toad-like skin.

"Don't turn around!" Spaeth said hoarsely. "Don't look at them."

They were just behind his back. He could smell mold. He fought not to turn and face them.

It was then he became aware of another light. He saw it first on Spaeth's face, diffuse and dim. Looking for its source, he realized that the front of his own shirt was glowing, as if he himself were emitting light. Quickly, he fumbled at his collar and brought out the stone pendant Goth had given him. It was shining with a clear, green light the colour of sun-shafts in the open sea.

The emerald light flowed into him, cleansing him from the inside out, putting his mind in a state of glow. He saw now that the green stone was far deeper than it looked, deeper than it possibly could be, as if an extra dimension were trapped inside. For a moment he lost his balance on the edge of a precipice, and when he caught himself he was standing on a marble pier in the light of a green spring morning. On his left, a pearly city rose in fragile leaps of spandrel and buttress up the mountain, its minarets like lace against the sky. On his right, the sun spangled the sea—but strangely, not a wave moved. Above him, swooping birds hung frozen. When he looked out beyond the harbour gates he saw the ominous purple line of an enormous wave on the horizon.

An old couple sat on a bench looking out at the sea, with their dog on a leash beside them. He turned to them, and they smiled, holding hands. "What is this place?" he said.

"Welcome," the old woman said. "You must be the owner of the stone."

There was no sound, no wind. The waves that should have been lapping at the shore hung in a state of never-arriving. "Why is everything still?" Nathaway said.

"Because this is the moment when we were imprisoned in the stone," the old woman said. "The moment just before our destruction." She gestured out toward the approaching wave in the distance, towering and impotent. "Nothing can change here, or our death would be upon us."

In a leap of dream-logic, Nathaway realized that this was Alta. Somehow, the ancients had managed to encode it all within the crystal matrix of the gemstone: the entire city and all its memories, preserved and yet not free to act or do.

He did not belong here. There were things waiting for him in the world where time had taken its course. Seeing that a dinghy was moored to a cleat close by, he said, "Can I take your boat?"

The old man and woman looked at each other, and the woman said, "Are you truly in need?"

"Yes," he said.

"Then take it with our blessing," she said. The dog wagged its tail.

As Nathaway unlooped the hawser, he felt a stir of sea breeze in his hair. The waves advanced, then froze again. He had changed something, and brought the city a moment closer to its death. He looked back at the old couple, but they were still smiling at him. They had known what would happen.

Back in the body he normally inhabited, he could feel Spaeth pressed tight against him. He still held the green stone in one hand, but now in the other hand was the hawser, looping away into the darkness. He held up the stone so that it lit the scene around him with the clear light of an ancient morning. The leprous bone-light slithered back. He followed the mooring line till it led to the dinghy, lying on the edge of black water. All around, vague shapes emerged from shadow—ships of every size and kind, lying on the sand. Some of them had tattered sails still set, the stubs of broken oars in the oarlocks. There were dhows and carrikers, pirogues and shallops, vessels of cork, reed, and metal.

"Get in!" Spaeth said. He climbed into the bow, and she launched them with a mighty shove, then scrambled in over the stern. A strong current quickly seized the hull and bore them away. As Nathaway looked back, he saw, dwindling behind them, three figures on the beach, holding bone torches aloft. He shivered with clammy revulsion, and looked away.

The stone around his neck no longer gave off light. He tucked it away in his shirt, thinking of all the souls caught in the crystal lattice. The lamps he and Spaeth had brought were extinguished. Absolute darkness closed in around them. Nathaway reached out to touch Spaeth's knee. "Are you all right?" he asked.

"Yes," she said, taking his hand in hers. Her skin was warm. "And you?"

"I feel . . ." He felt as adrift as the boat they were in. Every bit of knowledge he had ever used to steer himself was gone.

They floated on in the dark, holding hands. There was no sound now, neither surf nor wave. At times it seemed like they had stopped moving. Nathaway put his hand in the water, but if there was a current they were travelling with it. There was nothing left to do but wait, and simply be.

Spaeth gave a sudden move, and he looked up. Faintly outlined against the black was the arch of a masonry ceiling. Their boat was floating swiftly, stern-first, down a broad tunnel. The light came from around a bend ahead. It was an ordinary light this time, the light of their own world. They had ended up borne on the current of the underground River Em.

It was just before dawn when they emerged from the mouth of a huge culvert into the harbour. A low cloud of ash still hung above, and the water was scummy, but the eastern horizon glowed past the jagged outline of Loth. Nathaway breathed in the blessed normality of the scene. He had never expected to be so grateful just to know the rules of the world.

The current swept them toward a dock where a collection of ramshackle rowboats was moored. As they passed, Nathaway caught onto the gunwale of one of them. They bumped up against it, and Spaeth reached over to seize the oars. Fitting them into the locks of their own boat, she quickly brought them round and sent them spinning through the maze of pilings toward open water.

"There she is," Nathaway pointed ahead. "*Ripplewill*."

Her sleek, low shape looked marvellously familiar amid all the ships riding in the Outbay. As they drew close they could see two figures standing at the rail, outlined against the dawn. A gruff voice hailed them.

"Torr! Tway!" Spaeth called. "It's me!"

"Root and all, it's Spaeth!" Torr said, clutching his cap as if he thought it would spring off his head in surprise.

The figure beside Torr leaned over the rail to see. "Spaeth, is that Harg with you?"

"No, it's our Inning."

"Our *what*?"

They bumped up against the *Ripplewill*'s side. Spaeth eagerly reached out to the hands that helped her step from the dinghy onto the deck. She turned to Nathaway, holding out her own hand for him.

For a moment, he looked back at the city in the predawn light—the crowded commercial districts, the grand residences, all the towering tiers of buildings, crowned by the stern authority of the palace. It was his heritage—the world of structure, order, and power that he had been born to own. What had started last night as a rebellion against a single unjust act had turned into something far more serious. If he voluntarily left aboard a rebel ship, he would be severing himself from his birthright forever. They would never take him back.

"Nat!" Spaeth said, alarmed by his hesitation.

He couldn't leave her. The compulsion Goth had placed on him was too strong. And yet, he felt a painful wrench, like tearing fabric, as he turned away from the city to climb onto the boat.

"Blessed boots of Ashte!" Torr said to Spaeth. "I thought Harg was going to flay me for letting the prisoner escape. And you magicked him back for me!"

"He's not a prisoner any more," Spaeth said defensively, holding onto him as if he might still escape. "He's my bandhota now."

Tway and Torr both looked as if her statement had knocked the words right out of them. Tway's eyes automatically went to Spaeth's unblemished arm, then to Nathaway's bandaged one, then rose to his face with a disturbed frown. He couldn't meet her gaze, but drew closer to Spaeth.

"Are you ready to weigh anchor, Torr?" Spaeth asked.

"I've been ready these past six hours, since I heard the shooting. We've been waiting for Harg, Gill, and Calpe."

"What shooting? Where are they?"

"Why, the shooting in the city. It's been going on all night. And if we knew where they were—"

Nathaway was looking back over the harbour. "Torr," he interrupted tensely, "There's an Inning patrol boat heading toward us."

Torr seemed frozen at sight of the approaching skiff.

"We can't leave without Harg!" Tway said.

"If you wait," Nathaway said, "we'll all fall into their hands."

Torr looked at Nathaway, then at Spaeth, then down and away from Tway. "Cory! Galber!" he called to his crewmen. "Anchor up, double quick! Tway, help me hoist the mainsail."

Tway clenched her hands in furious protest, but Torr caught her by the arm. "He'll find a way home, Tway. Don't you worry, Harg's got luck to burn. Now go take it out on the halyard." As Tway moved forward, Torr shook his head and said softly, "Truth is, I think we've been waiting for the dead." He turned to unlash the boom.

The anchor winch rattled round and the mainsail shot up the mast. Catching the offshore breeze, the *Ripplewill* sighed and heeled over like a living thing drawing breath after sleep. Behind them, the patrol boat was flashing its light in a signal to stop. "Haul in, Tway!" Torr called from the helm. "Cory, Galber, the jib!"

When the patrol boat saw *Ripplewill's* jib go up, a shot echoed across the water. "Ha! Trying to stop us with pistols!" Torr laughed.

"It was a signal," Nathaway said. "There's a warship ahead. They're blockading the harbour exit. If you try to sail through, they'll fire."

Torr whipped out his spyglass, training it on the vessel ahead. "They're swarming like ants. Can they hit us if we sail right under the headland?"

"You can wager on it. If they aim right."

Torr drummed his fingers on the tiller, then said, "We'll have to risk it."

Nathaway had never seen an Inning warship from this perspective. Always before, he had been on their decks, or counting on the safety of their protection. From here, below and in target, the vessel towered over them, the black snub noses of the cannons pugnaciously extended. He said faintly, "Do you know what they can do to a boat this light?"

"We may find out," Torr said grimly. "Cory, Galber, get up every scrap of sail we have. At least the wind's in our camp."

They all flinched as a boom rolled out across the harbour. "I didn't see the flash," Torr said, spyglass on the warship. Then Tway said, "It's only the mountain."

Spaeth went to the starboard rail to look back on Mount Embo. Her face was tight with tension. Nathaway realized that the air felt like a breath too long held in; it throbbed against his ears.

The warship's brass stern chaser gave a sharp crack that echoed back from the shore. A column of water geysered skyward barely twenty yards in front of them, and *Ripplewill* bucked in the wake. "Horns!" Torr said. "They know how to aim."

"That was only a warning shot," Nathaway said.

"Oh, be quiet," Tway said.

Torr slapped his neck as if stung by a bee. "What's that?"

Something whacked against the deck, bouncing like a marble. Then there was a clatter, as if someone had thrown a handful of pebbles at them. "It's falling from the sky!" Tway shouted. They all craned to look up as a new spate of rock-hail fell, glowing as it streaked through the air. The sea around them hissed. "It's raining hot coals!" Tway said.

"Fire!" Torr roared, and his crewmen jumped for the fire pails to douse the coals that glowed in the scuppers. Torr rattled off orders as fast as he could talk. "Spaeth, run below. Get all the pails you can find, then wet some blankets. You there, Inning, help Tway get out the pump from the hold." In an instant, everyone was running.

There was another explosion from the warship, a diffuse *whoompf*. A bright light bloomed on the Inning deck, and the sound of alarm bells followed. "Their gunpowder!" Torr shouted. "The coals hit a charge. They won't be firing again in a hurry." In fact, a brisk fire had already started on the Inning deck, and was climbing the shrouds.

The coals were falling like a hailstorm now, beating a clattering tattoo on the deck. Wisps of steam rose from the sea where they hit.

"Water!" Torr thundered, still at the tiller. His hat was smouldering; Galber dumped a bucket over him, then raced forward to douse a column of smoke rising from a coil of tarry rope.

Soon each of them had a bucket and the water was flying across the small deck. But Torr was craning up at the sails. Little charred holes were showing. He glanced at the warship, now directly opposite them. "Cory, Galber, get the hose up there and wet down the sails," he ordered. "The rest of you, man the pump."

With the hose spout under his arm, Cory climbed the shrouds, made treacherous with weak spots. It was a small, two-man pump, and the rest of them took turns working the levers as Cory aimed the stream of water at the sails.

They were passing right under the Inning ship's guns. "Pray they're too busy," Torr growled, then roared, "Port mainstay! Wet the ropes too!"

No one spoke. The clanking of pails, the patter of coal-fall, and the wash of water were the only sounds. As the sails became soaked, they caught the wind better, making up for the loss of power created by the holes. The strained ropes groaned.

As the warship fell behind them, now blazing like a torch, they saw the sun rising between the headlands where Embo reached out to Loth. *Ripplewill* broke free into the morning. To Nathaway, the air had never seemed fresher, or the sky more beautiful and vast. At his side, Spaeth laughed aloud.

They were out of the harbour, past the blockade. Spaeth hugged Tway, then turned to Nathaway. She stopped, laughing at the sight of him. He laughed back. Their faces were all streaked with soot, clothes riddled with burns.

"We're not pretty, but we're free!" Spaeth said. "The Innings and the Mundua together couldn't stop us."

Torr was already barking orders, and Cory and Galber were scrambling for the sheets. They had changed course again, and were heading east with a strong tailwind.

"Where are we going, Torr?" Spaeth called.

"The Innings will soon be after us. I'm going to round the island and head home by the Windward Passage. They won't be looking for us there."

Just like a pirate to think first of evasion, Nathaway thought.

The *Ripplewill's* bow was bouncing down a shining path toward the sun; now her jib fluttered out on the starboard side like a huge white wing. Nathaway turned to Spaeth, standing at his side. She looked up with a euphoric smile. In her eyes he suddenly imagined himself glowing with a vitality his awkward body couldn't hide. He felt intensely desirable.

He was leaving the world of law and nation, setting out into a realm whose rules he didn't know, where he would be an exile. And it didn't matter, as long as she was there to make him new.

"Shall we go to Lashnish?" she asked.

"Anywhere," he said.

17
STRANGE ALLIES

In the mornings when she went out to milk the cows, Hegerly Ott usually stopped to look at the city of Tornabay from the back porch of her father's farmhouse on the south side of the bay. They lived close enough to see the city and the comings and goings of the ships at the wharves, but not so close that the crime and crowd affected them. Twice a week, her father took the cart into town to market their cheese and eggs, and she went with him if she wanted to buy something. Other than that, they stayed away.

This morning, a dirty black haze hid the city, and spread long fingers out into the harbour. Hegerly frowned and clumped down the back steps. She was worried. Her father should have returned last night from his marketing trip, but he had not appeared. All night there had been sporadic sounds of shooting and explosions from the city. She feared that the two circumstances were connected.

The morning air was chilly as she trudged to the barn, the tin pail bumping against her leg. As she undid the iron latch she wished she had brought gloves. Inside, the barn smelled of hay and cows—a musty, comfortable odour. She regretted having to leave the door ajar for the light, for it let in the cold outside air. As she bustled over to the stall where Ting, the best milker, was kept, she heard a rustle. She looked around and found herself face to face with a wild-eyed man holding a gun.

Hegerly screamed. The man leaped forward with an oath. She dropped the pail and whirled to run, but he seized her from behind, clamping a clammy hand over her mouth and pressing the pistol to the base of her skull. "Another sound and I'll blow your brains out," he snarled. Hegerly went limp with terror.

"Answer by moving your head," the man said in her ear. "Is there anyone in the house besides you?"

In her fright, it did not occur to Hegerly to lie, so she shook her head. "Are there any neighbours in sight of your farm?" he asked. "Are you expected anywhere today?"

To both questions she shook her head. "Good," he said. "Now we are going into the house, and you will give me some food and dry clothes. Understand?"

Numb with fright, Hegerly nodded. "Then move." The man prodded her with the pistol.

At that moment a deep voice said from the door behind them, "Stand right where you are!" The barrel of an old musket was protruding through the door.

In her joy at hearing her father's voice, Hegerly wrenched out of the stranger's grip. Taken by surprise, he made a desperate grab for her, but she dodged him and dived to safety behind a stall door.

"Drop that pistol," the stern voice from the doorway said. Hegerly watched the intruder through a crack between the boards. He no longer looked so formidable —just a bedraggled Adaina with an unkempt beard. His clothes were soaking wet. He looked at the musket pointed at him, then at the pistol in his hand. With a look of resignation, he tossed it to the ground.

Hegerly's father stepped into the barn, his musket still cautiously levelled at the stranger. "Are you all right, lass?" he said. When she nodded, he said, "Pick up the pistol. You, keep your hands in the air."

She crept forward to get the gun. The intruder said, "Don't worry, it's not loaded. Unless there are some fish in it."

Birek Ott scowled at him. "Who are you and why were you menacing my girl?"

The man's shoulders slumped; he looked as if he was trying to keep from shivering. "I wanted to get some food and clothes," he said. "If I have to stand another moment in this cold I'm going to turn to ice."

"Father," Hegerly said, "it's a Native Navy officer's pistol."

She held it up, and Birek glanced at it. He then turned back to the stranger, scrutinizing him. "Where did you get the gun?"

The man paused at this question, then finally said, "You won't believe this, but it's mine."

"You're in the navy?"

The intruder shrugged and nodded fatalistically.

"Are you a Talley's-man or a Tiarch's-man?"

The intruder looked up sharply at this question, searching Birek Ott's face. He seemed reluctant to answer. "Why don't you just shoot me?" he said.

"Answer the question."

"Tiarch's."

It was the right answer, for Hegerly's father lowered the musket. "I used to be Sergeant Birek, of the militia. A *true* Tiarch's-man. You didn't need to make threats; we would have helped you." He held out his hand.

Cautiously, the stranger reached out to touch it.

"Which ship?" Birek asked.

"The *Providence*, under Captain Quintock."

"Ah! I didn't know they were back. Well, come inside to the fire. You can tell us your tale. Your people are to rendezvous at Croom by tonight, you know." Turning to the door, Birek held out his hand for Hegerly. "My daughter doesn't yet know the news. She's probably wondering what's going on."

So, for that matter, was Harg.

An hour later, Harg sat in dry clothes by a roaring fire in the farmhouse kitchen, a bowl of Hegerly's porridge glowing inside him.

In his mind, the night before was a murky muddle of ash-fall, panic, and cold. He had spent what seemed like hours dodging pursuit, hiding in the forest of slimy pilings under the docks, gradually making his way southward to the outskirts of the city. The last he had seen of his friends had been when they parted outside the Gallowmarket. He could only hope they had escaped on their own to the *Ripplewill* and were now safely on their way home.

He jerked awake as Hegerly said, "The news, Father! Tell me what's happened."

"Well, lass," the farmer said, "Tiarch is no longer governor in Tornabay."

Hegerly looked as if her father had said, "The sky is no longer blue" or "The sun will not set today." Harg knew how she felt. As long as he could remember, Tiarch had been the government in Tornabay. "Tiarch" and "Inning" were synonyms.

"But who—?" Hegerly stammered.

"Admiral Talley," Harg said in a dead voice. He had said something of the sort to Tiarch, but he had never dreamed the warning would come true so soon, or so suddenly.

Birek's voice was bitter. "Twenty years she's ruled the isles faithfully in their name. Then in one night the Innings brand her traitor so they can seize the power themselves. It shows you what profit there is in serving faithless masters."

"Are they holding her?" Harg asked.

Birek eyed him in surprise. "Haven't you heard?"

"I've heard nothing. I spent the night rubbing noses with the carp in Tornabay harbour."

A smile spread across Birek's face. "No, they didn't catch her. I tell you, it takes fast footwork to outstrip our Governor. She figured out their plot almost as quick as they did. By the time they went to arrest her, she and her palace guard were on the road to Croom. The troop of militia they sent after her defected to her side. So did a lot of the city militia. You may have heard the firing. That was the Innings' marines, trying to get control of the city."

"The militia fought for Tiarch against the Innings?" Hegerly said, incredulous.

"Of course!" Birek answered forcefully. "It's our own native-born governor we owe allegiance to, not those arrogant newcomers. Of course, there were some who had no choice. The navy ships in harbour were blockaded in by those three ships from the Southern Squadron. But it looks like even they didn't go over without a fight." He glanced at Harg.

"You've got that right," Harg said.

"There were a few militia troops who got caught on the wrong side as well. But even some of the Innings' top officers, like that Commodore Joffrey who was the admiral's picked man, went over to Tiarch."

"He did?" Harg said—although it was the news of Joffrey's previous allegiance that made the biggest impression.

"You hadn't heard that either, eh?" Birek said appraisingly.

Harg sat forward. "Who controls Tornabay now?"

"The Innings," Birek admitted. "But that's all they control."

"And what's Tiarch doing?"

"Well, it seems she'd suspected what was in the wind for some time. For the last two weeks her ships have been gathering at Croom. She's been stockpiling arms and supplies there for months. Now the word's out that all faithful troops are to assemble there by nightfall."

"What then?" Harg asked.

Birek shrugged. "Who knows?"

Harg's mind was boiling with possibilities. Tiarch, a fugitive. The Torna-Inning coalition shattered. Half the navy wavering. It was an unbelievable chance. How could Admiral Talley have misread everyone's loyalties so disastrously? "I have to get to Croom," he said.

"I figured you'd say that," Birek smiled.

One thing was bothering Harg. It was the timing. "Why now?" he said.

"Well, you know what they were saying."

"No, what?"

"The rumours that Tiarch was negotiating with those rebels. That's the excuse the Innings used, of course: that she'd turned traitor. But what we heard was that she'd gotten too close to striking a deal. Admiral Talley doesn't want peace. He wants a rebellion so he can crush it and go home in glory. And now he's betrayed Tiarch and everything she built, to have the credit for putting down the South Chain."

Harg stood, unable to contain his impatience any longer. "How can I get to Croom?"

"I can take you," Hegerly said. Both men looked at her in surprise. She turned to her father. "I'll bet I can sell some milk and chickens there. They'll be paying bonus prices to stock the fleet. I can take the cart."

Frowning, Birek said, "The Rock alone knows what ruffians are roaming the roads."

"I can go by the back way. We know just about everyone along that road."

"I don't want you out there, just a girl—"

"Tiarch was just a girl once!" Hegerly said indignantly.

Harg tried to picture it, and couldn't. "I'll be outside," he said. As he walked out into the barnyard he could hear raised voices within, and was glad to be free from such tender ties.

He never knew how she did it, but an hour later he was sitting beside Hegerly in a donkey cart full of chickens, bound for Croom. Behind the seat lay the old musket Birek had insisted she take, sternly charging her to be home before nightfall. She whistled gaily as they bumped down the rutted road through the oak woods.

His companion's gaiety and the bright sun only brought out Harg's anxiety. So far, everything he had done in Tornabay had gone awry. Spaeth was still missing, and Goth unrescued. His three friends might be captured, or dead. He had no idea what he was going to do in Croom. There was no reason to think he could do anything.

"What are you thinking?" Hegerly asked.

Bunching his fists tensely, Harg said, "Don't ever become my friend, Hegerly. All my friends end up in trouble."

She was silent a moment, then said, "My father warned me you were a spy."

"What?" he looked at her, startled.

"It was the way you reacted to the news about Commodore Joffrey. Joffrey's got a whole network of spies, he said. He thinks you were probably an agent among the rebels, being Adaina and having a South Chain accent and all. He said you might be a go-between in the secret negotiations."

"Well, it's not true," Harg said. "I'm not a spy."

"He said you'd say that, too. Here, hold the reins." To Harg's astonishment, she squirmed out of her skirt, revealing boys' breeches underneath. She reached into the back of the cart, found a cap, and stuffed her hair up into it. Once the transformation was complete, she took the reins again and said, "I'm running away. I'm going to join the Navy."

Harg groaned. "You crazy girl! It's not some sort of game, you know."

"I know." She eyed him shyly. "I want to be a spy, like you. I'd be good; no one would suspect me. Will you take me to Commodore Joffrey?"

"No. You're not going anywhere but home."

"You can't make me."

"Listen, how old are you? Fifteen?"

"Sixteen," she said, offended.

"Well, you have to be eighteen to be a spy."

"Oh." She turned back to the driving, disappointed.

Croom lay on the south side of the island, and Hegerly knew a thousand backroad cutoffs. When they finally emerged onto a thoroughfare, it was crowded with traffic, mostly farm carts like their own. Though Harg kept a close watch, he saw no sign of Inning patrols. It seemed Birek's claim that the Innings were penned into the city was true.

They came to the south shore a little past noon. Here, the coast of Embo was ringed by a tall sea cliff like a sheer guardian wall. The line of traffic slowed almost to a stop where the road came to the edge. They could see far out across the Inner Chain, the misty blue shapes of islands dotting the water. The port nestled below, at the foot of the cliff. As they waited in line, Harg stood on the seat to look, swearing softly in astonishment.

Seventeen ships lay at anchor in the harbour below—three of the huge warships, seven armed frigates, the rest sloops and supply boats. It was at least three quarters of the Northern Squadron. The wharf was a mass of people, and lighters swarmed between the ships and shore.

Hegerly nosed the cart forward onto the steep switchback road that led down the cliff. It was packed with carts and caravans making their patient way down, like beads of water on a string. Caught in the long, single-file procession, Harg thought about what to do. The security around Tiarch would probably be tight, and the chances that he could get in to see her just by asking were nil. He was going to need a go-between, and some money.

"Hegerly," he said reluctantly, "I don't have any money on me. You'll be selling your chickens. . . ."

She eyed him. "Will you take me to Commodore Joffrey?"

"I'll pay you back as soon as I get in contact with my friends here."

"You mean Commodore Joffrey?"

Harg gritted his teeth. "Yes. All right, I'll take you to him."

They soon plunged into the seething activity of the port. As their cart clattered over the paving bricks along the waterfront, they were surrounded by the shouts of the longshoremen, the rumble of rolling barrels, and the staccato echo of hammers. A soldier directing traffic waved them toward a crowded market where Hegerly soon bargained away her chickens and milk. Harg had to restrain her from selling the cart and donkey as well. The money was a paltry bribe, but it would have to do.

The first soldier he asked about Joffrey's whereabouts simply laughed at him; the second brushed him off; the third ordered him away. After days of trying to avoid notice, Harg suddenly felt completely invisible. Standing in the crowded street, he felt like shouting out, "Here I am, Harg Ismol, rebel from the South Chain! Come and arrest me!" He suspected no one would bother. Other foes were on their minds now.

From her cart, Hegerly was watching him a little sceptically. "Don't you have code words and signals?" she asked.

"Yes, they're just so secret no one knows them."

"Oh," Hegerly said.

There was a crowd ahead where a mound of sacks and kegs was overflowing from a dock and obstructing the street. Watching, Harg realized the jam was caused by security officers inspecting every item being loaded. "That's the dock for Tiarch's flagship, I'll wager," Harg said. Then he was sprinting down the street toward it.

The security officer in charge was inspecting a crate of fruit when Harg sidled up and said in a low voice, "I've got a warning."

He suddenly turned visible. The officer looked him up and down, then said in a low voice, "What?"

"It's for Commodore Joffrey's ears alone. There's someone here he wants to know about. Someone from Thimish. Can you take me to Joffrey?"

"I can pass your information along to the appropriate authority," the officer said.

Harg pressed Hegerly's money into the man's hand. "Get the message to Joffrey, and you'll be rewarded. Call him 'Jobin' and he'll know it's real. I'll wait in that cart over there."

The officer turned back to his task without an answer, and Harg walked back to where Hegerly waited. "Well?" she said impatiently.

"Now we wait and see."

They waited over two hours. By the end, Harg was pacing tensely. At last Hegerly tapped his shoulder and said, "Someone's coming."

A six-oared skiff had pulled away from the flagship. As it threaded through the water traffic, Harg heard the tread of a guard troop approaching. They lined up on the dock and presented their muskets as the skiff drew up, oars aloft.

"By the root, I think we snagged our fish," Harg said. "That's Commodore Joffrey, Hegerly."

He had never seen Joffrey in uniform before. The man looked like every Torna officer who had every condescended to him in the navy, in his immaculate dress blues, his fastidious little moustache. The Commodore saluted the guard crisply, then turned to scan the waterfront. Harg stood leaning casually against the cart. Joffrey walked down the dock; the soldiers followed.

When they were face to face, Joffrey said, "I thought it would be you. None of your friends would be so insane." His expression was as stiff as his boots.

"Glad to see you, too, Jobin," Harg said.

"They reported you were drowned."

"Sorry to disappoint you."

"Oh, I'm quite happy you got in touch. Tiarch already issued standing orders in case you turned up. You realize, if we hand you over to the Innings it would put the lie to the claim that she turned traitor."

With a wary glance at the guard troop, Harg said, "Is that what Tiarch wants? To go back to serving a faithless master who cast her away once and would do it again?"

"With you as evidence, she could take her case over his head, to the High Court."

"Let me see," Harg mused, "What was the name of the Chief Justice? Oh, I remember now. Tennessen Talley."

"Very clever," Joffrey said. He turned to the sergeant in charge. "Arrest him."

Of all the things Harg had expected, outright treachery wasn't one. "Take me to Tiarch, you vile little insect!" he said. Then there was a bayonet under his chin.

"Stand back!" a voice said from behind him. The soldiers froze. "Go on, get back or I'll blow your officer to pieces," Hegerly said.

"Put the gun down, girl," Joffrey said, his face the colour of a raw clam.

"Oh, I forgot," Harg said. "Joffrey, this is Hegerly. She wants to be a spy."

"Tell her to put the musket away!"

The bayonet was still uncomfortably close. "If you'll behave like an officer, and take me to Tiarch."

Joffrey gave him a look of black hatred, but signalled his troops to stand back.

Harg turned around. "I'm sorry, Hegerly. I don't work for Joffrey. He doesn't even like me very much."

She lowered the gun, eyes wide. "I guess not."

"Go back and tell your father I'll send the money. Gods willing, I'll send it ten times over." He reached out and squeezed her hand. "Thanks for saving me."

The troop fell in and escorted him to the waiting skiff, this time without touching him. Joffrey said not a word the whole way over to the flagship.

When Harg stepped onto the broad oaken acreage of the warship deck, a troop of marine soldiers was waiting. "Keep him here," Joffrey ordered.

"Joffrey, you gave your word," Harg said.

"Oh, you'll get to see Tiarch," Joffrey said, drawing himself up as if his uniform prickled.

This time, Harg had not even a farm girl with an old musket to back him up. As he waited, he became acutely aware that he had not slept for at least thirty hours. He tried to marshal his thoughts for an interview with Tiarch. He had to be resourceful. He had to inspire confidence. He must not appear as exhausted as he felt. His thinking had gotten thus far when a marine officer appeared from below to lead him aft to the main cabin.

It was the most luxurious space Harg had ever seen aboard a ship. It was lined on three sides by casement windows. A thick, patterned carpet covered the parquet floor, and brass fixtures gleamed against the dark walnut paneling.

Tiarch and Joffrey were sitting together at the chart table. When Harg was ushered in Tiarch looked up, took a pair of spectacles off her nose, and said, "Oh, well done, Joffrey!" The Commodore smiled thinly.

She rose and came slowly over to face Harg. When she spoke again, her voice was hard as a file on metal. "So. The man who cost me my governorship."

It was not the greeting Harg had expected. "Corbin Talley is the one you should be blaming," he said.

"You gave him his excuse. If I'd turned you over when I first saw you, I would be sleeping in Tornabay palace tonight."

And I would be on a spit in the marketplace, Harg thought. "If it hadn't been me, it would have been something else," he said. "You were the issue, Tiarch, not me. They don't want islanders in charge of the islands. The only question now is what you're going to do about it."

She was regarding him with an expression of sceptical wonderment. At last she said, "Gods, I wish I were young again."

It was a non sequitur, and he didn't follow her thinking, so he stayed quiet.

She wheeled back to the table. "While you're on your way out, Joffrey, get the cook to send up some coffee for us."

Joffrey tensed at this dismissal, glancing from Tiarch to Harg and back. But he said nothing. A minute later, Harg was alone with Tiarch. He tried not to let the sudden change disorient him. She did it deliberately, he guessed, to keep everyone off balance. A moment ago, it was him she'd been trying to torment; now it was Joffrey.

"I wish you two young men were not at odds," Tiarch said.

Harg refrained from pointing out how she was setting them up against one another. "I've given him no cause to hate me," he said.

"Yes, you have," she answered. "You cost him his old appointment, and now he sees his new one slipping away. He wants to command the Northern Squadron. That's why he came with me, because I could give him that."

Trying to make his voice neutral, Harg said, "You think he's the right man for the job?"

"He's a talented administrator."

It wasn't an answer, and from her tone, he knew they saw eye to eye. He also saw how dangerous it would be for her to alienate Joffrey. "Well, I didn't come here looking for a position from you," he said.

"No, you've already got one, if I'm not mistaken," she said.

And yet, looking out the stern window at the humming harbour, Harg wanted this fleet more than anything in the world. The thought of what a lethal force he could fashion it into, and the purposes he could put it to, gave him a sharp desire, like hunger. If only she could see it.

He looked back at her; she was staring out the window, too. Outside, the sinking sun was painting the cliffs carmine.

At last she said huskily, "The tide turns within the hour, and I have to make up my mind. All day long the wind's been changing. This ship has been swinging like a pendulum. I'll look up one moment and see solid land; the next, nothing but sea."

Harg wondered if he was seeing the real Tiarch. Was there such a thing? "You haven't decided what to do, then?" he said.

"No. All that—" she gestured out at the hubbub on the wharf, where lanterns now glowed bright "—that is just to keep my options open."

"What are your options?"

"I could take this fleet around and attack Tornabay. But that route's no good; it would foreclose all compromise forever. Or I could send Joffrey to negotiate. He has a way with the Innings; he might be able to strike a bargain. Or I could surrender and trust the law to vindicate me. I could argue that Admiral Talley overstepped his authority by removing me."

"If you've got a decade to spare," Harg said.

She gave him an ironic glance. "Yes, I know. But it's not as hopeless as it sounds. There are Innings who don't want a Talley dynasty in Fluminos."

"You'd be a fool to trust them. But you haven't yet named your best option."

"I could, I suppose, sail off and join a pack of brigands in their hopeless, naïve rebellion against the empire. Is that what you mean?"

"You could look at who is really loyal to you. Your own people, Tiarch. We *were* just a pack of brigands yesterday. But with you we would be a power. You have the finances, the organization we need."

"And what do you have that I need?" she said.

"We have the justification, the cause. No one's going to fight to put one faction or another into power. They're going to fight for something bigger, for independence. For the isles."

As he spoke he felt a heady surge of certainty, erasing all his doubts, filling his exhausted body with fire. It was as if the words were flowing through him from somewhere else. "You can't survive without us, Tiarch. We are at your back, as the Innings are at your front. You are surrounded by enemies unless we are your friends. But if you come with us, everything will be different. Yesterday you were a tyrant in the isles, the puppet of a foreign power. Tomorrow you could be a patriot, a saviour, the one who put independence in our grasp. They will love you, Tiarch, all the people. They will flock to join us, Torna and Adaina both. I tell you, there will come a time when you will think nothing in your life succeeded as well as last night's failure."

Tiarch's eyes on him were narrow, but he saw in them a glint, a reflection of his own certainty. "By the Rock," she said softly. She turned around and looked out the window again, her back to Harg. The ship had swung round again, and the view was now of nightfall rising over the open sea. "Joffrey!" Tiarch barked suddenly.

The door opened so promptly that Harg cast a suspicious look in Joffrey's direction.

"Is the lading done?" Tiarch asked.

"Within the hour," Joffrey said.

"Then I want you to give the orders to set sail with the tide."

"Yes, Governor. Where are we bound?"

Tiarch turned to survey the two of them, both watching her tensely. If she said Harbourdown, Harg had won.

"Lashnish," she said.

There was a moment of silence.

"Well, go on!" Tiarch said.

"Yes, Governor," Joffrey said, and went.

Harg felt like an exploded gun. "Lashnish?"

"Yes," Tiarch said thoughtfully. "The ancient capital of the isles. The place where the Isons arose when the land was in danger, and summoned the Heirs of Gilgen to give dhota-nur. I have a strong and loyal garrison there. A much better base than Harbourdown."

There were machinations behind this, Harg realized, strategies within strategies. She was joining them, but on her own terms.

"I am joining the people of the Forsakens," she said, her eyes sharp on him. "I may be Torna, but I am still an islander. And we may never have a better chance to win our freedom."

Harg held out his hand to her. "Corbin Talley may be a clever man, but he never did anything more foolish than driving us together."

She started to reach out to touch palms, then hesitated. "What bargain are we touching on?" she asked.

Harg grinned. She didn't need to remind him she was Torna. "Friendship, that's all," he said. "If you'll promise me one thing: keep saying 'we' when you mean the people of the isles."

"All right," she said, "if you'll promise another."

"What's that?"

"Never say 'the people of the isles' when you mean Harg Ismol."

He stared at her a moment, then laughed. "Fair enough." They touched palms to seal the bargain.

It was too big. Harg could hardly grasp his success in his own mind. What would Barko say? Harg had set out as a fugitive rebel, and was returning home with an army of liberation.

to be continued in

Ison of the Isles

ABOUT THE AUTHOR

Growing up, Carolyn Ives Gilman spent her summers on an island in Lake Superior that was once the heart of the Ojibway Nation. Her interest in places where cultures overlap led to a career as a historian of the U.S.-Canada borderland and a writer of fiction about even more exotic borders.

Carolyn Ives Gilman has been publishing fantasy and science fiction for twenty years. Her first novel, *Halfway Human* (Avon/EOS 1998), was called "one of the most compelling explorations of gender and power in recent SF" by *Locus* magazine. Her short fiction has appeared in *Fantasy and Science Fiction*, *The Year's Best Science Fiction*, *Bending the Landscape*, *Interzone*, *Universe*, *Full Spectrum*, *Realms of Fantasy*, and others, and she has a collection of short fiction, *Aliens of the Heart*, from Aqueduct Press. Her work has been translated and reprinted in Russia, Romania, the Czech Republic, Sweden, Poland, and Germany. She has twice been a finalist for the Nebula Award.

In her professional career, Gilman is a historian specializing in 18th- and early 19th-century North American history, particularly frontier and Native history. Her nonfiction book *Lewis and Clark: Across the Divide*, published in 2003 by Smithsonian Books, was featured by the History Book Club and Book of the Month Club. She has been a guest lecturer at the Library of Congress, Harvard University, and Monticello, and has been interviewed on *All Things Considered*, *Talk of the Nation*, *History Detectives*, and the History Channel. Her history books have won the Missouri Governor's Humanities Award, the Missouri Conference on History Best Book Award, the Northeastern Minnesota Book Award, and the Outstanding Academic Book of the Year award from *Choice* magazine.

Carolyn Ives Gilman is a native of Minnesota who now lives in St. Louis and works for the Missouri History Museum.

EMBRACE THE ODD

AVAILABLE MARCH 15, 2011
FROM CHIZINE PUBLICATIONS

978-1-926851-10-5

ALSO AVAILABLE FROM CHIZINE PUBLICATIONS

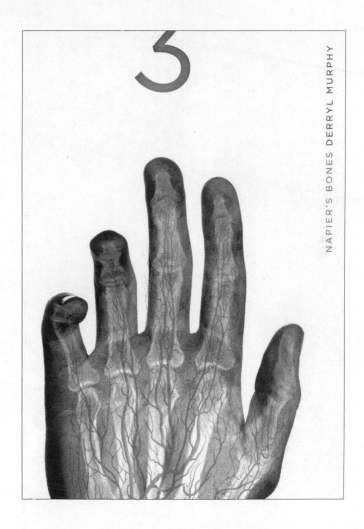

AVAILABLE MARCH 15, 2011
FROM CHIZINE PUBLICATIONS

978-1-926851-09-9

CHIZINEPUB.COM   CZP

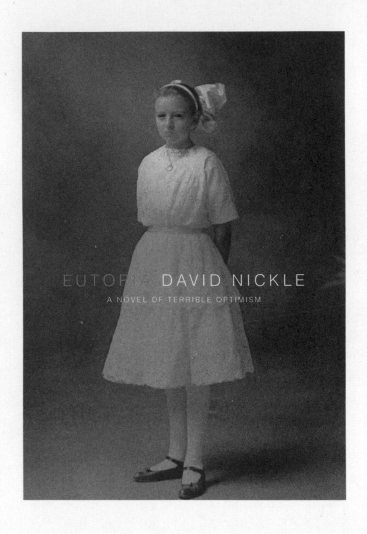

EUTOPIA DAVID NICKLE
A NOVEL OF TERRIBLE OPTIMISM

AVAILABLE APRIL 15, 2011
FROM CHIZINE PUBLICATIONS

978-1-926851-11-2

ALSO AVAILABLE FROM CHIZINE PUBLICATIONS

AVAILABLE APRIL 15, 2011
FROM CHIZINE PUBLICATIONS

978-1-926851-12-9

CHIZINEPUB.COM

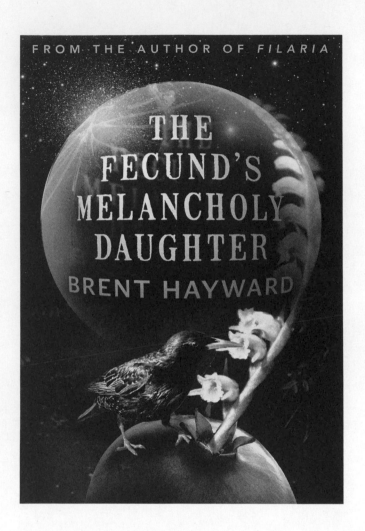

FROM THE AUTHOR OF *FILARIA*

THE FECUND'S MELANCHOLY DAUGHTER

BRENT HAYWARD

AVAILABLE MAY 15, 2011
FROM CHIZINE PUBLICATIONS

978-1-926851-13-6

ALSO AVAILABLE FROM CHIZINE PUBLICATIONS

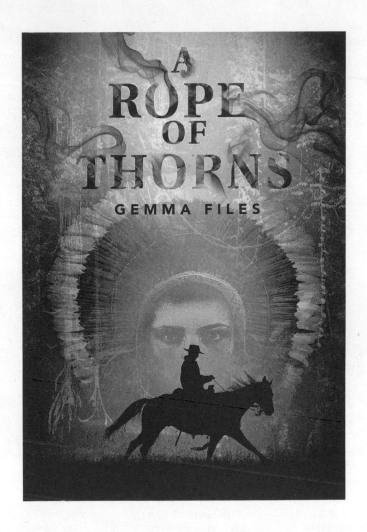

AVAILABLE MAY 15, 2011
FROM CHIZINE PUBLICATIONS
978-1-926851-14-3

CHIZINEPUB.COM CZP

978-0-9813746-6-6

GORD ZAJAC

MAJOR KARNAGE

978-0-9813746-8-0

ROBERT BOYCZUK

NEXUS: ASCENSION

978-1-926851-00-6

CRAIG DAVIDSON

SARAH COURT

978-1-926851-06-8

PAUL TREMBLAY

**IN THE
MEAN TIME**

978-1-926851-02-0

HALLI VILLEGAS

**THE HAIR WREATH
AND OTHER STORIES**

978-1-926851-04-4

TONY BURGESS

**PEOPLE LIVE STILL
IN CASHTOWN
CORNERS**

"IF I COULD SUBSCRIBE TO A PUBLISHER LIKE A MAGAZINE OR A BOOK CLUB—ONE FLAT ANNUAL FEE TO GET EVERYTHING THEY PUBLISH—I WOULD SUBSCRIBE TO CHIZINE PUBLICATIONS."

—ROSE FOX, *PUBLISHERS WEEKLY*

ALSO AVAILABLE FROM CHIZINE PUBLICATIONS

978-0-9812978-9-7

TIM LEBBON

**THE THIEF OF
BROKEN TOYS**

978-0-9812978-8-0

PHILIP NUTMAN

CITIES OF NIGHT

978-0-9812978-7-3

SIMON LOGAN

**KATJA FROM THE
PUNK BAND**

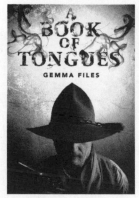

978-0-9812978-6-6

GEMMA FILES

**A BOOK OF
TONGUES**

978-0-9812978-5-9

DOUGLAS SMITH

CHIMERASCOPE

978-0-9812978-4-2

NICHOLAS KAUFMANN

**CHASING THE
DRAGON**

"IF YOUR TASTE IN FICTION RUNS TO THE DISTURBING, DARK, AND AT LEAST PAR-
TIALLY WEIRD, CHANCES ARE YOU'VE HEARD OF CHIZINE PUBLICATIONS—CZP—A
YOUNG IMPRINT THAT IS NONETHELESS PRODUCING STARTLINGLY BEAUTIFUL
BOOKS OF STARKLY, DARKLY LITERARY QUALITY."
    —DAVID MIDDLETON, *JANUARY MAGAZINE*

CHIZINEPUB.COM CZP

978-0-9812978-2-8

CLAUDE LALUMIÈRE

**OBJECTS OF
WORSHIP**

978-0-9809410-9-8

ROBERT J. WIERSEMA

**THE WORLD MORE
FULL OF WEEPING**

978-0-9809410-7-4

DANIEL A. RABUZZI

THE CHOIR BOATS

978-0-9809410-5-0

LAVIE TIDHAR AND NIR YANIV

**THE TEL AVIV
DOSSIER**

978-0-9809410-3-6

ROBERT BOYCZUK

**HORROR STORY
AND OTHER
HORROR STORIES**

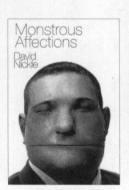

978-0-9812978-3-5

DAVID NICKLE

**MONSTROUS
AFFECTIONS**

978-0-9809410-1-2

BRENT HAYWARD

FILARIA

"CHIZINE PUBLICATIONS REPRESENTS SOMETHING WHICH IS COMMON
IN THE MUSIC INDUSTRY BUT SADLY RARER WITHIN THE PUBLISHING INDUS-
TRY: THAT A CLEVER INDEPENDENT CAN RUN RINGS ROUND THE MAJORS IN
TERMS OF STYLE AND CONTENT."

—MARTIN LEWIS, *SF SITE*

ALSO AVAILABLE FROM **CZP**